Gold Digger

ALSO BY SUSIE TATE

Daydreamer

Outlier
Coming August 2025

Gold Digger

SUSIE TATE

Arndell

Arndell

GOLD DIGGER
Copyright © 2024 by Sett Publishing,
excluding new exclusive content to this edition.
This edition has been published by Arndell,
an imprint of Keeperton, in 2025.
1527 New Hampshire Ave. NW
Washington, D.C. 20036

10 9 8 7 6 5 4 3 2 1

ISBN: 978-1-923232-15-0 (Paperback)

Excerpt from Outlier Copyright © 2025 by Sett Publishing

This novel is a work of fiction. Any reference to names, characters,
businesses, places, events and incidents are products of the author's
imagination or are used in a fictitious manner. Any resemblance to real
persons, living or dead, is entirely coincidental.

All rights are reserved. No part of this book may be reproduced or
transmitted in any form or by any means, graphic, electronic, or
mechanical, including but not limited to photocopying, recording,
taping, or by any information storage retrieval system such as AI,
without the express written permission of the Publisher.

Library of Congress Control Number: 2025933588

Printed in the United States of America

Edited by Joanna Edwards
Formatted by Kirby Jones
Cover design by Arndell
Cover image by Vitalii Arkhypenko, Unsplash

Sydney | Washington D.C. | London
www.keeperton.com/arndell

For Ollie.
Okay, you're a duke. Happy now?

CONTENT WARNING

This novel contains descriptions of sexual harassment, assault, domestic violence, alcoholism and childhood neglect. Please read at your own discretion.

CHAPTER ONE

Arse over tit

Lottie

Posh people were weird. They lived in huge houses with too many bedrooms and way too many toilets. I mean, the toilets in this house outnumbered the people five to one. It was ridiculous. But I wasn't complaining. Let them be weird if it meant I earned a decent wage. Because posh people might have liked a vast array of bogs to choose from, but they sure as fudge nuggets didn't like cleaning them.

That's where I came in.

Only on that particular day I had a small problem with my posh-bog-cleaning gig, in the form of a skinny, eight-year-old girl who had a tummy ache and didn't want to go to school. Just before we turned the corner into the square of posh people's houses, I squeezed her hand gently and then squatted down in front of her. My heart clenched when I saw a tear track down her cheek. She was all bundled up in her puffa coat but with her pyjamas underneath and clutching Keith, her very-much-in-need-of-a-wash soft toy pony.

"Right, lovebug," I said, carefully wiping the tear away and then settling my hands on her small shoulders. "Remember the plan? It's going to be like when we play hide and seek. Only you'll be hiding for a *really* long time. Still got some of that book left to read?"

Hayley nodded at me, her big, brown eyes huge and serious in her small, freckled face. I sighed, and my heart clenched again. Hayley had been through enough. If she had a tummy ache then she deserved to have a day at home with me, snuggled up on the sofa drinking Lucozade in the warm, not trudging through freezing London and having to hide in a scary, huge, posh-person house whilst I cleaned toilets. But I knew that Hayley's stomach ache had more to do with how much she hated school than anything, and I was not about to risk this job.

These particular aristocrats paid well above the odds, and I simply could not afford to be labelled as unreliable. Even if I *could* afford to drop today's hours, which I could *not,* the risk of losing the job altogether was too great. We were edging towards desperate, and there was no safety net, not for Hayley and me; there never had been.

"I've put loads of snacks in your bag. All your favourites plus a bottle of Lucozade, but if you feel like you're going to throw up, it might be better to wait to eat at home."

Please, please, God, don't let her throw up in that house. I'd been there when the interior decorator came last week. The woman had recommended a four-thousand-pound chaise lounge. If a weird, extra-long chair for *one person* cost four grand, then an eight-year-old vomit disaster could take me years to pay off.

"How's your tummy feeling?"

Hayley scrunched her freckled nose as her hand came up to make a so-so gesture.

I sighed again.

"Use your words, lovebug," I gently reminded her. Her eyes dropped from mine as she looked to the pavement, toeing a piece of gravel with her fluffy boot. I hated having to nag her, but I worried that if I didn't make her speak, at least to me, her vocal cords would atrophy from disuse.

"It's okay," she said eventually, her voice so small that it was almost drowned out by the city noises around us, despite the fact that we were on a quieter London street (posh people live on quiet, leafy streets in London – the bus noises, exhaust fumes, screeching tyres and shouting were for us lesser mortals). "I won't throw up. I promise."

I felt my nose start to sting and pulled her into me for a tight hug, smushing Keith the Pony between us. Blinking rapidly, I forced the tears back. I tried to never cry in front of Hayley if I could help it. She needed to believe I was strong, reliable. She'd been let down enough already by adults who couldn't cope. I would not have her believe I would let her down too.

Once I was sure that my tear ducts were back under control, I pulled back to stand up. Taking Hayley's hand in mine again, I squared my shoulders and turned into Buckingham Square.

Nestled in the heart of Kensington, Buckingham Square was beautiful. The large, ornate buildings surrounded a small central private garden in the centre. You had to be a resident of the square to use that gated piece of land. It was nothing like the common around the corner from our block of flats – rather more in the way of well-maintained roses and mature trees, and fewer used needles, burnt-out patches of grass, beer cans and homeless people. I'd yet to pluck up the courage to ask for the key so that I could maybe eat my lunch in there, restricting myself to only longing glimpses over the fence. It was like a little oasis of nature right smack in the middle of London. Even looking in from the outside fed my soul.

Hayley froze outside the imposing Buckingham House, and I glanced down to see her eyes wide and her mouth open.

"It's huge," she whispered, her unprompted words a testament to her shock. "I thought you said they weren't the royal family?"

"No, lovebug," I said, tugging her along towards the side staff entrance. The longer we were out here, the more chance there was of us getting caught. "Remember, that's *Buckingham Palace*? Buckingham House is different."

What I didn't say was that the residents of Buckingham House weren't *that* far down the line of succession. The duke was about thirty-fifth the last time I Googled him. I shivered at the thought of the duke. My obsession with him was way out of hand. But I challenge any red-blooded female to work for someone like that and not indulge in some light internet stalking. The man was almost inhumanely attractive – powerful, a multi-billionaire if Wikipedia is to be believed, practically fucking royal and, to top it all off, he had a dry sense of humour that rivalled even my own, which was of the desert variety. Not that he would ever share his humour with me. He barely even ever looked at me. I was staff and, therefore, practically invisible to god-like beings such as the Duke of Buckingham.

But there were a couple of times when I did feel seen. Last week I'd been emptying the bin in the corner of the kitchen as the duke and his creepy brother-in-law, Blake, came in. I was ignored, as usual, as they discussed the meetings they had on that afternoon, but then Blake said:

"I'm sorry, old boy," his posh accent booming through the space, "but it simply won't fit. You can try to squeeze it in, but it'll be unbelievably painful for everyone involved."

I tried, I really did, but it was too tempting. So, before I managed to rein myself in, I muttered, "That's what she said," under my breath.

The problem was, although I used to swear like a sailor, I'd managed to train myself out of it after Hayley came to live with me, but leaving a perfect *That's What She Said* joke hanging was just too much for me to manage.

I bit my lip, hoping neither of them had heard (staff were, after all, supposed to stay as invisible as possible – much like the house elves in *Harry Potter*). I tried to make a quick exit, but when I turned around and flicked a glance in the duke's direction, he was closer than I thought he'd been, and his blue gaze was pinning me to the spot. Blake clearly hadn't heard, thank God, and was blabbering on about some other nonsense, totally unaware that his brother-in-law was staring at me or that I even existed. But the duke wouldn't stop staring, and I couldn't seem to move.

Eventually, one of his dark eyebrows winged up, the corner of his sexy mouth quirked on one side, and I swear I almost passed out with a lust head-rush right there in the kitchen, holding a bag of rubbish which smelt like last night's curry.

Then, just like that, the moment was over. He looked back to Blake, and I sucked in some much-needed oxygen, having held my breath throughout the entire unspoken exchange. As I scurried out of the kitchen, I felt my face heat with embarrassment. Why did I have to draw attention to myself? I mean, if I was going to draw the duke's attention, I'd rather it hadn't been whilst I was wearing leggings and my cleaning t-shirt, which proclaimed my love for Take That and had a tear in the collar, with my hair piled on top of my head like I was some ridiculous pineapple, and holding a smelly bag of rubbish.

And anyway, getting your employer's attention when you were in a service role was never good. The last cleaning job I had proved this when the husband, who I'd thought a pretty nice guy up until then, started invading my personal space. For a while, I thought I was being paranoid or overly sensitive, right up until the day he grabbed my arse.

That's where friendly banter with employers had got me, and was one of the reasons I now kept my head down, even if the thought of the duke grabbing my arse – or any other part of me – made me lightheaded. The man was a walking wet dream. I should know as *my* dreams were full of him.

That was another result of my late-night internet stalking, falling asleep to dreams of him calling me into that dark-wood, oldy-worldy, big man office of his, grabbing the scarf I wore in my hair off my head, sealing his mouth over mine and bending me over his thousand-year-old priceless antique desk.

Ah, the consequences of an over-active imagination and the frustration of a non-existent sex life.

There was no room for smouldering blue-eyed, tall men with muscular frames, wearing immaculate suits and designer beards in my life. I needed to concentrate on survival.

Anyway, The Stepladder Incident a few weeks ago had taught me that the duke, rather than finding me irresistible like my last employer, in fact had a full-blown allergy to touching me. Which, whilst mind-blowingly embarrassing, was fine. At least, that's what I told myself.

The only interaction I allowed myself with him now was through our daily game of chess. Not that we sat down together to play. It's just the chess set was always out in the snug, and whenever I cleaned the room it was in, I made my move. There was always a countermove the next day. So far, I was winning three games to one.

Hayley and I scurried in through the kitchen. Luckily, the catering staff weren't here this early. Either posh people made their own breakfast, or they were happy to subsist on strong coffee from their fancy coffee maker until noon – I suspected the latter.

I hurried down the massive corridor to the double doors of the drawing room. No sitting room for these peeps – no, it was all *drawing rooms* and *snugs*. There were multiples of both; depressingly, the smallest snug had more square footage than our entire flat. Slipping inside, I towed Hayley along to the spiral staircase in the corner of the large, high-ceilinged room. There were various armchairs and uncomfortable-looking brocade sofas facing each other in the centre of the huge space, a large fireplace on one side and tall windows with views over the gardens on the other.

"Up here," I whispered to Hayley, motioning for her to climb up first – it was steep, and I was known for my clumsiness. If she fell, I'd rather she landed on me; and if I fell, I'd rather not take her down with me.

The mezzanine had rows of bookshelves, and a billiards table sitting in the middle. Since the bookshelves were largely filled with encyclopaedias, which, thanks to the internet had been surplus to requirement for years, and I didn't think anyone had played bar billiards since the 1800s, Hayley was likely to remain undiscovered up here.

She tucked herself into a corner with the cushions I'd swiped on the way up, and snuggled into Keith whilst I helped her out of her coat and laid it over her like a blanket.

"We made it," I whispered, trying to sound excited rather than the acute relief I was actually feeling. "That was fun, right? Secret mission complete."

I wanted Hayley to think this was all a bit of a game and not to worry too much. The problem was she was an observant little thing – just like me. We could both read people and atmospheres with almost supernatural accuracy. The social worker called it hypervigilance. Apparently it was common in people with our background. Hayley would have picked up on the tense line of my shoulders, the worry in my eyes. My bright, fake smile wouldn't be fooling her.

My hand pressed to the centre of my chest before I pressed it to the centre of Hayley's. It was our non-verbal *I love you*. Hayley was smiling a small smile by the time I was done, which was the most I could ask for. Big bright smiles, giggles and such were not part of Hayley's make-up anymore, but I was determined to change that. So I kissed her forehead and straightened up from kneeling to start back down the spiral staircase.

Unfortunately, I'd only managed to get halfway down when a rich, deep voice sounded from the corridor, getting closer. When the double doors opened and those blue eyes locked with mine, I did what I do best – I tripped, and fell arse over tit down the steps.

CHAPTER 2

Put the furniture polish down

Ollie

Her chocolate brown eyes widened for a moment as they met mine, and I felt the familiar jolt of arousal that seemed to be totally out of control around this woman. And then of course, of *course*, she fell. I'd never encountered a human being as clumsy as Lottie Forest. Only last week, I'd found her on a fucking stepladder in the living room. When I'd barked "What the hell are you doing?" at her (which, I'll admit, was probably not a great idea), the ladder wobbled, and I was only just in time to catch her when it crashed to the side.

Holding Lottie in my arms was *not* the best plan in terms of suppressing this ridiculous attraction to her. The flush on her cheeks, her lips parting in shock and the feel of her soft body against mine, combined with her fresh floral scent, was enough to make me almost lightheaded with lust as all the blood left my brain, heading south. Why the hell this woman with her baggy dungarees, multiple ear piercings, messy caramel hair that was permanently piled on top of her head in one of her colourful scarves, and zero make-up made my body react so violently (not least when I'd felt barely anything for my last put-together, effortlessly sexy, glamourous ex-girlfriend) was a complete mystery. I'd been so shocked by my visceral reaction that once she'd got her feet on the ground, I'd pushed her away like she was on fire.

"Be more bloody careful," I'd snapped.

"I wouldn't have fallen off the blooming ladder if you hadn't been blustering around shouting at me," she'd snapped back, and I felt another surge of attraction to her. In general, Lottie was deferential and quiet.

Although I regularly noticed some fire behind her eyes, she almost never broke the lowly cleaner persona. Her actually answering me back gave me way too much of a thrill. But after a moment of silence, the colour drained from her face, the fire in her eyes died and she looked down at the floor.

"Sorry, sir," she muttered. "Of course, you're right. I'll be more careful."

I had felt irrationally angry at her sudden compliance, my arms crossing over my chest as I looked down at her.

"Why the hell do you think you need to be up on a stepladder anyway? You clearly don't have the required coordination."

Her eyes had flicked up to mine, and for a moment, there'd been another flash of that fire before she closed them and gave her head a quick shake as if to clear it. "There are cobwebs on the ceiling. I was getting rid of them. Your mother said—"

"You do not work for my mother. You work for *me*. No more stepladders."

She'd taken a step back, her eyes still downcast, and I'd felt my chest tighten at her retreat. Some very basic part of my brain had screamed at me not to allow her to back away. In fact, her backing away had felt all kinds of wrong.

And now she'd fallen again, but this time I hadn't been near enough to catch her. I made it to her just as she crashed to the wooden floor, landing on one leg and then falling onto her outstretched wrist and her hip, hard.

"For Christ's sake," I said as I crouched next to her, concern making my tone unnecessarily harsh. "You are the most accident-prone person on the planet."

One of my hands went to her shoulder, the other moved to push back her hair that had, for once, escaped from the confines of that ridiculous topknot. She flinched away from the contact, and I felt that crazy sense of loss again as she shuffled back out of my reach. I clenched my jaw in frustration, but when her tear-filled eyes met mine, my stomach hollowed out.

"Hey, sorry," I said in a softer tone. "I'm being a dick."

Surprise crossed her expression, making me feel like even more of an arsehole.

"Listen, are you okay?"

"I'm fine," she lied, clearing her throat and swiping a tear from her cheek.

"Let me help you up," I said, offering her my hand.

"I said I'm *fine*," she forced out through her teeth, ignoring my hand and then wincing when she tried to push up to standing using the wrist she'd fallen on.

"Lottie, you need—" I reached for her again, but she rolled away, to transfer her weight to her other hand.

"I'm *fine*," she said in a stronger voice now. For some reason, she glanced behind her up to the mezzanine for a moment before refocusing on me. "I don't need any help."

I held up my hands. "Okay, okay," I muttered.

"Oliver, are you in here?" We both flinched at the sound of my mother's voice. "Oh! Lottie, are you quite alright?" Mum said as Lottie used her good hand to get to her feet, trying to mask another wince as she put weight through her ankle.

"No, Mum," I said. "She's not alright. She fell down the bloody stairs."

"Oh golly!" Mum cried, hurrying across the room to where Lottie and I were now standing facing each other. "What rotten luck, darling. Are you okay? Do we need to...?" Mum trailed off, her gaze focusing on the mezzanine above for a moment.

She frowned slightly, her head tilted to the side before her eyes widened and shot to me. I felt my forehead furrow in confusion and was about to turn to look at whatever caught Mum's eye when she snapped, "Oliver!"

"Yes, Mum?" I asked after a long pause. Mum bit her lip and glanced at Lottie, whose face had paled even more. Mum cleared her throat as she transferred her gaze back to me.

"Er... maybe you should get back to work. I'll take Lottie to the emergency department."

"Honestly, I'm fine, Margot," Lottie put in, her voice high-pitched and more than a little panicked.

I scowled. Lottie's easy familiarity with my mum was in sharp contrast to her stiff formality with me. I'd told her to call me Ollie ages ago, but she still insisted on *sir*. At least she wasn't using *Your Grace* anymore.

"No need for anything like that. Just a couple of bruises." She smiled despite the pain I could see etched on her features, and I wanted to shake her.

"You're not fine," I said, my waning patience making my voice harsh. "You've fallen down a set of metal bloody stairs. You should—"

"Honestly," she interrupted, taking one of the multitude of hairbands she kept on her wrist and using it to tie up her hair again, clearly favouring her good hand. I was unreasonably disappointed to see the long mass of caramel waves re-confined in its elastic prison. I hadn't realised how very long her hair was or how it would frame her delicate face. "I'll just get on if that's okay." She started to walk towards her cleaning cart, but when her left ankle almost gave way, she limped along instead.

"Stop," I snapped, but, as seemed to be typical for her, she ignored me. "I mean it, Lottie. Mum's right. You need an X-ray of your wrist and ankle."

She pulled the furniture polish out of her basket with her good hand and then hobbled over to the sideboard to start dusting. Fucking dusting.

I strode over to her and took hold of her elbow gently, trying to ignore the zing of electricity that shot from her bare skin to my hand. My intention was to support her and help her to the sofa so she could take the weight off her ankle. But the stubborn woman flinched away from me and nearly fell over again.

"Lottie," I said in a warning tone. "Put the furniture polish down, and let me help you over to the sofa so you can put your foot up."

The pain in her expression was making my chest feel tight. Why was she being so stubborn?

"Your Grace," she started, and my hands clenched into fists. Great, we were back to the *Your Grace* bullshit. "I'm perfectly fine. I do not need to put my foot up or have any X-rays. I'd much prefer to finish my shift."

I threw up my hands in frustration as she limped around me to start dusting again. "I wasn't aware that you had completed a medical degree, Miss Forest."

It was subtle, and she'd been side-on to me at the time, but I was pretty sure she rolled her eyes.

"I don't need a medical degree to know I'd be wasting everyone's time going to the hospital," she said through her teeth, belatedly adding on, "sir."

Then the bloody stubborn lunatic, no doubt attempting to walk without a limp, put all her weight through that ankle. She couldn't hide her wince this time as all the colour drained from her face. When she swayed on her feet, I'd had enough.

"Right, that's it." I strode forward and then swept her legs from under her to catch her in my arms. She gasped in shock as I spun around with her securely held against my chest.

"What the Fraggle Rock are you doing?" she said in a horrified whisper while I carefully deposited her on the sofa, then took a rapid step back. I cleared my throat and shoved my hands into my pockets.

"Er… darling?" Mum put in. "We can't just go around picking up the staff and plonking them onto furniture on a whim. Maybe last century, but I'm quite sure even your great-great-grandfather would have drawn the line there."

Lottie glanced at Mum and started to spin her legs around to put them on the floor.

Okay, maybe what I'd done wasn't completely appropriate, but I was not going to witness that stark pain on Lottie's face again. So, before she could touch the floor, I'd pulled my hands out of my pockets, leaned down, grasped her slim calves in my hands and placed them back up on the sofa, pulling a throw cushion from the side and putting it under her feet. This unexpected move meant that Lottie was forced to lie back against the arm of the sofa. She stared up at me in disbelief.

I heard a muffled snort from Mum, which I very much suspected was a laugh.

"*I'm* taking you to the hospital," I announced, and Lottie's mouth fell open in shock.

"Oh actually, darling, don't you have that meeting with the developers?" Mum said, and Lottie shot her a grateful look. What the fuck is wrong with this woman? I'm offering to personally take her to get checked out. Me, Oliver Harding, the Duke of Buckingham, offering to take his cleaner to the hospital and she was looking at me like I'd grown another head. Women – and, truth be told, people in general – tended to do what I wanted them to do.

"You are not taking me anywhere, sir," Lottie said, that fire back in her eyes. "I'm staying and finishing my shift."

"As your employer, I cannot in good conscience allow you to work with a possibly broken ankle and wrist." And there it was, another eye roll. Unbelievable. "You will be coming to the emergency department right fucking now."

Her eyes flashed. Flecks of green appearing in the brown. Bloody hell, she really was beautiful.

"Go to your meeting," she snapped, and my eyebrows shot up.

"Might I remind you, Miss Forest," I said in a soft but lethal tone. "You are *my* employee. The only orders issued between us are going to be from *me* to *you*, and they will be obeyed. If you want to continue in my employment, then that is how this is going to work."

I immediately regretted the softly delivered threat. Her face paled again, this time so badly that she looked a little grey, and that green fire died in her eyes to be replaced by a look of almost panic, which I found myself absolutely despising. She glanced up at the mezzanine for a split second before looking back at me. Before I could turn to see what she was looking at, she sat up, and her small hand shot out to enclose my wrist. Again, the contact was almost electric. My heart rate picked up as I felt her skin on mine.

"Of course," she said, her voice now devoid of the previous fight, and my chest tightened. "I understand. I'll... I'll leave for the day. I'll get an X-ray. I promise. B-but I can't allow you to take me."

I looked down at her hand on my wrist, and she immediately released her hold. When my gaze lifted to meet hers it was like time stood still. The warm brown of her expressive eyes was impossible to look away from. That feeling of... connection, even possession, swept through me.

But it was even more than that. It was as if my very soul was looking straight at hers through her eyes and simply saying, "Oh, it's *you*. There you are."

It was official: I was losing my damn mind.

"Just go to the meeting, darling," Mum put in. Lottie flinched, and the spell was broken. Christ, I'd forgotten Mum was even in the room. "You told me how important it is, and you can't leave Vicky to deal with it on her own."

I frowned in frustration. No, there was no way I could let Vicky walk in there without me. "Fine," I bit out, checking my Rolex to see that it was already five minutes later than I'd wanted to leave. I shook my head to clear it, attempting to claw back my sanity and ignore the slight panic I felt at Lottie being hurt. She was my cleaner for fuck's sake. And lately, she'd been taking up way too much of my headspace, which I could not afford to lose to a too-young, stubborn, scruffy girl who wouldn't even call me by my first name.

So, I forced myself to ignore the part of me that wanted to sack off the meeting, leaving Vicky right in the shit, in order to take care of my employee who didn't even seem to like me. It was also clear that I wasn't helping the situation. All I seemed to have done was piss her off and then scare her by threatening her job.

"I don't have time for this anyway," I muttered under my breath, before turning back to Lottie. "You'd better be going to the hospital," I said, pointing at her to emphasise my point. "And you," I transferred my point to Mum, "better make sure she takes one of the town cars."

"Yes, darling," Mum agreed in a bright voice, which immediately made me suspicious. My mother was not, in general, an agreeable human. I narrowed my eyes at her for a moment, but she just smiled. "Off you go then to make the family another pile of money it doesn't need." Now, that was more like the mother I knew and loved. "Toodle-pip."

I glanced between Mum and Lottie, unable to shake the feeling that something was happening here that I didn't understand, and then I stalked out of the room.

And, of course, the meeting was a complete disaster because my head wasn't in the game enough to stop Vicky from insulting everyone there. No, my head was still focused on the way Lottie's face had paled when she put weight through her ankle and what possible motivation she could have had to pretend not to be hurt.

CHAPTER 3

Rich people were ruthless

Lottie

"You can come down now, child," Margot called up to the mezzanine, and my heart sank. We were totally rumbled. When there was no movement from up there, I sighed, resigning myself to losing my job.

"It's okay, Hayley," I said. "You don't have to hide anymore. The jig is up."

Still no movement.

"I promise I don't bite," said a smiling Margot. "Hmm, if you don't come down, I'll have to eat all the cookies the cook made myself, and then my bottom will be even fatter, and *then* I won't be able to ride my horse, Bertie."

I heard a shuffling from above at that. It would have been talk of horses and not the cookies that tempted her out. Hayley was obsessed with horses. We watched as her little face appeared between the banisters, her wide eyes flicking between Margot and me.

"Come on then," said Margot smartly. "You're needed to save my bottom and Bertie's back, remember?"

Hayley looked at me. When I nodded, she turned and started to make her way down the stairs.

"Careful, Hails," I said, and she looked at me again, raising her eyebrows as if to say *I'm not a complete clumsy idiot like you. I can make it down a set of stairs without making a complete numpty of myself.*

I scowled at her.

"I got distracted, okay? I didn't expect him to be home and it gave me a shock."

Hayley rolled her eyes: *You're clumsy all the time, even without the shock of your intimidating actual duke employer scaring the bejesus out of you.*

"Whatever," I muttered. "As if you never fall over."

Hayley's eyebrows went even higher, and I huffed in annoyance. "Okay, I'll give you that. You might have received the lion's share of our coordination genes."

Hayley had amazing balance and hand-eye coordination. If I could afford it, or indeed convince her to go, I would have her at every dance, tennis and gym club under the sun. As it was, she point-blank refused, so she was stuck playing tennis with me in the park on a Saturday, which, given my complete lack of skill, was not ideal.

Margot cleared her throat as Hayley made her way over to me. "You two *seem* to be having a conversation, but only one of you is speaking," she observed. "It's quite uncanny."

Hayley skirted the edge of the sofa to come and sit next to me, still clutching Keith. My good hand enclosed hers, giving it a squeeze.

"Margot, this is my sister Hayley. She isn't much of a talker, I'm afraid," I said quietly.

Hayley squeezed my hand back, and her gaze dropped to the floor as her cheeks turned pink.

Margot looked between us again with kind eyes, then approached the sofa to squat in front of Hayley.

"Never mind," she said in a soft voice. "Too many chatterboxes out there talking about big bottoms and horses, I say."

That drew a very brief bit of eye contact from Hayley and a small smile.

I blinked. Hayley rarely smiled at anyone but me, and certainly not within the first five minutes of meeting them. Apart from me, her grandparents and her teachers at school, there weren't really many other adults in her life. And her grandparents had only really shown an interest in the last six months. I'd been trying to encourage them to bond, but it was hard going. Brenda and Tony had hated my mother and, by extension, me. After all, they weren't *my* grandparents, as they reminded me frequently. The starkest reminder had been two weeks ago on Christmas Day. I'd been lonely plenty of times in my life, but that day may have been my lowest point.

"Listen, Margot," I said. "I really appreciate you not saying anything to your son when you spotted Hayley earlier. I wouldn't normally bring her with me, but... she had a dreadful tummy ache last night and this morning, and I just couldn't take her to school like that."

"Lottie, my son is usually a very charming chap. I'm not sure why he's behaving like a high-handed tyrant from the last century with you at the moment, but you can take sick days if you need to. He would never object to that."

I broke eye contact with her to glance at Hayley, then cleared my throat. "I... um, that's good to know, but I—" God, this was awkward. I didn't want to outright call Margot a liar, but I was pretty sure her son *would* frown on me taking sick days. I'd learnt the hard way that rich people were ruthless.

I shivered when I remembered the parting speech of my last employer, Mrs Buchanon. "I'm afraid we need reliable staff and somebody with the ability to... maintain *standards*." She'd been eyeing my trainers with the soles coming away and the frayed sleeves of my jumper when she said "maintain standards", and I'd never felt so mortified in my life.

I'd like to see her maintain standards clothing-wise on the budget I was subsisting on back then. I'd barely had enough for food and rent. But unfortunately, I couldn't really argue the reliability aspect. Hayley had been even worse when I was working for them. I'd explained the situation to the Buchanons, and they'd seemed sympathetic at first. But in the end, the straw that broke the camel's back was the week off I took for our mother's funeral. Mrs Buchanon just didn't want to be inconvenienced anymore with my "frequent absences". I don't think her husband's habit of eyeing my arse with undisguised interest helped either.

So no, I wasn't falling into the trap of thinking there was room for mistakes. Not anymore.

I cleared my throat. "Hails, why don't you check out the bookshelf?" I said, giving her hand a squeeze.

Hayley loved books, and one of the walls of this room was a floor-to-ceiling bookcase. Her eyes lit up, but then she frowned, glancing at my ankle again and biting her lip.

"I'm fine, lovebug," I said softly. She freed her hand from mine and lifted it up with her little finger extended. I linked it with my little finger and whispered. "Pinky promise." She glanced between me and the books, and I sighed. "It's okay. Go and have a look. They might have a copy of *Black Beauty*."

That did the trick. Her eyes went back to the shelves, and she finally gave into temptation, getting up from the sofa and crossing the room to start examining the spines.

I turned back to Margot once Hayley was sufficiently out of earshot. "I just really need to keep this job," I whispered. My stomach was feeling tight at how I'd argued with the duke earlier. The last thing I needed was to piss him off.

But he was so blooming bossy. Of course, he wasn't to know that my eight-year-old sister was hiding in his mezzanine, and that leaving for hospital without her was completely out of the question. So my reaction probably hadn't made that much sense. But, honestly, fraggle off, mate. I'd been looking after myself since I was ten; I could deal with a measly sprained wrist and ankle. God.

Margot's eyes flicked between me and Hayley.

"Your parents?" she whispered back, and I shook my head. Her mouth tightened, and a look of determination came over her face. Since working here, I'd come to realise that Margot was quite something. Despite the fact she had her own house in the country, she spent a *lot* of time in London, her favourite pastime interfering in her son's life and siphoning his money off into the various charity foundations she'd set up under the Buckingham name.

She was a force to be reckoned with, and I had a feeling Hayley and I were about to experience that first-hand.

CHAPTER 4

Twenty-something snowflakes

Lottie

I hated waitressing. For a start, I'd had to leave Hayley with Ada, my crazy eighty-two-year-old neighbour. Ada didn't mind; it wasn't as though Hayley was difficult to look after – she went to bed at seven-thirty, so all Ada had to do was hang out in my flat and eat my food (which she did with gusto – I knew I'd have another trip to the Co-op in my near future, hopefully not costing me more than the fifteen pounds I had left for the rest of the month). Also, waitressing ate into my time in the evenings when I could study for the Open University psychology course I'd been doing part-time for the last two years, which required about sixteen hours a week. Luckily, I'd been able to sneak some of those hours into my time at Buckingham House (seriously, the man did not need a cleaner, his house was immaculate – as I've said before, posh people are weird) but I still had to do the bulk of the work late at night.

But even without all of that, I would still hate waitressing. The trick was to try and fade into the background. My outfit would hopefully help with that – white shirt and black skirt which screamed *staff member*; low ponytail and minimal make-up. I was careful to fill people's glasses without making eye contact. No smiling at the guests. Hopefully, it wouldn't be a complete disaster...

"Bloody hell, you seen the totty they've got serving tonight?"

Ah. Fading into the background wasn't quite working as well as I'd hoped. I swallowed and moved to the next group, one of whom was the bloke who'd just described me as *totty*. His back was to me, so he obviously hadn't realised I was there. I'd have loved to just slope off, but the whole group had empty glasses, and I was carrying a full bottle of champagne. It would have meant skirting around all of them without serving them to get to the rest of the room, which would look very obvious and weird. I swallowed and moved forward.

"Champagne?" I muttered the low question, eyes downcast, cheeks hopefully not too red.

A couple of throats cleared in embarrassment, likely having realised what I'd heard. A few muttered yes, and I started filling glasses. Unfortunately, you can't pour champagne quickly, and with the number of glasses held out my way, I wasn't getting out of there anytime soon.

"See what I mean?" muttered the same voice as before, and I flinched, almost missing the rim of the next glass. Clearly, he was not one of the embarrassed cohort.

"Nice," hissed his friend in a voice I recognized, and my heart sank as I poured with an unsteady hand. I'd yet to actually see their faces as not only was I focused on their glasses, but they were all a *lot* taller than me.

"What's nice, Blake?" I blinked at the female voice, and my eyes flicked up to see a blonde woman had joined the group. She was absolutely stunning. I don't think I'd ever seen a woman as beautiful in real life. Her long black dress hugged her slender body, her hair was swept to the side in a glossy bun.

"Nothing, Vics," Blake said dismissively, and she cocked her head to the side as she stared at him, a frown marring her forehead.

I cleared my throat.

"Champagne?" I asked her, and she transferred her familiar, crystal blue, piercing gaze to me.

"Hello," she said, her unblinking eye contact a little disconcerting.

"Er... hi," I said, surprised to be addressed directly. Nobody addressed the waitresses directly at these things, especially not the women.

"You are *very* pretty," she told me, and I blinked again. There was a muffled snort of laughter in the group, which I ignored.

"Thanks?" I tilted my head to the side as I studied her. "So are you."

"Yes," she agreed simply.

"So bloody weird," I heard muttered next to me, but the woman didn't seem to notice as she maintained eye contact with me.

"Er... right, I'd better get going," I said stupidly, lifting the champagne bottle and waving it slightly to indicate that I should be getting on with my actual job. The blonde woman just kept staring at me. Okaaaay. I moved away to the next group and went back to being invisible.

After a couple of hours, I was beginning to really despise my shoes. My ankle wasn't broken, but it still ached. Four-inch heels were not doing it any good. I nearly told the catering manager where he could stick his job when he'd specified high heels, but then I'd looked at my electricity bill and thought better of it. The other issue was my wrist. Of *course* I had to fall on my dominant hand, the one I needed for pouring champagne.

I glanced at the large ornate clock on the wall: only two more hours to go. Right, I could manage that. I'd dealt with way worse. I shook out my wrist, picked up a new full bottle of champagne, took a deep breath and then walked back out into the thick of it. The problem was that by this stage, the men were all well-oiled and a lot more disinhibited.

As I moved through the crowd, there were more blatant attempts now to stare down my blouse; even some of the men clearly accompanied by their wives were culprits. Then there was the standing way too close, smelling my hair (barf!), crowding me so I had to squeeze past them which created the opportunity for a good accidental boob graze.

It was all very tedious, and I was beginning to feel a little punchy. So when I wobbled on my heels after I'd just escaped a particularly irritating group, and a large hand enclosed my upper arm to bring me to a stop, I reacted without thinking. Spinning around, I smashed the thankfully empty champagne bottle into the grabber.

"Lottie, it's me," the deep, familiar voice shot through me as the duke's crystal blue eyes stared down at me. He dropped my arm and held both his hands up in surrender. "I'm sorry," his voice was surprisingly soft for someone who'd just been hit with a blunt object. "I didn't mean to scare you."

My eyes were wide as I stared up at him. I took a small step back, and he frowned. I swallowed before trying to speak.

"Are you going to get me fired?" I asked.

"Lottie I—"

"Please," I said, cutting him off in my desperation. "Please don't report me to the manager. I really *need* this job."

"Okay, Lottie," he said again in that soft tone. "Take a breath. Did you hear me? *I* apologised to *you*. I don't usually..." he broke off, and his hand went to the back of his neck. "I'm not in the habit of accosting women like that, okay? It just looked like you might fall and... well, you may have past form, clumsiness-wise."

He was smiling a small smile now, and my mouth went completely dry. Cheese and crackers, this guy was almost too beautiful to be real. I cleared my throat and readjusted my grip on the champagne. I needed to get my shizzle together.

"Right, er... well, thanks, I guess."

I looked left and right and bit my lip. We seemed to have

attracted a fair bit of attention. Shiitake mushrooms, I hoped Thomas the D-word hadn't seen what happened. That would not bode well for my future employment. It was drilled into us how exclusive this place was, how the patrons were pretty much all celebrities or actual royalty, how discretion was *absolutely essential* and how the customer was always, *always* right. No exceptions.

Never in all Thomas the D-word's pep talks did he mention that it would be acceptable to smash customers, especially the practically royal ones, with champagne bottles.

"I'd better get going." I waved the bottle, forced a tight smile and started to step to the side. Unfortunately, my ankle was still not entirely happy with the heel situation, and I winced when I put weight on it, well aware I was still under that sharp blue gaze.

"You need to take the weight off that foot," he said, moving to block my retreat. We were really starting to attract attention now.

"I'm fine," I said through a fake smile, unable to keep the irritation from my voice.

"And you shouldn't be wearing heels," he said, as if I hadn't even spoken. "Even if you hadn't hurt your ankle, *you* should *never* wear heels. You have enough trouble staying upright without adding stilts into the equation."

"I'm not normally this clumsy," I said without thinking. "It's just being around you that—" Uh-oh. My eyes went wide as one of the duke's eyebrows winged up, his small smile more of a smirk now.

"Oh *really*," he said in a low voice. "You're only clumsy around me? Now that's interesting."

"Fugger off," I muttered, and his smile widened.

"Fugger? I'm not familiar with fuggering. Is this something you indulge in?"

I felt my face heat. I really need to start swearing like an adult, but the alternatives I came up with for Hayley's benefit were too ingrained now.

"Ah! There you are, old boy!" one of the grim blokes from earlier said, slapping the duke on the back and blocking him from my view. "Now, where were we on the Lexington deal? Has that land been commissioned for redevelopment yet? Government bastards still giving you gyp?"

Now, this was a far more typical example of a customer here – happy to look down my blouse and cop a feel if they could get away with it, but beyond that, actual acknowledgement of my existence was rare. Unless they wanted a drink, of course.

"Giles," the duke said through gritted teeth. "I'm just in the middle of something. Could you...?"

I didn't hear the rest as I melted back into the crowd as fast as my hobbling gait would let me.

I managed to avoid the duke for another hour, but he caught up with me at the most mortifying moment possible. It was close to midnight by then, and what with the free-flowing champagne, the disinhibition from before was verging on outright vulgarity.

"Get over there and bloody well do your job," Thomas the D-word snapped at me, shoving another tray of drinks into my hands.

"I'd really rather not serve that group again," I said through my teeth.

"Suck it up, buttercup," he sneered. "Christ, you bloody twenty-something snowflakes. If you can't handle the occasional wandering hand, then don't bother coming in. Plenty of girls would put up with a lot more considering the tips you make here."

It wasn't worth arguing, so I squared my shoulders and limped my way over to the group in question – a table of only men, one of whom was Mr Buchanon (minus his wife), another was the disgusting Giles.

I'd seen the Buchanons together earlier in the evening, and they'd both ignored me, except when Mr B peered down my cleavage. Either Mrs Buchanon had got tired of her husband's

BS and gone home, or he'd sent her home so he could act like disgusting pond scum with impunity. His friends were all cut from the same cloth. I knew rich blokes like this. Off the leash for the rest of the night. Their next stop would be a strip club or a brothel.

"She's back!" one of them shouted as I approached. I gave him a tight smile, willing myself to go back to being invisible. I was carrying a tray laden with drinks, and my wrist was screaming at me.

"Finished cleaning the toilets yet?" Mr Buchanon asked, and they all laughed. "Such a shame Virginia fired you. It was nice having a bit of eye candy around the house."

"You lucky sod," Blake, Ollie's brother-in-law slurred; he seemed to be by far the worse for wear of any of them, practically sliding out of his chair and having difficulty keeping his head up.

"Excuse me," I muttered, trying to put the tray down on the table, but these bastards were not going to make it easy for me. There were empty glasses everywhere and nowhere to put the tray. Nobody made any move to clear a space. They barely made room for me to get the table at all. I had to squeeze in between two of them who were sitting in their leather chairs like the kings of the universe they considered themselves.

"Looks like you should have been a bit more on it with clearing the table, darling," one of them said with a smirk, still making no move to help. I flinched as a large hand clamped around the back of my leg behind my knee. When I frowned down at Giles and tried to jerk away, his grip tightened enough to cause bruises.

"Let me go," I bit out. My wrist was really aching now, and the tray had started to wobble.

"Way-hay!" some of the men called as the drinks swayed precariously. "Careful, darling." The hand slid up higher, and his grip tightened even more. That, combined with the smell of all the alcohol, made my stomach lurch, and I prayed I wouldn't vomit.

I swallowed my pride. "Please," I said, not above begging. "I can't..."

As his sweaty hand moved even higher, I jerked again. It was just exactly my luck the drink that fell was red wine and that it didn't fall onto any of these jerks. No, it fell back towards me. I gasped as the contents of the huge glass soaked my white shirt. There were catcalls from the whole table now, all of whom were loving this.

But just as my wrist was about to give out on me completely, the tray was whipped out of my hands and dumped on the table right on top of the empties, spilling most of the other drinks. There were shouts as the liquid ran out onto all of the men around the table.

At the same time, the hand on my leg was ripped away, and I stumbled back to see the duke towering over Giles, holding his wrist in an iron grip. Then, in a sudden movement, the duke pulled Giles out of his chair, pushed his arm behind him at an unnatural angle, and then shoved him face-first into the mess that was on the table. The duke held him there, almost casually, as Giles struggled to get free.

The table fell silent. In fact, the whole bar fell silent.

"Apologise to the lady, Giles, you piece of shit." The duke's voice was eerily calm, not like he was about to break this poor guy's arm or had him pinned with his face pressed against the wet table.

CHAPTER 5

The way the world works

Lottie

"Shit, my arm, Ollie, I—" he screamed as the duke readjusted his grip so Giles's arm was so far up his back it looked like his shoulder might dislocate.

"No," the duke said slowly, not seeming to need to expend much effort at all to keep Giles in place. "You can beg me in a moment. *First*, you will apologise to the lady."

"You're going to break my fucking arm!" Giles shouted.

"Then you'd better get on with it. Right fucking now, Smithe."

"I'm sorry," he gasped out. "Jesus Christ, please. I'm sorry, okay?"

The smell of the red wine was overpowering, and I really felt like I might vomit then or faint. But I couldn't let the duke break Giles's arm, however much he deserved it. The whole table was frozen in horror as they watched it play out. Mr Buchanon looked like he was going to vomit as well, and Blake's face had paled to an almost unnatural greenish colour.

"Ollie," I said softly, moving forward to put my hand on his arm. I could feel the muscles bunched under the suit fabric. "Please, just let him go. I'm fine."

He blinked at my use of his first name. I'd done it to get his attention, and it seemed to do the job. He frowned at me.

"You're *not* fine. Stop saying you're fine when you're not. It's infuriating."

I gave him a weak smile. Giles was still struggling under Ollie's grip, but it was like he didn't even notice – all his attention was on me.

"Okay, maybe I'm not fine. But please... everyone's looking."

"I don't give a fuck."

I squeezed his arm. "Well, I do. And... um, I don't feel so good."

I wobbled on my feet as a wave of lightheadedness and nausea came over me. The smell and the pain were really getting to me now.

"Shit," Ollie muttered, finally releasing Giles to reach for me and steady me by gently supporting both my arms under my elbows.

"I think I'm gonna be sick."

I'd barely managed to get the whispered words out before his arm was around me, and I was being propelled across the room. When I stumbled, he lifted me so he was practically carrying me.

I felt too awful to pull away, so I just let myself be pulled against his chest, trying to breathe in his glorious aftershave and block out the smell of red wine, but it was just too overpowering.

Instead of going into the public toilets, he took me through a door marked *Staff Only*, down a small corridor and into a large office. Thank the Lord, there was an ensuite bathroom. I pushed away from Ollie and flew into it, slamming the door behind me, and then I re-experienced my lunch in reverse, beyond caring that Ollie was only just behind the door and could hear me retching. At least I hadn't had time for dinner tonight – that was something.

When I was done, I flushed the toilet and managed to wash out my mouth at the sink but felt another wave of nausea as I smelt the red wine again. There was a reason I couldn't drink alcohol — the smell brought back such horrendous memories it wasn't worth it. But now, with my entire shirt soaked, I couldn't get away from it. Without thinking I ripped my shirt off, threw it into the corner of the bathroom, grabbed the hand towel off the rail next to me and sank down onto the cold tiles with it clutched to my chest.

"Lottie?" I heard his deep voice through the door. "Are you okay?"

"No," I whispered, too low for him to be able to hear. "I'm not okay. My life is a total shitshow, and I have no idea how to claw my way out."

I closed my eyes and let one tear fall down my cheek. Just a few moments of self-pity. I'd go back to being a "strong, competent, capable caregiver" after that. I snorted. If social services could see me now, they'd restart all their applications to have Hayley taken from me.

"Please, Lottie," he said, concern threaded through his tone now. "Just let me know you've not passed out in there."

Another tear slipped down my cheek, and I didn't trust myself to speak.

"Lottie," his voice was firmer now. "Answer me, or I will come in anyway."

Oh shit. I swallowed and tried to get my throat to work, but it was too late. The door swung open, and his huge frame filled the doorway. I swiped at my cheeks, but I knew it was too late. Crying on the bathroom floor in a wine-soaked bra was a new low, even for me.

"Hey," he said softly as he crouched down in front of me.

"Hey," I managed to choke out.

He glanced at the shirt I'd thrown into the corner, then back at me.

I clutched the towel tighter around me.

"I can't stand the smell of alcohol," I explained, my voice hoarse.

He cocked his head to the side.

"Unusual career choice working in a bar then," he said through a small, teasing smile.

I snorted. "Ha. Career choice. You're funny."

People like me didn't make *career choices*. People like me took what work we could get to survive. But then he wouldn't understand that. I flinched when he stood up in a sudden movement and then my mouth dropped open when he started undoing his tie.

"What are you doing?" I managed to get out in a horrified whisper.

His suit jacket was the next to go. He chucked it onto the floor of the bathroom. I caught sight of the Armani label and gritted my teeth. Here I was, stressing about how my only decent white shirt was covered in red wine, and he threw Armani suit jackets worth thousands of pounds onto dirty tiles without a second thought.

"Here," he said. I turned my attention from his jacket to look back up at him, and I stopped breathing altogether.

His shirt was off.

Dear God, his shirt was off, and I knew I should be horrified but I had never seen any man this perfect. Well aware that I should be screaming in this situation, my mouth stayed firmly closed. My eyes roamed over the bunched muscles of his biceps, his broad chest down to his defined abs. When I managed to force my gaze to his face, he was trying to suppress a smile.

"I'm not that kind of girl," I whispered, and he rolled his eyes.

"Lottie, I'm not getting undressed to assault you in a bathroom after you've just been assaulted in my bar. I'm offering you my shirt. If you've quite finished checking me out, you could take it."

I blinked and then realised that, yes, he was holding his shirt right in front of my face; I'd just been too fixated on his body to notice it. I cleared my throat.

"I can't take your shirt. I'll get wine on it."

"Take it, Lottie."

Realising that really this was my only choice, I clutched the towel to me with one hand and used the other to take the shirt. He moved back as soon as I'd taken it from him as if to emphasise his lack of interest in assaulting me. My face flushed with heat. Of *course* he wasn't propositioning me. As if he needed to proposition anyone. The man was in the top fifty eligible bachelors in the country, according to *Hello!* magazine.

Wow, I really needed to stop Googling my employer.

"Thanks," I said, my voice low and defeated. "For everything."

He snatched his jacket and tie off the floor before focusing back on me. "Put on the shirt and stay in the office. Do not go back out onto the floor. I'll be back." With that, he swept out of the room, and I heard the office door slam behind him.

"Right," I whispered. "Woman up, Forest."

I pulled off my heels and pushed up onto my feet. His shirt was massive on me. It fell to my knees, and I had to roll the sleeves up a ridiculous number of times to find my hands. I picked up my shoes, glanced at my ruined top but couldn't bring myself to pick it up yet. When I limped out of the bathroom, I came to an abrupt halt. The blonde woman from earlier was standing in the middle of the office staring at me, still looking immaculate.

"Er... hi," I said.

"Hi," she returned but then just kept staring at me.

"Right, I'm gonna go, so—"

"Ollie doesn't want you to go."

I blinked at her. Was she the duke's girlfriend? She certainly looked like she could be. Blonde, stunning, impeccably dressed.

"Er... sorry, lady, but I'm still gonna go."

She shook her head. "You can't go, and he said you need to sit down."

My eyebrows went up. "Listen, maybe your boyfriend can tell you what to do but—"

"Sit down, Lottie," the duke said as he strolled through the office door, back to full commanding, master of the universe mode. Now I'd been bossed around, manhandled and talked down to all night. This was the final straw.

"I'm *not* sitting down," I said through gritted teeth. "I've said thank you for what you did, but my only good white shirt is ruined, I stink of wine, my ankle and wrist hurt, I've been totally humiliated and I need to go home now." Ugh, my voice would have to break over those last few words. I really was pitiful.

"I know, Lottie," the duke's voice was back to soft now. Without me even really realising what he was doing, he'd gently manoeuvred me into the chair I was standing next to, pulled up another one, put a cushion on it, lifted my foot up onto the cushion and laid an ice pack over my throbbing joint. It was all done in the space of a few seconds. I tried to protest, but the weight off my ankle and the cold surrounding it felt so good that the words died on my lips. "My car's being brought around now, alright?"

"You should really listen to him," his stunning, maybe-girlfriend added. "Ollie *always* knows the best thing to do."

I gritted my teeth. I did not want to be lectured on Ollie's virtues by his girlfriend of all people. The white-hot jealousy actually scared me a little. What right did I have to be jealous over a blinking duke for flip's sake?

"I can get an Uber home."

The duke looked down at his phone, muttering, "No need. Car's here."

I was just about to speak again when the office door flew open.

"Your Grace," Thomas the D-word said as he burst into the room. When he saw me he froze. "Er..." he swallowed, then looked back at the duke. "I was told there was a problem with one of the staff?"

The duke straightened up from crouching next to me and I could feel a dangerous energy filling the room as he turned to Thomas the D-word.

"No, that is *not* what I said," he told him, his voice low and lethal. "I said there was a big fucking problem with the way this shithole is being managed."

I blinked. This was one of the most exclusive bars in London. Actual royalty was here tonight. Most of the wine cost £500 a bottle. The Nag's Head round the corner from me, now *that* was a shithole. This place, not so much.

Thomas the D-word cleared his throat. "I'm not sure what you—"

"There is no security."

"Oh, no, we've got security. They're—"

"You've got security on the door. There is no security on the floor."

"On the floor?" TTD repeated in confusion. "Why would we need security on the floor?"

"To police the dickheads you let in here."

"Police the..." TTD trailed off and then shook his head. His voice dropped to a whisper when he spoke again. "Y-you don't police these people."

"What the fuck are you talking about?" snapped the duke, clearly losing patience. TTD was shaking his head.

"The security is to keep the bar exclusive. The members inside the bar, on the floor. I-I-I... you don't police these people. I wouldn't dream of... I mean, there's no way I could set bouncers on any of them."

"Again, what the fuck are you talking about?" the duke's voice was rising now. "*Those people* have been routinely making one of your waitresses feel uncomfortable all night until one bastard touched her." He said *touched her* as if it was a capital offence. I rolled my eyes.

"Honestly, Your Grace," I said. "You must know that policing your mates out there is not an option. They pay an exorbitant membership fee to this place, and they're used to people putting up with their BS. They are not used to being told what to do. Give TTD a break, for flip's sake."

"TTD?" the duke asked, but I kept my mouth shut and he frowned. "Look, I don't care who they are. Nothing gives them the right to treat you like that."

"That's not the way the world works," I snapped, aware that my voice was rising but beyond caring. "People like *me* serve people like *you* and we do it with a smile on our faces, putting up with all manner of manure. Now, I don't have time to sit here listening to this nonsense. If I'm not working and therefore not earning, I want to go home in an Uber, and, seeing as I've very likely lost my job, I want to be paid for tonight before I leave and given my tips in cash. Because, Your Grace, there's a reason people like me work for unbelievable self-pleasurers like TTD here. We *need the money.* You might think you're the ruler of the entire known universe, but you can't upend the pecking order of this country on a whim."

"I might not be able to 'upend the pecking order of this country', Miss Forest," the duke said in a carefully controlled voice, "but I sure as *fuck* can tell *my* manager how to run *my* bar considering I bloody well own it."

There was a pause. Okay, I did not know that he owned this place. Come to think of it, hadn't he said "my bar" in the bathroom earlier? Not that it should have surprised me – he did own half of London.

I cleared my throat. "Oh," I said. "Right, well, in that case, carry on."

"Thank you," he said in a dry tone before turning back to TTD. "Security on the floor *now*, and I want the rest of those dickheads ejected from the club with a lifetime ban. Understand me?"

"Yes, of course," TTD said, glancing between me and the duke.

"*Now*, Thomas," the duke snapped, and TTD jumped into action, scurrying out of the room without a second look. The duke turned to me again and sighed.

"Lottie, I'm really sorry, but I'm going to have to insist you let my driver take you home." I looked between him and the blonde in confusion. She didn't look the least bit put out, just curious. Her head was still tilted to the side as she studied me – definitely a bit of an oddball. "He's outside now. I'll take you to him then I'd better go back and sort out this shitshow."

He extended his hand to me. I hesitated, but my mind flashed back to him nearly dislocating a man's arm in an effort to defend my honour, and I felt strangely comforted. I was officially losing it.

When I did place my hand in his, and his strong fingers closed over mine, I had the weirdest feeling. The only way I can describe it is that at that moment, with my hand in his, I felt as if everything was right. All the stress of the evening melted away. It was just me and him. No duke, no cleaner, no boundaries, no social norms, no shitty entitled parodies of the great and the good out beyond the office door.

Just Ollie and Lottie, hand in hand.

The feeling was so overwhelming that when my eyes met his, I couldn't help it; despite the awful evening I'd had, despite all my worries, despite his actual *girlfriend* standing not two feet away, I smiled at him.

And he smiled right back.

CHAPTER 6

My hand may have dropped

Lottie

"Cheese and crackers!" I shouted, leaping at least two feet in the air and dropping the Mr Muscle bathroom cleaner and the wet cloth I'd been carrying. Because there, right in front of me, having just emerged from his bathroom and wearing only a towel, was the man I'd been trying to avoid for the last month. The brief flash of his broad, muscular torso I'd had in the bathroom of his club had reigned supreme in all my fevered dreams and fantasies for weeks, but *this* – this visual with water droplets running into the grooves of his abs and his towel hanging low on his hips – I knew would escalate things significantly. I'd be lucky if I remembered my own name after this, let alone run my vastly complicated life whilst caring for a child.

I swallowed and forced my gaze up to his face.

"Get a good enough look?" the duke asked. His smirk was so outrageously sexy that if smouldering looks had the power to melt women, I would be a pool of goo at his feet. As it was, my face felt like it was on fire. Shock rendered me completely immobile. I just continued to stand there staring at him.

"You alive in there?" he teased as he took a step towards me. "Had a stroke or something?"

He was so close now that I could smell him: fresh man mixed with crisp shower gel. I'd only have to lift my hand up a few inches, and I'd be touching him. The thought of touching his bare chest, of being allowed to do that, gave me a headrush so strong I felt like I was going to pass out. So I jerked away and took a couple of rapid steps back. My heart felt like it was beating outside of my chest.

"Sugar, sugar, sugar," I repeated rapid fire as I used my hand to cover my eyes. "I'm sorry! I thought you were in Paris. Why aren't you in Paris?"

I was desperate to continue backing away but then remembered I'd dropped all the cleaning products, complete with a damp cloth, on his carpet, so with my eyes still covered, I crouched down, feeling blindly on the floor for my stuff.

I froze when a large hand caught mine. Then I separated the fingers of my other hand just enough to peer through them at a smiling duke crouched in front of me, his towel very much in danger of revealing more than it covered. I squeaked and snapped my fingers back into place as he chuckled. The Mr Muscle and the cloth were both put into my extended hand and I straightened up like a shot.

"I'm sorry I'm not in Paris, Lottie," the duke said.

Oh, my giddy aunt, the man was apologising to his cleaner for being in his own bedroom, in his own house. My mind flashed to the open textbook I'd left in the snug and I winced, praying he hadn't seen the evidence of my skiving.

"No, no. It's fine," I waved the Mr Muscle in front of me as I backed away. "You can be here... or in Paris. I-I-I—"

"Lottie!" he said sharply, but it was too late; my feet hit something soft behind me, and I went flying backwards. But before I could hit the floor, a strong hand was at my back, whilst another cradled my head, and I was suspended in midair. I could feel the heat of his body inches from mine, feel the large hand across the entire of my back and in my hair. I still had my fingers over my eyes.

"You must be the clumsiest human being I've ever met in my life," his low voice was shaking with humour, and I could feel his breath on my cheek. He was so close. "Er... Lottie?"

"Yes," I squeaked.

"I have a small towel issue."

"W-w-what do you mean?"

"As in, I no longer *have* a towel."

"Cheese and crackers," I breathed, and he chuckled again.

"I'm not sure what savoury snacking has to do with it, but I should warn you that my dick is very much out, so if you don't want an eyeful, I suggest you keep your hand in place as I lay you down. I'll go back to the bathroom and call when I'm out of sight, okay?"

I nodded.

Now, I'm a good girl. Really, I am. I don't swear. I look after my sister. I don't sleep around. I don't even drink. But I will admit that as that man gently laid me on the floor, the gap between my fingers widened, as did my eyes when I got a good view of what he was packing (and let's just say the man's big dick energy was wholly justified).

Then my hand may have dropped altogether as he walked back into the bathroom, sans towel.

*

"I looked at your ding dong." There, I said it. If he needed to fire me, he could.

"I see," he said as he strolled through the kitchen in his suit, looking so unfairly attractive and put-together that I felt like even more of a scruffy little perv.

"I would never have gone into your bedroom like that... without knocking, I mean, if I'd have known you weren't in Paris."

"You seem to be kept abreast of my movements pretty well," he said as he started making himself a coffee with his fancy coffee maker. I shifted uncomfortably on the spot.

"Er... well, your mum is... she's chatty."

Margot was around at least a couple of times a week at the house. She always seemed to have *important things* to do in London – mostly spending her money and hosting charity events. I liked Margot. She was one of those posh, no-nonsense, horsey women, and she was honest – *very* honest. With my ability to tell if people were lying, that was really quite refreshing.

"Hmm."

He was watching me over the rim of his cup as he drank his coffee. All the man was doing was drinking a cup of coffee, but I didn't think I'd ever found anything more attractive in my life. He had stubble today – thick, manly stubble. My mind wandered to how the stubble would feel against my cheek. Then, before I knew it, I was picturing him in all his naked glory again. I felt my cheeks heat and ducked my head.

"Right, well, best be getting on," I said, my voice unnaturally high as I backed away towards the door.

"Weren't you in the middle of cleaning the kitchen? Isn't this where you should be *getting on*."

"I... well, I-I-I..." I took another step back, and he frowned.

"Don't avoid me," he said in that commanding tone, and I had to grit my teeth to hold back a smart-arse response. I didn't know if it was his blue blood, his upbringing, his private school education, his general sense of entitlement or just his actual personality, but he was so blooming bossy.

"I'm not avoiding you."

"Yes, you are."

I narrowed my eyes at him.

"You know what? You can't order someone not to avoid you."

"Why not?"

"Holy guacamole. Why? Are you serious? Have you ever been told *no*?"

He tilted his head to the side and smiled. Honestly, this kind of sex appeal should be illegal. He wasn't safe for women with functioning ovaries to be around.

"Rarely," he conceded.

"Well, I'm not avoiding you. And even if I were, could you blame me? I don't think I've ever been so embarrassed as I was that night in the bar, which you own. Is there anything in London that you don't own?"

"Don't be embarrassed."

My eyebrows shot up. "Again, a little coaching on basic human interaction, which I fear may be a good thirty years too late, but you can't just order someone not to be embarrassed."

"I just did."

"Well, it doesn't work that way, you numpty." I froze before my eyes went wide. Was I trying to get fired?

"Numpty?" His smile was wide and glamorous now – it was like looking into the sun. "I don't think anyone's ever called me a numpty before. I like it."

Instead of the irritation or annoyance I would have expected to feel filling the room, all I could detect was amusement and… interest.

I blinked. Okay, so not fired.

"You're a bit of a rare one," I whispered, and then he did something almost magical: he laughed. It was deep and rumbly and glorious. I could have listened to it all day.

"You definitely know how to throw a compliment around," he finally said through his laughter, his eyes still dancing.

I shrugged as a small, involuntary smile tugged at my lips. It was literally impossible not to smile surrounded by that rich laughter. I took a step towards the kitchen island and away from the exit, shuffling carefully as if approaching an unpredictable large predator. The duke shifted away slightly like he was giving me space to come further into the room, trying not to spook me. I cleared my throat and squared my shoulders to do something I should have done a month ago.

"Thank you for helping me keep my job at the bar," I said quietly, putting my kitchen spray down on the marble of the island. His smile dropped as he lowered his mug to the counter and crossed his arms over his broad chest.

"You didn't do anything wrong."

One side of my mouth quirked up at that. The world didn't work that way. Just because I didn't do anything wrong didn't mean I wouldn't have been fired for causing a scene like that. People like me had to toe the line, however unfair that line was, and people like him would never understand that. There was no point explaining it to him.

"Is there better security on the floor now?" he asked, and I cocked my head to the side.

"Er... sure."

"You don't *sound* sure."

"I am," I said firmly. "It's a great place to work."

Okay, so yes, there were bouncers in the club now, and nobody touched the waitresses, but that didn't change the overall vibe of the place – rich, powerful men served by young women in four-inch heels. The physical harassment may have stopped, but the verbal...

He frowned. "I own the freehold, but I don't have much to do with the running of the bar. My brother-in-law, Blake, sorts that side of things."

I held back a cringe. His brother-in-law was a drunk (I was guessing that he wasn't one of the people who'd received a lifetime ban as I'd seen him since that night), but I was filing that info in the *not my blooming business* category. No way would I bad mouth the duke's family to his face.

"Why are you working there anyway?"

I held back an eye roll. Rich dudes, honestly.

"Oh, you know, it's always been my dream to serve overpriced drinks to rich people. I feel like I'm fulfilling my life's calling. It's where I'm *meant to be*."

"Lottie," he said in a warning tone, and that's when I did roll my eyes.

"I need the money, dufus. Why do you think I'm working there?"

He blinked again.

"Dufus?"

I bit my lip. What was wrong with me today? Luckily his frown had melted to a smile. For a duke, this guy seemed to really enjoy getting insulted. Despite his naturally overbearing nature, which he'd demonstrated on a few occasions now, the duke surprised me. For some reason he clearly didn't want me working at that bar, yet he hadn't ordered me not to. Instead, he did this:

"Would you like a cup of tea?"

"What?" I said in shock.

"You know, tea," he said in a patient tone. "Brown, British, hot liquid. You drink an inordinate amount of the stuff. Tea."

"How do you know I drink tea?"

"You leave little clues," he said as he pulled down one of the super-fancy, ultra-delicate china cups from the display cabinet just along from where all the standard mugs and kettle were. The teacup looked totally ridiculous in his huge hands as he raised it toward me. My face flooded with heat. I was the worst cleaner in the history of cleaning. Not only had I been using those beautiful, exquisite, antique china cups to drink my tea out of, but I'd been leaving them dirty around the house for my employer to find.

"Cheese and rice," I breathed as he flipped the kettle on to boiling. "I'm sorry. I know I shouldn't have been a) stealing your tea, b) drinking it out of priceless china or c) leaving said priceless china around your house."

He smirked as he pulled a matching saucer out of the same cabinet, then carelessly chucked the teacup onto it so that the china rattled.

"Careful!" I snapped before I could stop myself. "Or I mean, it *is* your china so I guess, er... be careful if you want to. It's just it's really pretty and..."

"I think my favourite teacup findage was the one I discovered in my shower, right there with the shampoo." He was opening up the teabag tin now and putting one directly into the cup. I bit my lip to stop myself from telling him that you don't make tea that way – you have to use the pretty teapot and the tea-cosy, then let it brew for at least five minutes, then add a splash of milk to the cup, then and only then do you add the tea. "You don't take sugar, do you?"

"You can't make me tea," I said in a horrified whisper.

He looked between me and the teacup and raised his eyebrows.

"Evidence would point to the contrary," he said in a dry voice.

Point to the contrary – he was so posh! Who spoke like that? Dukes, that's who.

He'd now chucked the teabag onto the counter (there was clearly a limit to a duke's kitchen abilities) and was about to hand the cup to me when he paused.

"Oh, I nearly forgot." He grabbed the biscuit tin, selected a custard cream, put it onto the saucer next to the cup and then brought it all over to me.

"You know that I eat your custard creams," I whispered, mortified.

He chuckled. "Lottie, you eat about three packets a week. Who do you think makes sure there's a steady supply?"

I slumped into the kitchen stool in front of my tea. What was the point of pretending to be the perfect professional now? May as well enjoy the tea (despite the substandard way it was prepared).

"So," he said, taking the stool next to me and making my heart skip a beat when his leg brushed mine. "About the chess game..."

CHAPTER 7

Duke of Fuckingham

Ollie

"I have a crush on my cleaner."

"You... what?" Felix's voice rose, and Mike choked on his coffee.

"My cleaner. I have a crush on her."

"*Mrs Higgins?*"

I stared at Felix. "Yes, dufus." Wow, I was really picking up her little non-swears now. "I have a crush on a sixty-five-year-old grandma who hates my guts."

"Totally tracks," Mike said without missing a beat. "You rich, aristocratic dudes are weird. Nanny fixations and all that. Who knows who you want to fuck? Probably gone through all the posh birds in London within your age bracket."

"Why don't you sod off back to Little Buckingham to your little woodwork projects, yeah?"

"You're just jealous I can actually make something with my hands like a *real man*. None of this namby pamby land-owner, finance bullshit."

Mike's custom-made furniture was actually pretty cool, but there was no way I would ever admit that to the smug bastard.

"I can do plenty with my hands, thank you very much."

"Oh yeah?" Mike smirked. "Lucky Mrs Higgins."

"I'm not fucking Mrs Higgins!"

"Who *are* you fucking then?" Felix asked, and I sighed.

"I'm not fucking anyone." Two sets of raised eyebrows greeted that statement, and I rolled my eyes. "Whatever, I'm not that much of a whore."

"Bucks, mate, you're a total whore," Felix said, and I gritted my teeth.

"Not anymore. I *told you*: I've got a crush."

"Okay," Mike put in. "Let me get this straight. You, Oliver Harding, the Duke of Fuckingham –"

I growled. This stupid nickname had plagued me for years. Ever since that bloody article ran in the *Daily Mail* with the headline 'Inside the Duke of Fuckingham's Sex Party', courtesy of my ex-girlfriend Cordelia, who (when she started doubting whether she was in line to be the next duchess) had decided to sell a hugely embellished version of that night's events to the paper, complete with grainy photos.

In reality, the party, while lively, was certainly not a *sex party*. It was held at Buckingham Manor, my country estate which had a pool – hence the bare-chested pictures of me – but it hadn't been the massive orgy the paper implied. Granted, since then I hadn't made much effort to improve my reputation. I maybe could have shagged fewer birds in my twenties, but my God, I hadn't slept with anyone now for over six months – *six months*. So, it was totally unwarranted now for Mike to use that nickname. Try telling these twats that, though.

"– you have a crush on an actual woman," Mike went on, "and you're not fucking her?"

"What, like some bullshit unrequited love situation?" spluttered out Felix. "Are you serious?"

"What's so surprising about that?" I asked.

"Ollie, when it comes to you, there's no pining, no crush, no unrequited anything. You fancy a bird, you fuck her – repeatedly if you should choose – then you move on."

I shifted on my chair. "I'm not a total bastard," I mumbled. It wasn't like I went around London sleeping with any woman I wanted with no consequences. I dated like anyone else. It was true my relationships usually didn't last longer than a few weeks, but I wasn't just bowling up to ladies' bedrooms, doing the deed and then buggering off. I was a gentleman. Plus, after the whole Cordelia debacle, trust had been a real issue for me.

"We're not saying you are," said Felix. "It's just... Ollie, there's no reason for you to have a crush."

"Why?"

"Because any woman would jump into bed with you, no effort required," said Mike. "Number one, you're pretty as fuck – even I can see that, and no, I do not want to fuck you; number two, you're the smoothest motherfucker I know – there's chat, and then there's Duke of Fuckingham chat, it's on another level, man; number three, you're an actual bloody *duke*. Any straight woman or gay man in this country would fuck you at the drop of a hat."

"I *knew* you thought I was pretty," I said through a smirk, and it was Mike's turn to roll his eyes.

All three of us were tall and built, but Felix and I were definitely in the well-groomed, pretty category compared to Mike. Our muscular physique was a product of hours in the gym, Mike's huge frame was the result of manual labour. And whilst Felix and I had thick, sharply groomed, designer stubble, Mike had a full-on beard, which he shaved off every couple of weeks, but it grew back within hours. Felix and I matched the other patrons of the restaurant we were in with our perfectly tailored suits, whilst Mike's bulky flannel-over-thermal top paired with ripped (and not in a designer way) paint-stained jeans stuck out like a sore thumb.

To be fair to Mike, he'd wanted to go to the café round the corner, which served god-awful coffee you could stand your spoon up in, along with sausages and bacon swimming in grease, but we'd made him meet us here instead. He'd actually asked the waitress for black pudding and beans when she'd taken our order – she'd just given him a blank stare until he'd grunted *bacon* at her. The artisan crispy pieces of bacon over poached eggs and sourdough that arrived at our table were certainly not the greased-covered, heart-attack-inducing thick slabs Mike wanted. He'd scowled at us and muttered *fancy London dickheads* under his breath before he ate the whole thing in two bites.

"The point is," Felix said. "It doesn't really track that you would have a crush on someone. It's not really your vibe."

"Yeah, well, it's more complicated than that. She works for me."

"I still don't understand who you mean. I was at your place last week when Mrs Higgins was cleaning your study. You asked her if she'd mind very much cleaning a different room, and she told you to sod off."

"Mrs H wanted to retire to spend more time with those horrendous grandkids of hers."

"Right, so what?"

"So, I replaced her."

"Er... if you replaced her, then why was she at your house?"

I shifted on my seat again. "The new girl, Lottie. She's not a great cleaner. I mean, she tries, but she's really clumsy. And... and she looks tired. I have all manner of dickheads, plus my family coming over, and the place often needs loads of work. Mrs H is indestructible whilst this girl..." I trailed off. It was difficult to explain, and I wasn't sure the guys would understand. But Lottie just seemed worn out, like life was chipping away at her. "Plus, I really don't want her cleaning up my pants and scrubbing my toilet." I shuddered at the thought.

"Because you have a crush on her?"

I shrugged. "I found her asleep on my sofa once. I'd slammed the door and everything, not knowing she was there. She was completely out. Nothing would have woken her up. And she looked..." I trailed off as a vision of Lottie filled my mind – curled in a small ball with her hands tucked under her cheek like a child, dark circles under her eyes, and naturally thick lashes casting shadows. Lying like that, she looked too small, too thin, which surprised me with the rate she got through custard creams.

"So, I asked Mrs H to come back and do the actual cleaning. By the time Lottie gets to my house, there's literally nothing for her to do. No washing up, bathrooms are spotless. And she doesn't eat enough, so I *might* have started leaving food for her."

I had a chef who I now paid to make double the amount of food. I told Lottie I would leave any dishes that needed eating up out on the counter for her to dispose of; made out that I just couldn't be bothered. Lasagnes, pies, pasta bakes. It did get a bit ridiculous last week when my chef was off, and I had to order in. I ordered from a restaurant for some friends, then boxed up Lottie's meal for her to take the next day – three courses of the finest Michelin food, which I passed off to her as leftovers.

Mike blinked at me. "Let me get this straight; you have a cleaner for your cleaner, just in case your actual cleaner might have to deal with your shit stain on the toilet or something?"

"It's not quite that, I—"

"And you're feeding this girl? So you're basically paying her to come to your house, sleep, and eat your food?"

"She studies as well."

"What?"

"She's doing an Open University course. Psychology. So, she studies as well."

Felix burst out laughing. "You've got it bad."

I scowled at him. "I know, dickhead. That's why I've made the mistake of talking to you twats about it. Clearly, I should have kept it to myself."

Both of them were in hysterics. Felix was almost crying he was laughing so hard.

"Well, just start fucking her then. What's the problem?"

"She works for me," I said through gritted teeth. "I can't just *fuck her* – that's harassment. And she still calls me *sir* and *Your Grace*."

"What the fuck?" Felix spluttered as they both started laughing again. "Nobody calls you that! Does she know that we're not in the eighteen hundreds anymore? Who told this chick to call you Your Grace."

"I'm calling you Your Grace from now on," Mike said through a wide smile. "That's gold right there."

"I've asked her to call me Ollie multiple times, but she completely refuses. I'm stuck. I can't ask her out. It's clear she really needs this job, so I can't fire her. I'm not sure if she's in debt or something, but she really needs money. She's got a second job waitressing at one of my bloody clubs of all places."

"Oh fuck. *She's* the reason you pinned Giles Bartholew-Smithe to the table last month. Not saying the bastard didn't deserve it, but it did seem a bit of overkill."

"That fucker deserved way worse," I muttered darkly. "All those dickheads did, and that includes your mate, Will, Felix."

Will worked at Felix's company and had been one of the losers sitting at that table along with my own drunk brother-in-law. Blake and I had had words – the poor guy had been off his face and not really aware of the situation. I'd let him off, seeing as he was celebrating landing a big deal with a supplier that day. Honestly, Blake was a bit of a fuck-up sometimes, but I knew he was harmless, and he'd never deliberately behave like a shitbag. Will, on the other hand, seemed anything but harmless.

"I'm not mates with Will," Felix said with a frown. "He's an employee. There's a difference. Anyway, what did he do?"

"It's what he didn't do," I said. "Lottie brought them all a massive tray of drinks, and those smug fuckers just sat there, not clearing any space for her to put it down. Then Giles grabbed her under her skirt."

"God, Smithe is such a slimy weasel. He's not going to be able to show his face in public soon if he keeps this up. I heard Verity Markham eviscerated him the other day at the opening of the LSE building for being a dodgy piece of shit. Christ, if *you* don't crush this guy, Harry York will be next in line. What an idiot."

"Yeah, well, I had to fire the manager and change the waitresses' uniform rules. Who the fuck thought it was a good idea for waitresses to carry heavy trays of drinks for hours on end in high heels? I'm not surprised a fair amount of women just plain hate men – who would blame them? We're clearly the lowest form of inconsiderate twat. Anyway, I also had to deal out some lifetime bans to some of the members, including Smithe and his whole table – that includes your mate, Felix."

"He's not my—"

"But the bottom line is, I don't want Lottie working there."

I closed my eyes, and a vision of Lottie in that club filled my mind. That caramel hair swept up in a high ponytail, her fresh face clean of make-up, taller than her normal pipsqueak stature with the high heels elongating her legs, a lethal combination of sinful and innocent making it impossible for her to just blend into the environment.

There was no ignoring Lottie. I watched as men I knew to be relatively normal most of the time lost their train of thought when she refilled their glasses and broke off important conversations to stare at her arse as she walked away. It was maddening. Because Lottie wasn't just some bright, shiny thing to be ogled. Yes, she was beautiful, but she was also funny, kind, amazing at chess, self-deprecating, quick-witted... fucking *perfect*.

"So, offer her money," Felix suggested, and Mike punched him in the arm. "Hey! What was that for?"

"How do you think that's gonna go, dickhead?" Mike asked. "The *duke* says to his *cleaner*, who, by the way, he wants to fuck something bad, 'Yo, cleaning-lady-I-want-to-fuck, how about I give you a shitload of money so you don't have to work? And guess what? You can fuck me instead!'"

Felix winced. "Okay, I see your point."

"Exactly," I said. "I'm stuck."

CHAPTER 8

Don't bullshit a bullshitter

Ollie

"Oliver Harding, what on earth are you doing?" my sister Claire asked as she, her daughter Florrie, and my other sister Vicky all blinked up at me from the front step of my house. Vicky I was expecting for the meeting that afternoon, but Claire and Florrie were showing up unannounced as usual.

I couldn't really blame them for being surprised. I was wearing a pair of yellow washing-up gloves and holding a bottle of bleach. I think that may have been the first time I'd ever worn washing-up gloves. And it's unlikely that my sisters or my niece had ever donned a pair either.

"Are you *cleaning*?" Claire seemed more shocked than when she'd seen me in a pair of ill-advised sarong trousers a few years ago in Goa.

"This is aberrant behaviour for you," Vicky put in.

I smiled before kissing Claire on the cheek and giving Vicky a firm, brief hug. Vicky didn't mind physical contact from me as long as there were no light touches involved. Firm hugs were much preferred to cheek kisses.

My niece, however, had no qualms about physical contact in any form. She jumped up at me and threw her skinny arms around my neck for a hug, whispering in my ear, "You're a weirdo." She was her mother's daughter, after all, and therefore programmed from birth to give me shit. I chuckled and gave her a squeeze before straightening up and mussing her hair.

"Oh my God, Uncle Ollie!" she shouted. "I've just got my fringe properly sweeping, and you've messed it up." Yes, definitely her mother's daughter.

"Nice outfit," I said with a smirk, and Florrie snorted.

"You know *nothing* about fashion," she said dismissively, flouncing past me into the house.

"Explain," Claire said, linking arms with me and giving me a side shove. I glanced up the stairs and then pulled her along to the kitchen, ushering Vicky to follow us.

"What's the rush?" Claire asked as I pushed them all into the kitchen and shut the door behind us.

"My cleaner's here," I explained.

Vicky glanced from my still washing-up glove-clad hands, then back to me and raised her eyebrows.

"Why are you cleaning if your cleaner is here?" she asked. "That is totally illogical."

"Keep your voice down," I snapped. "I sent her upstairs first so I could clean up the kitchen."

"Ols, you *do* understand the concept of a cleaner, don't you?" Claire put in.

I glared at her. "Yes, Claire, I know what a cleaner does. It's just that some of the guys came round last night, and this place was a serious shithole."

"Uncle Ollie! You said the s-word!" Florrie shouted in mock horror and I sighed

"Let me get this straight," Claire said. "You're cleaning for the first time in your life ever because you don't want your cleaner, whose actual job it is to clean your house, to have to clean your house."

I huffed "Normally Mrs Higgins would have been in earlier before Lottie got here, but she had to look after one of her dreadful, bratty grandchildren."

"Mrs Higgins?" Claire's voice rose. "But Mrs H retired weeks ago."

I muttered a curse as I slammed the dishwasher door shut, and the damn thing wouldn't start. What the fuck did all these buttons mean? For God's sake, I'd just negotiated a massive multifactorial agricultural investment deal, surely I could work my own kitchen appliance. I stabbed at it again, and it made a sad noise of discontent.

"Honestly, Ols," Claire said, shooing me to the side and then leaning down to look at the display. "It can't be that hard to..." she frowned, then straightened up.

Vicky came to join us. "What do the different pot symbols mean?" she asked. No help there, then.

We stood staring at the dishwasher for a full minute.

I sighed. "Christ, we're fucking useless," I muttered.

"Uncle Ollie!" shouted Florrie. "Children are present!"

"Yes, Ollie if you could tone it down," Claire said in an exasperated voice. "We don't want another call from the school."

"Little shit knows more swears than me," I muttered under my breath. Florrie's bat ears clearly heard me though and she stuck her tongue out at me.

"Why on earth are we trying to get this machine working again?" Claire asked. "And why do you have a cleaner for your cleaner?"

I cleared my throat, and my hand went to the back of my neck. "It's complicated."

"Complicated," Vicky tilted her head to the side as she stared at me. "Complicated how?"

"I just don't want her to..."

"You don't want her cleaning?" Claire paused with her eyebrows raised. "Your cleaner. You don't want her to actually clean."

"I'm gonna go practise," Florrie said, likely bored now with the lack of swearing.

"Don't go upstairs, darling," I called after her as she flounced out of the kitchen. Florrie was practising her TikTok dances.

Doing weird dances for TikTok, obsessing over Taylor Swift and following fashion seemed to be the fuel that Florrie ran on.

Claire crossed her arms as she stared at me, and I pulled the washing-up gloves off to chuck them in the sink.

"I told Claire what happened at the club," Vicky said.

"What does that have to do with anything?" Claire said dismissively. She was often dismissive of Vicky. "But by the way, Ollie – I do think you were a bit OTT. Pinning someone to a table. Honestly."

"Those fucking morons are barred. I don't care if Blake is mates with those dickheads. They were manhandling the waitress. Totally out of order."

Claire sighed. "They're not all bad. I mean, Giles is a piece of shit, and I'm not keen on that Will bloke, but the others are relatively harmless."

Visions of those *harmless guys* peering down Lottie's top all night, deliberately crowding her, touching her, flooded my brain and I had to force the red haze back.

"Your husband has shit taste in friends. He's lucky that he was too pissed to know what was going on by the time I came over there, or he'd be barred too." Claire's face lost colour, and she swallowed.

"Blake wasn't..." she trailed off and closed her eyes slowly. When she opened them again, I could see real concern there. Her voice dropped to a whisper. "He didn't do anything, did he?"

I frowned. "No, Claire. I would have told you." She sagged in relief, and I had an uneasy feeling. "He didn't stop the others, though." Claire looked away for a moment and nodded. "And, I'm sorry, darling, but he was pretty shitfaced."

"Yeah, I know," she muttered.

"Claire, is everything okay?"

My brother-in-law was a bit of an arrogant blighter, but I wasn't really one to talk on that score. Otherwise, he was a decent bloke. He *was* totally shitfaced that night, though, and if I thought back to the last few times we'd got together, he'd been very on it drink-wise. He'd got through a full bottle at Sunday lunch at Mum's a couple of weeks ago. I hadn't thought much about it at the time.

"If you want me to talk to Blake again, I can see if—"

"What? No, no way. Blake would *not* take that well. He already…"

She trailed off, and I blinked. "He already what?"

"Never mind," she said in a fake bright tone.

"Blake has a problem with alcohol," Vicky stated in that stark way she had of cutting right to the point. Claire shot her a dirty look.

My sisters had a tricky relationship. We'd met Vicky for the first time when I was twelve, Claire was thirteen and Vicky was six. Up until then we had no idea she even existed, seeing as she was the product of my dad's affair. Then, one summer, this small blonde girl who didn't speak a word was dropped off at Buckingham Manor, and Mum was expected to take care of her for the holidays.

Apparently, due to Vicky's problems, her own mother couldn't cope with her all year round and Dad certainly wasn't getting involved (he was barely home anyway by that stage). After that, Vicky spent two weeks of every summer with us, much to Claire's annoyance. She never forgave Dad. By the time he died suddenly of a heart attack five years ago, they were barely speaking.

I'd always felt protective over Vicky. It wasn't her fault that her parents were shit, and I was her big brother. Claire simply tolerated her.

"Why don't you keep your opinions to yourself, Vics," Claire snapped then turned away from her towards me. "Well, Ollie. Everyone's been saying you went totally Hulk on them. I was worried."

"I feel that Ollie was justified in his actions," Vicky said in her matter-of-fact way. "Although it was assault, Ollie, which could have resulted in a criminal record. The reason I brought it up is because the waitress was your cleaner, Lottie. Correct?"

"What?" Claire's eyebrows were in her hairline now. "Ollie that's—"

Her words cut off as the kitchen door opened, and we all turned to see Lottie shuffle through, carrying all her cleaning supplies.

"Fudge nuggets," she muttered as a couple of the bottles in her basket fell out of the side. As she bent to retrieve them, the rest of the basket tilted. I shot across the kitchen to right it before the entire contents ended up on the floor. She was so shocked when I crouched down in front of her that there was no resistance as I took the basket out of her hands. Her brown eyes went wide as they locked with mine, and it was like all the air was sucked out of the room.

"Hello."

Lottie broke eye contact at the sound of Vicky's voice, and the spell was broken.

"Er… hi," she squeaked, looking around me to see both Vicky and Claire.

"Hi there," Claire said with a smile and a small wave. "You must be Lottie."

Lottie nodded, then did a double-take when she saw Vicky. "Oh, I recognise…" she trailed off, and for some reason, her cheeks flushed red.

"Your foot is better." Stating the obvious was Vicky's special talent, as was making uncomfortable situations even more so. "And you are no longer covered in wine."

"Er… yes," Lottie said slowly, shooting Vicky a curious look.

Then she stood up and attempted to tug the basket out of my hands, but I wasn't letting it go. Instead, I grabbed the bottles she was holding and put them into the relevant slots then put the basket up on the counter.

Lottie frowned. "I can carry that, Your Grace."

I gritted my teeth as Claire stifled a laugh. "Oh my God. You call him *Your Grace*? I'm sorry, but that's priceless. I'm Claire, by the way, *His Grace's* sister. I know you've already met my daughter, Florrie." Lottie nodded, managing a small, nervous smile.

"Yes, your mum brought her over a couple of weeks ago. She's a great girl." Lottie bit her lip before continuing. "Listen, I'm so sorry for interrupting," she said quietly, her eyes darting to the exit and then back to me, Vicky and Claire.

Claire frowned. "You're not interrupting us. If anything, we're interrupting you. Anyhoo, now we have interrupted you, why don't you tell me about yourself?"

Lottie blinked. "I... er," her eyes flicked between all of us before she gave a helpless shrug. "You don't want to know about me, I promise. I'm boring." She lowered her voice. "And I know I'm supposed to stay invisible."

"Invisible? Who told you that?" Claire asked.

"Yes, Lottie," I cut in, crossing my arms over my chest. Her gaze fell on them, then fixed on my chest before she managed to look away. "Who told you you had to be invisible?"

"Mrs H sure as shit isn't invisible," Claire put in. "What is it she calls you, Ols?"

"Fancy, pretty-boy, trust-fund, namby-pamby git," Vicky said, as always remembering everything with perfect clarity.

"Who is Mrs H?" Lottie asked.

"Ollie's cleaner," Vicky replied.

"But... *I'm* Ollie's cleaner."

"Yes," I cut in, scowling at Vicky. "Yes, you're my cleaner, Lottie. Mrs H *used* to work for me."

"But you just said—" Vicky started, but I cut her off.

"Claire, I'm sure you have a lot to be getting on with. Vicky and I have that meeting with Felix. So maybe you'd like to bugger off?"

"I'll go and set up in the office," Vicky said before she swept out. Vicky could never really manage complex social situations where she wasn't sure of the rules, and this situation was more complex than most.

"Er..." Lottie's eyes darted out to the corridor again and then back to me. "Do you need any of the other rooms? You're not using the library, are you?"

I frowned. "What's wrong with the library?"

"Oh nothing, Your Grace," she said, trying to sound unbothered but the shake in her voice gave her away. "I just haven't dusted in there yet so—"

"We're not intending to use the library," I told her. How odd. Had she knocked something over in there?

She let out a relieved huff and then looked at the now pristine kitchen. "Shall I make a start in here?"

"Sure," I answered.

"It's just there doesn't seem to be an awful lot to do." She stared at me in confusion, then lowered her voice. "Listen, I've been dying to ask, but is this a rich person thing? Having a cleaner clean your already clean house?"

Claire snorted with suppressed laughter until I shot her a death glare.

"No, I just... I'm really tidy, so..."

"Okay," Lottie said slowly. She was frowning up at me now and I had the distinct impression she knew I was lying.

Claire's snort at that blatant lie was harder to cover up.

"Claire, I believe you were leaving?" I took matters into my own hands and grabbed Claire's arm to propel her out of the kitchen and away from Lottie. Once we were in the corridor, she turned to me with an excited expression.

"You *like* her!" she burst out.

"What are you talking about, Claire?"

"Don't bullshit a bullshitter, Bucky. You *like* her. There's no other explanation for keeping Mrs H on so that your cleaner, who you like, doesn't have to do any actual cleaning. And the way you guys looked at each other! I mean, you're my brother, but even I have to admit it was objectively fire emoji."

"Back off with this. I mean it." I tried to inject a sufficient amount of brotherly clout, but that had never worked on

Claire. Her smile was so wide now it was a bit unnerving.

"Oh, this is perfect! Wait until I tell the others. You haven't liked anyone properly since—"

"Don't say her name," I growled, and Claire pressed her lips together but still looked unreasonably excited.

"It's just we've all been worried, Ols. Since *you know who*, you haven't been right. You're... colder. Not my little Ollie."

"Claire, I'm well over six foot. I haven't been *your little Ollie* in over two decades."

Claire ignored me. She was bouncing on her toes in excitement. "You know what I mean. You've been a stubborn shit about women for too long."

"I'm well aware of your opinion on me and women. I can't walk out of my house without you or, worse, *Mum* trying to set me up. Have you two ever considered that maybe Vicky and I want to be single?"

"Don't be ridiculous. Vicky just needs to act a little less... *Vicky* and—"

"Claire," I said in a warning tone and she rolled her eyes.

"Ugh, you know what I mean. I'm not having a go, okay? It's just she tends to intimidate blokes with her mega-brain. And as far as you're concerned, you just need a *nice* girl this time. Not some bitch who sells you out. Anyway, none of the attempts we've made have been successful at all. You haven't liked any woman, full stop. Not in over five years, Ols." She'd stopped bouncing now and lowered her voice to a whisper. "I was worried that she broke you a little bit."

I sighed and pulled Claire in for a hug. "You lot worry too much," I said as I kissed the top of her head. "I was still a stupid kid back then. I thought I loved her, but..." I trailed off. Truth was, the sting of what happened had lasted for years. The humiliation, the heartbreak. But now... "What Cordelia did hurt me, but it didn't break me, Claire."

"I'm glad you can say her name now," Claire said softly. "That's progress right there. Maybe it's because of this girl?"

"Don't jump the gun, Claire Bear," I said sternly. "There's the small issue of her working for me."

"Oh pish! People meet at work all the time."

"There's a bit of a power imbalance."

"There's always a power imbalance, Ols. Let me think. You should get her flowers, right? And ask her to—"

"Oh my God, I am not discussing this with you," I groaned. "Right, how's Mum?"

We talked for a while about Buckingham Manor and the upkeep that Claire didn't think Mum was keeping on top of. Claire gave me some more shit about Lottie. I asked her if she thought anything was bothering Vicky who'd been quiet recently.

"How should I know?" said Claire dismissively and I sighed. Just when I thought my sisters were starting to get on a little better a few years ago, everything went to shit when Claire married Blake. Vicky did not like Blake and she wasn't particularly subtle about it.

"Right, come on. Let's go and find your demon spawn," I said after seeing the time and realising that Vicky would start the meeting on her own if I didn't get a move on. I pulled Claire down the corridor and followed the sound of Florrie's music into the library.

"Hi!" Florrie appeared abruptly from behind the sofa.

"What are you doing back there, darling?" Claire asked.

"Nothing!" Florrie squeaked, glancing down at the floor next to her and then back up at us. Her face was red and she was avoiding eye contact. The kid was a shit liar. Hopefully, she hadn't spilt nail polish on my hardwood floor like last time.

"Right, well we better go so—"

"Yes!" Florrie shouted, running over to us and shooing us out of the library. "You both need to go. *Right now.*"

"You just keep getting weirder, kid," I said as I mussed her hair again.

"Uncle Ollie! The hair!"

CHAPTER 9

They always jog on

Lottie

"For fuck's sake!" a deep voice boomed and I froze as the snug door slammed open.

I was holding the queen and about to make the move, putting my opponent into checkmate. The duke took a couple of agitated steps into the room and then came to an abrupt halt when he saw me. His eyes went from my face to my hand holding the chess piece, and despite his anger just a moment ago, he smiled.

"So, feel like finally admitting that you're the one beating me at chess?" he asked.

I was about to plop the queen back down where she'd been, but this move I was about to make was perfect, and it would put me two games ahead. I bit my lip, placed her down facing the bishop, then straightened up to take a step back.

"Checkmate," he muttered.

I backed away quickly as he approached, skittering behind the sofa. My movement seemed to reignite his irritation from before. His smile fell, and his brows drew together. He huffed as he threw himself into one of the armchairs next to the chessboard, sagging forward and rubbing his temples.

"I'll just be getting on, sir," I whispered, backing away further towards the door.

"Lottie?" he called just as I was reaching for the handle. "Could we just give all this deferential bullshit a rest for a bit? I've had a shitshow of a morning, and I'd really like to spend some time with someone who's not a complete dick."

I let out a surprised laugh. "How do you know I'm 'not a complete d-word'? Maybe I'm a total d-word."

"I just know. I get very minimal dickish vibes from you."

I hesitated for a moment before letting my hand fall from the door.

"Okay," I said slowly. "Maybe I don't have to shoot off straight away. But you should know I *can* be somewhat of a d-word... sometimes."

"Can't we all? My sisters would say it's something I excel at."

"Sisters?" I asked as I skirted him and took the chair opposite. "You have more than one?"

He frowned. "Yeah, of course."

"Oh, well, the sister I've met seems like a good time."

He tipped his head to the side. "But you've met both of them. Vicky was at the club then they were both here last week."

"Ohhhhh," I said slowly. "The blonde? I thought..." I stopped myself before I could reveal my stupid assumptions, trying to ignore the small bubble of hope and happiness at the knowledge that the duke *didn't* have a girlfriend.

"You thought what?"

"Well, I thought she and you were—"

"Oh shit. I assumed Vics would have explained who she was. Sorry, she's not really that great at ... er, well, she's not really *that* social. Doesn't *get* many situations. Vics is a genius in many ways, but human interactions often baffle her."

"She seemed nice." Without the white-hot jealousy, I realised that I did actually like Vicky. She was entirely without artifice and I could tell she definitely never lied.

His eyebrows went up. "Really?"

"I mean, she's blunt, I guess. Quite literal."

"That's an understatement. Unfortunately, Vics can be a bit of a liability. I love my sister, but she doesn't half piss people off." He paused for a moment as he looked at me, then seemed to make a decision. "She's Autistic. Her mother, not my mum but my dad's mistress, didn't believe in it, so Vicky was only diagnosed as an adult. We don't really tell people. I don't want her vulnerable, and she wants to keep it to herself anyway. But it can create problems. Vics is so truthful it can be… tricky."

"People can't handle the truth," I said.

"Yeah, well, now she's decided she's been 'smothered' for too long in the family business. She's joined my best friend's finance company to prove herself or some such bullshit. It's ridiculous."

"Is that why you're angry?"

"Sorry about that." He winced and looked away from me. "You don't need me storming around like a bear with a sore head."

"Er… it is your house, you realise?" I asked with a small smile. "You can storm as much as you want."

"Yeah, well, I don't want to be a—"

"D-word?"

He smiled. "That's right."

"Well, I don't think you are, if that's any consolation."

"High praise."

"The highest. So what else has happened to make you all door-slammy?"

The duke started rearranging all the chess pieces back into their relevant places. God, his hands were sexy. Tanned, with large, manly veins and everything. His chunky, expensive watch peeking out of his shirt sleeve added to the effect. Not to mention the subtle aftershave I could just about make out. His hair looked like he'd run his hands through it a few times, and his stubble was already edging towards five o'clock shadow territory. Seriously, it was almost indecent to be wandering around looking this good at two in the afternoon on a Tuesday.

He cleared his throat, and when I looked up into his blue eyes, I realised he was smiling.

"You okay there?" he asked. "You zoned out for a minute."

"S-sorry," I said, giving myself a mental shake to snap out of this.

"Your move," he said in a soft voice, and I blinked. Was he saying I should...

"I... er, I—"

"*Chess* move, Lottie." He gestured to the chessboard and raised an eyebrow.

I cleared my throat as heat flooded my face and hurried to grab the pawn, making a move with no thought at all.

"My brother-in-law *is* a bit of a dick. That's what made me door-slammy."

I pressed my lips together. No way was I giving my honest opinion on Blake. "Claire doesn't seem like she'd marry a d-word."

He shrugged his broad shoulders under his expensive suit. "He used to be okay, but lately..." he trailed off and looked to the side. "He was one of those dickheads in the club that didn't move the glasses out of the way for you."

"Oooh." I made an eek face, feigning surprise. "I see."

"Exactly, mega dickhead alert. But that's really only when he drinks. The deal he's just fucked up on the land that we need to develop the new bars has nothing to do with the booze."

I bit my lip. In my experience, booze could come into play in a lot more scenarios than people were aware of.

"Should never have let him take the lead on it, but he *said* it was under control. Even now, he thinks he can still salvage it."

"Maybe give him a chance," I said softly, and his eyebrows went up.

"Why are you defending him? He was a total prick that night at the club."

I shrugged. "He's your family. Family is important. You've got all these threads between you in families, weaving in and out, strengthening you all as a whole, giving everyone a safety net, a sense of belonging. Don't risk cutting any of the threads. Not when your sister could be the one to fall through the hole it creates."

He sat up and blinked at me. "I never thought of it like that," he said slowly.

My heart clutched in my chest, and my throat felt thick for a moment. If you've never had family and stability ripped from under you, you can't truly understand how important it is, how rudderless you are without it. I tried to shove the jealousy I was feeling down as I watched him consider my words.

"Is that how you are with your family?" he surprised me by asking. In my experience, men like to talk about themselves *exclusively*.

I shrugged. "I'd do anything for my family." That was true enough, even if my family extended to just Hayley. The threads that bound *us* were unbreakable.

"Hmm, well, I don't know how I'll keep my temper with him. But you're right – family *is* important."

"You could try what I do," I blurted out without thinking. He tilted his head to the side.

"And what would that be?"

"Well, when people pee me off, like in the club the other night…" I paused when a murderous look crossed the duke's face, "I, er, well, I have this little song I sing under my breath. I guess it's like counting to ten."

His frown was now replaced with a smile.

"Go on then," he encouraged.

"Oh, I'm not singing *you* my song." I picked up my knight and moved to engage his bishop on the chessboard.

"Hey, you can't hint at the secret to dealing with dickheads and then not give the actual deets."

He made a crap move with his rook, leaving his knight exposed; the man was total shiitake mushrooms at chess.

"Nope, not happening," I said. "Make up your own song."

"Come on, Lottie," he wheedled.

"No."

"Please."

"No."

"Pretty please?"

I huffed. "You're not going to let this go, are you?"

He raised his eyebrows.

"Fine, fine," I muttered, heat flooding my face. "So it's:
I won't punch this d-head in the face,
I'll just wait till he's gone.
Cause d-heads be d-heads,
But they always jog on."

His rich, deep laughter filled the room, and I stared at him in total awe. He was so beautiful it was almost unreal. "That's catchy," he said through his amusement. "Tell me, have you used that little rhyme when it comes to me?"

I cleared my throat and looked away. "No, of course not."

"You're a shit liar."

I smiled at him. "Even you have to admit that you sometimes warranted that poem."

"Oh really, would that include me being concerned that you might break your neck? Or wanting you to go to the hospital after you fell ten feet and couldn't put weight through your leg? Telling you off for standing on a ladder when – and baby, I mean no shade when I say this – you have a fair bit of trouble staying upright when you're on solid ground? I think my concern was warranted."

Suppressing the shiver that ran through my body when he called me baby, I rolled my eyes and made another chess move, this time taking his bishop.

"You're bossy," I told him.

"Yes," he told me, and I looked up at his face. His eyes captured mine, and we sat there staring at each other with me yet again completely under his spell. "Yes, Lottie. I'm *very* bossy."

Okay, so he hadn't said anything explicit, but it was the way he said it – dark-edged, low and commanding. I had a feeling we weren't talking about my clumsiness anymore. When I made my next chess move, my fingers were shaking and I knocked over the pawn I was reaching for.

Before I knew what was happening, he'd reached out and enclosed my hand in his. I should have snatched it away. If I'd had more willpower, I would have. But with his expensive cologne in the air, his strong hand swallowing mine in its warmth, the memory of his low, dark voice in my brain and his blue eyes staring straight at mine as his pupils dilated, there was really no way I could have pulled back. It was physiologically impossible. He stroked my palm with his thumb, and I felt so lightheaded I thought I might pass out sitting up. His touch felt electric, like a living, breathing force flowing into my hand and up my arm.

"Your hand is really small," he said, his voice still low.

"Er, I think it's average size," I said in a hoarse voice, then cleared my throat. "Yours is just too big."

He smiled at me then. "That's what she said," he muttered my joke from weeks ago back to me, and I lost it.

Years of careful control, of doing the right thing, of keeping my head above water, of never having anything for myself, of self-discipline, all unravelled. This man was simply too much. It was like a switch tripped in my brain – sensible Lottie left the building, leaving sex-starved, duke-obsessed Lottie in her place.

I surged out of my seat, my free hand diving into that glorious hair that I'd been dreaming about for months and my lips crashing onto his still-smiling mouth.

CHAPTER 10

Fantasy material

Lottie

It took a couple of seconds for my brain to catch up with what my body was doing.

"I-I'm sorry," I said as I tried to pull away. But then he gave a sharp tug to pull me towards his lap, and his other hand shot out to cup my jaw.

"God, you are so fucking beautiful," he muttered, his mouth nearly touching mine as he searched my face. Then another sharp tug on my hand had me falling forward, his arm enclosing me completely. He proceeded to tilt my jaw just how he wanted it, brush his nose against mine once, twice before finally his lips met mine again.

I could feel the taut muscles of his chest under my hands, the soft, firm pressure of his lips, the roughness of his stubble and that trip-switch in my brain shorted again. I melted against him, my lips parting on a small moan and letting his tongue inside. After a few minutes, his mouth moved to my jaw, then my ear. As I panted and tried not to pass out with lust, he kissed down my neck, his fingers moving from my jaw into my hair, pulling out the hairband and then wrapping the cascade of hair around his fist to hold me where he wanted me.

His kiss was like everything else about him – bossy, demanding, utterly glorious.

"We need more space," he said against the skin just below my ear, and I nodded vigorously.

Yes, yes, we needed *all* the space right now.

I squeaked as he surged up with me in his arms as if I weighed nothing; then, before I could tell which way was up, he'd laid me down on the sofa with his glorious weight settling on top of me. And he was kissing me again.

"Okay, okay," he said between kisses. "I've got to slow this down. I know that."

What was he talking about? I pulled at his hair to register how not on board I was with going slow. I mean, I had this *one chance* with him. Clearly, he'd had a shit day and was in the mood to try it on with the cleaner. It was *very* unlikely there would be a repeat performance. I was tired of playing it safe, doing the proper thing, always sacrificing my needs. And cheese and rice, did I need him. My body was screaming for him. The hair-pulling elicited a low growl, and his chest vibrating against my hands was deeply sexy.

"I'm trying to be good here," he said in a hoarse, almost pained voice.

"Ollie, I need you," I begged. Yup, I was reduced to begging now. My brain had officially left me to my own devices.

He groaned and moved against me, his hardness right at my centre where I needed it to be.

"Okay, baby," he said in a thick voice against my neck. "I've got you."

He licked up my neck, and then his teeth grazed my ear as I let out a moan so desperate, if I hadn't been mindless with need I would have melted into the sofa with embarrassment. When he started kissing down my neck, my body was coiled so tight I felt like the tension could snap at any moment. He pulled back, and I made a sound of protest but was cut off by him whipping my t-shirt up and over my head, leaving me in just my bra.

"Jesus fucking Christ," he breathed as he scanned my body. Before I could let insecurity and the fact my bra was of the white cotton, utilitarian variety, the heat of his body was back against mine, and his tongue was tracing my collarbone.

"Please," I moaned.

"That's it, baby," he said as his lips moved to my breast above my bra. When he pulled the cup down and his mouth fastened over my nipple, I totally lost it, arching up and letting out a whimper as I moved against him.

When he moved across to the other breast, his hand skirted down over my stomach, and I shivered in anticipation. I could feel the tension in his body, the muscles of his back bunching under his suit. And then his hand dipped into my leggings, past the waistband of my knickers. When the pads of his thick fingers zeroed in on my core in record time, I jolted like I'd been given an electric shock. Then he started slow circles as I ground against him.

"Good girl," he said against my breast. "Such a good girl for me. Help me get you there, baby." He slipped a finger inside me, his thumb moving to press where I needed it, and I felt it building.

When I came, it was like fireworks going off behind my eyes as bursts of pleasure overwhelmed my entire body. It was the single most incredible experience of my life.

My eyes had been clenched shut, but as I came down from the high, I blinked them open, and reality started to invade my consciousness. I sucked in a shocked breath and stiffened underneath him. His hand withdrew from me slowly, and his head came up from my chest as he moved so that our faces were level, his weight still pressing me down onto the sofa.

"Feel better now?" he asked in a husky voice, and then I had the gorgeous view of his handsome face smiling just inches from mine. But, however handsome he was, I was incapable of returning that smile. I'd just let my boss make me come, very *very* hard. What was wrong with me?

"What am I doing?" I asked in a horrified whisper. "Shit... ake mushrooms, I totally lost it."

"Hey, hey, hey," he said in a soft voice; his smile had dropped now, and his expression was clouded with concern. "Don't shut down on me, baby. Not after that. There's no going back after that."

I shook my head in jerky movements as his hand came up to sweep the hair out of my face at my temple so gently that it almost made me cry.

"Ollie, I mean, Y-Your Grace," I stammered. "I'm your forking cleaner. You're my boss. I realise this is my fault. I s-shouldn't have kissed you. I *know* that. I just…" I trailed off as true horror flooded my system. "Don't fire me. I need this job, Your Grace. Please don't fire me."

"Lottie, calm down," he said in his bossy tone. "*I* held your hand before you kissed me."

"But then I-I begged you to…"

He smiled again. "Yes, that was fun."

I smacked his chest. "This is not funny, you—you butthead."

He kissed me then, a soft brush of his lips against mine whilst he was still half smiling. "Okay, not funny."

"Can we please have this conversation in an upright position without you kissing me? I-I can't think when you—"

"Nope," he said against my mouth. "I don't think that would be a good idea."

"What?" my voice was a breathless squeak now; the weight of his body and the feel of him was beginning to addle my mind again.

"I think this is exactly how we should have this conversation. If I let you up, you'll start twisting things, and I can't let that happen. You're going to have to hear me out first."

"You're too heavy," I snapped, but it was half-hearted as I felt myself begin to melt again.

"You're hardly taking any of my weight, just enough to keep you still."

I huffed, and he searched my face again. His expression looked almost reverent, like he couldn't quite believe I was there underneath him.

"I'm going to start by saying that I really, really like you."

I blinked up at him, and my mouth fell open in shock. That was not what I was expecting him to say. In all honesty, I was expecting him to demand I return the favour he'd just given me. What would be the point of fooling around with your cleaner if you weren't going to get anything out of it?

"I'm not interested in just a casual thing with you," he said firmly.

Great Scott! Was he reading my mind?

"You're not?" My words were a little strangled, but I was having trouble believing that this was actually happening.

"I have feelings for you," he declared.

"You do?"

"Yes. Very strong feelings that I've had for a very long time. I know it's not ideal with you working for me, which is why I haven't made a move before now, but I can't stay away from you any longer."

"You can't?"

He smiled then and stroked my hair back from my temple again. "Have you got anything more to say than just two-word questions, darling?"

He called me darling. It was so posh and so sweet all at once. My throat felt tight, and I had to swallow before I could speak again. "You do realise that you're a duke?"

He chuckled. "Yes, I've known that for a while," he said in a dry tone.

"Your Gra—"

"Call me Your Grace one more time, baby, and see what happens," he said in a low, sexy voice as his hips pressed into mine. "Now, when I was kissing you and when I made you come, you called me Ollie." His face fell closer to mine then so that our lips were almost touching. "Do we need to go back to that? Is that the only way to get you to use my actual name?"

My stomach tightened with need.

"I-I... no more kissing or, er, the other stuff," I said, my voice pitched unnaturally high.

"Are you going to call me by my first name?" he said against my mouth.

"Yes," I whispered.

"Yes, what?"

"Yes, Ollie."

He smiled and kissed me softly as if in reward, triggering my mind to scramble again. My mouth opened, and his tongue swept inside as I started moving against him, my hands reaching to pull his shirt out from his belt and feel the skin of his back. But then suddenly, his jaw clenched tight and he pulled away.

"Right, right, no more fooling around for now," he said firmly. I suspected more to himself than to me. "We need to establish some stuff first."

"Oh my God," I breathed as humiliation washed over me. "You haven't even taken off your jacket."

Here I was practically naked beneath him, and the man was fully dressed. His pocket square was even still neatly in place. I felt at a complete disadvantage. As if sensing my extreme discomfort, Ollie muttered a curse and finally lifted away from me to let me sit up. I immediately missed his weight and his warmth, shivering slightly as I crossed my arms over my chest to pull my bra straps up. Ollie jumped up from the sofa and grabbed my t-shirt, putting it over my head and helping me into it like a child.

"Okay, sweetheart?" he asked cautiously as he took the seat next to me on the sofa and laid his hand over mine. "I'm sorry, I didn't even think of that."

He shrugged his suit jacket off and threw it on the floor; his tie followed, and then he undid a few buttons on his shirt, giving me a delicious view of some chest hair, his corded throat and the tanned muscle of his upper chest.

"Lottie?" he called, and I forced my eyes from his chest to his smiling ones. He gave my hand a squeeze. "Better?"

I let out a long breath and then bit my lip. "I think I'm just a bit confused."

"Right," he said, that firm tone back again. "I really don't want any confusion, so I'll spell it out again. I like you. I'm pretty much obsessed with you, actually. I think about you all the time. Your laugh, your dry sense of humour, your clumsiness, your eyes, your skin, the way I can tell if you think someone's a dickhead without you ever having to say a word. How we can share a joke with just one raise of your eyebrow. That you've got a sweary rhyme to stop yourself punching people who annoy you and that you blushed when you sang it to me because you never swear. I just..." He smiled and shrugged his shoulders. "I just *really* like you."

"Right, well, that's nice," I said weakly, and his sudden laughter made me flinch.

"Nice? Kill me now."

"Ollie, I—"

He gave my hand a squeeze at my use of his first name, and my chest tightened.

"I'm just trying to get my head around this."

I pulled my hand from his and stood up to pace across the room. I needed some space between us to force my brain into a normal functioning state.

"I'm sorry, Lottie," he said as he rose from the sofa, holding both his hands up in a calming gesture which did not have the desired effect. "I shouldn't be rushing you. I mean, I've had a long while to come to terms with how I feel and what the possible repercussions could be. It's all a shock to you. I'm sure you've not been thinking about me in the same—"

"You think I don't think about you?" I asked, my voice incredulous as I crossed my arms over my chest defensively. "Holy guacamole, Ollie, you've got the wrong end of the stick there." I let out a shaky laugh. "If you knew how much I..." I closed my eyes as embarrassment swept through me. But if Ollie could do this, then so could I. "Let's just say I think obsession-wise I'd be giving you a run for your money. You've starred in all my fantasies for months."

"I have?" he asked, a smug grin appearing as he took a few steps towards me. I held up my hand though, and he stopped with a frown.

"But *you're* fantasy material, Ollie. You have to see that. You're gorgeous and funny, and kind to your mum, sisters and niece; you do endless charity work and you actually care about it. The way you wear a suit is beyond drool-worthy. You're like the dream man. Not to mention, you are an actual duke. I'd be a disgrace to the sisterhood if I didn't have a raging crush on you, and you know it."

"Well," he said, stalking closer, his frown having melted away and a small smile playing on his lips. "We wouldn't want you to disgrace the sisterhood, would we?"

Then he was right there, his smell all around me again, and all I could see were his ice-blue eyes. When he took me in his arms and hugged me to him, I rested my hands on his chest, and I knew I was a goner.

"I want to hear more about these fantasies I've been starring in," he said with a raised eyebrow, and I let out a shaky laugh as I relaxed against him.

"Is that all you got from everything I just said?"

"I think my brain shut off after that comment, to be honest." He was staring at my mouth, his pupils so dilated that there was just a thin rim of blue visible, but as he started lowering his head to mine, he froze and shut his eyes tightly. "Okay, no more kissing."

"Okay," I breathed, and his arms gave me a squeeze.

"I'm serious, Lottie. Serious about you. And I want to do this the right way. So, you're going to go out on an official date with me before I let you have your way with me again."

I laughed at that and rolled my eyes. "Ollie, I work for you. It'll be weird."

He shrugged. "Well, let's see, shall we?"

"I need this job," I said in a small voice.

"Don't worry about it, Lottie. I'll sort it."

I didn't know what Ollie "sorting it" involved, but I definitely should have asked. And I really should have taken the chance then and there to explain just how complicated my life actually was.

CHAPTER 11

This is priceless

Lottie

"Fraggle Rock!" I shrieked, dropping the cleaning spray and cloth I was carrying to clutch my chest.

"Hello," Vicky said from one of the kitchen stools, staring at me with her head tilted to the side.

"Oh, you scared me," I said, bending down to pick up my stuff. "I didn't think anyone was here."

Vicky shrugged. "We came back here from a meeting. Ollie is shouting at Felix in his office. I decided to wait out here."

"Er... who's Felix?"

"Ollie's best friend."

"Why is Ollie shouting at him?"

"He doesn't want me working with Felix. He wants me to keep working for the Buckingham Estate."

"And you don't want that?"

Vicky shrugged again. "My half-brother can be overprotective."

I moved further into the kitchen and put the cloth and spray down on the granite worktop. There was something vulnerable about this woman. I couldn't quite put my finger on it, but the loneliness I felt a lot of the time seemed to cling to her for some reason. Like we were kindred spirits, which made no sense as

I knew Vicky had a family and was nowhere near as isolated as me. But looking into her deep blue eyes, it was almost startling how much sadness I could sense there.

"Why do you call Ollie your half-brother?" I blurted out then bit my lip. I needed to remember I was just an employee here. These people probably weren't used to the staff asking questions. But Vicky didn't look annoyed as she stared at me with that slightly unnerving focus she seemed to have.

"Because that's what he is," she said simply.

"It's just…" I looked to the side as I moved forward to take the stool across from her. Stuff worrying about how formal I should be, I felt a strange affinity for Vicky that I couldn't shake. "He calls *you* his sister. He doesn't make a distinction."

Vicky looked down at her hands, then said. "He is incorrect. There is a distinction."

I'd always had the ability to sense emotions, to read a room, and I could tell if someone was lying. It was harder with Vicky than with other people, but I could just about make out an undercurrent of hurt in her words.

"You don't think you belong in the Harding family," I said before I could stop myself. "That's why you don't want to work for the Buckingham Estate. It's nothing to do with Ollie being over-protective."

Vicky's eyes went wide as she stared at me. "How could you—?"

"Vics, honestly, you didn't have to bail on us. I know you don't like conflict. We just—" Ollie's voice cut Vicky off as he and another man stalked into the kitchen. They both came to a halt when they saw me sitting up at the kitchen island with Vicky. Then the shock on Ollie's face morphed into a wide smile as he unfroze and strode over to where I was sitting. Before I could make any sort of escape he'd come right up to me, his large hand wrapped around my shoulders and he kissed me on my temple.

He *kissed* me.

Right there in front of his sister and his best friend, as if I was his *wife* just hanging out in my own kitchen rather than the paid help taking an unsanctioned break to quiz his family member.

"You must be Lottie," the other guy said as he walked our way as well with his hand extended. "Hi, I'm Felix."

"Hi," I managed to squeak out as I raised my arm from where it was tucked into Ollie's side and leaned around him to shake Felix's hand. He was a similar height and build to Ollie, but with warm brown eyes rather than Ollie's startling blue. The two of them were quite the intimidating combo.

"Ollie's told me a lot about you," he said, still smiling as I dropped his hand, or rather was forced to drop his hand when Ollie pulled me back into his side again. Felix's eyebrows went up as he looked between us and his smile settled into a smirk.

"Really?" I asked, frowning in confusion. I mean, I'd only kissed Ollie a few days ago. What had he been telling his friend? What even was there to tell his friend about?

"Oh yes. I understand you're studying psychology?"

My mouth fell open before I managed to snap it shut. "H-how…?"

"Felix," Ollie growled. "Shut up, man. You're making me sound like a bloody stalker. Lottie," he turned to me, "I saw the books in your bag one day, and there may have been a couple of times I noticed them out on the coffee table in the library but—"

"Sh—sugar lumps," I whispered, fear gripping me. I did think I'd covered my tracks pretty well when I snuck in revision on the job. "Ollie, I'm so sorry. I swear I would only work for the odd hour or two and—"

Felix burst out laughing. "Oh wow. This is priceless. Lottie, I don't think you have any idea how gone for you my boy Ols is here. I promise you he gives zero fucks whether you clean his house or not. He doesn't even need a cleaner, for Christ's sake."

"Felix," Ollie said in a warning tone. "I think it's time for you to fuck off, mate."

Felix held up his hands, still chuckling. "Okay, okay. I get the message. Come on, Vics. We've got that meeting at three in the office."

Vicky was still staring at me in that disconcerting way of hers.

"Vics?" Felix called when she made no move to leave.

"I think psychology is a good choice for you," Vicky said. "I think you'll be very good at that."

I blinked at her. "Uh, thanks?"

She nodded then pushed off the stool to follow Felix out of the kitchen. Ollie let me go to stalk after her. He blocked her exit just before she could leave.

"You won't reconsider?" he said in a low voice.

"You don't need me there, Ollie," Vicky said firmly and Ollie sighed.

"If anything happens or someone's a dick to you, then you come to me, okay?"

"I'll be perfectly fine."

After she left, Ollie stared after her for a moment and ran his hand through his hair before turning back to me.

"What was that about?" I asked. I'd already crossed so many lines today, who cared if I added being supremely nosy into the mix.

Ollie turned back to me, then he walked over to where I was sitting, caged me in with his hands either side of me on the worktop and stared down at me, one side of his mouth hitching up in a small grin.

"You're so beautiful," he murmured, searching my face, his eyes burning bright blue.

I blinked up at him absorbing the totally bizarre scenario where a gorgeous duke in a three-piece suit, looking like he just stepped out of a modelling shoot, told me, Lottie Forest – baggy jeans, a sweatshirt which had bleach stains on it, no make-up and unbrushed hair balancing on top of my head in a messy bun (of the unsexy variety) – that I was beautiful. My mind blanked as I breathed in his aftershave and manly Ollie smell.

"You're so handsome that sometimes I feel like I can't breathe," I told him. Yes, that's what I said in a breathy little voice, completely saturated with my need for him. His eyes flashed as one of his hands went up and into my hair, the other to my jaw, tilting my face towards his as his lips brushed against mine, light at first and then he made a low noise at the back of his throat before he deepened the kiss.

My hands clutched at his shirt and my legs opened to let his hips between us so I could feel his heat against me where I needed it. I moved against him and felt a growl vibrate his chest as one of his large hands went around my back to pull me to him, lifting me up. I managed to get my hand from between us, going up under his shirt and waistcoat and eliciting another deep growl when I felt his hot skin and the bunched muscles underneath.

"Fuck," he breathed against my mouth as he moved against me and I let out a small moan. "Lottie, baby. I can't... I..." Then there was a crash on the tiles next to us and we broke apart with a start. I glanced down to see the delicate teacup I'd used earlier smashed across the hard surface then moved back to Ollie.

"I'm sorry," I breathed into his mouth.

"What?" he whispered, sounding pained.

"About the china. It's so pretty, and—"

He chuckled, low and deep and I felt him everywhere.

"Lottie, I give no fucks about the goddamn china." His lips brushed mine as he spoke and I shivered. His eyes started burning again as his breath stuttered, but just before I thought he was about to kiss me he jerked away. "Bollocks!"

"W-what's wrong?" I asked, my arms coming up around to hug myself in the cold that the absence of his large warm body left behind. "Did I do something that—?"

"No, of course not, baby," he said through a groan, pacing away from me and raking his hands through his thick hair. "It's me. I..." He shook his head then stared into my eyes. "Being around you here, it's... God, Lottie, I'm trying really hard to take things slowly. That does not include pinning you down and living out all the scenarios I fantasise about pretty much all the time. But having you here in my house is making things..." he laughed. "Well, it's making things hard – literally and figuratively."

I felt heat hit my cheeks as I pressed my lips together.

"Come out with me now."

"What?" I frowned. "But Ollie, I'm working."

"Well, I happen to know your boss and I know that he doesn't give a fuck if you skip a few hours of cleaning." His tone turned cajoling as he aimed a crooked smile at me. "Come on, Lottie. Just a few hours outside the house. I've cancelled the rest of my day. Don't leave me hanging. I promise it'll be fun."

I bit my lip. Fun. I honestly couldn't remember the last time I did something just for fun. Without obligation. Without worrying constantly. Ollie held out his hand to me and I hesitated for a moment.

But only for a moment.

CHAPTER 12

Fishmonger

Ollie

"What's wrong?"

Lottie had pulled me to a stop outside the restaurant. Her eyebrows were raised as she looked between me and the entrance before she huffed out a laugh.

"Ollie, I cannot go in there like this."

"Like what?" I asked, genuinely baffled.

She pulled her hand from mine to sweep it down her body and up again. "Like this!"

"You look great."

She rolled her eyes. "Ollie, I smell of bleach. I'm wearing a ratty old cat sweatshirt and even rattier jeans and the sole of my trainer is peeling away. I do not look *great*." Her hand went up to the messy bun on top of her head and she groaned. "Ugh, I don't even think I brushed my hair this morning."

"Nobody cares about that stuff."

"It's a Michelin star restaurant, you numpty. Trust me, they care."

I smiled. "I like it when you call me a numpty." I gave her hand a tug and drew her in for a hug, folding her small body into mine, uncaring of the looks we were getting from passersby on the pavement. "You and your dirty mouth."

She chuckled into my chest and shook her head against my suit. "You're so weird."

I sighed. "Come on, Lottie. I'm hungry. The last bird I took in there was wearing some sort of boiler suit, for God's sake. You look great in comparison."

"Little dating tip for you, big guy," Lottie said with some fire in her voice. "Not ideal to mention other women you've taken somewhere you're trying to take someone new."

I smiled. "Are you jealous?" I liked that idea. Smiling might not have been the best choice, though, considering how her eyes flashed green fire when I did it.

"Anyway, that *last bird,* as you so beautifully put it, was probably in a *designer* boiler suit that cost more than I make in six months. I doubt she was wearing clothes she scrounged up at Asda that have seen better days."

"I promise, nobody will care."

"Well, I'm definitely not going in there now that I know it's your regular hookup spot. No way."

Hmm. I recognised that stubborn tone. I had sisters after all. She wasn't going to change her mind. Bugger, this wasn't going the way I'd wanted it to. I thought I had dating down to a fine art: wow them with an exclusive restaurant, flash them a few smiles, get my way in all things. This negotiating thing was new to me. The woman wouldn't even set foot in the restaurant I'd chosen for a start, and I'd already pissed her off.

"I've got it," I said, "Come with me."

I took her hand in mine and tugged her along the pavement.

"This better not be another fancy place," Lottie grumbled as we made our way down the street. When she was level with me I took her by her shoulders and steered her around me so that I was on the traffic side of the pavement.

"What are you doing?" she asked.

"What do you mean?"

"All this manoeuvering me around. What's that about?"

"I don't understand."

"Just now, you moved me across to your other side."

I smiled down at her confused face. "Lottie, I'm sorry if I haven't given you this impression up until now, but I am, in fact, a gentleman."

Her eyebrows drew together in confusion. "What's that got to do with moving me around the pavement like a chess piece?"

I sighed. "The lady should walk on the inside, away from the traffic."

"What?" She laughed. "That's ridiculous."

I shrugged. "It's second nature to me, to be honest."

"So it's gentlemanly to be the first to get hit by a car?"

"Yes, of course it is."

Lottie snorted. "Posh people are weird."

"Here we are," I said, drawing us to a stop by Kensington farmer's market. "Right then, now we just have to find James."

"James?"

"My fishmonger friend."

*

"So let me get this straight," Lottie said after swallowing some of her smoked salmon bagel. "When you called James your 'fishmonger friend', what you actually meant was your aristocratic entrepreneur friend who smokes the most amazing tasting salmon for shits and giggles in smokehouses on his many country estates, and which sell like hotcakes at Harrods, Harvey Nicks and any other posh outlet you can think of?"

"That just about covers it," I said as I bit off more of my own bagel. "Like I said: fishmonger."

She rolled her eyes and relaxed back on the bench we were sitting on, closing her eyes, turning her face towards the sun and letting out a contented sigh.

"This is nice," she said with a wistful tone I didn't quite understand. She looked so peaceful and heartbreakingly beautiful that it took me a moment to clear my throat and speak again.

"It's not quite the date I planned," I grumbled.

She smiled and opened her eyes to look at me. "This is way better than being stuck inside a fancy restaurant. Your friend smokes good fish. I feel completely spoilt."

Spoilt? Sitting on a park bench in a shared garden, eating a smoked salmon bagel. I snorted.

"No, really it is," she told me. "I've been dying to use this garden since I started working for you."

"Why didn't you ask for the key?"

Her smile fell and she shrugged. "I didn't want to impose. Plus I'm not a resident. I'd stick out like a sore thumb around all the yummy mummies who use this." She let out a short laugh. "You should see the park near mine. No way you'd want to eat in there – too much dog shit, used condoms and drug dealers."

I stiffened. "That doesn't sound particularly safe."

She shrugged. "It's fine. Not all of us can live in Kensington. I can look after myself. I've been doing it for a long while."

My chest tightened. "How long?"

She looked away and shifted on her chair. "Since I was ten."

"Ten?"

She shrugged. "That's when I went into foster care." Her hands holding the bagel lowered as if she'd lost her appetite. "You should probably know that, Ollie. You could get some flak for my background if we go public. There can be a real stigma around foster kids."

"We bloody well will be going public," I said in a firm voice. "And nobody is going to say *anything* about your background."

I turned to her fully then, putting my bagel down to slide my hand under her jaw and turn her face to mine.

"I'm sorry that happened to you, darling," I said in a softer voice now. "That's totally shit."

She swallowed and her eyes became glassy with tears. One fell off the end of her long lashes and I wiped it away when it made it to her cheekbone. She cleared her throat.

"Fraggle Rock, sorry," she muttered. "You must think I'm a right wetwipe. I swear I don't usually blub like this."

She swallowed again and her eyes dropped down to her lap.

"I just... nobody's really said sorry like that to me before, or told me that what happened was shit. My mates, the other kids in the group home, were in the same boat, so they weren't going to say it. My social worker was always... well, she was just there to sort stuff out, and I was tricky to place so..."

A surge of anger swept through me at the thought of ten-year-old Lottie being placed into care, uprooted from her home with nobody to even say how sorry they were that it was happening to her.

"What happened to your parents?" I asked cautiously.

"Dad died when I was six," she said. "Mum couldn't really cope without him. She started drinking. It got really bad at home. She was never abusive, but she just couldn't function enough to wash my clothes and go to the shops to get food. The school started to notice the state I was in, the weight I lost and the fact I was always trying to steal food. When social services went round they couldn't wake Mum up she was so drunk. Rehab didn't help, and eventually I had to be placed somewhere."

"How's your mum now?"

"She got clean when I was fifteen. But she... er... she relapsed again a year and a half ago. Then ten months ago she got sick, really sick – liver failure. She had a bleed from her stomach and she died."

"Oh God. I'm so sorry, Lottie."

She shrugged and blinked away her tears as she squared her shoulders. "It happens. Alcoholism can be brutal. I lost Mum but I'm lucky in a lot of ways. I'm sitting in the sun in a posh garden eating smoked salmon. I work for the cleanest man in London who always has loads of leftovers and one of the finest arses I've ever seen. Life's good."

I took her hand and gave it a squeeze, leaning into her to kiss the side of her head. We sat like that for a long moment whilst I breathed in the floral scent of her hair.

"So you've been checking out my arse, have you?" I said eventually to lighten the atmosphere.

Lottie pulled back to look up at me and roll her eyes. "I promise you, Ollie. Any red-blooded straight female, or gay man for that matter, checks out your arse given the opportunity."

"Is that right?" I muttered, leaning in again until my lips were against hers.

"I've got salmon breath," she whispered against my mouth.

"So have I, baby," I told her. When my tongue darted out to lick the small spot of cream cheese from the corner of her mouth, she let out a quiet moan and closed her mouth over mine. She must have put down her bagel because her hands slid to my chest and grasped my shirt as I deepened the kiss, drawing her closer to me.

"Oh! Tarquin, come away from there!" The woman's voice cut through my haze of lust and we broke apart, flinching when we realised a small figure was standing right in front of us.

"You was kissin'," the toddler said accusingly, his stubby finger pointed at us and a deep scowl on his face.

"Hi," Lottie said softly. "Yes, we were kissing."

"Molly Henderson wants to kiss me, but I runs away," he told Lottie, then turned to me. "You should try running away. I had to climb up a tree. There's one there what's good for climbing."

"Thanks, mate," I said seriously. "I'll remember that if she tries to kiss me again."

"Tarquin!" the harassed-looking mum had made it over and grabbed Tarquin's hand. "So sorry," she said to both of us, her face now pink with embarrassment. "Carry on." She pulled Tarquin away with her, but as he was leaving, he turned back and mouthed, "Run away," to me, tilting his head toward the tree he had identified as good climbing potential earlier.

I snorted a laugh, then turned back to Lottie. She was smiling after Tarquin but her eyes had clouded over.

"You should, you know," she said softly. Although her smile was still in place, her voice seemed somehow sad.

"I should what?"

"Run away." She laughed again. "Tarquin's given you some solid advice there."

"Why would I want to do that?" I muttered against her temple before pressing my lips there in a kiss. She took a deep breath in and let it out slowly.

"Apart from the fact that I don't fit in your world filled with Tarquins and mums in activewear that probably cost as much as my rent for a month?"

"Of course you fit in my world."

She snorted. "Well, apart from that, I'm complicated. I've got all sorts of baggage, Ollie."

"I don't care about your baggage. There's nothing that would put me off. You can be as complicated as you like."

She smiled up at me, and I thought I'd settled it.

But just before she took another bite out of her bagel, I heard her mutter in a barely-there whisper. "We'll see."

CHAPTER 13

My life is... complicated

Ollie

"Hey, lovebug," Lottie said, and I froze outside the bathroom. Lovebug? Who would Lottie call *lovebug*? "That's really great. I'm so proud of you. We'll celebrate tonight, okay? We could go out?" She laughed softly. "Okay, okay, I'll cook for you, sweetie. Whatever you want. Okay, I'll see you later. I love you."

I frowned and took a step back. Maybe there was a good explanation? She might have been talking to a friend. But, would you call a friend lovebug? Unwanted memories were struggling to surface. I'd been burned by secret phone calls and sneaking around before. I shook my head to clear it. Lottie wasn't like that. If she had a boyfriend, she would have said. I just needed to ask her. I looked down at the flowers in my hand and winced. Making a split-second decision, I threw them into the empty laundry basket and shut the lid. Rubbing a hand down my face, I took a deep breath before pushing open the door to the bathroom.

"Hey," I said, and Lottie shrieked, spinning around, with her hand on her chest.

"Ollie, you scared shi—take mushrooms out of me," she said, giving her phone a nervous look where it sat on the counter before focusing back on me. I shoved my hands into my pockets to stop myself doing my usual of reaching for her to kiss her and nuzzle her neck hello. Lottie's clumsiness wasn't seeming quite so adorable at the moment. I took a deep breath in and let it out slowly.

"You still keen for tomorrow night?" I asked. After waiting almost two weeks after our bagels in the park, Lottie had finally agreed to a proper date. I wasn't sure why she was putting me off, but after hearing that phone call, I was beginning to have my suspicions.

"Yes, of course," she said. Her smile was like a punch in the gut, and I couldn't bring myself to return it.

"Are you sure?"

Lottie's smile dimmed, and she tilted her head to the side. Over the last two weeks, I'd been coming home for lunch with Lottie as often as I could, and I could feel her shields gradually coming down. I kept our interactions kitchen-based, not wanting to go further with her physically in case she thought I was just wanting to have a bit on the side with a member of staff. I did let myself kiss her, hold her hand, and put my hand on her lower back to lead her where I wanted her to go – all of which gave her a slightly dazed, almost reverent look on her face, like she couldn't quite believe this was happening.

The more time I spent with her, the deeper I fell for her. She had a bizarre way of sensing my mood – almost as if she could read me. I was talking to her about a housing project the other day, and she'd cut me off: "But you don't want to invest in it," she told me.

"What makes you say that?" I asked in complete surprise.

"I just know that you don't," she said simply. "If I had to guess, I'd say you don't agree with their green space plan."

I blinked. Yes, I had some reservations about the amount of green space planned for the project, which was about half what I considered to be sufficient.

"How on earth do you know that?"

She shrugged. "I'm good at reading people. Don't invest in something that makes you unhappy."

I was also feeding her up. Lottie was too bloody thin. When I wanted to give this woman diamonds, I was, in fact, providing smoked salmon bagels from James and takeout from the local Italian. It broke my heart a little bit yesterday when she asked if she could take the leftover lasagne home. Lottie shouldn't be eating leftovers. But that was all going to be sorted soon. Lottie would be a full-time student once I got my way. And I always got my way. My *girlfriend* wasn't going to be cleaning houses or eating leftovers or any of that shit. I just had to tread carefully with how I approached it. And maybe I needed to find out why she might be calling someone lovebug on the phone?

"Ollie, what's the matter?" Her brows drew together as she looked up at me, and I forced a smile. "Is this because I said I'm not coming to the gala dinner tonight? It would have been a bit public for a first date anyway, don't you think?" She gave a nervous laugh, which I ignored.

"You'd tell me if you were involved with someone else, wouldn't you?" I asked, hating the unsure quality in my voice. Her eyebrows went up.

"Involved with someone else? What are you talking about?" She laughed. "Ollie, I barely have the time to be involved with *you*."

I cleared my throat. "Who were you talking to just now?"

Her eyes were wary now, and her expression shuttered. My throat felt tight.

"Ollie, I told you, my life is… complicated. I…" she closed her eyes for a moment, then moved to me. After a brief hesitation, no doubt in response to my defensive posture, she put her small hands on my chest. "There're lots of things you need to know, alright?" My arms moved of their own accord. Having her hands on me, her soft flowery scent around me and her beautiful face blinking up at me was impossible to resist. One of my hands went into her gorgeous soft, thick hair, the other splayed across her back, pulling her further into me. She smiled again, this time with relief, and my chest felt tight.

"Does this *complicated* have anything to do with why it's taken over two weeks for you to have a free evening?" I tried to keep resentment out of my tone, but I was tired of waiting to be with her. She nodded.

"Yes." She squeezed her eyes shut, and when she opened them, they were full of determination. "Yes, and I should have told you already, but I was afraid that..."

I leaned down to rest my forehead against her. "What are you afraid of, darling?" I said softly. She opened her mouth to speak, but before she could say anything, the shrill sound of the alarm on her phone cut through the atmosphere and broke the spell between us.

"Fudge nuggets," she muttered, pulling away from me to silence her phone. "Ollie, I've got to go, but I promise, I *promise* to tell you everything tomorrow night. Then you can decide if you—" she paused for a moment to swallow. "If you still want to be with me." Her voice broke on the last sentence, and I frowned in confusion. Had I not made it clear how desperately I wanted to be with her?

I crossed my arms over my chest as she gathered her stuff, in a real rush now. Maybe I should give her the flowers? But before I could retrieve them, she was already running for the door. I jogged after her and caught her hand to stop her, but she shook me off.

"I've got to go," she said in a panic. "I can't be late *again*. I'll explain everything tomorrow night, okay?"

"Okay," I said to the thin air she left behind.

I was grumpy for the rest of the day and even grumpier that I had to go to the gala dinner without Lottie. I mean, I'd told her last week that this evening was really important. She knew how much it meant to me, yet she'd still blown me off. So that was why when Arabella, who's always wound me up, grabbed me in front of the photographers I thought, why not? Maybe a little jealousy would do Lottie some good. Nothing else seemed to be working.

I must admit, the way Arabella burrowed into my side made me feel slightly uneasy. I was relatively quick to pull away, so the paps probably didn't catch it. Still, I definitely regretted it once we were inside. The woman was like an octopus and clearly shitfaced before she even arrived. Her perfume made me feel a bit sick after about five minutes. Claire had to come to the rescue in the end.

"Why on earth are you letting Scary Airy put her paws all over you?" she asked once she'd told Arabella in no uncertain terms to bugger off.

I shuffled my feet and avoided eye contact. It seemed a bit petty now. "At least *she* wants to be here with me."

Claire's eyebrows went up. "What's that supposed to mean?"

"It means I wanted Lottie to come to this stupid shitshow, but she keeps blowing me off."

"Ah." Claire smiled. "You know what, baby bro? This is a good learning experience for you. Not everything can fall into your lap without effort. I'm beginning to really like Lottie. Anyone who can take you down a peg or two is okay in my book."

I huffed. "I just can't understand why she won't make the time for me."

"Have you considered that she may have some shit going on in her own life?"

"She works another job, Claire, but I *know* she's not working tonight as that other job happens to be in a bar *I own*."

"Just try to have a little patience," Claire said.

"Well, Mum thinks—"

"Oh my God, Ols, do not tell me that you spoke to Mum about this?"

"What's wrong with talking to Mum?"

Well, I was about to find out.

CHAPTER 14

A severance package from a person?

Lottie

Hayley and I both startled at the knock on the door and then exchanged worried looks. Unannounced visitors often did not bode well for us, unfortunately. Not since Brenda and Tony had filed concerns with social services last month in a bid for Hayley to live with them full-time. Laura, our social worker, was lovely, but it was still a scary process. And a slap in the face, to be honest.

I knew Brenda and Tony didn't like me, but I'd gone out of my way to encourage their relationship with Hayley. It wasn't easy or cheap for me to schlep all the way across London to facilitate contact, and I'd been nothing but nice to them.

When they'd first come back into Hayley's life, I was actually excited. I was naïve enough to think that they might be extra support, even that they might become like family. But I was wrong. They may have considered Hayley family, but the same could certainly not be said for me.

Anyway, I wasn't in the best of moods after seeing the pictures of Ollie online. I knew he was going to the foundation gala, and I knew it was a high-profile event. I couldn't go. Not only did I have nothing to wear to something like that, but I'd had to be with Hayley for her session with the new counsellor, and it was lucky I was there given that she made a huge breakthrough.

Ollie wasn't pleased, and I knew I needed to give him a better explanation, but I just hadn't been ready to make everything so heavy between us by telling him about Hayley. And my life was heavy. I had a *lot* of baggage. Granted, I would do anything for that particular baggage – she was my only family, and I loved her to pieces. But the story of why I was my sister's guardian, why she needed specialist counselling, what we'd both been through... I needed some time to explain all that. Time when I wasn't supposed to be on the clock cleaning his freaking house.

"Don't worry, lovebug," I muttered. "It's probably just Ada about tonight."

It was frivolous, I knew, letting Ada babysit when it wasn't for work. But I never did anything for myself, and I simply wanted Ollie. I knew it wasn't going anywhere – people like me did not end up with people like him. But the last few years had ground me down so much that this chink of light, something that wasn't just the unrelenting pressure and struggle, was impossible to pass up.

I know Ollie had *said* he was obsessed with me, those words had replayed in my brain over and over again for the last two weeks, but I also lived in the real world. I was essentially a single mother, and there were skeletons in my cupboard that would very likely be deal breakers. But I was going to let myself stay in the light for just a little longer.

The walk from our makeshift kitchen table to the door was only a couple of steps; everything in this flat was only a couple of steps. I wasn't joking when I said the snug at Ollie's house was double the size of my entire space. I frowned as there was another knock on the door.

"Ada, I... oh!" I snapped my mouth shut and stared at the Dowager of Buckingham on my doorstep. "Er, Lady Harding. Hi."

"Hello, dear," she said, peering around me to wave at Hayley. "Please try to remember to call me Margot. And hello, Hayley. Sorry to pop in like this. Unforgivably rude of me, but I'm afraid this just wouldn't wait."

"Oh, right," I said, moving back from the door. "Please, come in. I'm sorry, but we don't have that much space. Can I get you a cup of tea? I've got some custard creams." I was rambling now, but having an actual *lady* in my tiny flat, not least one who was the mum of the man I was fairly certain I'd fallen in love with, was a little overwhelming.

She gave me a kind smile as she moved into the cramped space, glancing around at my charity shop sofa, the chair which I'd tried to jazz up with colourful throws, the tiny kitchen complete with a small, scuffed table and rickety chairs that I'm ashamed to say I retrieved from a skip. I cleared my throat. "Would you like to come and sit down?"

"Thank you," she said, showing no reaction to any of the décor. "But don't let me interrupt Hayley's dinner."

"Oh, she's finished anyway," I said quickly. "Haven't you, Hails?" Hayley nodded as her eyes flicked between me and Margot. I hated that her default was suspicious caution, but that was how she was eyeing Margot despite how much she'd seemed to like her the last time they met.

"Thank you, Hayley," said Margot through a smile. "Do you mind if I borrow your sister for a minute?" Hayley shook her head. "I brought you something." Margot walked over to Hayley, fished in her handbag for a minute and then pulled out a beautiful sketchpad, a huge set of colouring pens and one of the toffee sweets she knew Hayley liked. "I found the drawings you left up in the mezzanine that day. My particular favourite was the rainbow unicorn. I thought you might like these." Hayley's eyes went wide as she took the gifts and hugged them to her chest. She looked up at Margot as her free hand went to her chin and out.

I cleared my throat. "She's signing, *thank you*," I said.

"You're welcome, darling," said Margot, then she turned back to me.

"Hails, why don't you go to your room and make a new picture for the fridge." Hayley smiled at me and shot out of the room. Any excuse not to be around a relative stranger and to draw, she would jump on. Once alone, I cleared my throat again.

"Tea?"

"Lovely, dear."

"Please take a seat. Oh no not that one!" I stopped Margot just in time before she could sit on the dodgy chair. She looked at me, and I grimaced. "Sorry, it's just that one is liable to collapse – only Hayley's got the knack. Maybe we'd be safer on the sofa?"

I ushered her over, feeling my cheeks heat with embarrassment. "Er, could you sit on the left side? It's just the springs are a bit better there."

I finished making the tea and brought it over to her. She smiled kindly at me as she took it, then her eyes drifted around the space as she sipped from the chipped mug, which had Best Sister Ever painted on it in Hayley's rubbish writing from the time I made the mistake of taking her to one of those make-your-own-pottery places. I mean it was great, but they're rip-off merchants – fifteen quid for a mug? Daylight robbery.

"Lottie, I understand that my son is taking you out tonight." Her gaze was fixed on me now, and there was a sharp quality to it I couldn't quite put my finger on. I nodded, not really knowing what to say. The last thing I expected was a visit from someone's mum before they picked me up for a date. Is this how the upper class did things? Bizarre. "You may or may not know that my Oliver has had some unfortunate experiences… with women."

My eyebrows went up. "Oh, no, sorry we… I mean, we haven't discussed exes yet. It's all a bit new at the moment. But I promise you I could give him a run for his money in the dodgy ex-stakes; some of mine are real pieces of work."

The dowager nodded. "So you'll understand why I have to exercise caution. Last time, everything was so horrendous… he hasn't been himself for years. I know he comes across as a bit…" she paused, searched for the right words, "…sure of himself." I stifled a laugh; there was an understatement if ever I heard one. "But really, he's quite a sensitive boy."

"Oh right, well…" I trailed off, not knowing how to reply. I stared at the dowager, focusing on the energy coming off her – anxiety, pity (annoying, but okay, I get it, given the state of my flat), determination and just the vaguest hint of hostility. She had not come here to tell me how excited she was that Ollie was showing an interest in me. I squared my shoulders. "Margot, why are you here?"

She flinched at my direct approach, then cleared her throat as she set her tea down on the small coffee table. "I know you need money," she said, and I blinked.

"W-what do you mean?"

"You need money for Hayley. The funding you're getting via the school isn't enough to deal with her selective mutism. You are going to have to fund that privately, and that is *very* expensive. I know you've had some sessions with a therapist, but you're going to struggle to afford more. There is also the matter of funding the next module of your Open University degree course." Margot indicated to the numerous textbooks strewn over the coffee table.

"How on earth do you know all this?" I said in alarm, starting to feel a little sick.

"I have extensive resources, Lottie," Margot went on almost casually. "My investigators are extremely thorough."

"B-but that's all *private* information," I spluttered. "You can't—"

"I can, and I did," Margot stated firmly, and, as had happened so many times before in my life, I sensed the powerlessness I had in this situation. My chest felt tight. I had thought that Margot liked me.

"What has this got to do with me and Ollie going on a date?" I managed to get out in a stiff tone.

"I also know about Hayley's grandparents and how they want custody of Hayley and how you're having to prove that you're a better caregiver than they are."

I shot out of my seat. Some tea spilt over my hand before I could shove it onto the coffee table, but I barely felt it.

"Y-you can't just go poking around in someone's life like this!"

She sighed. "I'm sorry if it upsets you, but I'm very protective when it comes to my children. Given your situation with Hayley, I'm sure you can understand."

"I-I-I can't... I'm sorry, but that is not okay!"

She shrugged. "I apologise for the intrusion, but I felt it necessary to have all the facts. You can't be so naïve to think that a man with Oliver's wealth and influence can get involved with people without them being vetted first? I'm not quite sure you know what you're getting yourself into. This family has held its hereditary title for over five hundred years. It was created by Henry VI himself in 1444. We own an embarrassing amount of London, most of Surrey as well as properties in Asia, Europe and North America. We have investments in food and agricultural companies all over the world. Oliver's net worth is estimated at over nine billion pounds."

I felt the colour drain out of my face as I walked back slowly to the sofa to sit down.

"What?" I breathed. Nine billion? That was more money than I could comprehend. How could anyone be worth that much? I let out a shaky laugh thinking about the five pounds seventy-five pence I had in my wallet and the meagre amount sitting in my bank account. "Cheese and rice."

"So, as you can see," she continued, all business now, "we *do* have to vet people. It's just what—"

"Just because you're rich doesn't actually give you the right to have people investigated, you know," I told her, my shock receding and my anger rising now. "It doesn't change the fact that it's just plain rude. Having money doesn't make you above everyone else; it doesn't make you better people. It just means that your great-great-great-great-great-grandparents were mates with the king, and he gave you a load of dosh and land, whereas my great-great-great-great-great-grandparents worked the land or something."

The dowager blinked at me, and then she shocked me by smiling. "I knew I liked you," she said, and my eyebrows went up. "And yes, you're right, it was rude. I am sorry."

I huffed.

"But, just so you know, not all Oliver's wealth is inherited," she added. "He's nearly doubled the family's holdings with his investments."

"'Cause you really needed to double your money," I said dryly. "God forbid you couldn't buy and sell entire countries. What would the neighbours say?"

She laughed. "Touché, Lottie. I can see how you'd think that. But Oliver's set up more charitable foundations than any of his predecessors as well. We *are* trying not just to hoard all our wealth."

I rolled my eyes. Clearly, with a net worth of nine billion, he wasn't trying *that* hard.

"I'll ask again," my tone was firm now. "What do you want? You didn't come here just to list all the ways you're a boatload wealthier than me."

"Right, well..." she looked away and cleared her throat before looking back at me. "There's no easy way to approach this, Lottie. But I'm here to offer you a severance package."

"A... what?"

"A severance package... from your employment."

"Listen, Ollie said there wouldn't be a problem with me keeping my job. He promised that—"

"Oliver doesn't know I'm here. This would be a private arrangement between you and me."

I blinked at her. "What?" I whispered.

"If you leave your job now, I will transfer fifty thousand pounds into your account. Today." She was serious, I could sense that, but there was something else too, almost like... hope? What was she hopeful for?

"Why would you do that?"

She looked to the side. "For my son," she said when she looked back at me.

"How is this helping your son?"

"It wouldn't be just severance from your job, Lottie. It would be severance from *Oliver*."

"A severance package from a person? Is that a thing?"

"It can be, yes."

"You want me to stay away from your son."

I felt an ache in my chest at my words. Ollie's mum was here to bribe me to stay away from him. She hated me that much? I never got that vibe from her and I could always sense how people felt.

Always.

It was then it really came home to me how deluded I'd actually been. I knew Ollie had a close family. There were blooming loads of them: cousins, sisters, all sorts came to the house. So many threads in his family tapestry holding everything together. And over the last week, I'd started to let myself imagine a world where Hayley and I were weaved into a family like that. A world where this woman allowed us to be a part of her family, maybe even welcomed it.

I turned away from the dowager when my eyes started stinging. What planet did I think I was living on where a family like this with a hereditary title going back five hundred years would welcome a nobody like me?

Well, Hayley and I had been alone for this long, and we'd been let down plenty already. At least this way, I was finding out early about what kind of *family* these people were. The last thing Hayley needed was another disappointment. I squared my shoulders and looked back at Margot. The pictures I'd seen online of Ollie and that other woman raced through my brain, along with the cost of Hayley's ongoing therapy.

Her voice was softer when she spoke again. "Listen, Lottie, it's not just Oliver I'm doing this for, you know." She glanced at my ancient laptop which I'd nudged when I sat down and was embarrassingly showing the article I'd been looking at a picture of Ollie and the beautiful blonde from last night. Then she looked back at me. I felt my face heat. "I just don't think he's serious enough about you. I'm worried he'll let you down, and with your little sister relying on you... I wouldn't want you to be put in a difficult position. I really do like you and your sister, you see."

"Fine," I snapped.

The dowager's head jerked and she blinked at me. Even without my ability to read people, it wouldn't have been hard to tell that she was shocked. She expected me to decline. But underneath the shock, there was something that confused me. There was disappointment. Why would the woman offer me fifty grand to get rid of me and then be disappointed when I took it?

"So, you'll cut off contact with Oliver?" she asked slowly, her eyes narrowing on me.

My throat felt tight as Ollie's gorgeous face, his eyes, his smile, his laugh and his inability to play competent chess all flashed through my mind, followed swiftly by visions of him and that blonde with the tagline *Duke of Fuckingham Strikes Again* underneath. It wasn't just the fact that he had another woman tucked into his side the day after he'd brought me lunch and kissed me again, although that hurt, a lot. Deep down, it was the ingrained knowledge that the likes of him were not for the likes of me. The woman hanging off him at that event was wearing a five-thousand-pound dress according to the article. Five *thousand* pounds. That was five months' rent for me. And she was clearly happy in front of the cameras. There was no way

I would want to be photographed. In my situation, it literally couldn't happen.

Oliver Harding was a dead end. And we needed that money. A few years ago, heck, even six months ago I would have been too proud to take it. But, you know what? Now, it wasn't about me and my pride. Now it was about a little girl and the fact she simply *couldn't* speak to anyone but me. It was about trying to establish a normal life for her, and it was time-critical. The longer Hayley was without help, the more ingrained the behaviour would become.

"Yes," I said after a long pause. "You have my word."

CHAPTER 15

Well, that's a relief

Lottie

After I'd accepted the money from his mother, I texted Ollie to tell him that I was resigning from my job but would work my two weeks' notice, and that I didn't think us going out was a good idea. He tried to ring me, but I just didn't pick up. The next morning, I still turned up to clean his house. When I arrived there, though, a grumpy-looking lady in her sixties, clutching a bottle of bleach was barring the doorway.

"Er, hi," I'd said to her as she glared at me. "I'm Lottie, the cleaner. Are you—"

"I know who you are," the woman snapped.

"Well, are you the new cleaner?"

She snorted. "New? I've worked for the Hardings for forty years, young lady."

"Does Ollie know that—"

"*His Grace* told me to tell you that your services are no longer required. He will honour a full month's pay which I think is more than generous since he's been paying you to do sod all for months. So you can jog on."

"Mrs Higgins," Ollie's voice sounded behind the lady and she huffed in annoyance, "give us a moment please."

"Fine," Mrs Higgins snapped, moving away from the door and muttering to herself about gold-digging harlots as she shuffled away down the corridor.

"Lottie," Ollie said, his large frame filling the doorway as he crossed his arms over his chest. Our height difference was even more exaggerated by the fact I was a step down from him where he stood. I swallowed.

"Your mum told you then?" I asked in a small voice and his eyes flashed with anger.

"That she paid you off? Yes, Lottie. Mum made sure to tell me that." His voice was so cold. Warm, teasing, kind Ollie was gone, replaced by this cold stranger who was staring at me like I was a squashed bug on the pavement.

I cleared my throat and willed the tears I could feel building back.

"I'm so sorry," I said and despite my effort it was barely above a whisper. "Ollie, I feel terrible but I really needed to—"

"How could you?" The coldness in his tone was replaced by white-hot anger as his whole body tightened with tension. "How could you take it? Did everything mean nothing? Did you..." his voice broke off and he looked away from me, squaring his shoulders before he looked back but this time not giving me any eye contact. If I thought his voice from before was cold, the next time he spoke it was positively Arctic. "I believe my mother's terms include no further contact. I suggest then that you leave. Unless you'd like to repay the fifty grand?"

God, Margot had told him everything. I felt like I was going to throw up. But he was right. I'd made a deal. I had my reasons, I'd apologised to Ollie. Now I needed to move on.

"I can't repay that money," I said in a small voice. "But, Ollie, I promise it meant something to me. *You* meant something."

He snorted. "Clearly," he said in a dry tone. "I meant so much that you were willing to be bought off for a measly fifty grand. I feel so bloody special."

And there it was: the difference between us. A *measly* fifty grand? I'd been living in cloud cuckoo land if I thought the Duke of Buckingham and I stood a chance. We didn't inhabit the same planet, or even the same universe.

I swallowed down the tightness in my throat and forced my feet to move down the steps away from Ollie. On the way down I had a small kernel of hope that he'd run after me. That he'd sweep me up in his arms and tell me everything was going to be okay.

But when I reached the pavement I flinched at the sound of the front door of Buckingham House slamming shut.

*

From then on, the only other time I saw Ollie was at the club where I still waitressed. The look he gave me was so full of hatred that I hadn't been brave enough to keep eye contact for more than a few seconds, and when I checked back to the same spot, he was gone, and I hadn't seen him in there since.

At first, I'd had visions of him missing me and then turning up at my flat and calling up to me from the pavement, *Romeo and Juliet* style (I was quite sure that if his mother could track me down, then Ollie would have had no trouble in obtaining my address). But that never happened, which I told myself was for the best.

But not long after Margot's visit another Harding *did* track me down. Vicky showed up at my flat about a week later.

"This is very small," was the first thing she'd said on entering it, and despite my depressed mood, it had startled a laugh out of me. When Hayley popped her head out of her room, Vicky waved, saying, "You don't have to greet me if you don't want to. I know how annoying it is when people expect you to speak when you'd rather not. I didn't used to speak much either."

Hayley had been shocked for a moment, then surprised me by smiling and offering Vicky a biscuit.

When Vicky told her, "I don't eat refined sugar," Hayley handed her an apple instead, which Vicky took. There was this unspoken acceptance between them, as if they could each sense that the other just did things a little differently, and that was okay.

"Why are you here, Vicky?" I'd asked as she munched on her apple after Hayley had gone to her room, sitting where her mother had sat a week before.

"I read your file."

"The one that Margot compiled on me?"

"Yes," she said, totally unrepentant. "You have a criminal record."

I froze and stared at her. "Can you keep your voice down?" I hissed.

"It will be hard for you to gain other employment which pays as well as the cleaning job for my half-brother."

"So, you know what happened with Margot?"

Vicky nodded, then tilted her head to the side. Now, Vicky was harder to read than other people. There were few subtle signs to give her away. But I could sense she wanted something from me. Very badly.

"You have abilities," she said, and I blinked.

"W-what?"

"You can notice nonverbal cues. As a child, you were described as watchful. One report says that you survived living with your mother due to your ability to read people. You're now doing a psychology course, I presume in order to capitalise on these abilities as these are where your strengths lie."

I stood up from the sofa quickly and paced away from Vicky. "Let me get this straight. Margot accessed my *personal, confidential* files from when I was known to social services as a child?"

Vicky nodded. "School reports too: *Lottie has the uncanny ability to sense exactly what people need in a conversation. She can adapt to any circumstance. She has such strong emotional intelligence, it's almost as though she can read people's minds.*"

My mouth fell open. "How many times have you read my school reports?"

"I have a photographic memory."

"Of course you do." I sighed. "Much as I'd love to sue you and Margot for invading my privacy, to be honest, I don't have the time, the energy or the money. So, if we could just move this along? Tell me why you're here. You want something from me."

"You can read people. I cannot," Vicky stated bluntly, which seemed to be the only way she stated anything. "I am Autistic. But you would know that already. You would have sensed it."

I nodded.

"I don't tell anyone that and it's only recently been diagnosed formally. I would prefer that you didn't share this information with anyone."

"Of course," I said.

"My half-brother has tried to protect me since I was dropped off at his family home at the age of six, but he has done enough now. I don't want to work for the Buckingham Estate when I'm not a proper member of the Harding family."

"Who says you're not a proper member?"

"I'm the result of an affair. Technically I'm not sure I should even have their last name. Anyway, I need my own career, away from them. I'm very good with numbers, and I know how to make money."

"I can understand you wanting to branch out from your family, but haven't you got enough money?" I said wearily.

"Yes, I do," she agreed. "But I need more. A lot more."

"Of course you do," I repeated. "So what does this have to do with me?"

"I want to hire you to help me. Investors are not always logical. They do not choose the companies to use just based on objective facts. There seems to be a subjective element which I can't grasp. Also…" she looked away for a moment, then back at me, "people don't like me."

"Oh." I felt my annoyance and anger deflate slightly at that bald statement. "Vicky, I'm sure—"

"It's okay. I know that I'm different. I state facts, always. But I really can't understand why anyone wouldn't. I can't lie, or at least I see no point in it. But..." she swallowed before continuing and I could sense sadness and discomfort, "but I hurt people's feelings sometimes, and I don't realise I'm doing it. People don't always want to hear the truth."

"No, they don't," I said more softly now. I could see that hurting people upset Vicky.

"And most of the time, I don't even know I've hurt somebody's feelings because they don't tell me. It's easier with Margot and my half-siblings. They know that they need to spell everything out to me and be really clear. But even then, I can run into trouble. My half-sister sometimes takes things the wrong way. She got married to Blake last year and told me before one of her dress fittings that she wanted me there and she loved me, but she didn't want any honest opinions about the dress. So I didn't say anything. After half an hour she begged me for my honest opinion."

I winced. "Which was?"

"It looks itchy."

"Ah."

"It did. There was a lot of lace. I'm afraid that when I look at lace, all I can think about is that it looks really itchy. I couldn't *see* anything else. That's literally all I could think about when I was looking at her."

"She was upset," I concluded, and Vicky's face clouded.

"It wasn't just the dress she wanted an honest opinion on. It was Blake too."

"You don't like him?"

Vicky shrugged. "I do not feel he is an adequate partner for my half-sister or stepfather for my niece, and I couldn't come up with any quality I admired about him other than the fact his tie coordinates well with his shirt."

"Oof," I said with another wince.

"The thing is, if I can't even manage with people who know me well, then how can I deal with clients or potential clients?"

I gave her a long look. She was telling the truth, but there was something she was holding back.

"This is not the only reason you want to hire me."

Vicky looked away from me again, and for the first time, she seemed uncomfortable.

"I don't have any friends," she said, her voice smaller than before. "And I've never had a boyfriend. People think I'm cold and rude. Hence the *Ice Princess* nickname."

"You think I can help you with that?" I said softly.

She shrugged. "I need a people person. My half-brother has tried to help me… but he's just too overprotective. I need to hire someone. Someone with 'almost unnatural intuition'."

"You really did a deep dive on those school reports, didn't you?"

"I know that you need money for your sister, and I know how much Margot has given you, but it won't be enough for ongoing care. I will pay you more than enough for your sister's therapy, to continue your psychology course and for you to move out of this flat."

I stiffened. "What makes you think I want to move out of this place?"

"It has damp. You sleep on a sofa. The area is not safe."

"Don't hold back," I muttered.

"That's kind of the problem," she said. "I never do."

"If I take this job, I can't work long hours in the day. I have to be here for Hayley. So it's school hours only. The odd evening is fine – I can get a sitter after she's in bed, but I can't miss her coming home from school."

"Okay."

"And I want to be able to study whilst I'm on the job."

"Yes, I thought you would. Your degree course requires sixteen hours a week."

"Of course, you'd know that," I muttered. "You probably know what I ate for breakfast."

She shook her head. "The only one of your consumption habits I know of is that you don't drink alcohol, which I assume is to do with your moth—"

"I'm going to start my job of stopping you from putting your foot in your mouth right now, Vicky," I interrupted, my voice rising. "Do not ever, *ever* mention my mother." I never talked about Mum. The fact that I told Ollie that day on the bench was a minor miracle.

"Right," she said quietly, drawing back slightly from me and my sharp tone. Subtle cues were lost on Vicky, but she knew when someone was telling her off. She was rigid in her seat now. I could sense discomfort and maybe a little fear.

"It's okay, Vicky," I said softer now. "I know you didn't realise how much that would upset me. I'm sorry I raised my voice."

She shook her head. "It's okay. I'm just... sensitive with sound."

I tilted my head to the side. "I'll remember that, okay? I wouldn't have raised my voice, but I really don't ever want to talk about my mother. Right?"

Vicky nodded, and her stiff posture relaxed somewhat.

"What will my job title be? I can't very well go around saying I'm your *empath*."

"No, I suppose not. You'll be my personal assistant."

"And one more thing. Will I have to see your brother?"

"I can't guarantee you won't see my half-brother. I see him a lot, and my business partner is his best friend."

"My agreement with your stepmother is that I could not see your brother again."

"Romantically."

"What?"

"You were not allowed to see my half-brother again romantically. You won't be seeing him romantically when you're with me. He hates you now, so there is definitely not going to be any romantic element to you seeing him."

All the air left my lungs in a sudden whoosh as if Vicky had physically winded me. To hear so bluntly that Ollie hated me was worse than I imagined it would be. I looked away, blinking rapidly to force the tears back before I looked at Vicky again.

"Well, that's a relief," I said with a forced smile.

CHAPTER 16

Nobody likes a stale Jaffa Cake

Lottie

"Vicky," I said through gritted teeth. "You did not tell me that your brother was going to be here."

Since I'd started working for Vicky three months ago, I'd managed to avoid Ollie as now I didn't even have to waitress at that awful bar anymore – and I was keen to keep it that way.

"No, I didn't," she said, stating plain facts as always, no apology in her voice.

"Well, why the heck not?"

"You would have refused to come, and I needed you here."

I rolled my eyes. "I knew you weren't telling me something."

"I know you did. You can sense omission."

"Vicky," I said slowly as Ollie scowled at me across the room. "This is where you apologise."

"Oh, right," Vicky said and then paused. "But I'm *not* sorry. I need you here." Vicky had a tendency to see things her way. If she needed me to be somewhere then that to her was the priority.

"Lie to me."

"You know I can't do that, and also, you can tell if people are lying."

I gave up and took a big glug of my elderflower instead, swiping the tiny canapés as the tray went past and shoving one in my mouth. "I could be at home right now eating Chinese food with Hayley."

Vicky frowned. "Chinese food has MSG in it. You and Hayley should not be eating it." She paused for a moment, then turned to me. "I do *not* want you eating it. I like you and Hayley. I don't want you to get sick or have reduced life expectancies."

"Vics, there're a lot of things I'd do for you, babe. But abstaining from Chinese food for life is not one of them."

She huffed. "I'll send you a meal plan tomorrow."

"We've already got the last three you sent over, love. And I hate to break it to you, but there's no universe where Hayley is going to eat spinach."

"Why not?"

"Because she's eight, Vicky."

"Even more important that she eat green vegetables."

"Can we maybe concentrate on why we're here? I'd prefer to be able to get away the right side of midnight and before I run into your brother."

"Right, yes," Vicky said. She looked over my shoulder and then bit her lip. "Er... there might be a problem."

"What problem?"

"Mr Arkins is talking to my half-brother."

"Mother trucker," I muttered. Mr Arkins was the whole aim of tonight. Vicky wanted to invest this man's money for him. This shouldn't have been a problem, seeing as Vicky was the best investment broker in the business. But Mr Arkins was not going to be impressed with just the stats and cold, hard facts that Vicky could provide. The man needed schmoosing. Now, schmoosing was not Vicky's strong point, which is where I came in. I closed my eyes for a long moment.

I squared my shoulders and told myself to woman up. Vicky was paying me to help her with this stuff – I didn't need to let another employer down. So I forced a smile.

"Come on then," I said briskly. "I've got to face your brother at some point, might as well be now." Anyone else might have heard the shaky nature of my voice or noticed how my hands were bunched into tight fists, but Vicky, bless her, was totally oblivious. In her mind, if I said it was fine to go and see her brother, then it was fine.

So we made our way over there, but it was only when I was a few feet away from Ollie that I realised I'd made a mistake. Being this close to him again was not a good idea. He was glaring at me, his body language screaming for me to stay away, hatred coming off him in waves, but my heart hadn't seemed to have caught up to the fact that he wasn't the potential love of my life. All I wanted to do was fall into him and let him hold me against his broad chest, let him kiss my temple in that unbearably sweet way he had and absorb all the regret and longing inside me, bursting to get out. The feeling was so strong it was all I could concentrate on as I stared at him dumbly. I even felt myself sway towards him slightly, only clawing it back when I saw that his lip had curled with disgust and he had actually shifted back in the wake of my advance.

Abrupt greetings were exchanged between the four of us. I was barely able to form coherent words, let alone be of use to Vicky. And before I could stop her, Vicky had launched into the stats behind her investment strategies, and Mr Arkins' eyes had started glazing over. I shook my head to clear it and shifted my focus from the furious man across from me to the one I *should* be focusing on.

Mr Arkins was leaning slightly away from Vicky. I could feel annoyance, boredom and some frustration rolling off him. So I reached for Vicky's wrist and gave it a squeeze. Vicky was fine with touch as long as it was firm and deliberate, not light and unexpected. She knew to expect the wrist squeeze in this situation. It was the signal that we had come up with together to use if she needed to stop and take a breath. Once Vicky started on a subject, she tended to run with it at an alarming pace. She could lose her audience very quickly if we weren't careful, and right now we were dangerously close to losing Mr Arkins. His eyes were already flicking to either side, looking for some sort of escape. But they snapped back to us when Vicky's verbal diarrhoea cut off abruptly.

"Sorry, I went off on one," Vicky explained to Mr Arkins who was looking at her curiously. "Lottie tells me when I do it by squeezing my wrist. I'm not very good at letting other people talk." He blinked. Vicky looked at him seriously. "Apparently, I bore people."

"That's bullshit, Vics," Ollie snapped at her, then turned to me. "How dare you say that to my sister."

I ignored Ollie's furious gaze. All my focus on Mr Arkins. He was a big man, not as tall as Ollie but just as broad, and he didn't look particularly comfortable in a suit. One of his ears had been mauled at one stage; it wasn't a full-on cauliflower ear, but it wasn't that pretty either. And he had a scar on his lip, suggesting it had been busted a couple of times before.

I forced a laugh. "It's just there's so much flying around that huge brain of hers," I explained. "She knows all there is to know about investing people's money. But then there's all sorts that Vics knows about. Don't get her started on the latest rugby stats."

"You like rugby?" Mr Arkins asked, his eyebrows going up in surprise.

Vicky opened her mouth to speak, but I cut her off. She *didn't* like rugby, but that didn't mean she didn't know everything there was to know about it.

"Oh, she loves it." I put my hand on her shoulder in a firm pat — this was another signal that said *don't correct the speaker in the lie they've just told*. "Don't get her started on the starting line-up for the World Cup team in the semi-finals at the weekend."

"But the starting line-up is not logical," Vicky put in. "Just because Sam Vaughton has played well for the last two games does not mean he's earned a place there. If you look at his stats, he's the least reliable player by about thirty-three per cent."

"That's what I've been saying!" cried Mr Arkins. "Finally, someone who agrees. He's too much of a wildcard. They need a steadying influence."

Vicky nodded and opened her mouth, probably to launch into another rugby-related rant, but I gave her a light poke under her arm on her ribs – the poke was a prompt to either ask a question or to agree with someone (Vicky had a really hard time agreeing with something that she felt was untrue, but we'd been practising and she could just about manage a nod and a "that's interesting").

"Which players would you choose?" she asked. And it was Mr Arkins' turn to launch into his own rant. I cleared my throat and Vicky glanced at me, then copied my body language – head tilted to the side, steady eye contact with him, small nods of agreement as if she were hanging off his every word. When I risked a glance at Ollie, his eyes were narrowed on me and he didn't look very happy.

Luckily, someone else came to claim his attention just as Mr Arkins and Vicky had launched into another debate about the front row. I had to poke her twice before she managed her nod and a "that's interesting", which Mr Arkins took as her agreement with his superior rugby knowledge when it very much was *not*.

"Well, if you're as sensible about the markets as you are about rugby, then maybe I should reconsider your proposal. I'll get back to you on Monday."

I breathed a sigh of relief when that was done, and we were one step closer to leaving. Needing a bit of a breather, I downed the glass of elderflower I'd been holding and told Vicky I was going to find the bathroom without looking at Ollie. Not wanting to leave her for too long, I hustled across the room, unreasonably relieved when I found the door to the bathroom straight away.

Once there, I just sat on the side of the ornate bath and concentrated on my own breathing. After a minute of silence my heart rate had calmed down and I was no longer hyperventilating, but the ache in my chest that had started when I first saw Ollie glare at me was still there. I was tempted to just stay hidden, but Hayley's face flashed through my mind and I gritted my teeth. Quitting was not an option.

So I forced myself off that bath and back out into the fray. But just as I was about to search for Vicky, my upper arm was enclosed in a large hand and I was brought to an abrupt halt. At my startled flinch, Ollie's hand fell away, but he still blocked my path in the narrow corridor.

"Why did you do it?" he snapped, his anger palpable. "Why did you take the money?"

"I-I need to go," I muttered, avoiding eye contact now, my face feeling like it was on fire.

But then Ollie surprised me again. His expression softened and his hand went to the back of his neck, a move which never failed to exhibit all his arm and chest muscles to their full potential, even when trapped under that suit.

"Listen, Lottie. I've been thinking and if you're in some sort of trouble. If you need the money for something and... well, *I* can give you fifty grand. You don't have to—"

"Fifty grand for what?" I said, hardening myself to his concern. He hadn't seemed so concerned over the last three months when he was out being photographed all over the place with other women hanging off his arm. I mean, he had a blooming date here, for cheese's sake. There was a lipstick mark on his collar. What kind of fool did he think I was? "To be your bit of rough on the side? I might have taken that money, but I have some pride, you know." If I wanted to shake him off, I was going to have to squash this completely and be a total bitch. I could actually feel the atmosphere around us change as his mood darkened – the air was thick with his anger.

"If you had *pride*, you wouldn't have taken fifty grand in the first place. I expect that was your plan all along, to extort money out of my family." He looked me up and down with a sneer. "Was any of it true? The quirky dungarees, the multiple earrings, the cat sweatshirts – was any of that really you? Because you seem to have morphed into Corporate Barbie a bit too seamlessly if you ask me."

I faked a smile. "Glad you approve. Corporate Barbie was *exactly* the look I was going for."

I decided he didn't need to know that it was Vicky's stylist who had dictated everything I was wearing, from my pale pink nail varnish to my form-fitting but reserved little black dress. The job with Vicky had included the makeover and clothes. Vicky explained that it was pretty much essential. She called it *armour*. I hated it. But then, so did Vicky – and for her it really was a struggle as she couldn't bear restrictive clothing. When I went over to her house with Hayley last night to plan for today, she had been in a buttery soft hoodie with leggings, and I could feel how much more relaxed she was.

"And I didn't extort any money. I was offered money as a severance package."

"Well, you made a big mistake. Fifty is pocket change for us – you could have extorted a lot more. But you know that, don't you? That's why you've latched onto my sister."

"I work for Vicky," I said defensively, and he tilted his head to the side.

"What exactly are you doing for Vics? Seeing as you have no university degree and you're totally unskilled. How arrogant *are you* to think that you could offer her anything? She's a fucking genius."

"I *am* helping her, you douchebag. Not everything requires a university education."

His eyes flashed, and he moved again, too suddenly for me to anticipate. One minute he was glaring at me from a few feet away, the next he was right in my space, crowding me against the wall, his smell all around me, his breath on my cheek. My heart felt like it was beating outside of my chest, which was rising and falling with rapid breaths. What I should have done was tear right out of there or kneed him in the balls, but when my eyes locked with his, I was frozen completely. His hand came up to the side of my face slowly, and I stopped breathing altogether as his fingers brushed my temple, sweeping some hair that had fallen into my eyes back behind my ear, so achingly gentle that I felt my eyes start to sting. Even with these heels on (something I was yet to be totally reliable in), he still loomed over me; my head tilted right back as he bent forward.

"Beautiful little liar," he breathed, searching my face as if trying to see everything I was hiding. "Now, I'm going to tell you this once. Understand?" I nodded, still under his spell. "You're going to stay away from my family. Don't think you can get any more out of us. You've already been paid off. There won't be a second payday. Whatever you think you're going to get out of Vicky, you're wrong. Everyone in my family knows what a grasping, scheming gold digger you are, so don't mess with us again."

The worst thing was the delivery – it was slow, calculated and controlled, as if every word had been carefully weighed with maximum precision to hurt me as much as possible.

"*Vicky* doesn't think that," I said, my voice shaky despite my best efforts to keep it steady. "And the rest of you can sod off. I hope you always have stale Jaffa Cakes, your Marmite toast ratio is always slightly off and your tea is perpetually too weak."

He blinked, his angry expression cracking for a moment. "Is that the best you can come up with – weak tea, poorly spread Marmite and stale Jaffa Cakes?"

"*Nobody* likes a stale Jaffa Cake."

"True."

He looked like he wanted to laugh. I could feel the battle within him – hatred mixed with reluctant affection. Then he frowned and shook his head as if to clear it, giving me one last furious look before he pushed away and stood back.

Totally wrung out and desperate to get away, I forgot the footwear situation as I launched myself away from the wall and nearly went headfirst onto the solid wood floor. But, of course, I didn't fall. Just like in the past, Ollie caught me, his strong arm hooking me around my middle and setting me back on my feet. The heat from the contact flashed through me, his hard body against mine for a long moment before the pressure of his arm fell away and I took stumbling steps back, doing my very best to remain upright this time.

"You really shouldn't be wearing heels," he grumbled.

When I glanced back, he had his hand on the back of his neck again, frowning at me, his expression conflicted.

"Lottie—" he started, but I couldn't take any more, not that night. I needed to get home.

I needed to concentrate on what mattered: my family. Not on dreams that weren't for grasping, scheming gold diggers like me.

CHAPTER 17

Harding family reunion

Lottie

"Vicky, why is he doing this?" Felix asked again for what seemed like the hundredth time.

"Just accept it, Moretti," Harry York taunted from the other end of the conference table with a smirk. "Your company is *so* shit that you can't even be guaranteed to invest someone's money when their *sister* is your business partner."

We were at Moretti Harding in the conference room, waiting for Ollie to show up for this meeting. I twisted my fingers together on the table and bit my lip. I enjoyed working here, mostly. Being Vicky's assistant was great, and I'm not being big-headed when I say I was killing it. My ability to read people was actually one of the most valuable attributes you could have in business. When I started three months ago, I could tell everyone was a little shocked. My lack of qualifications and experience were glaringly obvious, and, despite the best efforts of Vicky's stylist, I didn't quite fit in with the corporate vibe. But gradually, I'd been gaining respect.

A week into my time there, I'd been at a meeting with Felix and Vicky about the projections for a development they were considering. I was feeling like a bit of a spare part, to be honest, because Vicky didn't need to suppress any of her abrupt ways in that circumstance; the men we were meeting were trying to convince her to take the deal, not the other way around.

But about ten minutes in, I knew they were lying. The tells were so clear that I couldn't understand why at least Felix wasn't catching it. The problem was that some stuff was going to be signed there and then so I had to move fast. I'd squeezed Vicky's wrist, and she looked at me with a frown, seeing as there was no need for our normal cue. I shook my head side to side before tipping it towards the men on the opposite side of the table. It was a testament to Vicky's faith in me that she stood immediately and announced that we needed some privacy before signing. Once the men had reluctantly filed out, Felix turned to Vicky and me.

"Vics, what the fuck?" he asked, frustration rolling off him in waves.

Vicky ignored him and turned to me. "Lottie?"

Felix huffed. "You stopped a multi-million-pound deal to chat with an unqualified intern? Vics, honestly, I've put up with this situ—"

"They're lying," I blurted out.

"What?" he said, turning to me with both his eyebrows raised.

"Those men are lying."

His brows snapped together. "What about?"

I shook my head. "Look, I'm sorry it doesn't work like that. I can just tell that they're lying. I don't know what about."

"Really fucking helpful then. Thanks for—"

"But it's something about the land drainage. They react whenever that's mentioned. So no, I can't tell you *exactly*, but I can say they are not telling you the truth, and they're scared when drainage is mentioned."

"How the hell do you know this?" he snapped.

"I can read people."

"Read minds?"

"No, of course not. I just… I've always been able to sense how people are feeling, and part of that is identifying whether they're lying." I shrugged. "I've been like this since I was a child."

It'd served me well in the childhood I had. With every different caregiver came a whole different set of expectations. Anticipating people's moods, especially people I didn't know very well, was very important and occasionally essential for survival.

He stared at me for a long moment. "You'd better not be wrong."

Felix and Vicky turned down the deal despite the men's dire warnings that other companies were interested and that they were making the biggest mistake of their careers. Felix was a bit frosty towards me until a few days later when he came to Vicky's office (which we shared – at that point, Vicky was happier if I was there for even her phone calls) and apologised. The men *had* been lying about the land – the drainage system was illegally installed and was posing a flood risk. The deal would have lost Moretti Harding millions. Since then, Felix was absolutely not averse to poaching me from Vicky whenever he could. And, given my ability to tell if people were bluffing, he said yesterday that no negotiation should ever happen without me.

"Fuck you, York," Felix muttered. He hated Harry York. The two had been at each other's throats for years since Harry advised one of his clients against investing in a land development project of Felix's. And now Ollie had decided to antagonise the situation even more by using Harry for some of his investment portfolio. I was furious with him because I just knew this was a dig at Vicky about me.

Of course Ollie didn't want me anywhere near him or his family, but with Vicky, it was more. He was protective of her. He saw her differences as something that made her vulnerable and thought I was positioning myself to exploit her. But he had no idea how protective I now was of his sister too. Or that Vicky was my first real friend in the city. Since I moved to London two years ago for Hayley, I'd been working so hard that I didn't have time to build any connections, not like the ones I'd had back home. It was lonely being left with all the responsibility, feeling like you had to prove yourself all the time, having no family support at all – in fact, the exact opposite.

And I really liked Vicky. I liked that her tells were more difficult for me to interpret, so I couldn't always decipher what she was thinking. And she never lied, which was refreshing – there are so many small lies in everyday conversations with normal people that I could find it a bit exhausting shutting it all out, but with Vicky it was honesty all the way.

"Well, he's twenty minutes late. Maybe neither of us are going to find out his plan," Harry suggested just as the double doors to the conference room opened, and Ollie strolled in. Ignoring everyone else, he moved around the table to his sister, grabbed her hand, pulled her out of the chair and gave her a tight hug. Vicky was good with hugs, especially tight ones. In fact, in stressful situations, a tight hug could calm her down, something her brother clearly understood.

"Hey, Vics," he said, smiling down at her as he pulled back, still ignoring everyone else in the room.

"Hi, Ollie," she said. The hug had worked somewhat. There was much less nervous energy rolling off her now.

When Ollie turned to me, his smile was more like a baring of teeth, the soft expression reserved for his sister long gone.

"If the Harding family reunion is quite finished," Harry said, clearly irritated. "I hope you haven't called me here just to yank my chain, Buckingham?"

"Yes, Ollie," Vicky put in as Ollie made his way back around the table via Harry York, clapping the man on the back as he moved past by way of greeting and giving Felix a chin lift. "You actually can't hug people in business meetings."

His hard expression went soft again when he looked at his sister. "This is my meeting, darling and I can do what the fuck I want."

"You can't say the f-word in meetings either," Vicky told him.

"Fuck that."

There was more posturing and ridiculous fighting over nothing between Felix and Harry York. I managed to tune them out until Harry York dragged me into it.

"I heard you almost lost a cool ten mill on that dud bit of land the other day, Felix. Apparently, your intern clawed it back for you." Harry York nodded towards me, and I froze. Ollie's gaze flew back to me as well, and his eyes narrowed.

"Lottie's not an intern," Vicky put in, and I wished for once she'd just let something go and not make everything worse – but if something was incorrect, there was no stopping the woman. "She's my *executive* assistant."

Ollie rolled his eyes and I felt my face heat.

"Ah, sorry," Harry said, smiling at me and I saw Ollie stiffen. "Maybe we could recruit you to York Evans Investments? Save you the effort of having to bail out these numpties on the reg." More angry vibes rolled off Ollie which made no sense. Firstly, Harry was married, very happily married if reports were true; secondly, seeing as Ollie *hated* me, what on earth did he have to be jealous or territorial over?

"The fucking cheek of you," Felix snapped. "You come here, steal my clients, try to poach my staff. Don't think I haven't got some shit on you as well, York. You want to get into the weeds about poor client management? We can go there, you tosser."

"Enough!" Vicky said, that one word cracking through the room, silencing the meeting.

"Will, is that tea on its way?" Felix asked, and Will Brent (one of the executives on the partner track and, in my opinion, a real dick – I still remembered him from that night at the club) – nodded.

"It's handled," he said just as the door to the room opened again, and Lucy, Will's assistant, shuffled in with the tea trolley before freezing like a deer in the headlights when she saw the number of executives sitting at the conference table. Her eyes came to rest on Felix, and I had to hide my smile. The poor girl had the biggest crush on him I'd ever seen in my life. All Felix did was scowl at her, which did nothing for the girl's confidence, something that was already in her boots. It was a shame because I really liked Lucy but, in truth, I wasn't sure how much longer she was going to last here.

From there the meeting went the way I thought it would – straight to shit. When Ollie wasn't scowling at me, he was combative and needling towards Felix, while Harry York seemed to be an expert in winding everyone up.

The only thing to break the tension was the squeak of the tea trolley as Lucy pushed it around the room, sporting an obvious limp before peering down at Vicky's tea colour chart with confusion. To Vicky, providing an actual colour chart for her preferred tea and the exact shade it needed to be according to the time of day was not a *tea diva move*; it was providing detailed instructions on how she wanted something done – something Vicky would want from other people – so she couldn't understand why anyone would think it made her difficult.

"If anything, it makes me easier," she'd told me in frustration when I tried to explain to her that she couldn't pull out her chart when she was visiting other companies or, *worse*, people's homes and was offered a cup of tea. "I'm providing an objective measurement with which to gauge my tea preference. I would be *grateful* if someone gave me a colour chart when I was making their tea."

Once Lucy had spent an inordinate amount of time making a cup of tea (Lucy was not the most practical of people – in fact, she may have been the worst assistant I'd ever seen in action), she started making her way to our side of the table. That was when Felix noticed the limp, and he lost his mind, interrupting the meeting to interrogate her about her injury. When Slimy Will, Lucy's direct boss, said, "Felix, let Hop-a-long serve the tea. She's been limping all morning. She's fine." I thought Felix was going to punch him in the face.

"Lucy Mayweather!" Ollie's deep voice filled the room. He was grinning at Lucy from across the table. "What the fuck are you doing here? Last time I spoke to Mike he told me you never left the village."

"Er..." Lucy glanced around at all the faces staring at their exchange and blushed. "Hi." She gave Ollie a small wave, and he grinned across at her. When he got up and hugged her I knew I shouldn't care, really there was no logical reason for me to care, but that didn't stop the rush of white-hot jealousy from tearing through me.

By the time the meeting was over, I felt like I'd run a marathon. All I could do was hope and pray that this would be my last encounter with Ollie for a good long while. Because being around him and his animosity felt like it was slowly breaking me.

But my hopes and prayers had never been answered before, so I don't know why I thought they would be now.

CHAPTER 18

I spoke to her

Lottie

"Where are you going?" Ollie snapped. I glanced over my shoulder and growled under my breath when I saw him striding after me, a furious expression on his face. It was two weeks after Vicky had told her brother and Felix off in the meeting. I'd just left Vicky in another conference room to renegotiate with some of Ollie's advisors.

"None of your fudging business. Why don't you... argh!"

Yes, it had to be that exact moment I stepped on an uneven bit of pavement and twisted my bad ankle.

"Mother trucking, fudging heels!"

I was tempted to take them off and throw them into the road, but the last thing I needed was for dillweed here to witness me walking barefoot through London like some vagrant. Unfortunately, thanks to his abnormally long legs, he'd managed to catch up to me and was holding my arm to stop me falling. I jerked it out of his grip.

"Don't touch me," I hissed as I attempted to storm away, now with a slight limp. This is what happens when girls like me and Lucy are forced into misogynistic shoes by the patriarchy.

"You shouldn't be wearing heels if you can't walk in them," he said in that fudging superior tone that peed me off so much.

"Cheese and rice, you condescending butthead. Do you think I *want* to wear this stuff? It's my *Corporate Barbie* uniform, as you put it."

He shook his head. "You can wear whatever you want."

"Says the man in a three-piece suit," I muttered. "Why are you following me?"

"My sister's paying you to do a job, and you're just buggering off and leaving her halfway through the working day? Pretty shit assistant if you ask me."

"I thought you didn't want me near your sister?" I said, glancing at my watch and picking up the pace when I saw the time.

"No, I don't want you anywhere near anyone in my family."

I rubbed my chest absently as if to ease the pain. I don't know why I wasn't used to his casual cruelty by now. Thanks to Vicky, I was around him way more often than was healthy, and he never failed to remind me exactly what he thought of me.

"But you've made her rely on you. She needs you now, so you can't just sod off in the middle of the day."

I sighed as I came to a stop to turn to him. "I haven't made her rely on me, Ollie."

He flinched at my use of his name, and I realised that I hadn't said it since before everything fell apart.

"And anyway, not only was I leaving her with you and Felix, both of whom can look after her perfectly well, but also some of those guys in there could probably use some of Vicky's truth bombs – do them the power of good."

Ollie shook his head. "So, you just run off whenever you want? It's not even the end of the working day."

"It is the end of *my* working day. This is what I negotiated with Vicky before I even started with this job. I *have* to leave by three, she knows that. Most of the time we work around it, arrange meetings in the morning."

"Well, I could only meet in the afternoon, so…" he trailed off, shoving his hands into his pockets. I raised both eyebrows.

"Right," I said slowly. "Well, I'm afraid I *can't*. I have other commitments. I would have thought you would be breathing a sigh of relief." I tilted my head to the side as I stared up at his frowning face.

"What other commitments?" he said, crossing his arms over his broad chest.

"If I didn't know better," I said, my voice soft. "I would think that you wanted me at that meeting for *you*." My tone became taunting then because I'd had enough. Fork this guy. So I took a step forward until we were inches apart, so close I could smell his aftershave. "Is that it, Your Grace? You want me there? Can't stay away from me?"

I watched in fascination as his eyes darkened and a muscle ticked in his jaw.

"Careful, baby," he growled, and I felt a head rush as my stomach clenched with desire. "You want to go there? We can go there. But you'd better know what you're asking for. I'm not blind to the kind of girl you are now. No more bullshit romance and fake feelings. But if you want to go, we'll go. Just say the word." His voice dropped then, dark and low. "I know for a fact nobody's ever made you come as hard as I have. If I close my eyes, I can still see the shock on your face, hear the scream I had to stifle with my mouth. So I can't promise any more flowery words, but I can guarantee you'll be *more* than satisfied."

"Oh yeah?" I said, going for confidence, but the breathless quality of my voice let me down. "Bring it on."

I could feel my pulse beating in my chest as my face caught fire. Images of dirty, angry sex with Ollie flooded my brain until there was a low ringing in my ears, and I felt almost high. Nothing existed beyond Ollie and me. Not the London crowd moving all around us on the pavement, not the traffic, not the car horns. Everything was drowned out by my absolute need for him. *I* was drowning in his blue eyes.

Then my gaze dropped to his mouth. He was smirking, but as time remained suspended, the smirk gradually fell away.

And then time just stopped.

I felt myself go up on my toes as if I no longer had control of my body, and he started leaning down. It was like there was an invisible gravitational pull between us, something that neither of us could fight. The air crackled, and I stopped breathing altogether.

"God, you're so fucking beautiful," he muttered low just as our lips were about to touch.

The way he said it was so full of resentment that it snapped me out of my trance. I blinked, and the spell was broken. I had to use every ounce of self-control to wrench myself away and out of our cocoon of suspended animation. When I did step back, of course, it was into the path of the oncoming foot traffic. I was knocked to the side as a businessman clipped my shoulder. When I stumbled I would have fallen without Ollie's strong hand shooting out to hold me. Unfortunately my handbag did fly off my shoulder and crash to the ground, the contents spilling everywhere.

"You can go," I said in a shaky voice as I shook off his hand and crouched down to stuff my belongings back into my bag.

To my surprise, he crouched down with me and silently started helping me, his mouth set in a grim line and two flags of colour high on his cheekbones. His hand landed on the glitter and pasta necklace Hayley had made for me, the one I had to wear when I picked her up and had convinced her I wore all day, every day. He paused, staring at it intently, then looked back at me with a questioning look. I snatched it from him, hiding it in the depths of my bag and avoiding eye contact with him.

"Lottie, I—"

"I have to go," I whispered, straightening up and turning away from him to join the stream of human traffic. When I made it to the bus stop, Ollie was nowhere to be seen. I breathed a sigh of relief, telling myself I was glad and ignoring the relentless ache in my chest.

"Hey, lovebug," I said as I hugged Hayley outside the school gates. When we separated and I moved to straighten up, she stopped me with her hands on either side of my face. Our brown eyes stared at each other for a long moment, and she frowned, tilting her head to the side. I felt the concern rolling off her, and I sighed. Just like me, Hayley could often see what others were blind to. A fake smile wouldn't fool her, not for a second.

"I'm okay," I whispered, but she just frowned at the lie. I felt my nose sting but held it together. "Alright, kid, you win. But I *will* be. We both will be. And fudge nuggets to everyone else."

That got a little smile from her finally.

"How was today, lovebug?" I asked as we started to walk home. Hayley shrugged, and I squeezed her hand. "Words, love," I said in a gentle but firm tone and heard her blow out a frustrated breath.

"Fine."

"More words, please."

"When can I see Florrie again?"

I drew to a sudden stop, ice trickling through my veins. "Hayley, what are you talking about?"

"Florrie," she repeated, her voice was a little hoarse from disuse, but the name was clear enough. "I liked her."

I prayed that this was just a weird coincidence, but I had a bad feeling in the pit of my stomach.

"Is that a girl from school?"

"No, the girl in the big house."

I closed my eyes and blew out a breath.

"Why have we stopped?" Hayley asked. "And why are you cross?"

"I'm not cross," I said in a forced, bright tone as I started walking again.

"Yes, you are."

We were level with the entrance to our block of flats now. I pressed the buzzer to open the door, but there was no sound. Rolling my eyes, I pushed on the door and it swung open.

Great security.

I expected it would take another few months to fix the blooming thing, just like last time. I'd made a game of piling up furniture against our flat door when it happened before, but that had been a while ago, and I wondered if Hayley would see straight through that now. She would definitely sense my fear. Her intuition got better every day. The lack of speech seemed to compound the observational skills. Every day, her ability to read people seemed to improve at an exponential rate.

"How did you meet Florrie?" I asked as we climbed the stairs (the lift had long since given up the ghost, and we were well into the third month of taking the pee-smelling stairs).

"She came to the big room while you were cleaning."

I took my keys out and, finally, we were in our little oasis. Once inside, I turned the deadbolt and put the chain on. I'd move the chest of drawers across once Hayley was in bed later.

"Florrie speaks a lot," Hayley told me. I laughed at that – Hayley wasn't wrong. The time I'd met Florrie with Margot she'd certainly had a lot to say. "So she said it didn't matter if I was quiet – she'd make up for it. We learnt a dance. She had a phone and played some music on it, and she taught it to me."

It was the most words I'd ever heard Hayley say at one time, and I felt like my heart was breaking. Why did the first kid she connected with in years have to be the niece of a man who hates me and the granddaughter of a woman who'd prefer to pay me off than take the small risk of me being a part of her family one day?

"You can't see Florrie again," I told her. "What about the kids at school?"

She looked away, and her little shoulders dropped. For a mad moment, I considered ringing Ollie and saying, "Hey, listen. I know you hate me and your family hates me, but how about we arrange a playdate between my sister (who you aren't aware exists) and your niece? Sound good?" Yeah, never going to happen. But then Hayley said something in a low whisper that I only just caught, and it changed everything.

"I spoke to her."

"You what?" I flew to where she was curled up on the sofa. "Hayley, you spoke to her?"

"It was only one word," she mumbled as if it was no big deal, when it was a very, *very* big deal. Hayley hadn't said one word to anyone other than me in two years. "It was after she showed me the dance."

I felt my throat swell and my eyes sting but I managed to ask, "What did you say?"

"Cool."

I let out a watery laugh. "And you didn't think to tell me?"

She shrugged, and I gathered her up in my arms, hugging her to me.

"So, can I see her again?"

I closed my eyes and hugged her tighter as her little arms came around my neck to cling onto me.

"We'll see, lovebug. We'll see."

CHAPTER 19

I'm only a cleaner, remember?

Lottie

"Why don't you ever drive, Vics?" I asked as we glided to a stop outside the pub. Vicky tended to travel in the Buckingham town cars with a driver, so we were both sitting in the back.

"I can drive, but I rarely do and never at night."

I felt some discomfort coming off her. "Okay, hun, you don't have to—"

"I have meltdowns," she blurted out. I was a bit more attuned to Vicky now. She may have been difficult to read, but she wasn't impossible. This subject made her uncomfortable. I wished I could take back the question.

"Okay, honestly, if you don't want to talk about it, that's fine."

She shrugged as if it was nothing and that shrug was the first half-lie she'd ever told me. "I had them a lot as a child, but they're very rare now. You know, standard stuff – hand flapping, shaking, covering my ears. It can be triggered by bright lights, very loud noises, aggressive situations where physical violence is a threat. So, I can drive, but I never drive at night. The headlights, the streetlights, the unpredictability of the environment just mean I'm not comfortable."

"Okay," I said softly. "Well, that sounds like a pretty sensible decision then."

"I always make sensible decisions."

"Right, yes, of course," I said, hiding a smile. To be self-effacing was, in Vicky's book, just another form of lying: she couldn't see the point in it. "Thanks, Rich," I said to the driver. "You coming in for a pint?" Richard smiled at me.

"No thanks, Lottie."

"I could sneak you out a pie and chips?"

Richard's face flickered at the mention of chips, and his eyes went down and to the left when he said, "No, I'm fine. I'll just be around here for when you two are finished."

I winked at him. "I'll bring you out some chips."

He laughed as we exited the car and made our way to the door.

"Why are you going to bring him chips when he said he didn't want chips?" Vicky asked in a perplexed voice as we pushed through the double door.

"Because he really *does* want chips," I replied.

"If a man says to me *no* and *I'm fine,* then I would assume he's fine. I don't understand."

"He was lying when he said he was fine. I can see more than just people's words."

Vicky sighed. "All I can see is their words. I'm the most literal person I know."

I linked my arm with her and gave hers a firm squeeze. Vicky liked linking arms, just like she liked firm hugs – shaking hands she disliked but could manage. Holding hands was a big no-no for her with anyone, as was somebody touching her unexpectedly. I took a deep breath as we approached the group. Felix was standing with his arm around Lucy. Ollie was there too, looking at them with his head tilted to the side and a curious expression on his face. Lucy was looking nervous but not uncomfortable with being tucked into Felix's side. To me this was not a surprise – I'd felt the vibes between them for ages, but clearly Ollie was taken aback, and Vicky…

"Hello," Vicky's voice cut through the tension. "Lucy, you're here."

"Er, hi," Lucy replied with a small wave.

"Felix has his arm around you," Vicky put in, blunt and to the point as always. "Are you sleeping together?" Lucy's eyes went wide, and her face flooded with colour.

"Vicky," I said slowly. "Remember, we talked about questions that are okay?"

Vicky turned to me. "But you want to know this too, correct? As far as we knew, Felix was *not* sleeping with Lucy. But he's here, and he has an arm around her. Why can't I be direct?"

"Lucy's embarrassed, hun," I said softly, squeezing Vicky's arm briefly. Vicky looked at me.

"Oh," she said.

"You ask whatever questions you want to, Vics," Ollie said in an irritated tone. He shot me an aggravated look, which softened when he transferred his gaze to Vicky and touched her arm to get her attention. They made eye contact, and he hesitated until Vicky gave a small, almost imperceptible nod, then he hugged her exactly as he knew she preferred. When he moved back, he gave me another filthy look. "Don't tell her what to do, Forest."

My chest tightened at another small rejection, but with Ollie, I'd found the best solution was a grey rock approach – I tried not to show any external reaction to his barbs. So I acted as if Ollie hadn't spoken, turning to Felix and Lucy instead.

"I knew that jumper would suit you," I said as I hugged Lucy. "You look like a fierce, wool-wearing badass."

Lucy laughed. "I'm not sure how many badasses wear fleece-lined tights."

"So, am I allowed to ask if Lucy is your girlfriend?" Vicky said. I sighed as I felt Lucy stiffen. Felix grabbed Lucy's hand and pulled her to his side.

"Yes, Vicky," he said with a conviction which made me have to stifle a smile. "Lucy is my girlfriend."

"I am?" Lucy squeaked, and he frowned down at her.

"Of course you are." Then it was like we didn't even exist for her anymore. She stared up at Felix with a soft look. A slow smile spread across her face, her eyes shining with happiness.

"Awesome," she breathed. No artifice, no game playing, no hiding how absolutely into him she was. And, as if he couldn't really help himself, he kissed her.

My chest tightened with jealousy. To have someone that into you. To have a man look at me the way Felix was looking at Lucy would mean everything. Then, moment ruining bastard that he was, Ollie cleared his throat, snapping Lucy and Felix back to reality as they broke apart.

"Does Mike know about this?" Ollie asked, a hint of accusation in his tone. Mike was Lucy's older brother. Felix, Mike and Ollie had grown up together in a village called Little Buckingham. The protectiveness in Ollie's tone made my throat tight. I'd never had anyone be protective of me and here Lucy was with basically two big brothers ready to jump to her defence.

"Not yet," Felix said. "But he will, alright? I'll sort it."

Ollie whistled. "He's going to lose his shit. Please, let me have a front-row seat to that nightmare."

"Mike's not my keeper," Lucy put in. "And *I'll* tell him. He's my brother."

"I'll come to your funeral, mate," Ollie said, and Lucy growled in frustration. I kept my eyes lowered and bit my lip. She clearly had no idea how lucky she was.

"Well then," Vicky said. "That's fine." Lucy tore her gaze from Felix to look at Vicky. "I'm sorry, Lucy," Vicky explained. "But I'm much better with social interactions if all the dynamics are made super clear at the start."

"Vicky's not good with grey areas. It's just that…" I broke off midsentence when Ollie made an annoyed noise at the back of his throat. I slid him a nervous look then forced a smile. "Shall we sit?"

"I can't sit here," Vicky snapped, glancing at the table and the empty plates.

"I know, hun," I muttered. "We'll sit in a booth, all right?"

Vicky nodded, and some tension seemed to leave her shoulders. She couldn't have sat with the table so crowded with plates and cutlery. Vicky was very prescriptive about food and could find it difficult even being around lots of food debris.

Once we were settled in the booth, and despite the frosty atmosphere between me and Ollie, the conversation flowed. To my surprise, Lucy came out of her shell more than I'd ever seen her manage before. Whether it was the smaller, more relaxed environment, the fact that Felix kept his arm casually draped around her shoulders or that Vicky and I were there, I wasn't sure. But it was clear that in the right environment, Lucy could be coaxed out of her extreme shyness, and she asked *a lot* of questions.

Whilst I managed to deftly avoid most of them (I did have extensive experience of this, after all), she did coax a surprising amount of information out of the others: boarding school, polo playing, what it was like to be an *actual* duke. The only titbit of info she did manage to extract from me was how I met Vicky.

"Oh, wow," Lucy said. "I had no idea you worked for the Buckingham Estate before. Did you ever go to Little Buckingham?"

"I only worked at the London house," I replied in a small voice as I shifted in my chair.

"Less said about that the better," muttered Ollie into his beer and my face heated as I shrank further into my seat. "And now you're a personal assistant to one of the leading financial brokers in London. Cleaner to executive. Perfectly logical transition."

My face flooded with heat at that, and when my eyes started to sting I prayed I could keep it together.

"Lottie's very qualified for what she does, Ollie," Vicky said, frowning at her brother. Vicky often didn't pick up on Ollie's digs as they were too subtle for her literal brain to catch, but this one didn't seem to go over her head.

"*Right*," Ollie drew out the word. That was my cue to stand.

"I think I'd better leave," I said in a soft voice, avoiding eye contact with Ollie and turning to Vicky. "I'll see you tomorrow."

"But—" Vicky started, looking a little panicked. I leaned down towards her. "Ollie's here, hun," I said softly. "You'll be good with him. You know that." Vicky glanced at Ollie and visibly relaxed.

"Of course, I'll sort you out, Vics," he said. "Let the girl go home."

Just *the girl*, not even my name.

That's all I was now – just that girl who screwed him over.

I grabbed my jacket off the coat rack at the entrance, but when I turned to step outside I ran into what felt like a brick wall. I staggered back but large hands shot out to enclose my upper arms and stop me from falling.

"What the—?" I started to say then stopped as I looked up into those piercing blue eyes.

"Why are you still wearing this fucking coat?" he snapped. I jerked back from him, and he released my arms immediately, which meant I could dodge around him and out of the double doors. But he wasn't finished with me. Once I was out on the pavement he was again blocking my path.

"Go away, Ollie," I said, if anything my voice was tired. I was so over these stressful interactions. So over his judgement, his disappointment in me, his censure. This man who'd never struggled a day in his life chose to judge me? What a prick. How had I ever fancied myself in love with him?

He blinked as he frowned down at me, seeming a little thrown by the resignation and lack of fire in my tone. His hand went to the back of his neck, and I found myself immune to the arm and chest muscles that move inevitably displayed. Well... almost.

"Buy a better coat, for God's sake," he said, his words now more frustrated than angry.

I rolled my eyes. "My coat is none of your business."

He sighed as if *I* was the one inconveniencing *him*. What on earth? *I* wasn't blocking *his* way and banging on about *his* clothing. The fact was that I didn't need a new warm winter coat as all the business interactions we had were indoors, so I only had to buy *the uniform*, as I saw it, for those. I wouldn't accept company money for my coat, and I sure as heck wasn't buying one out of my own money.

Hayley had a new coat, that was all that mattered. And I had to save the rest for her one-to-one therapy, and maybe, if I was careful, I might be able to afford a private school. Her therapist had advised that smaller class sizes would benefit her. Plus, I wasn't sure what was happening at her school, but it was clear she hated it there. Even my degree was on hold for the moment. I didn't want to waste any of the money paying for the next module when I might need private school fees, and unfortunately, my ageing laptop had finally given up the ghost as well.

"You've plenty of money to buy a coat now," he told me in that superior bloody tone. "What's the point of blackmailing my family if you're not going to spend the money?"

"I didn't blackmail your family," I said through gritted teeth, although why I bothered I had no idea. We'd been over this before and he wasn't going to believe me. "And you have no idea what I need money for."

His grumpy expression flickered for a moment as his brows drew lower. "What do you need money for?" His voice was no less frustrated, but it had softened with something almost like concern now, and I had to swallow past the lump in my throat.

"Leave it alone, *Your Grace*," I said, cursing my unsteady voice. "After all, I'm only a *cleaner*, remember? Not qualified for anything else according to you."

Ollie let out a huff. "I'm..." he cleared his throat and looked to the side, "I'm sorry, okay? I shouldn't have said that."

I blinked in surprise. "Wow, the great Duke of Buckingham apologises."

"I mean it, Lottie. I shouldn't have embarrassed you like that."

I narrowed my eyes at him then and took a step towards him. "I'm not embarrassed by the fact I cleaned for a living. It's honest work. I needed the money and I didn't have many other options."

Fuelled by my anger, I didn't realise how close we were now. I was on tiptoes with my face just inches from his. We'd moved towards each other almost unconsciously. It was only when his gaze dropped to my mouth that I realised my mistake.

"Lottie," he breathed, an almost desperate quality to his voice. In that moment there was just me and Ollie in our own bubble. The strength of desire between us so tangible I could almost taste it.

"Sorry, love," a man's voice snapped me out of my trance when he bumped my shoulder on his way past. Ollie opened his mouth to speak again but I was *done*. As I darted around him he caught my hand. I looked back at him for a moment, my body swayed forwards, but then a vision of Hayley flooded my mind and I snatched my fingers from his.

I could *not* afford to be distracted by Oliver Harding. Not again.

CHAPTER 20

Is she here?

Ollie

"Mrs H, I really don't have time for this," I snapped. "I'm sure there'll be ample opportunity to insult me over my lifestyle choices and berate me for the recycling later." Mrs H did not approve of the bottles that accumulated when you lived like I did. I knew she was right – I was hitting it too hard in order to block out the dreams of *her*.

I had no idea what was wrong with me, but the bone-deep yearning was getting ridiculous. I'd only seen her a handful of times since the pub three months ago, but that didn't seem to make any difference. To try and forget, I went out nearly every night, accepted every invitation, put up with the paparazzi and let women drape themselves over me in bars and clubs, hoping to feel *something*... something other than the ache I felt for her. But it never ended with me taking any of those women home. No, I invariably either stumbled home alone, or with some mates in tow to work our way through the pile of now empty bottles that Mrs H objected to so strongly.

But still, her face, her eyes, the way she tripped over her own feet, the way her head tilted to the side when she was listening – everything about her was replaying in my brain obsessively.

It was exhausting. I wasn't sleeping properly. When I closed my eyes all I saw was her, then when I finally did sleep it was littered with fevered dreams of her. I'd wake up sweating and rock hard with my arms empty and the ache of loss in my chest. I could not carry on like this, but I had no idea how to break the cycle.

It was getting to the stage where I was having trouble remembering why I cared that she'd accepted the bribe. What right did I have to judge her? And it was also painfully clear to me that I knew next to nothing about her. The desperate quality of her voice when she spoke about needing the money was haunting me.

What did I know about needing money? All my energy was directed at protecting my legacy, and it had been drilled into me that meant maintaining and, in my case, accumulating more wealth. That's the terrible fear that drives us heirs in the aristocracy – the worry that after hundreds of years, we'll be the ones to fuck up the dynasty, to lose it all. The weight of our ancestors' expectations seems massive. But honestly, just like Lottie once said, those guys are dead – they don't care if I've added another billion to the empire they built. Is that really what I want my legacy to be? How is that benefiting anyone other than me and my family?

I'd also been thinking about Cordelia, who I still saw at events now. And it struck me how even five years ago, just after she'd sold me out to the *Daily Mail* and I broke off the engagement, I'd never felt half the level of betrayal that I did when Lottie took my mother's payoff. And I certainly never picked a fight with Cordelia. Why did I continue to berate Lottie when the payout she'd received was a fraction of Cordelia's and did far less damage to my reputation?

Mrs H put her hands on her hips and blocked my way in the corridor. "We have a problem," she said in a firm tone. "And it's nothing to do with your bad habits, although rest assured your mother *will* be hearing about the recycling later."

I looked up at the ceiling to seek patience, my hand on the back of my neck.

"What problem? Honestly, Mrs H, I don't have time to—"

"There's someone in the house," her voice had dropped to a whisper, and my eyes snapped back to hers as I frowned.

"Christ," I bit out. "Where? Have you called the police?"

Mrs H pointed to the library door behind her as she shook her head. I moved quickly to position myself between her and the door. I'd had crazy stalkers in the past, but none had ever actually managed to break in. The last thing I wanted was for one of them to hurt Mrs H.

"Go to the kitchen and call the police. Don't come out until I tell you to."

Luckily my golf clubs were in the hallway. I took out a five-iron as I moved to the library door but stopped when Mrs H grabbed my arm. She was still shaking her head.

"Put that down," she snapped as if I was still a naughty little boy she needed to rein in. "I'm not calling the police. And you're not to go in half-cocked with a bloody golf club. You'll scare her half to death, the poor thing."

My eyebrows went up. "Mrs H, these people can be dangerous. Do as I say and go to the kitchen. Call the police."

"Oliver Harding!" she shouted after me as I stalked to the library, golf club still in hand. But when I threw open the door and stormed in, it was empty. I frowned as I slowly lowered the golf club. Mrs H, as always not following orders, was right behind me and tapped my shoulder.

"Up there," she whispered, pointing at the mezzanine.

I squinted up in the direction she'd indicated. At first, I couldn't see anything, then I blinked as a small shoe came into focus, which was quickly pulled back into the shadows.

"What the fuck?" I whispered as I started to walk towards the spiral staircase.

"Don't scare her," Mrs H whispered, still on my heels as I made my way up the steps. I waved her away, still not sure if it was safe, but she just tutted in my wake. Once I was at the top and my eyes adjusted to the shadows up there, I saw her. She was huddled in the corner, her arms wrapped around her knees, her big brown eyes staring up at me under her mop of caramel hair. Those eyes flicked to the golf club I realised I was still holding. She looked terrified.

"It's okay," I murmured, lowering the golf club to the floor and then holding my hands up to show I meant no harm. "I'm not going to hurt you."

I stepped towards her, but she shrank back from me, her eyes widening with more fear. Realising that our size difference was freaking her out, I lowered down to a crouch, with my arms resting on my bent legs and my hands dangling between. I tilted my head to the side.

"Want to tell me what you're doing in my library, sweetheart?"

She shook her head in a rapid, jerky movement, her caramel curls spilling all over her shoulders. Looking into those eyes, I felt a jolt of recognition and I frowned.

"Do I know you?" I asked, and she shook her head again. I smiled at her, hoping to put her at ease, but it just seemed to scare her more. "How did you get in?"

Her eyes flicked over, past my shoulder to where Mrs H was standing, which wasn't a surprise. The woman was the least security-conscious employee I'd ever had. I'd frequently come home to the front door left wide open whilst she was on the job.

"Well, that was very clever of you."

She focused back on me again, a little curiosity cutting through the fear in her expression as her head lifted slightly. She was wearing pink and white trainers, a thick winter coat and mittens. There was a book open next to her. She flinched slightly when I moved to pick it up.

"*The Lion the Witch and the Wardrobe*," I said as I examined the cover. "You must be good at reading if you're halfway through this at age... six?" I hid my smile as she scowled at me. She looked closer to Florrie's age, but I knew this would get a rise out of her. "Hmm, not six then. Five?"

Her head came right off her knees at that, and I could finally see her whole face. That jolt of recognition hit me again as her brown eyes flashed with indignation.

"I'm just kidding, sweetheart," I said placatingly. "But even for your age, this is pretty good reading. Is that why you hid up here?"

She bit her lip and looked to the side, her nose scrunching in her pretty face.

"Listen, why don't you come down from here and Mrs H will get you some cookies."

She shook her head again, but as if on cue, her stomach rumbled.

"Come on," I said in a soft, cajoling voice. "I know you must be hungry. I promise you're not in trouble, but we can't leave you up here."

"It's okay, lovie," Mrs H put in, her voice softer than I'd ever heard it before. "He's an alright sort really, the big lout."

The lack of respect for me in my own house was staggering but I didn't care when I saw the little girl's face break into a small smile. She uncurled herself and pushed up to her feet as I straightened from my crouch. There was a touch of fear back in her expression once I was at my full height again, but I smiled down at her, and her small shoulders relaxed just a little. She held on tightly to the bannister as she made her way down the staircase, then Mrs H bustled her through to the kitchen, coaxing her out of her bulky coat with dire warnings about how she "wouldn't feel the benefit" if she stayed bundled up in it.

She looked tiny in my massive kitchen. On instinct, I lifted her up onto one of the stools, just as I would with Florrie. She weighed nothing and I frowned in concern as I set her down. Mrs H slid a plate of cookies and a glass of milk in front of her and she began nibbling one of them, her eyes flicking nervously between me and Mrs H.

"Your mum's got to be frantic with worry, lovie," Mrs H said. The little girl shook her head, and I frowned.

"She won't be worried?" I asked, and she looked away and to the side. "Right, okay, so not your mum then. Is there someone who *will* be worried?" She bit her lip and shrugged, but her discomfort was telling. Clearly, someone *would* be desperately worried about this girl's whereabouts.

I sighed. "You're not very chatty, are you?"

She shook her head again.

"Listen, I'm sorry, sweetheart, but if you don't tell us who to contact, we'll have to phone social services to see if—"

My words cut off as she leapt off her stool towards me, grabbed my arm and shook her head furiously. Her face had drained of all colour now, and there was real fear in her eyes. The hand she was gripping my arm with was shaking. What in the world?

"Okay, okay. Calm down," I said softly, crouching again so that I was eye-level with her. "No social services, I promise. But you're going to have to—"

I broke off again as the doorbell started sounding repeatedly, accompanied by loud banging on the front door.

"What on earth?" I muttered, turning to look over my shoulder towards the source of the commotion. When I looked back at the girl, she was also looking over my shoulder towards the front door with a guilty expression. I had a feeling that whoever *did* care about this child's whereabouts had somehow found themselves at my house. "Wait here with Mrs H," I told her as I turned and strode to the front door.

The banging and the doorbell ringing was becoming frenzied, and when I finally pulled open the door a woman practically fell into my arms, clearly being mid-door pound. The familiar lavender smell filled my nostrils as I lifted the small woman back up onto her feet and then I was staring into the same brown eyes I'd been looking at moments before. This was why I recognised that little girl.

"Is she here?" Lottie's voice was frantic, her eyes wild as she gripped onto my suit jacket, balling the material in her fists and shaking. "Did she come here? Please, Ollie, please, please, please tell me she's here?"

I heard small footsteps behind me, and then Lottie wrenched herself out of my arms to tear around me. She skidded onto her knees on the polished wood of the corridor and flung her arms around the little girl who'd emerged from the kitchen.

"You're okay. You're okay. You're here. You're okay," she chanted over and over again, her words shaking with tears.

The little girl was gripping Lottie so tight around her neck that her knuckles were white. I walked to them slowly as Lottie pulled back and took the little girl by both shoulders, giving her a gentle shake.

"You can't do that to me, Hayley," she said, relief, frustration and anger lacing her words. "We're a team, remember? You can't just bail on the team."

Her face crumpled then as two tears tracked down her cheeks.

"What would I have done if something happened to you, lovebug?" she said in a broken voice and the puzzle pieces of the phone call I'd overheard months ago fell into place. "You're my world. I'd have nothing without you."

Hayley looked at her feet as a fat tear rolled down her face too.

"I know things are tough," Lottie went on, her tone softer now. "But we can do tough, can't we? As long as we've got each other we can do *anything*."

Hayley looked up at Lottie then and frowned.

"I know, hun. But you *have* to go to school. Everybody has to go to school."

Hayley bit her lip and looked to the side, clearly not in agreement with Lottie there.

I cleared my throat, and both caramel-hair-coloured, brown-eyed girls flinched as their gazes shot to me. Lottie's eyes went wide as if she was just now becoming aware of her surroundings again. She straightened and stood with Hayley's hand in hers, glancing nervously between me and Mrs H.

"I'm sorry," she whispered, her pale, tear-streaked face filled with mortification. "Hayley shouldn't have come here. She's having a tough time at school, and she just—" she broke off and shook her head once. "Jeepers, you don't want to hear about all that. We've wasted enough of your time."

She took a step away, towards the front door, but I moved to block her path, my arms crossed over my chest.

"Neither of you are going anywhere until you explain," I told her, and her eyes widened. "Now, Hayley was halfway through her plate of cookies. I suggest we go back to the kitchen and have a long overdue chat about what the fu..." I broke off and cleared my throat – so this was why Lottie never swore, "... fudge is going on."

"Ollie, I'm sorry, but—"

"Your Grace?" We all turned to look back at the still-open front door and the two police officers now filling it.

CHAPTER 21

Little stowaway

Ollie

"There we go," said Mrs H as she bustled into the room armed with a tray of tea. "Nothing that a nice cuppa can't sort now is there?"

Lottie gave her a weak smile whilst Hayley just burrowed further into her side on the sofa. After the police arrived, I suggested we all go and sit in the drawing room. Lottie had called them this morning in a flat panic after she found Hayley missing from their flat when she went to wake her up for school. She'd then checked with the school, her neighbours and anywhere else Hayley could have gone, before finding a note Hayley had written to Lottie and left on her bedside table:

Gone to the big house to find Florrie.

So, Lottie had rushed over here in an Uber, calling the police on the way to let them know she'd found Hayley. The police informed us that they still had to do a welfare check on the child if they were reported missing, hence their arrival at my house.

"So, you are Hayley's legal guardian?" the policewoman, who'd introduced herself as Mary, asked Lottie.

She cleared her throat and wrapped her arm around Hayley. "Yes, Hayley's my sister. I've been her legal guardian for two years."

"Does she speak at all?" the other policeman, Grant, asked.

"She has selective mutism," Lottie said quietly.

"Selective?" Mary put in. "Who does she speak to?"

"Me. Only me. But not if I'm with other people. Only if we're alone."

"Right," Grant said slowly. "Learning difficulties?"

I frowned at him. It was beginning to annoy me that they were talking about Hayley as if she wasn't there, and it was clearly making Lottie very uncomfortable.

"She does not have learning difficulties," I put in. "She's halfway through *The Lion the Witch and the Wardrobe*. Does that sound like learning difficulties to you?"

"And how did Hayley get out of the flat in the first place?" Grant asked Lottie, completely ignoring me.

Lottie shifted on the sofa. "Um... our flat's security isn't that great."

I stiffened. I had no idea where Lottie lived, but hearing her security described as *not great* was like a shot of ice into my veins. Why had I never insisted on knowing where she lived? I was such a self-absorbed arsehole.

"The door has a double lock," Lottie went on, "but there's no alarm, and the coded door at the entrance to the block hasn't worked in ages. I've told the management company but they take months to do anything." Her voice dropped down to an embarrassed whisper that made my breath catch in my chest. "We don't exactly live in the Hilton. I guess it was easy for her to slip out."

"Hmm," Grant's disapproval of this set-up was made clear with his next statement. "Of course, we'll have to report this to social services. I presume you have a social worker assigned to your case."

Lottie nodded, her pale face tightening as she drew Hayley into her side. "Y-yes, we do. I'll give you her details. B-but..." she swallowed, blinking rapidly in an obvious attempt to push back tears. "Honestly, this has never happened before, and I will talk to the building management about the security there. Hayley wasn't hurt and—"

"We'll relay the facts about what happened as we're duty bound to do," Mary said, more softly now in the face of Lottie's obvious distress. "But we do have to—"

"Please," Lottie whispered. The whole room went quiet at the desperation in that one word. She swallowed before she continued. "There's... been a complication in the last few months. Hayley's grandparents are back on the scene, and they..." she broke off and shot a quick look at Hayley, obviously not wanting to say too much in front of her. "I just really don't need any *incidents* reported to social services negatively right now."

Grant sighed. "The trouble is that we have to let them know the concerns we have with your home environment, and the fact that Hayley ran away to a random house is also concerning. I just can't—"

"This house isn't random," I said.

In the last few minutes, as I watched the panic build in Lottie's expression, I'd made my decision. I knew that Lottie would never agree to it, so my only chance was a surprise attack. An added benefit was that it would result in a better story for social services. I wasn't sure what was going on with the grandparents, but the way Hayley had shrunk further into Lottie when they were mentioned only cemented my plan.

I stood from my chair and walked over to Lottie, who was looking up at me with wide eyes that went even wider as I sat right next to her on the sofa and took her hand in mine.

"I'm Lottie's fiancé, you see, so really, this is Hayley's second home. In fact, this is all just a big misunderstanding, seeing as Hayley didn't *actually* run away. She merely relocated herself to her other home. A home in which she will be living very soon anyway. So, your concerns about her fleeing to a random house and the security of her current home are null and void." I turned to smile down at Lottie, who was still staring up at me but now with her mouth open in shock.

"Ah, well, that does change things," Mary said with a smile – I'd definitely won Mary over.

"Is that the case, Miss Forest?" asked the more sceptical Grant. "Are you engaged to this gentleman?"

Lottie's mouth opened then closed twice as she transferred her gaze from me to Grant, then back again.

I gave her hand a firm squeeze.

"Er..." she started, looking totally bewildered. Luckily for me, Mrs H was a bloody marvel.

"Well, of course they're engaged," she said as if it was the most obvious thing in the world. "And this one's always around." She ruffled Hayley's hair. "Loves my cookies, don't you, lovie?"

Hayley looked up at Mrs H and back at the police officers with wide eyes. But it was only after she looked at her sister with a tilted head and a question in her gaze and something unspoken passed between them that she finally nodded.

"Okay then," said Mary with a smile. "We'll still have to file a report, but we won't include ongoing safety concerns. You'll need to update your address with social services, of course."

"Right," Lottie managed in a high-pitched voice. "Will do."

I saw them out, and when I came back into the room, the sisters were still huddled together on the sofa. Two pairs of brown eyes came to me as I walked in – one curious, the other furious.

"What the fudge have you done?" Lottie said through her teeth.

"Mrs H," I said casually, "can you take Hayley back to the kitchen so she can finish her cookies."

"Come on then, lovie," Mrs H said with a smile as she reached for Hayley's hand, but the child just burrowed further into her sister's side. So I walked over to her and crouched down to her eye level.

"Hey, little stowaway," I said softly, and her face emerged from the folds of her sister's jumper to peek at me. "I know that was all a bit scary. But there's nothing to worry about now. You've seen me before, haven't you? Maybe when your sister was working? That's how you knew your way here?"

She gave a tentative nod confirming my suspicion, and I smiled.

"Well, now you don't have to hide when you come here, right? Because you and your sister are going to live here."

"Your Grace, I—"

I shot Lottie a warning look, and she shut her mouth, pressing her lips together in a thin line, her eyes flashing with fury.

"And I'm Ollie, okay? Sometimes, your sister is silly and calls me Your Grace, but that's not my name. To you, I'm Ollie. And I've got a niece about your age. She can tell you what a fantastic uncle I am."

Hayley's eyes went wide at the mention of Florrie, then she looked away quickly.

"Ah, of course," I said slowly, "you've already met Florrie, haven't you?"

She bit her lip and looked up at her sister.

"It's okay, lovebug," Lottie muttered as she stroked Hayley's hair back from her face.

Hayley turned back to me and nodded. Christ, how often had she hidden in my library? Why the fuck didn't Lottie tell me that her sister needed to come with her to work? I forced a smile.

"Well, that's good because you'll be seeing a lot more of her."

Then, to my surprise, Hayley did something I'd yet to see – she smiled.

My eyebrows went up.

"You like Florrie?"

She emerged further from her sister to sit up straighter and gave an enthusiastic nod, and I chuckled. I couldn't think of two more opposite personalities. Florrie was *a lot*, but clearly that appealed to Hayley. I guessed children don't always need words to get along. And anyway, Florrie likely had enough words for both of them.

"Well, that's great news."

Hayley's smile got bigger, and my chest tightened. I decided then and there that making this little girl smile was going to be my new favourite pastime.

CHAPTER 22

Frustration and hurt pride

Lottie

"What the fudge is going on?" I said as Ollie strolled back over to me after ushering Hayley and the indomitable Mrs H out of the door. I was standing now, my fists clenched at my sides, adrenaline pulsing through me. How dare he promise Hayley things like that? How dare he lie to the police? We were in deep manure now because of him. I closed my eyes when they started to sting and swallowed down the sob that was threatening to work its way out of my throat. "Are you punishing me?" I whispered and saw his eyes flash when I focused back on him.

"Of course not, Lottie," he snapped, crossing his arms over his chest. "I saved your arse just now. A thank you would be great." He raised one eyebrow, and my hand tingled with the urge to slap his smug face.

"You lied to the police," I said in a low voice, shaking with fury. "You made *me* lie to the police. You have no idea how tenuous our situation is."

"No, I don't," he snapped back, uncrossing his arms as he stormed over to me, the smug expression giving way to an angry one. "Because you never fucking *told me*. You even made your sister hide when she came over here. What kind of monster do you think I am that you have to hide your little sister from me?"

I threw my hands up and took a step back, making his eyes flash again. "I was your employee. I relied on the money I earned here. You can't just bring along a child to your place of work when she won't go to school. I needed this job."

"I never gave you any indication that I would be enough of a prick to send your sister away. Jesus Christ, Lottie, I thought you knew me better than that. I thought we meant something to each other. You lied to me. Over and over again, you lied."

There was some hurt leaking into his tone now. Angry Ollie, I could handle but hurt Ollie…

I backed away another couple of steps until I came up against the coffee table. My hand went up to my temple to push my hair back, and when I saw Ollie watch its progress, I realised it was shaking, so I lowered it to my side and fisted it again.

"I couldn't risk it," I said. "You don't understand."

"Explain it to me then!" he shouted, and I flinched at the loss of his normal control. "Fucking *talk to me* for once. I really liked you, Lottie, and you held everything important back from me. Then you left me. Don't you think I would have given you that goddamn money myself if you'd asked me rather than take a payoff from my fucking mother and make me look like a goddamn idiot?"

"I didn't mean to—"

"Well, you did." His face was a mask of fury now. "You threw us away for a measly fucking fifty grand. You confirmed everything my family suspected about grasping gold diggers. I thought we had something special, but you were never honest with me. You never even told me about your sister. So this whole shitshow today is *your* fault. If you'd been honest from the beginning, this would never have happened."

Your fault.

Ollie's words hit me with such force that I rocked back on my heels like he'd struck me. I'd been trying so desperately hard to hold everything together for Hayley for the last few months, but the stress and pressure just kept building and building, and now I'd taken my eye off the ball for a moment and the police were involved. They were going to file a report with social services, which would include actual lies. The chances of me losing Hayley to those fudging bastards who thought she was just *putting on* her selective mutism and that she needed a *firmer hand* were now much, much higher.

And Ollie was right. It was my fault. A wave of nausea swept over me, and I realised that it wasn't just my hands that were shaking now. My throat was tight, and my eyes started stinging as Ollie's angry face blurred with the tears I was trying to hold back.

"Don't you think I know that?" I said in a hoarse voice.

"Lottie, maybe we should—" Ollie's voice was softer now, which somehow made everything worse. As his hand closed over mine, I felt something inside me snap, and I lost it.

"Don't you think I know it's my fault?" I screamed, ripping my hand away from his. "It's all on me! It's always all on me!" I was shouting now, shaking my head from side to side as the tears fell in rivers down my cheeks. "Because there's *no one else*. There's nobody to catch me when I fall. No family that gives one single shit about me. No safety net. And I can't do it all. I'm not strong enough." My words were broken through my sobs now.

"Lottie, baby, please let me hold you." Ollie's voice was still soft but now edged with real concern. He was right in front of me, but I was crying so hard that I couldn't see the expression on his face.

I skirted the coffee table and continued backing away from him with my hand up to ward him off, shaking my head from side to side in jerky movements. I couldn't let him hold me up. I couldn't lose control. I had to rely on myself. I'd relied on myself since I was ten years old.

"I've let her down again and again," I continued in that awful, broken voice. "And she shouldn't have to go through any more. Not after what she went through already. She needs specialist counselling. Do you know how long the waiting list is for that on the NHS?"

"Listen, Lottie, let's just take a minute to—" he was sounding panicked now, probably regretting letting this crazy, ranting lady into his home.

"Nearly two years. *Two years* of Hayley not speaking to anyone but me. I had to get her help sooner. I *had* to take that money. I had to, I had to, I had to…" I was chanting that over and over again as Ollie made it clear that he'd finally had enough of me keeping my distance. Ignoring my hand, he walked right into it, bent down and simply picked me up, cradling me to his chest. I still couldn't see properly through my tears, but I felt him stride across the room, and I was jostled as he sat down on the sofa with me in his lap.

I knew I should be stronger. I knew better than to show this type of weakness. But the feel of his strong arms around me, the deep, soothing quality of his voice as he said words of reassurance about how "everything was going to be okay now", the sheer bulk of his large body cocooning mine, his glorious, clean, masculine scent – all of it combined to rip a huge tear in my self-control. So, I shoved my face in his throat and let the sobs work their way free finally, my arms clutching around his neck and my body pressing into his.

"I had to," I repeated into the warm skin of his neck.

"I know, darling," he said as he stroked my back. "It's okay now. I'm sorry I shouted – it was frustration and hurt pride. And, of course, I can be a dick if I'm not getting my own way, as you know."

My sobs were subsiding, and I nearly managed a small smile. Nearly.

"You've been strong for a long time, Lottie," his voice was achingly soft now. "It's not your fault."

I shook my head at that as more tears flowed, no doubt soaking his shirt, but he didn't seem to mind.

"No, Lottie," he said in a firm voice. "It's not your fault. You did the best you could, and you were scared. Anyone would have done the same thing. But it's enough now. Now you *do* have people that care about you. You've got that safety net, and so does Hayley."

"I can't let you—"

"Baby, I'm sorry, but it's gone way past you *letting* me do anything. As soon as you and your sister turned up at my house today, it was a done deal. You've both been dealt a shit hand, and life is going to be a fuck of a lot easier for you from now on. So, you didn't lie to the police. You *are* moving in here."

"W-what?" I pulled away from him to look up at his face, scrubbing the tears from my eyes so I could actually see him.

"You and Hayley will be moving in here."

I blinked. "You c-can't... I mean, we..."

"I can do whatever the fuck I want to do, Lottie."

"But, your mother," I whispered, biting my lip and bracing for his reaction. The woman had paid me a substantial sum to stay away from her son. I did not think me moving in with said son was really sticking to that agreement.

"I'll deal with my mother," Ollie snapped, that anger from before making his words hard.

"Ollie, I think we should talk about this," I said slowly. When I tried to ease out of his arms, they only enclosed me tighter. I cleared my throat. "Maybe we should talk about this whilst I'm not being held on your lap?"

"No," Ollie said firmly, and my eyebrows went up. His arms gave me a squeeze, and he planted a brief kiss on my lips. "You're much more reasonable when you're in my arms."

"Ollie, I just had a total mental breakdown in your arms."

"Yes, and it was the first time you've been really honest with me. Plus, I much prefer conversations with you like this."

"You're mad," I whispered, and he smiled down at me before kissing me softly again. I was so emotionally drained and mentally exhausted that all my resistance melted away with the feel of his lips on mine, and I kissed him back.

Yes, that's right. My sister ran away and hid in this man's house. I practically banged his door down to get to her. The police had invaded his home to question us, and now he was holding me in his arms, kissing me. He really was mad. But, then again, so was I.

CHAPTER 23

You made the choices you thought you had to

Ollie

I scowled up at the shithole block of flats I was standing outside. Movement caught my eye from an alleyway, and when I looked over I saw two men exchanging something before one of them melted back into the shadows – drug dealers. Lottie and Hayley lived in a neighbourhood with drug dealers out in the street on a goddamn Tuesday afternoon in broad daylight.

"Fucking hell," I muttered as I pressed the intercom, which remained blank. Fury shot through me as I gave the door in front of me a light shove, and it swung fully open. A big 'out of order' sign was on the lift, so I jogged up the five flights of stairs to their flat, then banged on the flimsy piece of shit wood.

"What are you doing here?" Lottie breathed as she blinked up at me with a shocked expression. Hayley peeked at me from behind her sister and gave me a small wave which I managed to return, even accompanied with a smile despite my anger.

"Hey, stowaway," I said softly. She blushed and gave me another tiny smile. It would do for now, but future Hayley was going to be smiling big all the fucking time and not doing it in this unsafe dump of a flat.

"Ollie, I thought we agreed to give it a few days," Lottie said through gritted teeth, and I shrugged as I gently moved her and Hayley back so I could make it into the tiny space and shut the door behind me, scowling at it as it creaked on its hinges.

"No, *you* decided that," I told her, taking a few steps into their home (really, that was all the steps it was possible to take – the place was smaller than our larder). "*I* didn't agree to anything." As I looked around the space my stomach pitched. Lottie had made the best of the tiny room. Colourful throws over the shitty sofa, a threadbare rug that had seen better days but brightened up the place, but there was still some obvious damp with peeling wallpaper and a draft from the window which was rattling in the wind.

"Wow, kiddo," I said, turning to Hayley as I walked over to the fridge and touched one of the many paintings of horses stuck onto it. "These are bloody good."

Hayley's face flushed with pleasure, and that small smile tugged at the corners of her mouth again despite the obvious tension between me and her sister.

"Got any more of these to show me?"

She gave a quick nod and then rushed out of the room to the only door other than the entrance. The folded bedding next to the sofa told me all I needed to know – one bedroom, which Hayley used; Lottie slept on the sofa. My resolve hardened as I turned to Lottie, whose mouth was now set in a stubborn line.

"You and Hayley are coming home with me today," my tone had gone from the soft, encouraging way I spoke to Hayley to now hard and uncompromising.

I'd been willing to be gentle with Lottie yesterday. Her complete breakdown after I'd shouted at her like the absolute prick that I was, gutted me. Lottie Forest was carrying the weight of the world on her shoulders, and she had been for a long fucking time. And I'd watched right there in my home as that weight finally took its toll and crushed her. I never *ever* wanted to see her like that again. Now that I'd finally got off my arse and looked into Lottie properly (something I should have done months ago but my hurt pride hadn't even considered because, again, I was a massive prick), I knew that any normal person would have broken *way* before she had.

Lottie and Hayley had been taken home by my driver yesterday – Hayley had a therapy appointment and, to be honest, I knew that they both needed time to regroup, so I allowed them space for now. The first call I made was to my mother. As I suspected, she did have some information and she had known about Hayley, but she didn't have the full picture. Unlimited funds and contacts everywhere meant that by lunchtime the next day, I had a comprehensive file on both sisters, and it wasn't pretty reading.

Just like Lottie had said, she had been on her own since the age of ten. That was when she was removed from her mother's care after repeated concerns raised by the school. Her mother was an alcoholic, father passed away when she was six. From aged ten to sixteen Lottie was in and out of foster care until she returned to her mother's care. Her mother had been sober for a year and in that time had managed to find a new husband and get pregnant with Hayley.

She did stay sober for the next six years, but then her husband ran away with another woman and emigrated to Australia, of all places. Contact was minimal after that, and he never paid any child support, despite court summons to do so.

Lottie's mother fell off the wagon in a dramatic fashion, rocking up to Hayley's primary school completely shitfaced on multiple occasions and, yet again, her child was taken into foster care. Only this time a sister was waiting in the wings. Lottie had only just turned twenty-two, but she took in her now selectively mute, grieving, extremely damaged sister.

Over the last two years, the scrutiny from social services had been intense, but Lottie had managed to meet all of their standards. She'd given up any hope of attending university to take low-paid jobs and make ends meet as best she could. The only time she slipped up was when she was caught shoplifting a pair of school shoes for her sister. Meanwhile, her mother fell deeper and deeper into alcoholism.

Hayley's grandparents had cropped up more recently. They hadn't been involved with the child for her entire life, having disapproved of the mother, but they had got back in touch ten months ago demanding visitation rights. This was after Lottie and Hayley's mother died from alcoholic liver disease.

When I thought of those two cremating their mother all alone, I felt even more rage than I had before. I'd already started to make a few moves to ruin Buchanon's business after I'd uncovered the fact that they fired Lottie two weeks after her mother died. From the looks Buchanon gave Lottie that night at my bar, I was pretty sure that her absence from work for a goddamn funeral wasn't the only reason his wife got rid of her.

As if all that wasn't enough to deal with, after a few months the grandparents reported Lottie as poor parenting material and made new demands – this time for full custody. Judging by Hayley's reaction to the mention of them yesterday, I imagined that this was not what either sister wanted, but it was clear that Lottie was terrified it would happen.

Well, all of that shit, all of those worries were over now. With my money and my connections those girls were going to do exactly as they pleased, and nobody was going to threaten them ever again. There certainly would not be any problem obtaining fucking school shoes. There was just the small hurdle of convincing Lottie to trust me.

"W-we are not coming home with you," Lottie's voice was high-pitched with disbelief. "That's insane. We can't just pack up and move out."

"Lottie," I said in my most reasonable tone. "The police will have already filed their report with social services. When it comes to child protection issues, they are usually very prompt."

She frowned up at me, looking adorably confused. In fact, at home and out of her Corporate Barbie uniform, Lottie was just plain adorable. Her glorious caramel hair was piled on top of her head, and her delicate face free of any make-up; she had on a pair of checked pyjama bottoms paired with a tight tank top and a fluffy, oversized cardigan, and her slippers were unicorns, which I noticed matched those of her sister. I'd never seen anything as ridiculous or as completely endearing in my life, and it only firmed my resolve that these two would be under my roof by the end of the day.

"How do you know about the police process for child protection?"

I shrugged. "Just a guess," I lied – my team had done extensive research on police processes, local social services, family court, fostering, applying for adoption and grandparental rights. My personal assistant was an unrelenting arsehole, but she did not like injustice. Once Jenna had heard Lottie's story she was all over the research. She'd even compiled a file on the grandparents, digging up all sorts of decades-old shit that I had no idea how she'd uncovered, but that may well come in useful if they continued to threaten Hayley and Lottie.

I'd been the one to research selective mutism – but I'd save that conversation for another time; Lottie was clearly struggling with how fast things were moving now, and she hadn't even moved in yet.

"The point is, you and Hayley are not staying here another night. Did you know there are actual drug dealers on the street outside?"

Lottie frowned at me. "Er, yes. We're in the dodgiest part of south London. Of course, there're dealers."

I threw up my hands. "What do you mean 'of course there're dealers'? They're dangerous."

Lottie narrowed her eyes at me and crossed her arms over her chest.

"Listen, posh boy. I've been living in dodgy parts of London for years. The chuffing dealers aren't the threat around here. Unless you're buying drugs or trying to sell drugs on their patch, you're invisible to them. Seeing as I have never had any intention of doing either, they're a complete non-issue."

"What *is* the threat then?" I said in a low, dangerous voice.

"What?"

"You said drug dealers aren't the threat around here. Implying there was another threat. I want to know what it is."

She looked down and to the left, and I ground my teeth. I'd never met anyone as stubborn as her. As if on cue, Hayley came running out of the bedroom, skidding to a halt in front of me in her unicorn slippers.

"Hey, stowaway," I said, crouching down to her level. She lost a little of her nerve then. The piece of paper she'd been clutching lowered as she bit her lip. I held out my hand and smiled at her. "Is that for me?" Very slowly, she lifted the paper up for me to look at. My heart tripped as I looked at what she'd drawn. "That's amazing, Hayley. You know what? We can put this one on the fridge in *my* house. Would you like to come over tonight?"

She nodded straight away.

"Hails," Lottie snapped. "We've been over this. What His Grace said to those policemen wasn't true. It was just to help us out, which is naughty because we shouldn't lie. But we are not moving in with him." Hayley's eyes darted over to the door, then back to Lottie. "Fudge nuggets," Lottie whispered to herself as she covered the distance to Hayley, took her hand and tried to lead her away from me. But Hayley's face fell into a stubborn expression reminiscent of her sister and she planted her feet as her gaze flicked over to the door again. I straightened from my crouch as I looked in the direction of her gaze. There was a chest of drawers at a funny angle next to the door that I hadn't noticed before. It was almost as though someone had dragged it across and not bothered to put it back against the wall. I blinked. Surely not...

"Lovebug," Lottie's voice had softened now as she dropped down in front of her sister and pushed some of her curls out of her face with a gentle hand. I had to strain to hear her next whispered words. "That was only for a couple of nights. We were safe, I promise. It was just *in case*. You should have told me you knew. I thought you were asleep."

"Please tell me this isn't what it looks like, Lottie," I said through gritted teeth. Lottie gave me a wary look, and I tried to tamp down my rising temper. But visions of Lottie waiting until Hayley was asleep and then dragging a huge chest of drawers, which, even being likely twice her weight, would not keep anyone other than my ninety-five-year-old grandma out, flew through my mind.

"It was just a precaution," Lottie explained. "I didn't really think anything would happen, but there was the odd… er… kerfuffle in the corridor and, well, someone did try the door handle a couple of times."

"Define 'kerfuffle'," I said in a tight voice and Lottie bit her lip.

"Just some drunk dudes, shouting and horsing around."

"Christ," I snapped, my hand going to the back of my neck.

"It wasn't that bad," she rushed to say. "And I've probably been a bit extra cautious with the barricading thing." She turned to Hayley and softened her tone. "I didn't know you noticed that, lovebug. You've got to tell me if something's worrying you. We're a team, remember?"

Quite rightly, Hayley's eyebrows went up as she shot the chest of drawers a significant look. Lottie sighed. I was starting to see how this non-verbal communication worked.

"Yes, okay," she admitted. "I wasn't honest with you either, but still, you should have told me if you were worried."

Hayley crossed her arms over her chest and scowled at her sister.

"Because I'm the adult, Hails," Lottie said in a firmer voice. "You're a kid. I get to make the tough choices." With that, Hayley rolled her eyes and stormed out of the room in disgust, slamming the bedroom door behind her. At Hayley's exit,

Lottie just seemed to deflate. The fight went out of her eyes, and she sank down onto the small sofa with a huff, taking her head in her hands. The anger coursing through me at the vision of Lottie pushing that huge chest of drawers in front of her door melted away as I took in her defeated pose.

"Hey," I said softly as I sat next to her on the sofa, putting my hand on her back.

"She was scared," Lottie said in a whisper that was only just loud enough for me to make out.

"It's not your fault, darling," I said, rubbing circles on her back now. "You did the best you could."

"She's still scared," Lottie went on as if she hadn't heard me. "I should have found somewhere else to live but, cheese and rice, you wouldn't believe the rent they charge in some places." She swallowed. "I needed to make that fifty grand last, and I couldn't rely on Vicky employing me forever, so I—"

"You made the choices you thought you had to," I said, cutting her off. I couldn't hear any more about how she expected the worst. Lottie's entire life had trained her to do that. *Of course* when my mother stepped in with a solid financial offer, she would take it. She *had* to take it. I could see that now, see beyond my hurt pride to how much that amount of money meant to Lottie. How much stability it gave her and her sister. "But I'm offering you an alternative. Everyone needs some help sometimes, Lottie. I don't want Hayley to be scared, and neither do you."

The last sentence was a low blow to get my way, and I knew it, but I had to use everything at my disposal to convince her. I was *not* leaving this building without both sisters.

"Why do you want to help us?" Lottie said, lifting her face from her hands to look at me. "You hate me. You wanted me to stay away from you and your family. Wait..." she blinked up at me as her face paled, "is this some bullshit guilt thing now that you know about my sister?"

"Firstly, I never hated you. Ever."

"Could have fooled me."

"I didn't. I was frustrated with you, but I *never* hated you."

"You thought I was a threat to your family." Her voice cracked at the end, and she cleared her throat to try to cover it, and I felt a burn in the pit of my stomach. When she spoke again, her voice was small. "I did that. I know I did, by taking the money. It was a test, and I failed it. I even *knew* it was a test when your mum offered the money, but I couldn't turn it down. I just—" Her breath hitched, and she pressed her trembling lips together. I suspected that the last thing Lottie wanted to do was cry in front of me again. The burn had worked its way up to my throat now and I had to swallow it down before I spoke again.

"It was unfair of Mum to offer you that money, Lottie," I said in a tight voice. Past establishing that Mum had known about Hayley in our brief call yesterday, I hadn't spoken to her again. I was absolutely bloody furious with her. She went to Lottie with that offer, knowing how desperate she was, knowing how impossible it would be for her to say no. The casual cruelty with which she'd treated Lottie was almost unbelievable to me. It didn't gel with my vision of my mum. "Especially when she knew how desperately you might need it. It's…" I broke off, jumping up from the sofa and pacing away as far as the small living room would allow, my hand rubbing the back of my neck, searching for the right words, then turned and locked eyes with Lottie. "It's playing with people's lives. She pushed you around with her money. Took advantage of you when she should have been *helping* you."

"Ollie, I didn't have to take that money," Lottie said softly.

My eyebrows went up as I looked pointedly around the flat and the dresser that was at an awkward angle, then nodded towards the shut bedroom door. Her cheeks flushed red.

"I would have managed."

"Would Hayley have the therapy she needs?" I asked gently, pacing back to her and taking my seat on the sofa again. She bit her lip and looked down at the floor. "That's not a criticism,

Lottie. Hayley's had ongoing therapy for weeks now because of that decision you made."

Lottie swallowed, but to my relief, when she looked at me, some of the torment had left her eyes. "Thanks," she said softly.

"So, now that we've got that sorted. You need to pack."

"Ollie, I—"

"I'm not leaving you here."

Lottie rolled her eyes. "This is not a warzone. We've lived here for nearly a year with hardly any problems."

"Hardly any? There have been some, then?"

She looked down and to the left, her mouth set in that stubborn line. I realised that if I wanted my way, and I always wanted my way, I was going to have to change tactics. And I was good at manipulating situations. I'd been doing it since I was a child, just as Lottie had been reading people and situations to keep herself safe.

"Listen, I'm sorry, Lottie, but I told the police that you were moving in with me and that we're engaged. So, for the moment, both of those things need to happen, or I could be accused of lying to the police. That has some serious consequences for me and my family." I was definitely stretching the truth to breaking point there; I had full control of my estate, my investments and the dukedom. My family had never been so secure. None of this could touch me or them. But Lottie didn't need to know that. I knew I was on the right track as I watched her face pale.

"B-but that's *your* fault," Lottie said, and she had a point, but it was not one I was willing to concede.

"The fact is that Hayley came to *my* door, putting you and her under my protection. End of story."

Her mouth opened, closed and then opened again before she finally spoke. "You want me to pose as your fake fiancée?"

Hmm, she could think it was fake if that would keep her from freaking out for now. But to be honest, since yesterday, I'd had a massive sense of satisfaction thinking about Lottie as my future wife without "fake" once coming into the equation.

But I was well aware that I'd been a dick to her for weeks and that my intention to keep her and Hayley for good at this stage might make me look a little crazy – with good reason.

"Sure." I shrugged. "It'll keep Mum from setting me up with a string of annoying women. You can deter my crazy ex-girlfriend, who's been a real problem recently. I've got a million charity galas coming up, which you'll make vastly less dull." She blinked at that, and her lips tipped up just slightly. She liked me saying that she'd make something less dull. Not the most effusive compliment but it had clearly worked on Lottie, and I guess compared to all the insults I'd hurled at her recently it was a big improvement. "And you can help *me* like you help Vicky."

She jerked in surprise at that as her gaze snapped to mine. "What do you mean? You don't need the same help as Vicky."

"I know you do more than help Vics interact with people. Your abilities are valuable in business. You must realise that?"

There was that small smile again just as the bedroom door opened, and Hayley emerged, dragging a massive bin liner which was overflowing with toys. She huffed and puffed her way to her sister, dumped the bag at her feet and then planted her feet wide with her hands on her hips. When she looked at me, I gave her a wink and a grin. When she smiled just like her sister, I knew that I'd won.

CHAPTER 24

I made your sister sad, didn't I?

Lottie

It was weird coming here and not immediately starting to clean the place. Hayley clutched my hand after we'd helped to lug the last of our belongings into the hallway. This space looked even more imposing with our pile of possessions stacked in the centre of it. I felt a hot, reflex snap of shame as I looked at everything we owned. We had some suitcases and boxes, but the rest was in bin liners. I hated fudging bin liners. Foster children get far, *far* too acquainted with them, seeing as that was invariably what our stuff would be packed up into when we had to move. By the end of my years in foster care, one of my bin liners was stuffed full of soft toys. You might think that was a good thing, but the bigger the collection of cuddly animals you had, the more you'd had to move. Every new home would produce one for you on your arrival. I developed a hatred of that bag of toys, but whilst I was still in foster care, I'd never had the heart to throw them away.

It hadn't taken more than two trips to move the stuff from Ollie's car, and the pile itself only took up a tiny percentage of his hallway floorspace. Granted, the hallway was blooming massive, but it still made me feel slightly pathetic. And that was after Ollie had pulled my laptop out of a box I'd earmarked for the dump with a raised eyebrow. I'd had to explain how it had died which led to a deeply uncomfortable conversation about my psychology course being "on hold". Ollie had just looked at me for a long moment, the tic in his jaw the only sign of his extreme annoyance, before he gave me a short nod and hauled the box to his car.

"Well, I guess you know all the rooms, Lottie," Ollie said as he strolled in with another full bin liner to add to the pile. "Which ones will work for you?" I mentally flipped through the house's ten bedrooms and scrunched my nose. The truth was, there simply wasn't a single room in this house that Hayley would feel comfortable in. I bit my lip as I glanced down at her. She was staring at the library – probably wanting to go and tuck herself away with the books up in the mezzanine again. I cleared my throat to speak, but my words stuck in my throat when the front door swung open, and in came Margot.

"Yoo-hoo!" she called as she swept into the hallway, a big smile on her face.

I took a step back, pushing Hayley behind me.

Her smile dropped somewhat as she took in my retreat. To my surprise, Ollie let out a low growl. When my eyes flew to him, I realised he was furious.

"Mother," he snapped, and I blinked. I don't think I've ever heard him snap at her or call her *Mother* before – it was always Mum. "I told you to stay away from the house for the moment whilst Lottie and Hayley settle in."

"Pish posh," Margot said, waving away his concerns. "I'm allowed to pop in and say hi."

She leaned to the side to get a better look at Hayley, who was glued to the back of my legs. Hayley saw a lot more than adults gave her credit for. And she'd liked Margot that day when she'd driven us to minor injuries. Margot had even managed to get a couple of smiles out of her, which back then was almost unheard of. After Margot dropped us back at the flat that day, and it was just us again, Hayley had referred to her as the "nice lady with sparkly ears" (her diamond earrings were huge) "and toffee sweets in her bag", which coming from Hayley was high praise.

But then, when she came to the flat a few weeks later, despite the fact that she was just as smiley with Hayley and gave her a toffee sweet like before, Hayley could feel the tension in the air, could feel the threat. I found that sweet in the bin later still in its wrapper, and there were no more mentions of the nice lady.

"Hello there, Hayley. I swear you've grown a whole foot since…" She cleared her throat, and her gaze shot to me, clearly not wanting to complete that sentence and bring up our last encounter. "Hello, Lottie," she said softly, as if worried she might spook me.

"Hi," I managed to get out past my thick throat.

Hayley tugged on my jeans.

When I turned to look down at her, she gave a quick shake of her head, going back another step and tugging me to move with her. Hayley was totally ready to walk away from the thick atmosphere, and I couldn't say I blamed her.

Margot's eyes moved to the pile of our belongings in the hallway, and if the floor could have swallowed me up at that moment, I would have jumped at the chance. The tension was too thick now, and I didn't want Hayley exposed to it. So I turned to her and dropped down to her level to speak softly.

"Why don't you check out the books again, lovebug."

She was still eyeing Margot over my shoulder, but at the mention of books, her eyes shot to mine and her expression lit up.

"Off you go."

Hayley threw one last wary look from Margot to me, and I shook my head, dropping my voice to a whisper.

"It's okay. I'll be fine."

She leaned forward to put her hand to the centre of my chest then to hers: her non-verbal I love you. As she dashed off into the library, I felt her loss as a buffer acutely. But I'd been through worse than this. I'd had people judge me my entire life.

I cleared my throat as I straightened to face Margot. "Lady Harding," I said and, thank Elton John's glasses, my voice was steady, "I realise that I'm violating the terms of our agreement by coming here. I want you to know that I will pay the money back. It's not all there at present as I've had some expenses that were time critical and—"

"Your sister," Margot said softly, taking a tentative step towards me.

"Mum," Ollie said in warning, and she stopped in her approach. I couldn't feel the anger or annoyance I would have expected from her; all I could feel was warmth, discomfort and regret.

"I know why you needed the money, remember?" she continued, still in that soft voice.

I nodded, and she took a deep breath, but I cut her off before she could speak again.

"Yes, so some of it is gone – I had back payments to her therapist. But I can set up a payment schedule. I'm earning more now, you see, and—"

"Yes, you're working for my stepdaughter now. Aren't you?"

I nodded slowly. "Yes, but the agreement was just your son, as I understood it. You never specified that—"

"No, Lottie, I'm not angry that you're working with Vicky," she said with a frown. "How could you think…?" she closed her eyes for a moment, "Of course you'd think that. I've given you no reason not to, have I?"

I didn't know how to reply. I mean, of course I assumed she would be angry that I was working with Vicky. If the woman disliked me enough to buy me off one of her children, of course she wasn't going to be happy with me spending every working day with another.

"Lottie, you're really helping Vicky," she said. "I'm not angry about that." She took another small step towards me but then halted when Ollie made another warning noise. "I've never been very good with figures," she said, and I tilted my head to the side in confusion. "But my daughter tells me that you've made her company over three point three million pounds since you started 'helping' her."

My eyebrows went up. "Er... Lady Harding, I don't do any wheeler-dealing. I don't cut any deals. I just help Vicky read the room."

"Does reading the room help cut the deal?" Margot asked, and I shrugged. "Be honest. Would most of those deals have progressed if you weren't there?"

"I don't—"

"Well, that's settled then. Three point three million, minus fifty thousand is three million two hundred and fifty thousand. Shall I transfer that amount to you?"

"Of course not! I—"

"Okay, we'll just leave things as they are for now then," she cut me off briskly. I was starting to see that when it came to getting her own way and being high-handed, Margot was cut from the same cloth as her son.

"I work for Vicky for a set wage," I said through gritted teeth. "I do not take a share of the profits."

Margot waved her hand. "Oh well, none of this matters now, seeing as we're going to be family, and it's all family money anyway."

My eyes flew wide at that, and I jerked my head to look at Ollie, who was standing in the hallway with his hands shoved in his pockets and a completely unconcerned smirk on his face.

"F-family?" I said slowly, looking between the dowager and Ollie. The dowager beamed at me.

"No need to be coy, dear," she said. "Oh, I nearly forgot. Here you are, darling." She handed Ollie a ring box and I took a sharp breath in. Very few people surprise me. I'm always able to predict what they'll do.

Always.

But I did not see this coming.

"Thanks, Mum," Ollie said, grabbing the box from her and then strolling over to me.

I took a small step back, but he grabbed my hand to stop me. Before I knew it an antique ring was on the ring finger of my left hand, the sapphire and surrounding diamonds glinting in the sunlight streaming in through the windows.

"What are you doing?" I squeaked. Then looked round his large frame to his mum. "Lady Harding, this is not what it looks like. I—"

"I know, I know," she said, waving her hand dismissively. "Fake engagement, yadda yadda. I've read enough romance books to know how this works, darling. Let's just see how it pans out, shall we?" She winked at me then, and I blinked in shock. "Okay, best be off. I've got a committee meeting for the fundraiser next week." She was striding towards me then and didn't stop coming until we were toe to toe, and she pulled me in for a hug. I thought posh people only air-kissed, but this woman was a good hugger. I hadn't had a maternal hug in years. Embarrassingly, before I could get a hold of myself, my eyes started to sting.

We both pulled back when we heard the library door open. Hayley popped her head out and turned to us.

"It's okay, Hails," I said in a shaky voice. I glanced back at Margot, and she was scanning my face with soft eyes. I cleared my throat and blinked to push back the tears, but I was pretty sure she still saw them, especially after her hand came up to pat my cheek and her other hand squeezed mine at my side.

"Right," she said in a bright voice that was just very slightly choked as she turned to Hayley. "It was nice to see you again, young lady."

She pulled away from me and skirted her son to get to Hayley, crouching down in front of her.

Hayley studied her, still wary. When she glanced up at me, I gave her a small nod to say that this was okay.

"Have you met my daughter, Vicky?"

Hayley nodded slowly. Vicky and Lucy had been coming over to the flat for movie nights regularly for the last few months and treated Hayley like a surrogate niece.

"Well, my Vicky wasn't very chatty when she was little either, but she liked tight hugs. Do you like tight hugs? Sometimes it can be a bit scary to move somewhere, and hugs help us feel better. Would you like a hug, darling?" Hayley bit her lip and took a step back. "Okay, maybe next time."

I could feel the sadness and regret pouring off Margot as she reached out very slowly to Hayley's face, giving her time to step back again, and tucked her hair behind her ear, which Hayley allowed.

"You've very pretty hair, just like your sister. I made your sister sad, didn't I?" Hayley nodded, and I felt my throat close over. "I'm sorry about that, Hayley." Her gaze went up to me, "Really, I am so sorry." Then she looked back at Hayley. "Well, now, *my* little boy, Ollie—"

That got a snort out of Hayley, who was grinning now, and my heart felt like it stopped beating. Even noises like that were rare from Hayley, especially around people she didn't trust. And Margot seemed to understand her perfectly.

"He's still my little boy," she explained, her eyes twinkling. "He may be twice my size, but he'll always be my funny little boy with messy hair and missing front teeth who peed himself on stage when he was a shepherd in the preschool nativity."

"Mum," Ollie protested, but she ignored him, and to be honest, so did I as just then, Hayley let out a tiny giggle. My hand flew to my mouth. Giggling with anyone but me was unheard of. Unaware of how momentous this was, Margot simply stroked her cheek again and stood up.

"As I was saying, my little boy and I are going to make your sister happy, okay?" Hayley nodded and Margot smiled down at her with a soft expression before hitching her handbag back onto her shoulder. "Toodle-pip then, darlings," she singsonged, and swept out of the house.

CHAPTER 25

No more kissing

Ollie

"Hey, stowaway," I called across the kitchen. "I can see you there, you know."

Hayley peeked back round the door again, her big eyes blinking up at me. One side of her hair was poofed out in a massive tangle, the other in her normal waves. She was in her pyjamas with her fluffy unicorn slippers and even fluffier dressing gown, which swallowed her small frame whole.

Lottie had told me last night that Hayley was small for her age. She was certainly a lot smaller than my niece. Lottie was worried she wasn't eating enough. To be honest, Lottie was worried about a lot of things, not all of which she would admit to me. But after Hayley went to bed last night I'd basically forced Lottie to play chess. Her chosen activity would have been arguing with me about the ring on her finger, but she was tired enough to cave when I put that particular dispute on hold.

Her exhaustion and the fact the last few days had been an emotional minefield meant that all her defences were down. So, despite how wary she was of me, a few chess moves and it all came flooding out, including how Hayley stops eating when she's stressed, and how even when she does eat she's fussy. It was another way that Lottie felt like she was failing her sister. She took everything on her shoulders. By the time we'd finished chess, she looked totally done in.

"Hails wakes up early," she'd told me through a yawn as she stumbled up the stairs, too tired to object to my arm going around her shoulders to practically carry her up. "But don't worry. I'll set my alarm to make sure she doesn't disturb you." I smiled at her outside her room and shoved my hands in my pockets to stop myself from reaching for her.

"Okay, darling," I said softly. She blinked at the endearment but then disappeared into her room. An hour later, I pushed open her door to see her fast asleep, looking tiny in the huge bed, her glorious hair spread across the pillow. She didn't stir at the creaks of the floorboards as I walked over to her beside table, nor did she when I grabbed her phone. Lottie needed sleep, and I was perfectly capable of looking after an eight-year-old girl.

Hayley shuffled into the kitchen, looking around at the huge space with wide eyes. She was clutching a toy pony to her chest like a life preserver.

"So Mrs H isn't around yet to make breakfast, but you're in luck. Breakfast is my speciality. You hungry?"

She shook her head rapidly, clutching her pony tighter.

"Hmm, okay," I muttered.

Her eyes flicked to the Nutella and maple syrup I had in front of me.

"I guess I'll just have to eat some pancakes on my own then."

Her eyes lit at the word pancakes, and she shuffled a bit closer.

"And I'll have to eat this Nutella on my own." I scooped out a big spoonful of Nutella and shoved it in my mouth.

Hayley gasped in shock and then pointed at the spoon, shaking her head. I grinned.

"Who says I'm not allowed? There's no Nutella police to stop me."

She frowned in disapproval but then started eyeing the Nutella with interest.

I stretched over the island, putting a spoon in front of one of the kitchen stools, then leaned back.

She hesitated for a moment, then shuffled forward, put her pony up on the counter and then climbed up the stool so that she was sitting facing me with the spoon clutched in one hand. She gave a furtive look behind her, clearly checking for her sister, who I doubt condoned straight-up Nutella for breakfast, and then back at the Nutella jar, which I pushed over to her. She shoved the spoon in, took a big scoop and put it in her mouth. Then she grinned at me around the spoon, and my chest felt too tight.

Her smile was so like her sister's, and I'd missed that smile way too much. I doubted that a spoonful of Nutella was going to be all it took to convince Lottie to smile at me again, though. Last night my brain had played its favourite new game with me, where it ran through all the different ways I'd been a dick to Lottie. It actually made me feel physically sick to think about it. Some of the things I said to her...

Well, I was a good negotiator. I'd pulled myself out of some sticky wickets in my time, and this would be no different.

Okay, so maybe I blackmailed her to come and live here with her sister, but I'd had to get them out of that shitty flat. It was totally unsafe.

Now, back to pancakes. I frowned.

"Hey, stowaway, you know how to make these things?" I asked and Hayley rolled her eyes as she took another spoonful and shoved it in her mouth. But she hopped off the stool and came over to me.

She took an egg out of the box and cracked it into the bowl. When she took another one, though, it slipped through her small fingers and smashed on the granite work surface. As soon as it happened, her whole demeanour changed. She shot me a terrified look, scuttled back before running around to the other side of the kitchen island and grabbing her pony.

"It's okay, sweetheart," I said very softly.

The poor thing looked terrified. Her hand formed a fist at her chest, and she made a circular movement with it, obviously trying to tell me something, but I couldn't understand what she was saying. I needed to learn some sign language – this was frustrating as hell.

"You're not in trouble." She didn't seem to believe me, taking another step back and eyeing the door. I sighed. "You've still got to help me make the pancakes."

Still just fear. Ah, fuck it. I grabbed an egg and chucked it onto the granite myself. I may have miscalculated the force required, however, and it splattered everywhere, covering me and most of the counter with egg.

"Happy now?" I asked as egg dripped down my forehead, a piece of shell sliding its way off my shirt.

Her eyes were wide as she watched me; after a few beats of silence, the most wonderful sound filled the kitchen – an eight-year-old giggle. So, because I was totally addicted to that sound, and *maybe* because I'd never in my life had to clean up after myself anyway, I cracked another egg on the counter, grabbed the bag of flour, and stalked over to her.

"You think that's funny, do you?" I asked, and Hayley didn't pause in her giggling to nod.

"What the bleeding hell is going on here?" Mrs H stormed over to me like the force of nature that she was. She went up on her tiptoes to clip me round the ear, but when she couldn't quite reach, I leaned down for her to finish the job. "I told your mother that you'd end up spoiled rotten. Look at this mess!"

Hayley was wide-eyed as she watched me being chastised by this small but fierce woman. When Mrs H turned to her, however, her attitude changed completely.

"Ah, hello there, lovie." She bustled round to Hayley's side of the counter to stroke the wild side of Hayley's hair. "Goodness gracious, we've a job on our hands this morning to brush this out. You're lucky to have such pretty, thick hair, mind."

"Why are you being so nice to her and mean to me?" I grumbled. "She started it."

Mrs H shot me a narrow-eyed look. "She did *not*. And don't be a tattletale. Now what on earth were you trying to make the child?"

With Mrs H's help, we managed to make pancakes. I told Hayley that we were on a special mission to let her sister sleep this morning, which she seemed extremely invested in, tiptoeing past Lottie's door to get dressed into the uniform that Lottie had laid out the night before. I cancelled my first two meetings and then dug through the files I had on Lottie and Hayley on my phone to find out the name of her school. I frowned when I saw the Ofsted rating, which was especially poor for children with special educational needs.

My mood nose-dived even further when we arrived at the school. I wasn't allowed to walk Hayley in, which, from a security perspective, seemed like a pretty poor show. And the transformation from giggling Hayley to sombre *scared* Hayley was even more worrying. She clutched her backpack in front of her as she shuffled across the playground with her little shoulders hunched defensively. And when some little bastard ran past her and bumped her shoulder before laughing and running off, I nearly lost my shit. I contented myself with shooting a short email to my assistant to research local private schools. Local to *my* area of London and not this shithole.

I realised my mistake when I arrived home, and Lottie came flying at me down the corridor, eyes wild and voice high-pitched with panic.

"Ollie, she's gone," she said as she grabbed the lapels of my suit jacket. "She's not in her room and—"

"Hey, it's okay," I said, taking the opportunity to wrap my arms around her and pull her close. It was a ruthless move. If Lottie wasn't completely out of her mind with worry, she would never have flown at me or put her hands on me, but I was happy to take advantage of the opportunity. "I've taken her to school. Mrs H made her pancakes. She's fine."

Lottie sagged against me with acute relief. "Thank God," she breathed. "I thought she'd run away again."

Shit. Her voice had a broken quality to it now, and I felt like a total dick for not leaving a note. I told Mrs H to let her know, but she must have still been cleaning up the bombsite in the kitchen.

"I'm sorry, baby," I said softly, tightening my arms around her and pulling her closer as I kissed the top of her head. "I didn't mean to panic you. It's just you looked so tired, Lottie. So, so tired. You needed to sleep."

"I thought I set my alarm clock." Her voice was steadier now, and she was clearly coming back to herself. I breathed in her hair, realising I probably only had this for a few more moments with her in my arms. I didn't want to admit anything, but there were already too many lies between us. "But when I woke up my phone was gone and there was a laptop there in its place."

"I *might* have taken it. And that laptop is yours."

"You what?" Lottie stiffened and tried to pull back. "Why the Fraggle Rock would you do that? And you can't give me a laptop."

I smiled. The cute non-swearing was a good sign. It was like she'd given up the other day when she swore during her breakdown, and I'd hated it.

She slapped my chest. "Let me go," she snapped.

I sighed and loosened my arms so she could step away.

She took a good few rapid steps back, putting some real distance between us, and crossed her arms.

I thought this was an opportune time to return her phone. When I pulled it out of my back pocket and held it out to her she snatched it from me with a scowl.

"Let me get this right," she said in a low, angry voice. "You came into my room and took my phone?"

"Yes, I did, and I'd do it again."

Her eyebrows were practically in her hairline now. "You are the most high-handed, insufferable jerk on the planet."

I inclined my head in acknowledgement and started stalking towards her. Her eyes went wide as she took some more steps back, nearly falling over a small hall chair. When she stumbled, I decided that enough was enough. I caught her arm to steady her before she could go down. One of my hands went to her jawline, the other splayed the middle of her back, holding her to me. Her breathing was rapid now, her pupils so dilated there was only a thin ring of warm brown around them.

"I completely agree."

"W-what?" she breathed, and I smiled down at her.

"I *am* insufferable, but if that means that you actually get some sleep, then I can live with it."

Then, because she wasn't pulling away, because I could feel her soft body through her ridiculous fluffy dressing gown, because I could count the green flecks in her brown eyes, I had to kiss her. It was a light brush of my lips against hers, but when she shivered in my arms, and her lips parted very slightly on a low moan, I took full advantage, deepening the kiss and sliding my hand into her glorious, soft as silk hair. But just as I was sliding my other hand into the dressing gown, a door slamming across the house caused Lottie to jerk in my arms, her lips wrenching from mine.

"What am I doing?" she whispered, more to herself than me. I rested my forehead on hers, my hands going to either side of her face to tilt it to mine so that I could look into her eyes.

"*We're* doing what we should have been doing for the last six months if I hadn't been such a self-absorbed arsehole and my mother wasn't a manipulative piece of work."

She sighed and closed her eyes. "Ollie, you can't take my phone, you can't give me a laptop and you can't take Hayley to school without my permission. And you definitely *can't* kiss me."

I kissed her again, lightning quick, then leaned back to smile at her.

"I'm sorry I scared you by taking your phone," I said softly. "But you're exhausted. You needed to sleep. You've been running on fumes for months." I gave her a squeeze. "You would never have crumbled like that the other day if you weren't at breaking point. I know that. So, I'm sorry if I scared you, but I'm not sorry that you had an extra couple of hours in bed. And I'm not sorry about giving you a laptop or kissing you."

I thought I'd wait to tell her that I'd actually already enrolled her back in her psychology course and paid for the rest of the year of modules — her head might have exploded.

"Couple of hours?" she said, her face draining of its remaining colour. "Cheese and rice, Vicky!"

"Don't worry about Vicky. I've sorted her out. She knows you need rest. She's been worried about you as well." My smile dropped completely then, and I gentled my voice. "She says you haven't been eating, darling."

"I do eat," Lottie said defensively. "I just... I'm like Hayley, if I'm stressed, I feel a bit sick and..." she shrugged. "I just—"

"Look, I don't want to be a dick or anything. God knows I've been enough of one already. But you've got to look after yourself better. Hayley needs you healthy. Right?"

"Okay, okay." She nodded, her cheeks heating as she looked away from me.

"Hey, don't be embarrassed. This is not another thing to beat yourself up about, okay? You just need to start looking after yourself and making yourself a priority for once. Right?"

She bit her lip. "Right," she said slowly. "But no more kissing."

"Sure," I promised with a small smile, before leaning forward and kissing her again.

CHAPTER 26

Let go of her

Lottie

Hayley squeezed my hand so hard I almost winced. Of course, there was a bloody pool. I should have expected that. Posh people have country houses with pools. That's just a fact of life. And it was a boiling mid-July day. Two kids streaked past us, chucking t-shirts over their heads in their mad dash to get in the water. Hayley stopped dead in her tracks.

"Everything okay?" Ollie asked when he doubled back after noticing our abrupt stop. "I forgot to tell you to bring your swimmers, but we have plenty of spares for you and Hayley."

"It's fine," I whispered through my fixed smile. "You go on and see everyone. We'll be there in a bit."

Embarrassment flooded me in waves. It wasn't just Hayley's fear of the water that was making me feel so humiliated. *I* wasn't exactly the Little Mermaid either. The fact was that neither Hayley nor I could swim. There simply hadn't been the opportunities for us that there were for other children.

To be honest, Hayley had more experience than *me* in water. I'd managed to scrape together the cash for some swimming lessons at the local leisure centre, but it was painfully clear how behind the other kids she was when she was stuck in group lessons with a much younger group. Hayley didn't do well in groups anyway, but after she'd swallowed some water and nearly vomited on the side of the pool, she cried if I ever even mentioned swimming again.

"Hey, lovebug," I said, keeping my voice light as I kneeled in front of her. "You don't have to go into the water if you don't want to. Okay?"

She looked down at the floor and kicked the perfectly manicured lawn. Everything about this place was perfectly manicured. There was topiary along the driveway, for cheese's sake. A driveway that went on and on until an imposing house loomed in the distance like something out of Downton Abbey.

Apparently, Buckingham Manor was the Buckingham "country seat", and this was their annual summer family party. When Ollie had suggested it, I'd naively thought he meant a picnic with maybe a dozen or so peeps. I did not anticipate it to be fully catered with nearly a hundred people, waiter service, a pool and of course, *of course*, croquet (they were the British aristocracy, after all).

A family party for me and Hayley would be the two of us and some cheese sarnies. The difference was staggering. What must it feel like to have this many people woven into your life? This many people you could call family? My heart ached even thinking about it.

Hayley glanced behind her and then back at me, her eyes wide and pleading.

"No, lovebug. We're not going home. Ollie wants to see his family, okay? We can have some fun. We don't have to go to the pool. You know I don't like the water any more than you do, right?"

I felt Ollie's hand on my back and swivelled my head to look at him over my shoulder.

"Is there a problem with the pool?" he asked softly, frowning in confusion. "We've got spare costumes in the house. There're loads to choose from."

I pushed up to my feet so that I could whisper to him and not embarrass Hayley. "She can't swim."

"Oh. I..." He trailed off, clearly shocked that this life skill had passed an eight-year-old child by, which just demonstrated how out of touch he, and people like him, could be. No doubt he was under the impression that every child in the UK simply *had* to learn to swim.

"Listen, I tried, but when Hails came to live with me, she'd never been in the water and swimming lessons are expensive. We did some, but it was in big groups and she hated it, then refused to try again. Now she's dead set against it." All of this came out in a garbled, frantic mess. I just didn't want him to think that I didn't try. "I would have taken her myself but I..." I looked away from him, feeling my cheeks heat as shame washed over me and my voice dropped to a whisper, "I can't swim either."

"Hey, hey, hey," he said softly, his hand reaching for mine to interlink our fingers. "Don't worry about it. You did the best you could, darling. That you got her to *any* lessons is amazing."

Then he skirted around me to crouch down in front of Hayley himself.

"So, I hear you're not that keen on water, stowaway?" he said gently.

Hayley sniffed and turned her head away, shrugging her shoulders.

"I used to hate the water too," he told her, and her eyes snapped back to his as her head tilted to the side. "No bullshit, I promise."

I rolled my eyes; honestly, what was the point of me substituting all my swear words when she was going to learn them from him now? But the s-word did earn a small smile from Hayley, and that twinkle was back in her eye, so I forgave him.

"Mum had to get me *two* private teachers and bribe me with Fruit Pastilles to get me anywhere near the pool, and *I* grew up with a pool. What a numpty, huh?"

Hayley nodded, and Ollie laughed.

"So, maybe you'd let me teach you another day?"

She scrunched her nose.

"Okay, we'll leave that for later negotiation involving Fruit Pastilles. But for now, you don't have to go in the pool unless you want to paddle in the shallow end. So you can just have fun."

Hayley still looked unsure, but her shoulders were no longer up near her ears, and she wasn't tugging me to go back to the car, so as far as I was concerned, he'd worked a minor miracle.

"Hayley!"

Ollie was nearly bowled out of the way by a flash of neon pink as his niece homed in on Hayley like a missile. Then, to my complete and utter surprise, Florrie hugged Hayley. It took a second, but Hayley hugged her back. I blinked. It was the first time I'd seen Hayley hug anyone other than me. Florrie pulled back but kept hold of Hayley's hands as she rattled on.

"It's so cool you're here! There's a bouncy castle set up near the back paddock, well I hope there is – see, we've got a pony called Legolas on loan from Hetty next door, and I was supposed to put him away before the bouncy castle people came, but I *might* have forgotten and he won't be caught now cause he likes to be part of the action. So Legolas may have chewed through the bouncy castle by now. But there's the pool too and—" Florrie broke off and stared at Hayley for a moment, her eyebrows furrowed. After a moment's pause, she spoke again, but her voice was much softer. "Okay, so no pool. That's cool. I wasn't that into it anyway. But we need to get to the bouncy castle before Legolas deflates it."

My eyes started stinging, and my hand went to my throat. Who was this kid? I'd never come across a child as perceptive.

"So shall we go?" She grabbed Hayley's hand and gave it a tug. Hayley was smiling and nodding.

"Er... hi, squirt," Ollie said with mock disgruntlement. "Where's *my* hug?"

Florrie rolled her eyes. "We're on a schedule here, Uncle Ollie," she told him as she gave him a quick hug, which he took advantage of to lift her off her feet and spin her around as she giggled. "You're wasting our time, you weirdo!" she shrieked as he threw her up into the air as if she was still a toddler, caught her and set her back on her feet. Hayley looked on with wide eyes and just a hint of longing that made my heart break.

"Okay, now you can go," he said.

"Ugh, you're the worst! You've messed with my hair," Florrie grumbled, but she was grinning. Ollie ruffled her long blonde hair again for good measure as she squealed in annoyance then he turned to Hayley.

"You happy to go with her, stowaway?" he said gently as he ruffled her hair as well. Hayley grinned and nodded as Florrie grabbed her hand again.

"Of course she is," Florrie snapped. "As if she wants to stay with boring old people. No offence, Lottie, and um hi, by the way."

I smiled at her and dropped down to her level in a crouch.

"Hi, love. Do you have a quick hug for me too? I promise not to mess with your hair." She smiled and threw her arms around my neck. I hugged her back and whispered, "Thank you," in her ear.

When she pulled away she gave me a small nod, and then both the girls shot off across the lawn hand in hand. They looked so completely different it was almost jarring: Florrie in head-to-toe designer pink and purple with subtle sparkly eyeshadow, pink lipstick, blond waves interspersed with the occasional artful braid; then Hayley wearing an old band t-shirt with black jeans in July and her scuffed trainers, her caramel hair shoved back into a ponytail which was as much styling as she would tolerate. But they were both giggling as they ran, perfectly happy together.

"Your niece is pretty great," I said as I stood up.

"Yeah, she's an absolute diamond, that one," Ollie agreed, deep affection in his voice. "Just like her mum, but don't you let Claire know I told you that."

"Told her what?" Claire's voice cut in, and we both spun around to see her and her husband approach.

"What a little shit you are," Ollie said without a pause, snatching her into a tight hug. She rolled her eyes as she pulled away, then turned to me and, to my surprise, hugged me too.

It took a second, but my arms closed around her just in time. When we separated, she scanned my face for a moment.

"Bit overwhelming, aren't we," she said with a small smile. It seemed that she was more like her daughter than I realised. "You'll get used to it, though."

A muffled laugh came from her husband, and Claire's eyes flickered with annoyance before she masked it.

"Something to say, Blake?" Ollie said in a low voice.

"Well, whilst I agree this family *is* a bit much, I'm not sure why you think this one will get used to it." He was sneering at me, and his words were slurred. "I thought this engagement deal was all a load of bullshit. She's not going to have the chance to get used to anything. Unless she starts cleaning for you lot again, I guess." He snorted again at that, and I felt my face flood with heat. Ollie stiffened.

"What the fuck has got into you, mate?" he growled, taking my hand in his. Blake glanced at our interlinked fingers, and his lip curled. But he wiped his expression clear before Ollie could catch it.

"Sorry, sorry," he said, forcing a smile. "Always putting my foot in it. Mum's the word, eh?"

"Blake, we talked about this," Claire said, glancing at me in discomfort. That was when I felt it. My gaze snapped to Blake, who was now glaring at his wife. The atmosphere had changed. It was crackling with animosity. Shit, something was very, very wrong here. Claire caught his look and her face paled before she looked down at her feet, her shoulders slumping. Then, just as soon as he'd flipped it, his expression went back to *smiling, damn good chap*.

"Of course, we did, darling," he said; the fake warmth in his tone actually caused a shiver up my spine. Claire winced, and on instinct my eyes shot to her hand which was held in his. Her fingers were all bunched together and white from the pressure he was squeezing them with. When I looked up again, her face was pale and pinched with pain.

"Let go of her!" I burst out, and everyone started in shock. Claire's wide eyes flew to mine. Blake didn't let go of her hand, but he did loosen his grip. I let out a breath I hadn't realised I'd been holding.

Ollie cleared his throat. "Lottie?" he said hesitantly. "You okay?" He clearly thought I was losing it. Claire was avoiding eye contact now; her colour returned as she blushed.

"I-I-I don't..." I broke off as I stared up at Ollie's confused expression. "He was holding her hand too tight," I whispered. It sounded a bit mad now, I realised, wishing I could claw the words back. Ollie's gaze snapped to his sister, and he frowned.

"Claire? Everything alright?" he asked, looking between his sister and her husband.

"I'm fine," Claire said, with a nervous laugh. "I think maybe Lottie's just a bit overwhelmed with everything. We *are* a lot to take." She was grinning at me now, but it was a fixed grin that looked painful to maintain. I tilted my head to the side, silently telling her that I knew what I saw, that I knew what was going on and I was ready to say something. She stared at me for a moment, that fixed grin still on her face, but then she gave a very brief, almost imperceptible shake of her head. *Not here*, it said. *Not now.* I glanced between her and Blake, and my lips pressed in a thin line before I spoke again.

"Yeah, sorry about that," I said lightly. "Must be the heat getting to me."

Ollie was still frowning in confusion as he looked between the three of us. He was completely oblivious. But I knew a predator when I saw one. I knew a dangerous atmosphere when I felt it. And I could sense fear acutely.

Blake was dangerous. And Claire was afraid.

CHAPTER 27

Position of power

Lottie

"Do you play, Charlotte?"

I smiled at the woman in front of me, clutching my glass of champagne in a death grip. Since the little run-in earlier with Claire and her scary husband, she'd been avoiding me, which felt a little like feeding me to the wolves, to be honest. I mean, all I did was object when her husband was about to break her fingers. I'd even caught sight of her cradling her hand when her family weren't looking earlier. It wasn't as if I imagined it.

"Er... no," I replied, forcing myself to smile. "The closest I've got to a horse was a donkey ride when I was nine."

It had been one of my better memories of Mum. She'd been sober for a year, and we'd gone to Wales for a holiday. I remember being totally ecstatic to be out of London. I loved the sea, even if I wasn't brave or competent enough to go in it, and I thought the tiny caravan we were staying in was the lap of luxury. Unfortunately, there was a pub around the corner, so it all went to shit fairly rapidly. The stench of alcohol coming off Mum on the train journey the next day was horrendous and acutely embarrassing. I glanced at the glass of champagne in my hand and sighed.

"I'm sure Ollie will teach you to ride, darling," Margot put in. My eyes went wide, and I had to press my lips together hard to stop a startled laugh from escaping.

"Yes, of course, I will," Ollie said smoothly as he rejoined the group, having been commandeered by various cousins for the last hour. His eyes were twinkling as he made that comment, and I couldn't help it – I snorted out a laugh and had to cover it with a cough.

"Oh, you really should," Cecelia, his horsey cousin, continued, completely oblivious. "It's such tremendous fun. Don't you think Ollie?"

"Yeah, Cece," he said through a smile, his hand settling on the small of my back and his fingers flexing in the material of my t-shirt. "It certainly *is* tremendous." My lips were trembling, but I forced the giggles back. In fact, I was so involved in my battle against laughter that I didn't pay attention to Vicky. I really, *really* should have done.

"Okay, I can get this one," Vicky said. When I looked at her, I could feel the gears in her brain turning. "Cece is talking about riding horses," Vicky started. Fraggle Rock, I was too late. "But Ollie means the sexual type of riding. That's a double meaning. That's why you're trying not to laugh."

There was a shocked silence. Ollie's shoulders were shaking, and he had his hand over his mouth.

"What?" Vicky asked, bewildered, then turned to me. "You taught me about double meanings the other day. And I know that your face looks like that when you don't want to laugh. I asked you about it last week when you were trying not to laugh at that man in the meeting and I thought you needed the toilet for a number two."

Cecelia gave a nervous titter and then backed away with a vague but still horsey excuse – something to do with *going on a hack*.

"Nice one, Vics." Ollie said.

"What *are* you teaching her, Lottie?" Margot was looking at me with suspicion again. Grumpy barnacles, I was tired of this bloody party. I was wearing the wrong clothes – everyone else looked like they could be going to a wedding. I was the only one in cutoff shorts, a Taylor Swift t-shirt and flip-flops. I was absolutely parched but only had the now warm champagne, which I wouldn't touch because I didn't blooming well drink.

I didn't know where Hayley was and I was starting to get worried. Everyone asked me where I went to school and looked puzzled when I told them Southwark Comprehensive. I mean, Cecelia was nice, but really? Did I *look* like I played polo? Then there was my name. I was not called Charlotte, but for some reason, that's what Margot was introducing me as. I wanted to be at least called by my own fudging name. I levelled Margot with a don't fudge with me look.

"She just likes working things out. Vicky hates all the hidden meanings that go on around her. I didn't tell her to go around pointing it out. I just explained the concept."

"Are you implying I don't know my stepdaughter?" I'd clearly hit a nerve with Margot who had been going out of her way to try and win back my trust over the last two weeks.

"That's enough, Mum," Ollie snapped, but I was done.

"Excuse me," I muttered and walked away from them towards the pool. Margot had clearly tired of trying to win me over. One time questioning her about her family and her back was up.

Now, I didn't want to go anywhere near the blinking pool, but I was boiling and dying of thirst, and all the drinks were set up over there. Once I got some water down me I was going to find Hayley and get out of here. I just hoped that Uber came out as far as Little Buckingham.

I gave the bartender a brief smile as I swapped my champagne for iced water. Stepping away from the makeshift bar, I drank it down past my dry throat and closed my eyes in relief. But then something slammed hard into my ribs, shoving me to the side. My eyes flew open as I stumbled backwards. My balance was rubbish at the best of times, and with a sharp jab like that, the force of it nearly winding me, there was no chance of me staying upright. But instead of hitting the hard patio, I gasped as my body crashed into the water.

There wasn't even time to suck in a breath before I went under. Everything seemed blurry and upside down. My lungs were burning. I kicked my legs haphazardly and flapped my arms around. When I broke the surface, I sucked in some much-needed air, but then I was under again. Crap, what had Hayley's teacher said? Legs like flippers? Kick from the hip?

I could see blurry figures above me. For the love of Marmite, I was going to die at the bottom of this pool with posh people watching me drown like it was some sort of sport. When I came up again to breathe, I heard someone say:

"What *is* she doing?"

"No idea. Some sort of synchronised swimming?"

Cheese and rice, I was doomed. None of this lot would ever think that a grown adult woman wouldn't be able to swim. I sank under again. My movements seemed to be pushing me downwards more than they were helping me break the surface now. But before I could reach the bottom of the pool, a strong arm closed around me, and suddenly I was surging up to the surface. When my face was back in blessed air again, I coughed and spluttered all the water I'd swallowed between deep, stuttering breaths. That strong arm was dragging me from the deep end, and then I was lifted up out of the water, cradled in Ollie's arms.

"By Jove," an older man said from the gathered crowd. "Is she alright? We were wondering what she was up to."

"She can't fucking swim, you idiots," Ollie shouted, and there were various gasps of surprise. Ollie then walked out of the pool up the steps from the shallow end and over to one of the wicker chairs at the side where he sat down with me in his lap.

I was still coughing and choking, and he alternated between giving my back firm slaps when I was choking and rubbing gentle circles when I took deep breaths. Tears were streaming down my face and I felt utterly humiliated. Then, just as I was starting to get my breath back, a little girl missile flew across the courtyard, her arms closing tightly around my neck, her little body shaking with sobs.

"Hey, hey, hey," I chanted in a croaky voice. "I'm fine, lovebug."

But however much I tried to reassure her, she just sobbed harder. It was only when Ollie gathered us both to him and he spoke in his firm voice, ringing with certainty, that she started to settle.

"I would *never* let anything happen to *either* of you. Lottie's swallowed some water, but we're going to take care of her now. And you're both going to learn to swim so that this will never ever happen again." Hayley stiffened at that, but Ollie's arms gave us a squeeze before he pulled back slightly to make eye contact with her. "Hayley, both of you are going to learn to swim, and neither of you are going to be scared of water ever again. Understand me?"

To my absolute surprise Hayley nodded slowly.

"Good girl," Ollie said.

"Lottie?" I turned towards Claire who was standing next to us, holding out a towel, her face pale. "Are you okay? I'm so sorry I was out on the lawn and—"

"Quite the drama," Blake interrupted as he came to stand next to her.

I took the towel from Claire with a low, "thanks". I was wiping the tears and water from my face so it took a moment to notice Hayley's reaction. But when I glanced down at her I saw she was staring up at Blake, her eyes burning with anger, and her mouth set in a thin line.

"Hails?" I croaked and she tore her furious gaze from Blake to look at me. I frowned and tilted my head to the side. She looked between me and Blake with jerky movements of her head, her little hands were fisted at her sides. My eyebrows went up and she nodded once. Okay, so now I knew who that blow to my ribs was from.

"Hayley!" Florrie called as she skipped over to us. She was smiling and had a whole gaggle of other children with her. "Oh good, you found Lottie. Did you tell her that we want to go out to the backfield and—"

Florrie's words cut off as she turned to me. "Oh, did you jump in with your clothes on? Richie did that earlier. His mum was super cross."

"Lottie had a bit of an accident, darling," said Ollie. Hayley was shaking her head furiously and for once I was grateful that she wouldn't speak. This was *not* the time to throw accusations around.

"Hails, why don't you go with Florrie a minute. I need to have a quick chat with Ollie and then we'll have to get going soon, okay?"

Hayley looked between me and Blake, the anger in her expression morphing to concern.

"It's okay, lovebug," I said, trying to make my voice as reassuring as it could be with the croakiness still there. "Ollie's here."

She looked to Ollie who was frowning slightly, not quite understanding the interaction.

"Yes, it's fine, stowaway," he said gently. "You go and see Legolas with Florrie."

It took a moment but with Florrie tugging her hand and me encouraging her she did go. The party had resumed around us now, so it was just the four of us. I stood up, not wanting to do this from Ollie's lap. I needed to stand my own ground. Unfortunately, Margot chose that moment to bustle over.

"Darling, I heard what happened," she said, pulling me into a hug, seemingly uncaring that I soaked her outfit. And, just like that, I was reminded of the warm, wonderful mother she really was underneath the whole bribery and changing my name thing.

"Lottie tripped into the pool, Mum," Ollie said, and I stiffened slightly as he spoke for me. "If the goddamn drinks weren't so bloody close to the edge, then—"

"Actually, Ollie," I started as I pulled back gently from Margot. "I didn't trip. Someone jabbed me and knocked me into the pool."

There was a stunned silence for a moment. "What the fuck?" snapped Ollie.

I was staring at Blake. His eyes flashed and I raised an eyebrow in challenge. *I see you, arsehole*, I communicated silently.

"Er... Lottie, are you sure?" Margot asked. "I mean, you have been known to be a little on the clumsy side. There's no shame in just having tripped."

Claire was looking between me and Blake, her face draining of colour.

"Did you see who it was?" Ollie asked, still furious.

"No," I said slowly. "But I think Hayley did."

"What a load of bollocks," Blake said, dismissively. "You didn't even speak to the kid when she was here."

"Hayley and I communicate just fine without words."

He rolled his eyes. "Well, if she's going to go around making up stories, perhaps she shouldn't be playing with *my* stepdaughter."

"Blake, what the fuck's crawled up your arse, mate?" Ollie said, anger and confusion running through his tone. But Blake's eyes were locked with mine and I could see everything he was trying to say: *this is my family, back off or I will annihilate you*.

So I had a choice to make: should I say something now, and trust Ollie to choose me if I went up against this psychopath? Or should I stay quiet? In that moment, I ran through everything that I had to lose here. I'd had another family meeting summons from social services this week. As much as I'd protested against the fake engagement, I now acknowledged that it really was my best chance at keeping Hayley. It was a lifeline.

Yes, this guy needed calling out. Yes, I was worried about Claire and Florrie. But I simply wasn't in a position of power here. This was their family. I wasn't family. I wasn't blood. And I'd experienced over and over again how people would prioritise their real family over some random foster kid. I might not be the foster kid anymore, but that didn't change the dynamic. And Florrie was the first friend Hayley had ever spoken to. I couldn't take that away from her. So, in the end, I was the first to break eye contact with Blake.

"Maybe I did trip," I muttered at my feet. "And it was pretty crowded over there. It was probably an accident." The words felt bitter on my tongue. That was no accident — my ribs were still throbbing.

Ollie closed his hand around mine and squeezed.

"You sure, darling?" he asked, and I nodded. Maybe I'd tell him later, but with the memory of Margot's hug fresh in my mind, I decided that fitting in would be better. Giving in would be easier.

I caught Blake's smug look as Ollie led me away from the pool and took the opportunity when nobody was looking. Just because I didn't say swear words didn't mean I couldn't mouth them.

CHAPTER 28

People think I'm rude

Ollie

I've never been so terrified as when I saw Lottie sinking to the bottom of that pool. I still felt like I couldn't breathe even now that she was safe and in my sister's dry clothes. Luckily Vics had come over just as we were walking up to the house and sorted Lottie out. Vicky had been nearly as furious as me when she heard what happened. She displayed more emotion than I'd seen out of her in years, even shouting at me to demand an explanation as to why I let it happen. And now she was here, she clearly did not think me up to the job of looking after Lottie. She hadn't moved from her side since they came back from the house.

"Why are you calling her that?" Vicky snapped at Mum.

"Er... what darling?" Mum asked, frowning at her in confusion.

"Why are you calling Lottie 'Charlotte'? It's not her name."

We were in a large group with some of my cousins, and Mum had been introducing Lottie to everyone. I'd thought it was a bit weird that she was using Charlotte, but seeing as Lottie didn't say anything, I hadn't thought to question it.

Mum gave a nervous laugh. "Well, it *is* her name."

"No, it's not," Vicky replied. Lottie sidled closer to her and put her hand on her wrist.

"Honestly, Vics, it's fine," she murmured. "I don't mind."

Vicky's eyebrows went up. "But your name isn't Charlotte."

Mum was looking confused, and the rest of the group were shifting uncomfortably. "Of course it is. Lottie is short for Charlotte, surely."

Lottie gave a small shrug. "Well…"

"*Lottie* is her legal name," Vicky said firmly then turned to Lottie. "Why would you let her call you Charlotte?"

Lottie's face was bright red now as she looked down at her champagne glass which had been doled out to her when she came back from changing, seeing as she dropped her other glass by the pool.

"And why are you giving her champagne? She doesn't drink." Vicky turned to me. "You know she doesn't drink, and she hates the smell too because her mother was an alcoholic."

Lottie was now looking like she wanted the ground to swallow her up. Everyone around us had gone totally silent.

"Vicky, that's enough," I growled.

"What?" she glared at me. "You're the one calling her by her wrong name and giving her drinks she can't stand. Why are you having a go at me?"

Her gaze then snapped to Lottie, and I realised that she must have made a signal via her hand on her arm. I knew they had all sorts of non-verbal cues but I hadn't found out what meant what yet.

"Why should I leave it?" Vicky asked. "You nearly drowned. You don't have a drink you can drink on a boiling day, and you're not even being called by your actual name. And people think *I'm* rude."

Lottie forced out a laugh. "It's fine Vics honestly," she said, lightening the atmosphere. "Siblings, eh?" she said to the group in general. "Always bickering."

Everyone around us relaxed, the discomfort dissipated. Then Lottie asked one of my cousins about the upcoming polo season, using the knowledge she'd managed to extract from Cecelia earlier to segue straight into a very involved conversation about polo ponies and their training. Vicky was still glaring at me, and my mother was still in shock.

When a waiter passed, I stopped him and grabbed an elderflower drink from his tray, to switch with Lottie's champagne. Why hadn't I thought of that? But also, why hadn't Lottie objected to being given champagne? Just like with the name thing. Why would you accept being called something that wasn't your name? And now she was talking about polo like it was the most interesting conversation she'd ever had. I could guarantee she had zero fucking interest in *polo*.

"Legolas!" A tiny pony bowled through the group, followed by a rather larger billionaire in the form of Felix. Nobody was particularly surprised. Well, apart from Lottie. Everyone just raised their drinks to protect them from the fat-bodied, furry force of destruction and carried on their conversations.

"What the Fraggle Rock?" I heard Lottie mutter and then, "Oh, Lucy?"

Lucy Mayweather stumbled into the group following the path of her runaway pony and Felix, then stopped to lean on Lottie.

"Oh my God," she gasped. "I am not built for cardiovascular exercise. That bloody pony."

We both looked in the direction of Legolas's travel to see him upending a table of sandwiches, which he started munching his way through. When Felix tried to grab his halter he snorted and started off at a run again.

"Nice that you guys could make it," I said dryly to Lucy as her pony continued to destroy most of the catering.

"I'm sorry, Ols," Lucy said in between her gasping breaths. "But you know what that little shit is like. He behaves for the girls but as soon as he saw Felix he broke free. It's like a red rag to a bull for some reason."

Since they'd got back together, Felix and Lucy spent far more time in Little Buckingham, following a bleak couple of months apart.

Lucy's mum Hetty lived on the edge of the Buckingham Estate which bordered Felix's land as well. She had a whole menagerie of weird and wonderful animals. Felix and Legolas the pony had a strained relationship to say the least.

"Have a drink, darling," Mum said brightly. "Let Felix chase after Legolas. It does entertain the children so."

Both Florrie and Hayley had joined the chase now, armed with apples and various other pony treats. Felix and Legolas were facing off next to the cake stand.

"Oh bugger," Claire muttered. "I haven't had a piece of that Victoria sponge yet."

Felix growled as he stalked forward towards Legolas, who stood perfectly still. But just as Felix's fingers were about to close over his halter, the bastard ducked down and charged under Felix's arm to collide full force with the table of cakes. Luckily the majority of the guests were used to Legolas and his destructive tendencies, so at least half the cakes on the table were already held aloft by those nearest to the destruction zone.

"Mum, can you get that pony under control," Lucy snapped at Hetty who had appeared and was busy profusely apologising to my mum.

"I'm so sorry, Margot," Hetty said, ignoring her daughter. "But Legolas has psychological issues, and the kids just don't quite know how to manage him."

"Mum," growled Lucy. "Felix is thirty-four years old and I'm twenty-eight. We're not exactly kids. And the only *psychological issue* that pony has is that he's an absolute *arse*."

Felix had Legolas cornered near Mum's rose bushes now.

"It's quite alright, Hetty," Mum said as we watched Legolas easily dart around Felix again. "But I'm not risking my roses." Mum put her drink down, clapped her hands twice and shouted, "Here, boy!" across the courtyard. Legolas immediately abandoned what he clearly viewed as a game with Felix and trotted over to Mum, who snapped a lead rein to his halter and passed it to Hetty. Felix stumbled over to us. He was covered in twigs and leaves, his knees were caked in dirt, and his shirt was ripped.

"How did you do that?" he said to Mum as he took a glass of champagne from a passing waiter and downed the entire thing.

"You just have to have a commanding tone, dear," Mum told Felix, the CEO of a multinational company.

When I felt Lottie shaking next to me and looked down at her dancing eyes, she let out a snort. I raised an eyebrow, and that set her off. Once Lottie started laughing, everyone joined in. It was the most relaxed I'd seen her at this bloody party. And for once, I was grateful that our neighbours couldn't control their livestock.

CHAPTER 29

Unless we're agreeable

Ollie

"Why didn't you say anything?" I asked, not for the first time. But I thought I might finally get an answer out of her now. Hayley was in bed. She'd fallen asleep in the car on the way home, clutching Keith the pony with the horseshoe that Florrie had given her, and I'd carried her upstairs and tucked her in under the covers. Now Lottie and I were both downstairs, and I wanted answers.

She sighed. "What does it matter what your mother introduces me as? Honestly, I don't care."

"But that's not your name."

She shrugged as if people calling her by her actual name was neither here nor there.

"And why accept the champagne?"

She rolled her eyes. "I said I didn't drink *twice*. Nobody listened. It was easier to hold a glass of champagne than be a pushy dingus."

"You don't like the smell, Lottie." I remembered how she reacted in the bar when that wine had been spilt on her. She'd thrown up, for God's sake.

"It's fine."

"It's not fucking fine," I snapped. I was still supremely pissed off that my sister had called me out for how Lottie was being treated. "You need to stop being so goddamn agreeable all the time. Tell my mother to fuck off if she calls you the wrong name. Shove the glass of champagne back at the person that offers it."

She laughed then, but it wasn't her genuine laugh; no, this one was hollow and bitter. "You have no blooming idea how important being agreeable has been to me. I'd be totally Fraggle-Rocked if I hadn't been *agreeable*. You have the privilege of being an awkward, bossy arsehole. Some of us have to tread more carefully. Even now you could chuck me and Hayley out. Your mother could turn you against me again. Your sister and brother-in-law could take Florrie away from Hayley. Out of everyone there today, Hayley and I are the only ones who won't be invited to another family party unless we're *agreeable*.

"I know first-hand what happens when people like me don't blend in, when we aren't easy. That's why the situation with Hayley scares me so much. It's hard to be agreeable when you won't even speak. Maybe that's *why* she won't? Maybe the pressure is too much? Who the heck knows? But it's on *me* to make sure that we're accepted, at least temporarily."

"Fuck," I barked out, my hand going to the back of my neck. I tried and failed to rein in my temper, but it was a losing battle. It wasn't Lottie I was angry with, though. It was her mother who had let her and Hayley down so badly, the foster care system that had taught her to conform to what everyone else wanted her to be, and my mother for confirming all her fears about how easily we could try to cut someone like her out – but, most of all, me for being a stupid prick.

So I stalked over to her, and her eyes went wide with alarm at the look on my face, but that didn't stop me. I'd now have to add scaring her to the list of crap I'd put her through, but there was no way I could stay away from her in that moment. She backed away, her hand coming up to ward me off, but it was ineffectual when it came up against my chest. I simply kept coming at her until she was backed up against the door with nowhere else to go. Both her hands were flat against my chest now, prepared to push me away. I slid a hand to her jaw and then into the soft, thick caramel waves of her hair; my other hand went to her back, holding her to me and I leaned down to rest my forehead on hers.

"Ollie, I—" she breathed, her tone alarmed, but I cut her off with a soft kiss in direct contrast to how I'd just aggressively caged her in. When I pulled back, she was blinking up at me, and I knew I had a small window of stunned silence to get through to her.

"I'm *so* fucking sorry, Lottie," I said firmly. It was an odd apology, seeing as it was made through gritted teeth by an angry man, but it would have to do. "You've been let down so many times, and I'm just another fuckwit in a long line of fuckwits to do it to you again."

"Ollie, what are you talking about? You're *helping* Hayley and me. You—"

"I let you down when I didn't ask why you needed the money. When I believed Mum that you were seeing another bloke—"

"She said what—?"

"She showed me photos of you with Hayley's therapist. She didn't know who he was at the time, nor did I. You were hugging him on the street."

"Hugging Marc? But I... Oh, that was the day she spoke to him. Hayley said her first word to Marc in that session. Well, not to Marc, it was to me, but Marc was there. It was huge. I... wait, why did your mother have pictures of me and Marc?"

I winced. "She had you followed."

"What?" Lottie tried to pull away, but I kept her in place.

"You've got to understand," I said quickly. "It's shit, but there are some real crazies out there, and Mum is super cautious. My ex-fiancée went to the *Daily Mail* with all sorts of stories about me, complete with pictures from a party I'd thrown. The irony was I didn't even want to have the party; Cordelia had pushed and pushed for it. 'Duke of Fuckingham' was the headline they ran with. I mean, I was a bit wild back then, but it was all hammed up. It was just after Dad died, and… Well, Cordelia didn't mean to be found out, but our family have links with all the press. It didn't take much digging to know who sold the story. When I confronted her, she said it was an insurance policy in case I didn't follow through with a proposal." I broke off and swallowed. "Well, anyway, as I said, Mum's cautious, and she thought you were on the make."

"Ollie," Lottie said softly. "I'm sorry about Cordelia, really I am, but I *was* on the make. Your mum offered me money, and I literally took it. That's kind of the definition."

"My mother went to you the day after those photos were taken. So that means that was the day after Hayley had her breakthrough. I bet Marc suggested more sessions, didn't he?"

Lottie broke eye contact with me then, but I gave her waist a squeeze, and she dragged her gaze back to mine.

"You weren't on the make. You were looking after your sister. My mother was the dick in this scenario, even *she* admits that. And I was a bigger dick for cutting you off."

"*I* was the one that cut *you* off, Ollie."

"And I was the one that didn't even bother to fight for you. Didn't bother to find out why you needed the money. And then the way I behaved, I—" I took a deep breath and let it out slowly. "There's no bloody excuse for the way I behaved. I was hurt and angry. Pissed off that I couldn't have you when I wanted you so badly. Pissed off that I still wanted you when I thought I shouldn't. And I took it out on you. You know what? I saw Cordelia a few weeks after all the *Daily Mail* stuff happened, and I just shrugged and said no hard feelings. That girl sold me out, damaged my reputation, hurt my family for way more money than Mum gave you, and I just shrugged my shoulders. But with you, I was a vindictive, cruel piece of shit."

"Ollie, I don't—"

"But I didn't feel anything for her by then. That's the difference, Lottie. I was an arsehole, and I'm so *so* sorry, but I wasn't indifferent because I had fallen in love with you."

"What?" Lottie breathed, her eyes wide with shock, her pupils dilating. "You can't—"

"I'm in love with you, Lottie," I told her. "And I'll spend forever making it up to you. I'll spend forever proving that you can trust me. I let you down *again* today, but that's just because I was being an oblivious arsehole, not a vindictive one like I was before. So, you'll just have to forgive me for that too."

I didn't give her a chance to reply. We'd done enough talking and it wasn't getting us anywhere. So, I kissed her. Her lips were already parted in shock, so it didn't take much to deepen the kiss. For a moment, she stiffened in my arms, her hands on my chest starting to exert some pressure to push me away. I pulled back slightly to kiss the corner of her mouth, then across her cheek to her ear and her neck.

"I've missed this," I whispered in the shell of her ear, gently biting the soft lobe before continuing. "I thought about you constantly. Even when I told myself I hated you, I couldn't stop thinking about you: how you felt, the sounds you made. It drove me crazy. You drive me crazy."

I rocked against her, and when I bit the soft lobe of her ear, she let out a small moan. Her hands had stopped pushing me away. I smiled against her neck before licking her below her ear then kissing back along her jawline.

"I've got you, Lottie," I said softly against her mouth. "I promise you're safe with me, baby. You can let go."

She blinked up at me, her pupils huge and her expression slightly dazed.

"You're so beautiful," she whispered, almost as though she couldn't quite believe I was real. I smiled against her mouth.

"I think that's my line," I said, then kissed her again. This time she melted against me as I swallowed another of those small moans. Her hands slid from my chest up around to my back to pull me closer. She was plastered against me now, her soft breasts pressed against my chest, her breathing fast and erratic. I turned the key in the lock next to us, but she barely noticed – too involved in her pursuit of getting her hands under my shirt to feel the skin of my back. Once the door was secured, I slid one arm under her and lifted her up so she was straddling my hips and I could carry her over to the huge sofa. I laid her down on the cushions, smoothing her hair back from her face and kissing her softly as I let her take some of my weight, rocking into her again and eliciting more of those small noises from her parted lips. Her hands were frantic now on the buttons of my shirt.

"Ollie, please," she said, her voice hoarse. "I need to see you. I never got to *see* you."

I remembered last time. How she was half-dressed and vulnerable and I, arse that I was, had kept my bloody suit on. I'd thought it gentlemanly at the time, but now I could see that to her it must have looked like I had all the power and wanted to keep it that way. I wasn't going to make the same mistake again, so I reached back and yanked off my shirt in one go.

"Cheese and rice," she whispered reverently as her eyes roamed over the muscles of my chest and stomach. Her small hand came up to trace from my shoulder, down to my nipple and then over my pecs and onto my abs, which flexed at her light touch. I stopped her hand when it came to my belt buckle, and when she frowned up at me, I smiled.

"Baby, it'll be over embarrassingly quickly if we get him involved at this stage."

She pouted, looking adorably put out. "But, I—"

"We'll get to him soon," I said as I lowered myself back onto her again, this time kissing her neck down to her collarbone. "Arms up," I said, and she complied immediately so I could whip her t-shirt over her head. It was my turn to stare then as I traced from her neck over her bra and down to the slope of her stomach. "Christ," I breathed. My hands moved then to her back, releasing her bra and flinging it over the side of the sofa. "Fucking hell."

Just then, I noticed a red mark over her ribs on her side, and I frowned.

"Hey, what's this?"

"What?" she breathed.

"You've got a mark here on your ribs. What happened? Was this when–?"

"Oh, I... er, I think I must have banged my side when I fell in the pool. It doesn't hurt. I promise."

"Fuck, I'm sorry, baby." I traced the mark lightly. "I'm so fucking sorry that–"

"You've really got to..." she broke off as I settled my weight on her again and kissed her neck, "stop." With super-human effort, I pulled back.

"Stop?" I croaked in a hoarse voice filled with need. She frowned up at me.

"Don't stop *that*," she snapped, and I smiled. "Stop *swearing*, you muppet."

I fell back to her again; my skin against hers felt incredible. My lips went to her collarbone now, and she shuddered underneath me. "I've missed you calling me a muppet," I said against her skin as I moved down further. When my mouth closed over her nipple, and she arched off the sofa, I almost lost it totally. Her hands were in my hair, then down to my shoulders, smoothing across the skin as I moved to the other side.

"Oh my God," she breathed as I kissed down her smooth stomach. I undid the button on her shorts and pulled them down and off with her knickers. I felt almost feral as I stared down at her on my sofa. My hands slid down between her legs, my fingers finding her centre until my mouth replaced them.

"Fucking hell."

It was the first f-word I'd heard out of her gorgeous mouth, and it almost made me smile, but I was too intent on what my tongue was doing. I licked the length of her, pushing my tongue inside in a steady rhythm before I moved up to concentrate on her clit. After a minute I increased the pace and she started to stiffen.

"Oh shit, Ollie. Yes, I..." She broke off as I sucked down hard, my fingers pushing in, sending her over the edge. Her thighs squeezed as she contracted around me, a muted scream coming from the back of her throat as she arched off the sofa again.

When I moved up over her, she was boneless, her eyes hazy. I pushed some hair back from her now slightly sweaty forehead, and she searched my face with an almost reverent expression.

"That was bloody brilliant," she said in an unsteady voice, and I burst out laughing. Her smile was lazy as she fixated on my mouth. My laughter died as I moved over her again and kissed her with her taste still on my tongue.

She started moving underneath me again, her hands coming to my belt, but she wasn't getting anywhere. I snapped open the buckle, pulled off my trousers along with my boxers, fished out a condom from the pocket and then rolled it on, fisting my cock as I moved on top of her again. My lips came to hers, and I kissed her more gently this time, trying to keep my savage need to claim her in check.

"Are you sure?" I said against her lips, my voice strained to breaking point.

"Please, Ollie," she whimpered, her hands going to my back to pull me to her.

"Christ, Lottie baby, wait," I choked out. "I need to make sure it's right. I don't want to rush you. I need you to—"

Her hands went to my face which she pulled to hers to kiss me.

"Your Grace," she said against my lips. "Fuck me, right bloody now. Or I swear to God I—" I slammed into her then, knocking the breath out of her as her eyes rolled back into her head.

"Look at me," I ground out, seated fully inside her tight body. She blinked her eyes open, her pupils were huge, her expression wild. "Are you okay?"

I'd been rough; she was so small. She frowned at me as her hands went to my lower back, then even lower.

"I'm fine, Ollie. I *need* you," she gritted out, and that's when my control snapped completely. I hooked one of her legs over my arm as my hips started moving.

"You're mine," I growled. "Say it, Lottie." When she didn't answer, I thrust into her fully and then froze. "Say it," I said against her mouth.

"Ollie, please," she breathed, undulating under me with desperate movements.

"Say you're mine," I repeated ruthlessly.

"I'm yours," she groaned. "I'm yours. Please, I'm—" She broke off as I started my rhythm again. "Oh, God, Ollie." She was clawing at me now as her body tightened around mine. "I'm going to…" she let out a small scream as her back bowed off the sofa.

Watching her and feeling her pushed me over the edge, too, and with a shout, I experienced the most intense orgasm of my life. I collapsed onto her, letting her take my weight for a moment before I pushed up slightly to scan her face.

"Wow," she breathed, blinking up at me, her cheeks flushed, her eyes bright as her hand came up to trace over my face from my temple down to my jawline. My eyes actually started to sting – a totally unfamiliar sensation. But my heart felt unbelievably full as I looked down at her. I'd never felt so strongly for anyone before in my life. And I *knew* it would be like this between us. I'd known she was meant for me from the first time I heard her laugh.

"I love you, Lottie," I said in a hoarse voice, and her eyes went wide as her mouth fell open in shock.

I moved away to deal with the condom, but before she could have any time to think too deeply, I was back and pulling her onto my chest on the sofa, covering us both with the huge blanket from the back of it. I tucked her face into my neck and kissed her hair. I could feel the nervous tension in her again, feel the frantic beating of her heart and stroked her back to try to help her settle.

"I know you don't believe it. I know you don't trust me yet. But I *will* prove it to you. And you *are* mine. You said so yourself."

"Ollie, that was coercion," she snapped but snuggled into me all the same.

"I'm yours as well, you know," I said softly as I kissed her hair again. Her fingers flexed and then relaxed on my chest, but she didn't pull away. "Hayley's too. You're both mine, but I'm yours as well."

"Okay," she whispered, her breath hitching. She kept her face buried in my chest and hidden from me. I didn't say anything when I felt her silent tears on my skin. But I did frown at the ceiling, her words from earlier filtering through my mind:

I know first-hand what happens when people like me don't blend in, when we aren't easy.

I wanted to punch everyone who'd ever made her feel that way, but I knew I'd have to punch myself in the process.

CHAPTER 30

You know your job's secure, right?

Lottie

"Yeah, no, they turned us down," I said to Felix.

He frowned at me. "Why are you smiling then?"

"Am I?" I reached up to my face as if to check.

Lucy giggled from her corner. Since Lucy had taken Felix back, he'd set her up in a corner of his office with a desk for her to write at, but she mostly curled up on the sofa with the many, *many* blankets and cushions he piled in for her there. Felix's office was set at twenty-five degrees, but Lucy still had a thick jumper, woollen socks and at least two blankets over her. To be honest, this was a better solution than the one Felix came up with a few months ago when he super-heated the entire office space for Lucy's benefit. Pete from accounting had to wear actual sweat bands it was so stifling.

Felix crossed his arms over his chest and glared at me. I would have found his glare intimidating before, but now that his girlfriend was one of my best friends and I'd seen how much of a big softie he really was, it didn't have the same effect.

"It makes you a bit of a dick to be beaming away about us losing a massive client to Harry bloody York."

"Sorry," I said, pressing my lips together to try and prevent the smile, but it was a losing battle.

"Oh, pish," Lucy said from her corner. "Let her smile. Who cares about your silly money people? Lottie's happy."

"Lucy," Felix said in a strained tone, clearly scrambling for patience. "They're not *silly money people*, they are billionaire businessmen with serious capital to invest. The ROI for the Stantington group would have been—" He broke off as Lucy yawned, and I stifled a laugh. "You can go if I'm so bloody boring," he grumbled, and Lucy narrowed her eyes at him.

"Fine," she snapped, starting to push her blankets down. Felix's annoyed expression dropped, and he strode across the room to pull them back over her and tuck them into her sides.

"I'm sorry, Luce," he said, contrite now with the prospect of her walking out. "You're right. They are silly money peeps, and ROI *is* boring. Please don't go."

"Be nice to Lottie."

"I am being nice to Lottie," he said through gritted teeth.

"If anyone should understand, it's you," Vicky put in, and we all turned to her. She was sitting in Felix's chair, spinning one way and then the other.

"What do you mean?" Felix asked.

"Well, you smile all the time now too," she said simply. Felix's eyebrows went up. "Because of Lucy," Vicky clarified. "Now Lottie has all the sex and endorphin-releasing activities with Ollie, so she smiles as well. Wow. And here I was thinking I was the one bad at reading people."

"Vicky," I hissed, my cheeks on fire.

"And anyway, Lottie told me that the Stantington Group representative was lying. That's why I didn't encourage them in the meeting or offer them acceptable terms. And look, their stock value crashed about an hour ago. So, actually, even if Lottie was not smiling because of her happy sex hormones, she should be smiling because she stopped us from taking on an unstable, high-maintenance client."

"Just another typical day in the finance world, I see," Ollie appeared in the doorway to Felix's office wearing his own huge smile; my face could have probably fried a full cooked breakfast at that stage. Without pausing to greet anyone else he came straight to me, wrapped his arms around me, gave me a brief but firm kiss and then put his mouth to my ear to say, "I want to hear more about these *happy sex hormones.*"

"Ollie!" I protested, giving him a light shove but his arms remained around me. "You can't just barge in, kiss me and talk about sex hormones. I'm at work."

"Felix does it all the time," he argued. "I've caught him snogging at work twice in the last month, and he's the bloody boss."

"It's true," Lucy put in. "I've given up telling him off for it." She shrugged.

"Lucy, you're not employed here now," I said, finally pulling back from Ollie but he simply took my hand and held it in his instead.

"I *was* employed here, if you remember?" Lucy said. "I was a gloriously bad assistant, and Felix was a totally inappropriate boss – complete HR nightmare."

Felix laughed. "HR loves me now," he said in a smug voice.

"Only because you made all the changes *I* told you to."

It was his turn to shrug. "I am exceptionally good at taking advice."

"God, you're arrogant about *everything*," Lucy complained. "You've even got to be the best at taking advice."

"*Si*, I am."

"Well, *I* can't afford to be inappropriate at work." I tried to keep my tone light, but when Felix's narrowed gaze came to me, I realised that some of the fear may have leaked into it.

"Hey, Lots," Felix said carefully, "you know you don't have to worry, right? We're only joking around. I don't give a shit if your boyfriend—"

"Fiancé," Ollie put in, and Felix rolled his eyes.

"Fiancé wants to be a pest. It doesn't reflect on you, and you know your job's secure, right?"

"Yes, sure, of course," I answered too quickly. Felix crossed his arms over his chest and Ollie gave my hand a squeeze.

"I'm serious, Lots," he said, clearly starting to get annoyed now. "You're one of the most important members of the team."

I sighed. "Okay, Felix. I get it." I resisted the urge to roll my own eyes. I was unqualified for this job. The only reason I was even there was Vicky. My position was in *no way* secure. Nothing about my life was ever secure.

Felix opened his mouth to say more, but Lucy cut him off. "Drop it, Felix," she said in a soft voice, her gaze fixed on me. Luce could often retreat to her own little world, but when she was focused on the world around her, she was surprisingly observant.

"Right, anyway, are we prepping for the meeting now or what?" I put in. "Harry will be here in a minute." Moretti Harding meetings with Harry York were still often tense due to both Felix and Harry leaning towards dickhead tendencies. They got on better than they used to, but they could still rub each other up the wrong way. So invariably I needed to be there to cut the tension, or they wouldn't get anything done.

"Hi all," Harry said as he casually strode into the office, ignoring Felix in favour of making a beeline for Lucy. Harry was a massive L P Mayweather (Lucy's pen name for her fantasy books) fan.

"Harry!" Lucy said, her face lighting up.

"Hey there, little genius." Lucy was still on the sofa, so Harry leaned down to give her a hug and a kiss on the cheek.

"York," Felix snapped. His hands were balled into fists, but he knew better than to drag Harry away from Lucy – he'd had a long period of silent treatment from her the last time that happened. "You can't just bowl about my office like you own it."

"Well, nobody was in the conference room," Harry said, straightening in his own good time from Lucy. "Not my fault if your organisation is sloppy, Moretti."

"Sloppy? Jesus, you're one to talk. The Lexington deal last week was a complete shitshow." Harry had turned fully to Felix now. Both men had their hands on their hips. Things were about to deteriorate.

I opened my mouth to speak, but my phone vibrated against my hip. Frowning, I pulled it out, and my heart sank when I saw the number on the screen. Mumbling to the others that I had to take the call (Harry and Felix were well into their argument now, so they barely noticed), I pulled my hand from Ollie's and stepped towards the door.

"Hello?"

"Ah, Miss Forest." I recognised the school administrator's nasal, superior voice. "I'm afraid there's a problem with Hayley."

"Is she okay?"

"Well, it's quite serious, but obviously, with Hayley's difficulties, it's hard to ascertain—"

"What happened?" I snapped. "Is she okay?" In my panic, I'd stopped walking, so I was still in Felix's office, and my voice had risen to a near shout. I was too worried to notice the silence around me, but I did feel Ollie's large hand on my back.

"There was an altercation. Hayley is perfectly fine – just a few bumps and scrapes. One of the other children, however, has a bloody nose."

I felt like I was going to be sick. "A few bumps and scrapes?" My gentle Hayley had been hurt.

"Yes, she's absolutely fine, but unfortunately, she needs to be collected. She's quite beside herself."

"She's hurt?" My voice came out as a strangled whisper. I couldn't process anything. All this time and effort keeping her safe, and she'd been hurt anyway. I shook my head in denial and I was about to reply when the phone was snatched out of my hand.

"This is Oliver Harding the Duke of Buckingham, Miss Forest's fiancé and Hayley's other guardian. We will be at the school in twenty minutes. Please keep the child safe until we arrive."

"All the children are kept safe here," the officious bitch snapped.

"Clearly not," Ollie said in a low voice, shaky with fury as he hung up on her.

"Okay, baby," he said to me as he turned me towards him by my shoulders. I blinked up at him. My eyes were stinging. Hayley had been hurt. "We're going now." I nodded, still feeling numb with shock. "It's going to be fine. We're going to sort it out. Hayley will be fine."

"Right," I whispered. He nodded, then tucked me under his arm to steer me out of the office.

"Oh, sugar," I said, turning to Felix as I left. "The meeting, Felix, I—"

"Fuck the meeting," Felix said, and I nodded, but my heart sank.

The irony was that the more Hayley needed me, the more I had to flake out on work, but also the more I desperately needed the financial stability of work.

CHAPTER 31

Not for over five hundred years

Lottie

"Obviously, if violence is involved, we really need to see if we're meeting Hayley's needs because—"

"Who hurt my sister?" I said in a low, furious voice. Hayley squeezed my hand, and I looked down at her. She gave me a quick shake of her head, which only infuriated me further – that head shake meant, *don't bother, there's no point*. I clenched my teeth in frustration. Both Hayley's knees were scraped, and she had a bruise blooming under her left eye.

"I don't think that rehashing the specifics is really of any value. The other children involved are—"

"Children?" My voice was rising now. "Multiple children attacked my sister?"

The head teacher shifted uncomfortably. "Well, the other children are *also* injured. I believe it was a playground dispute that escalated and—"

"And how the hell would a playground dispute escalate or even start when my sister *doesn't speak*?" I was shouting now. I knew shouting was counterproductive, but I couldn't help it – these people were supposed to keep Hayley safe.

Playground dispute, my arse. Hayley had been targeted by bullies again. My chest constricted and I started to feel like I couldn't breathe. Then I felt his hand on my back.

"Breathe, Lottie," he murmured in my ear, and I felt my eyes sting but blinked the tears away.

"If we could keep this civilised," the headteacher said, her mouth set in a disproving line. "There's no need for raised voices."

"But you're not *hearing* me," I said through my clenched teeth. "Hayley couldn't have started a playground dispute – she doesn't speak to the other kids. She's being bullied. You're supposed to keep her safe and you're not doing it. You need to keep her safe." My voice broke on the last few words which only made me angrier. I did not want to appear weak in front of these people. I needed them to listen to me.

"Miss Forest," Hayley's class teacher put in. "You have to understand, there are over thirty children in each class and—"

"What is the SEN budget allocated for Hayley?" Ollie's voice was calm but firm.

When we first arrived at the school and saw Hayley, she ran to me and gave me a tight hug. Ollie's furious expression as he looked down at us was so fierce I had thought he might lose his shit there and then. But by the time Hayley had pulled back and looked up at him he'd managed a tight smile for her as he smoothed her hair back from her tear-stained face.

"Don't you worry, stowaway," he'd said, taking her hand in his. "We'll sort this out." Then we'd been led to the headteacher's office by the form teacher and now he seemed to be the picture of calm.

"Er... I'm not—"

He smiled a smile that didn't reach his eyes. "Shall I remind you? Hayley has a SEN budget of six thousand a year. Where was her teaching assistant when this playground incident occurred?"

"She doesn't have a teaching assistant."

Ollie's eyebrows went up in mock surprise. I had a feeling he knew very well that Hayley didn't have a teaching assistant –

something I'd been pushing for months. "What is the money being spent on then?"

The headteacher's face started getting red. "We don't allocate the budget on an individual basis. The money goes into a pot for the whole school, and we can use it according to need at the time."

"Ah, I see, and when has Hayley had a 'need at the time', requiring *any* of the budget allocated to her to be spent on her? Has she had any additional input *at all*? Anything above and beyond the other children to reflect the six thousand your school is given for that very purpose?"

"We are going wildly off the point here," the headteacher snapped. "I don't—"

"It's not fair; we know that," the form teacher blurted out. "Hayley isn't disruptive. She gets on with her work. She's bright. She just…"

"Doesn't speak," Ollie said. "And because Hayley's pain is silent, she doesn't warrant the help that she has been deemed to need? In fact, I would hazard a guess that the money is actually being spent on the children who bullied Hayley today. Am I right?"

The form teacher looked to be on the verge of tears now, and the headteacher's face had paled.

"Excuse me, Mr Harding, but I didn't quite catch your relationship with—"

"The correct way to address me is *Your Grace*, and I'm engaged to Miss Forest. Both Lottie and Hayley are part of my family," he said firmly. His voice lowered then, his next words vibrating with fury. "And nobody fucks with my family, Mrs Franklin."

"Well, I don't think there's any need for that kind of language. I—"

"My language is the least of your problems," Ollie said. "I'm not sure what kind of shitshow you think you're running here, where the level of supervision allows an eight-year-old girl to be beaten up by a group of children – and, as I understand it, this is *not* the first episode of bullying. But I am sure that OFSTED *will* be interested, and I'm also sure that Hayley will never enter this school or be under your care ever again. Good day."

He swept both of us out of the office then, leaving Mrs Franklin and Miss Lever behind with open mouths. There were two boys and a girl outside the office, flanked by their parents. I was happy to see that at least one of the boys had a bloody nose. Good. Just like me, Hayley could be scrappy when pushed.

Ollie stopped in his tracks, focusing on the kids and his eyes narrowed. "You little shits ever bully another kid, and I will know. Understand me? I'll know and I'll rain hell down on you and your families." His gaze snapped to the parents. "Control your children."

We got into his town car in a complete daze. Hayley and I snuggled together on the backseat and Ollie took the one facing us, telling his driver to take us back to his home.

"You will never be hurt like that ever again," he said to Hayley, his voice low and firm. "And if anyone even looks at you wrong, you come to me. Understand? Nobody fucks with us, Hayley. Nobody *ever* fucks with my family. Not for over five hundred years."

I blinked at Ollie but kept my mouth shut. Hayley stared at him, and I knew she could feel the absolute certainty coming off him in waves. She tilted her head to the side and then she did something that made my world explode.

"Okay," she said to Ollie with a firm nod. I stiffened, and my arm that was around her automatically tightened. Ollie's eyes lit with intensity on hearing that one word from my sister, and he leaned forward to take both her hands in his.

"You understand, don't you," he said to her. "You and Lottie are my family."

"Family," Hayley repeated, and then she smiled. And it wasn't one of her small smiles she used to placate me; no, this was a proper happy, teeth-showing beam.

"You're a tough stowaway, aren't you?" Ollie said, ruffling her hair. "I saw that little shit's nose. You got your punches in too, huh?"

Hayley shrugged. "I kicked the other one in his privacies," she said proudly. That explained why the other boy hadn't been able to sit up straight.

"Good. I'm quite sure that his privacies deserved it," he said firmly. "Well, you'll both be having self-defence classes anyway. You can teach your sister some of your moves." I rolled my eyes. "But that will just be a precaution. Florrie will kick any bully's arse in your new school, so you don't need to worry about bullying anymore. That girl rules the place."

My eyes went wide and my mouth dropped open. Florrie went to a private school. An extremely exclusive private school. There was no possible way I could manage those fees yet. What was he doing? And promising that he was our family. He couldn't do that either. It was cruel to do that to a child. Hayley and I weren't his family. And both of us had had too many broken promises to have to deal with another one.

"Ollie, I don't think—"

"Later," he said, glancing at Hayley then back to me. I pressed my lips together and gave him a curt nod.

When we returned to the house, Mrs H was there, and my resilient, brave Hayley was happy to skip off to the kitchen with her for cookies. In Hayley's mind her hero had struck again, and it had only cemented her knowledge that we could rely on Ollie. Once we were alone, I let my anger and fear show.

"You can't do that," I snapped as I spun around to face him in the library. He crossed his arms over his broad chest and fixed me with a patient stare. Ugh, it was so unfair how attractive he was. His blue eyes were burning from his earlier fury, his muscles pulling his suit jacket taut.

"Do what?" he said, and his calm tone only ramped up my anger.

"Tell us we're family. Build up Hayley's hopes."

"You *are* my family."

"No, we're not!" My voice was rising for the second time that morning, but I felt completely out of control. All I ever wanted to do was protect Hayley, but now I'd exposed her to the biggest risk of all. My eyes began to sting, but I was not going to cry in front of him. "It will break her, Ollie," I said, no longer shouting but the unsteadiness in my voice was perhaps worse. His expression softened, and he uncrossed his arms as he came towards me, but I backed away, and he frowned.

"What will break her?" he asked in a soft voice.

"Losing you," I managed to get out past the lump in my throat. "Losing you will break her heart. Last time her heart was broken she stopped speaking. What will happen next time? You *have* to take it back."

He advanced then, ignoring my outstretched hand and pulling me into his chest. I resisted for a moment, but he was so solid against me, his arms so strong.

"You have to take it back," I repeated, even as I let myself sink into him, my hands coming up to grip the lapels of his jacket. One of his arms was wrapped around my back holding me up. The other pushed my hair back from my face at my temple and then kept stroking there.

"Everything's going to be okay, darling," he said, his voice heartbreakingly soft now.

"I can't afford Florrie's school," I said into his chest.

"You won't be paying for the school, Lottie."

"What if she's bullied there as well?"

He sighed. "I know private schools have bullying too. But this would be a fresh start for her, and Florrie would make sure she was okay. It's a small school. She won't get lost there. There are state schools with better SEN provision that would be great, but there'll be waiting lists. This way, she can move immediately. And this is the school the Harding family attend. Hayley won't be any different."

"You can't tell us we're your family." My voice broke as a rogue tear made it down my cheek.

"Yes, I can." He pulled back slightly so that he could look into my eyes. The blue burning even more fiercely now as our gazes locked. "I'm not going to let you down, Lottie. I know that you and Hayley have been let down before. Too many fucking times. But I'm not going to do that. And my word means something. Listen, even if things don't work out between us, which, if I have anything to do with it, they fucking well will, I wouldn't abandon Hayley. I'd still be in her life."

My breath hitched.

"I want to believe you," I whispered, and his arms tightened around me again.

"Then do it. I'm here. You just have to trust me."

I closed my eyes as another tear fell. "They hurt her," I said, my voice breaking again.

"Yes, they did." The fury from earlier was leaking into his tone again. "But believe me, that's the last fucking time anyone ever hurts either of you ever again."

CHAPTER 32

Now you're gone again

Lottie

"Wow, you're learning a lot faster than I did," Florrie said from the side of the pool where she was sitting with her feet dangling in the water. Hayley smiled at her but shook her head, no doubt knowing that Florrie was just trying to make her feel better.

Florrie was good at that – trying to make everyone feel better, looking after other people. She'd been doing it for the last month with Hayley at school as well. Ollie had been right; Florrie *did* rule that school, but only because she was so blooming likeable. And when she'd marched in on Hayley's first day and announced that Hayley was her friend and *just a bit quiet*, none of the kids had said a word about Hayley's lack of speech.

The transformation in Hayley had been tremendous. Even though I'd known about the bullying at her old school, it was obvious that she hid the worst from me – Florrie wasn't the only one who liked to take care of others.

So now, in her new environment, she was slowly coming out of herself. Her new teachers said that she still wasn't talking, but I knew she spoke to Florrie, and last week she'd started to speak to the other kids at break times. Not often, but it happened. They certainly giggled together. A group of them had come over after school this week to Ollie's house and the giggling when I listened outside Hayley's door had been next level. I spent so long listening that Ollie eventually went in search of me, finding me with my ear pressed against Hayley's door and happy tears tracking down my face.

"You are learning fast," Ollie told Hayley firmly. "You'll be a fish before you know it. Now, this time, put your whole face in, kick your legs and swim to Felix. I'm right here. You'll be fine."

Hayley's face set with determination as she gave him a firm nod. When she made it across the whole width of the pool with her face in the water, we all started clapping and cheering. Her head popped up, and she blinked in surprise at the attention, but despite her red cheeks, she wore a pleased smile. She high-fived a grinning Felix, and Lucy sighed from her seat next to mine.

"Felix should always be in tight swim shorts, teaching children to swim and looking like an Italian god," Lucy said.

I laughed, but Vicky frowned in confusion.

"Lucy, that would be extremely impractical."

"Hello, ladies," Mike's deep voice came from behind us, and we swivelled to watch him strolling to the water in his own pair of tight swim shorts. Vicky squeaked. It was an actual squeak. And so un-Vicky like that both Lucy and I turned to look at her.

"Er... Vics, you okay?" I whispered.

Vicky was staring at Mike with the kind of fierce focus I usually only saw her display at work when she was absorbed in her numbers. The only other time I'd seen her this focused on something was when she'd seen a hedgehog in Ollie's garden out in the daytime (apparently that's a bad sign with hedgehogs). She'd stayed up all night to look after it and cancelled all our meetings the next day to tend to it and take it to the local RSPCA rescue centre. Vicky *really* liked hedgehogs. It was almost an obsession. But then again, she really, *really* liked Mike. Maybe even more than hedgehogs.

Men asked Vicky out all the time. Despite her mean-spirited nickname, Ice Princess, and the mutterings I heard behind her back about her being cold and stuck-up, she *was* incredibly beautiful and filthy rich. But she'd never shown even the slightest interest in any man, nothing like the interest she showed in Mike.

"Okay," she breathed. "I can see what you're saying. Your brother should also be restricted to these swim shorts. I can see the logic in this now."

Lucy made a gagging sound.

"Please, no more about my brother. Honestly, Vicky, what do you see in the big lout?"

Vicky's crush on Mike was not a secret. She didn't try to be even slightly discreet about it. Unfortunately, Mike had also made his feelings clear, and it was a big no from him, which was disappointing. But Vics was just not moving on. One of the problems was that Mike still held a grudge against her over how his sister had been treated when she worked for Vicky and Felix. He felt that they didn't protect her when she needed them to. What annoyed me as I watched Mike muck about with Felix and Ollie in the pool (Hayley was now sitting giggling with Florrie on the side) was that whilst Felix had been completely forgiven, Vicky was still given the cold shoulder.

"Uncle Ollie, do the thing! DO the thing!" Florrie shouted, then squealed as he plucked her off the side of the pool, lifted her high above his head and then launched her into the deep end, where she swam to Mike, stood on his shoulders and was launched into the air again.

"Want to give it a try, stowaway?" Ollie asked Hayley, who was watching Florrie with wide eyes. I knew she was scared, but my Hayley was brave. So, so brave. And she trusted Ollie. So she gave him a firm nod.

When he launched her, it was only to the shallow end and much more gently than with Florrie, but it was still a massive achievement for a girl who would never even have considered putting her face under the water a few weeks ago.

We'd been coming down to Little Buckingham for the last couple of weekends. Ollie said it was because the city was "too bloody hot", but I knew he would never have left if it wasn't for us. Hayley loved it here with the ponies and the space. She'd restarted swimming lessons in London, but the vast majority of her swimming progress was made here in the pool with Ollie. My swimming was making much slower progress, mainly because I was too embarrassed to learn in front of other people, so when I was in the pool it was just Ollie and me. The two of us alone together, half naked in warm water meant more time spent fooling around than anything else.

My attention had been on memories of fooling around so I wasn't paying attention to the guys' banter in the pool. But when I heard Vicky's name and she leapt to her feet I frowned. Before I could say anything, she'd shoved one of Ollie's huge t-shirts over her head and practically run off towards the house.

Five minutes later, Mike hauled himself out of the pool, grabbed a towel and stalked off in the same direction. I made a mental note to ask Vicky about it later and considered going after her now, but then the girls' giggling shut off abruptly, and I frowned. Florrie was focused on something behind me.

"Come on, Hails," she said, her expression now grim. "We'd better go and muck out Legolas and Bertie. We said we would."

Hayley looked at her friend and then glanced behind us as well. Now my sister's expression wasn't just grim – it was furious. I turned to see Claire and Blake walking towards the pool. He had a hold of her upper arm. It could have been seen as solicitous to help her across the uneven ground. But as she winced and shook him off, I realised it was anything but. I frowned, my nails digging into my palms.

To be honest, I was really, really hoping that I was wrong about Blake. For once, I wanted my intuition to have failed me.

But versions of Blake had littered my childhood; I knew exactly what he was. My mother's boyfriends may not have had posh accents, but they were the same deal wrapped up in different packages.

My childhood had gone through cycles. Mum would be sober for a few months then I'd notice the smell and her speech would change. Gradually there'd be less food in the house and more men. The men were often nice. One even bought me a McDonalds after he caught me eating frozen peas out of the freezer. But a couple were... not so nice. Luckily, I had really good instincts. I only got backhanded once when I didn't manage to dodge, and I screamed so loudly when one came into my bedroom late at night that the neighbours came round. So I knew a bad man when I saw one. I knew the vibe they gave off, and I knew deep down that I wasn't wrong about Blake.

By the time they reached us, Blake was all smiles and charm. Claire was reaching for her usual bubbly personality but falling short. Something had clearly happened that morning. I was glad Hayley had left with Florrie. The last thing I needed was for her to be around a man like this one. Whilst hugging Claire hello, I glanced at Blake and saw what most people would miss: the slightly bloodshot eyes, exaggerated, jerky movements and the smell. This really wasn't something someone else would notice, especially as we were outside, but I *knew* that smell; I'd lived with that smell – it was like sour vinegar, and as the wind changed direction, blowing his scent across the lawn to me, I almost gagged.

Despite Mum's perfume, no matter how many showers she took, I could always tell if she was actively drinking or hungover. Later, when she got sick, it was an almost sickly sweet smell mixed with the vinegar as she became increasingly jaundiced. The vinegar smell from Blake could just be there from a hangover, but this guy had had a few this morning – of that, I was completely sure. I moved back slightly, putting the sun lounger and small table between me and him. Blake needed to be avoided. There was no way I would ever voluntarily be within grabbing distance of a mean drunk again.

Ollie and Felix had got out of the pool now. Felix went straight to Lucy, making her squeal when he gathered her into his wet body. Ollie was clapping his brother-in-law on the back now and smiling at him. They were talking about a redesign of one of the bars that Blake was managing.

"I trust you with it now, mate," Ollie said. "I know you won't bugger it up."

I pressed my lips together and looked to the side in the direction the girls had gone. They looked over at me, waved, and then darted off. Personally, I wouldn't trust Blake as far as I could throw him. I found it strange that Ollie could be so perceptive about some things, but not this. I always thought Ollie was so different to Vicky, but I was starting to realise that blind spots when it came to reading people might be a common character trait in all three of the siblings. After all, Claire had married this guy, and apparently Florrie's dad had also been a waste of space and barely saw her now.

It was actually Vicky, in this instance, who seemed the most perceptive. She certainly didn't have much time for Blake. But then that may have been because he was unrelentingly crap at his job, and Vicky hated incompetence.

Margot rounded the corner then in her riding gear having clearly come from the stables and walked towards us.

I caught movement out of the corner of my eye and turned to see the girls emerging from the pool house dressed and ready to go. Florrie had pink leopard skin leggings paired with a crop top and a matching Alice band, whereas Hayley was rocking her baggy jeans and Nirvana t-shirt. They both glanced over at us, Florrie whispered something in Hayley's ear and to my delight Hayley whispered something back. In front of everyone and not behind a closed door.

I was smiling when I turned back to the others. I opened my mouth to interrupt Ollie and tell him but caught myself just in time. He was deep in conversation now. Yes, this was momentous to me, but to him... Don't get me wrong, I knew he'd care, just not quite in the breathlessly excited way that I did. So, I bit my lip and held my tongue. Despite my joy at seeing Hayley speak to another child out in the open, I felt my chest compress. There just wasn't anyone as invested in Hayley as me, and it felt so very, very lonely, even surrounded by people.

"I'm just going to go and check on the girls," I said, keeping my voice low so as not to give away my excitement. There were a few muttered acknowledgements, and my chest felt even tighter. I looked down at my feet but blinked as a pair of riding boots came into view in front of me. Before I could look up, my hands were grabbed and I was pulled up into a hug.

"Did you see?" Margot said, her voice breathless and excited as she swayed me side to side.

"W-what?" I asked, hugging her back automatically, even through my confusion. Maternal hugs hadn't been a feature of my life in so long I'd forgotten how good they felt.

"Hayley and Florrie," Margot said, pulling back to look at my face. "Hayley spoke to her. Didn't you see it?"

"Y-yes, but I—"

"Hayley's speaking to Florrie? In front of everyone?" Ollie put in, abandoning his business chat to come over to us. "You saw it?"

I looked at Ollie in surprise. Margot gave my hands a squeeze again. "We both saw it."

"Fan-bloody-tastic!" Ollie said through a wide smile. "I knew she could do it."

"Well, I... she's actually been speaking to her peers for a while now." Everyone had come over to us now. Ollie blinked at me.

"She has?"

I nodded slowly as his wide smile faded to a frown.

"That's why I was happy crying outside her room the other day. I could hear them through the door."

"I just thought you were happy she was with her friends. Why didn't you say anything?"

"Oh... I guess I..." I shrugged. "I guess I didn't think it would be headline news. You guys are so busy, and I just..." Ollie was looking angry now, and he'd crossed his arms over his unfairly muscular chest, which still had some rivulets of water running down it – I wished he'd put a shirt on. It would be easier to think if he weren't half-naked. Especially after the way he woke me up this morning. "I just didn't think you'd be that interested or—"

His eyes flashed as he reached for me, his arm going around my waist to pull me away from his mum. He half carried me off into the pool house, then set me down on my feet, slamming the door behind me.

"Why the fuck wouldn't I be interested in Hayley speaking to her peers?" he asked.

"Ollie, you're really kind to Hayley. I can't tell you how much we appreciate it – how much it means to us. And I know what you said before, but I also know this is still a temporary arrangement. I know you care about Hayley to a certain extent, but you don't have to pretend to—"

"A certain extent?" he said in a low, dangerous voice.

"Yes, well, maybe I—"

"I want to renegotiate the terms of our deal."

"W-what?"

"Our deal. The temporary engagement."

"Er... what, you want to cut it shorter or something?"

Pain lanced through me as I said those words, but if Ollie wanted us gone, then I guessed it was better sooner rather than later. Hayley was already way too attached. And he'd promised to honour the school fees and I believed him. My salary now was significantly higher. We would be fine. We would be better than fine. Why, then, did it feel like my heart had been ripped out of my chest and lay bleeding on the floor in front of me?

"No, Lottie," he said, his voice edged with real irritation now as he stalked forward towards me. "I do *not* want to cut anything short."

A bolt of relief flashed through me so strong my whole body sagged with it and I blew out a breath I hadn't even realised I'd been holding.

"What I want to know," he said as he crowded me back against the door of the pool house, "is why the fuck you immediately jump to me cutting things short and why you think I don't care about Hayley speaking to Florrie which is a *massive* fucking deal."

"You're using the f-word a lot again," I whispered as his arms caged me in, and he leaned his body into mine.

"Fuck right I am," he snapped just before he kissed me. His lips were firm against mine; his warmth and strength surrounded me. I could feel his muscles moving under the warm skin of his chest as I slid my hands up into his hair and opened my mouth under his. Once he'd thoroughly scrambled my brain with that kiss, he pulled back slightly to look down at me, his forehead resting against mine; one of his large hands was holding me to him at my lower back, and the other was in my hair.

Everything about the way he held me was ultra-possessive, almost caveman-like, and so the opposite of the sophisticated, urbane aristocrat that the rest of the world got to see. A wave of absolute desire and need left me feeling almost weak in his hold. My breaths were coming fast as my lips parted. It was the most turned-on I think I'd ever been in my life.

"Did it feel temporary when I fucked you in the shower this morning?" he growled. "Did it feel temporary when I told you I loved you?"

I shook my head, not trusting myself to speak.

"Good. I'll tell Mum to start planning a wedding."

My eyes went wide.

"B-but you don't... I mean... you want me to marry you? For real? Now? Th-th-that's mad."

"You're *going* to marry me, and it's perfectly sane." He was growling again.

"Ollie, are you proposing to me?" my voice pitched high. "If so, I wouldn't say this is the most conventional way to do it."

There was a pause, and then his face relaxed from his fiercely possessive expression to a wide smile, and his hand on my neck loosened. "We'll see."

He brushed his lips against mine then stared down at me again. "For the moment, I'll settle for no more talk about this being temporary – apparently, it makes me a little ragey."

"Okay," I said hesitantly. "If you really mean it then maybe we could ease back on the temporary chat."

"I know I lost your trust, Lottie," he said carefully. "But I care about you and Hayley. I don't know why you didn't tell me that Hayley talks to her peers. But please don't keep things from me, okay?"

I looked up at him and could hear the sincerity in his voice. My eyes slid from his to go down and to the left. You didn't have to be as good as me at reading body language to know I was hiding something.

"Lottie?" He was frowning at me now. "Is there something else you're not telling me?"

I took in a deep breath and let it out slowly. "Your brother-in-law is an alcoholic."

He blinked, and I held my breath. His hand at my back and the one that was now in my hair flexed as he opened his mouth and then snapped it shut.

"Lottie, I... er, listen Blake drinks, but I don't think he's an alcoholic."

I closed my eyes slowly. Ollie didn't realise he was doing it, but he'd withdrawn from me. Walls had gone up. He'd even shifted back slightly, putting physical space between us. His hands loosened on my back, falling to his side and the other hand went from my neck to his. I watched the muscles of his arm tighten as he squeezed. And I immediately regretted saying anything.

But then I remembered Blake's grip on Claire's arm and her wince of pain. Ollie said I could trust him – I had to learn to trust *somebody*. And he'd *promised*.

So I leaned into him, trying to close the distance he'd put between us, and I wrapped my hand around his arm.

"I *know* he's an alcoholic, Ollie," I said firmly. "And I... I just have a bad feeling about him and your sister."

Ollie's eyebrows went up. "A bad feeling? Lottie, you're not giving me much to go on here."

I sighed. "Look, if *I* get a bad feeling, then something is wrong. And Florrie's in the mix. I just—"

But Ollie was already shaking his head. He wasn't going to believe me. "Sorry, darling, I know you have crazy good intuition, but I've known Blake since we were kids. Maybe his drinking is a bit out of hand – I'll have another chat with him about it. But if you're suggesting he'd ever hurt his family, you're way off base. He's been good for Claire. Her divorce was messy, and she was depressed for a long time. Blake really stepped up for her."

"He wasn't drinking alcohol when you were kids, Ollie," I said, desperate to make him understand. "It changes people. Good people. I know you don't think that—"

"Baby, don't you think you might be projecting here?"

"What?"

Ollie sighed, his muscles flexing as he squeezed the back of his neck again.

"Your mum," he said softly. "I can understand why you'd be really sensitive about that kind of thing, why you'd maybe see things that aren't there. But honestly, Blake's fine."

I let my head fall forward onto his chest, inhaling his scent and trying to block out my hurt feelings. I knew I didn't have the right to feel so let down – whatever he said, I wasn't his family. Of course, his loyalty wouldn't lie with me.

"Yes, I'm sure you're right," I said, my voice flat now as I retreated mentally. There was no point arguing my case any further with Ollie. He wanted me to confide in him, but this kind of inconvenient truth was probably a step too far.

"Lottie?" He put a hand to my jaw to tilt my head back, so I was looking at him. He scanned my face, which I tried to blank of all expression. "I know you're worried about this. I'm not minimising anything, I promise. I'll talk to Blake. It's just, I know him better than you."

"Of course," I said.

Ollie growled, and I frowned up at him.

"What?"

"I've lost you," he muttered, scanning my face again. "Fuck's sake. I had you and now you're gone again."

"I'm right here, you numpty." I tried to force a smile, but by the look on Ollie's face, I didn't quite manage it.

CHAPTER 33

Who wants to be normal?

Lottie

I squeezed Vicky's wrist lightly. When she turned to me, I gave my head a very subtle shake. She tilted hers to the side with a small frown, but her mouth snapped shut. Then she turned back to the men in our circle and smiled. They all looked a bit startled for a moment at the abrupt change from Vicky's tirade of information on the financial markets to that smile. We were going to have to work on her transitions a bit more. But at least she'd stopped just in time. She'd lost most of these guys right around the time she started on the economic principle of comparative advantage in trade. But their expressions weren't glazed now. Nowhere near. Vicky's smile, even this fake smile, could bring entire rooms to a standstill. She was simply that beautiful.

I was glad we managed to get her out tonight to be honest. Something was wrong with Vicky and none of us could work it out. Ever since I'd known her she would occasionally go into herself. There didn't seem to be an obvious trigger. Once it was after a phone call she'd had in the office. I'd asked her about it when she went abnormally quiet for the next few hours, but she'd just shrugged and told me it was her mother on the phone. When I'd gone on to ask if everything was okay with her mother, she said it was "fine".

That had been a lie.

I'd been surprised to be honest – Vicky very rarely lied. Ollie said she could occasionally withdraw. The last time it happened was over a year ago. Nobody saw her for nearly a week. Ollie had been distracted by work at the time and never got to the bottom of what happened.

Then a couple of weeks ago Ollie and I had gone to her house after she went AWOL for twenty-four hours, not even calling into work to let them know she wasn't coming in which was so out of character to be alarming. Ollie used his key when she didn't answer the door. We found her underneath a coffee table which for some reason was in the middle of her hallway.

Ollie had to physically lift her out from under it and over to the sofa. She was almost completely unresponsive – just staring off into space. No tears but so much pain behind her eyes it was scary. She'd only started crying when Ollie picked her up and hugged her on his lap. I'd picked up Hayley from school and brought her back to Vicky's house. The three of us stayed with her that night and Hayley's presence seemed to gradually bring her back from wherever she went. She'd recovered since, but she still wasn't herself, and she absolutely refused to tell us what the trigger was.

"I'm sorry, gentlemen," she said in that self-effacing tone we'd practised – Vicky was not self-effacing at all, so that had been a real struggle for her. She really didn't understand the point of it. But I had to explain that if she wanted people on her side, it was one of the tools that needed to be in her arsenal. "I tend to get carried away with economics."

"Money is Vicky's jam," I added with my own smile. I heard a snort from the side. My eyes flicked over to see Mike next to his sister, and I blinked in surprise. I don't think I'd ever seen Mike in anything other than t-shirts, overalls and flannel shirts. Yet here he was in a DJ, his beard under control for once. Rough Mike was attractive, but I could never really see Vicky's outright obsession. But *this* Mike, Fraggle Rock, he was hot. However, he didn't seem too happy in his new get-up. He was pulling at his collar and shifting in his shiny, Italian leather shoes. I knew the Hardings had asked him to come tonight, but Mike was normally consistent in turning down this type of invite.

"Well, I can attest to that," one of the investors said with a smile and an adoring look in Vicky's direction. "The investments you've managed for us have doubled in the last quarter." A couple of the other suits in the circle perked up at that and I smiled. This was perfect. This fundraiser was the ideal environment to plant the seed with Mr Harrington that Vicky was the right choice when it came to his fund. All Vicky had to do was...

"You're wearing a suit," Vicky blurted out, staring at Mike with that focused expression which seemed to be reserved for universal income, hedgehogs and Michael Mayweather. I looked up at the ceiling, seeking patience. *Not now, Vicky.*

Mike's eyebrows went up. "Er... well, yeah. It's kind of required," he said in his gruff voice.

"You never wear suits."

Everyone around us was beginning to look more and more confused. All Vicky's attention was on Mike now as if none of the others were even there. I reached to subtly squeeze her wrist, but she didn't even acknowledge me. Vicky in hyper-focused mode was *not* distractable.

"I prefer you in your normal clothes," she said, frowning across at him. "In particular, I like the thermal shirt you wear that has a small rip in the left sleeve."

"Jesus Christ," Mike muttered, and I didn't think it was possible but the man actually blushed under his beard. Everyone else was listening to the exchange with open mouths. I knew for a fact that over half the men at this function had propositioned

Vicky at one time or another. Most of the time she didn't even realise they were doing it; she'd certainly never shown any level of interest in any man. Her reputation as an untouchable ice princess was legendary.

"Who *is* this guy?" I heard the investor from earlier, who'd made no secret of his interest in Vicky, whisper to his colleague.

"Vics," I said in a low voice, trying to draw her out of her fixation. "We need to keep an eye on the time, yeah? Gentleman, ladies, excuse us for a second." I pulled on Vicky's arm. For a moment, I thought she was going to ignore me and carry on staring at Mike. "Victoria," I snapped, and she blinked before turning to me. "We need to *go*." She nodded, and I breathed a sigh of relief as we made our excuses and left the circle.

"I was doing it again, wasn't I?" Vicky asked in a dejected tone. I winced as I turned us towards the exit. There was a good thirty minutes until the fireworks, but I didn't want to be caught out. We had to leave before the display started. Ollie had been vehemently opposed to Vicky even coming tonight. He knew what could happen. He'd confronted me about it yesterday.

"Lottie, I know Vics has come a long way, but she still shouldn't be going to the gala. I can't look after her – I've got to give the speech straight after the fireworks. She has to leave before then, and she loses track of time, you know she does."

"Trust me, I know Vicky," I said through a smile. "And I think it'll be good for her after what happened last month."

He shook his head. "You've never seen one of her meltdowns. Last month was nothing in comparison. If it happens at the fundraiser, then I don't know what—"

"*Trust me.* I've got it. She wants to go."

He hadn't been happy about it, but I'd kissed him, effectively cutting off his argument as I started unbuttoning his shirt.

"I've never let Vicky down before. I won't do it now," I muttered against his mouth as my hands slid into his shirt. He groaned, backing me up to the bed.

"You have a very effective way of winning an argument, Miss Forest," he muttered against my neck as his weight settled on mine.

That was the last objection he'd officially lodged, but it was clear tonight that he still wasn't happy, despite my repeated assurances on the way here.

Once Vicky and I were around the corner in the corridor leading to the toilets, I turned to her and gave her hand a quick squeeze (Vicky couldn't bear to have her hand held for any length of time, but a brief squeeze with the right amount of pressure was okay). "It's okay, hun," I said in a soft voice.

"It's not okay." Her hands bunched into fists at her sides now. "I'm never going to convince him to sleep with me if he thinks I'm defective."

I frowned. "Vicky, you're not defective."

She stared at me. "Yes, I am. I'm defective and weird."

"Who wants to be normal? What even *is* normal?" I said with a smile, trying to coax her out of this mood. "It's probably blooming boring. I'd rather hang out with you than someone boring. And you are *not* defective, Vicky. Not at all."

I linked arms with her and propelled us to the ladies.

"Why are we going to the toilets?" she asked.

"It's what women do to catch their breath," I explained, and Vicky wrinkled her nose.

"Sometimes I think that the whole world is weird and I'm the only normal one."

I snorted a laugh as we pushed through into the cavernous bathroom. I moved to the mirrors whilst Vicky headed to the toilet.

"You're not even going to try and use the opportunity to empty your bladder?" she asked, completely incredulous and I laughed as she disappeared. Just as the door to her stall closed another opened and Claire walked out.

"Hey," she said as she came to stand next to me at the mirror. "I thought I could hear you guys." Our reflections locked eyes, and she gave me a tight smile. Her eyes were red-rimmed, and her shoulders were so tense they were almost up around her ears.

"Hi, love," I said gently as I pulled out my lipstick, more for something to do than anything. Glancing at her again I lowered my voice. "Claire, are you okay?"

"Of course," she said, her obvious attempt at a bright tone falling flat and the strain around her eyes increasing. I abandoned the lipstick and turned to her fully. "If you need someone to talk to, I'm here," I said quickly, aware that Vicky would be out any minute and Claire would clam up completely. She looked away from me but not before I saw the tears in her eyes that she quickly blinked away. I laid my hand over her arm. "If Blake is—"

"Listen," she snapped, "why don't you pay attention to your own situation and keep your nose out of mine." I pulled my hand off her arm and took a rapid step away. "I know what you told Ollie. Your interference was totally unhelpful."

Her hand fluttered up to the side of her face in an unconscious movement, and that's when I saw it. She'd done a great job with her make-up, you could barely tell, but in the harsh light of the bathroom I could see the darkened area from her left temple down to her cheekbone.

"Oh, Claire," I said, my voice rough with emotion and concern. "Honey, what did he do?"

"Stop it," she hissed just as Vicky was coming out of the stall. "Leave me alone."

"Claire?" Vicky asked with a perplexed expression. "Why have you got a bruise on your cheek?"

Vicky might not have been able to read people's body language, but she catalogued everything about physical appearance in great detail. Claire looked between me and Vicky with a hunted expression, then tore out of the bathroom.

I turned to Vicky and put my hand on her arm. She was looking after Claire with a frown. "Vics, we need to go really soon. Why don't you find Ollie and let him know, and I'll go after Claire." Vicky looked at me for a moment, then gave a sharp nod. She clearly wanted to ask me more about Claire, but she trusted me to sort it out. When we left the bathroom, Vicky disappeared into the crowd towards the bar where Ollie was earlier.

It took me a moment to spot Claire across the room, but as I started towards her, I was hauled back by someone grabbing my elbow. It was so jarring that my head snapped back, and I nearly lost my balance on my high heels.

"Who the fuck do you think you are?" Blake slurred in my ear, and I gagged from the stench of his alcohol-infused breath.

"Get off me, Blake," I said in a low, furious tone. I jerked my arm to dislodge his hand, but he hung on and tightened his grip so hard that I winced.

"Your magical snatch may have my brother-in-law fooled, but I know you're just some fucking townie with a chip on her shoulder."

"Blake," I said slowly as I turned to him and met his red-rimmed gaze with my steady one. "Get *the fuck* off my arm or you'll find out exactly what kind of townie I really am. You might scare your wife, but I've dealt with *way worse* pieces of shit than you in my life. I promise you, you don't want to dance this dance with me."

Blake made a big mistake then – he held on.

CHAPTER 34

My family are none of your fucking business

Lottie

"Ollie came to me about my fucking *drinking habits*. Apparently, you noticed *the signs* or some bullshit. I've been putting the groundwork in on that family for fucking decades. I'll not have some common slut blow it all to hell for me."

"You're the one blowing it all to hell, Blake. You're an alcoholic, and you beat your wife. There are people like you everywhere in every walk of life. Just because you have old money doesn't make your shit stink any less than anyone else's, and it doesn't make your behaviour any less reprehensible than all the other bottom-feeders I've come across in my life."

"You and that nutjob brat need to stay away from my family," he said, and as his grip tightened even more, his spit landed on the side of my face, and he gave another vicious shake before he lifted his other hand, drawing it back.

I actually hadn't thought he would be stupid enough to hit me in public and my shock meant that I didn't quite dodge quickly enough. He didn't manage to make full contact but his fingers did clip my chin.

How fucking dare he?

I'd had enough.

What these people didn't appreciate was that I'd been having to look out for myself since I was ten years old. I wasn't some helpless girl they could push around and backhand. So, I lifted my foot and brought my spiked heel crashing down onto his shin. He shouted out and dropped my arm, which gave me the opportunity I needed. I spun around and kneed him in the balls. He made an almost inhuman noise and went down to the ground.

I'm not proud of what I did next but, in my defence, my chin was stinging and I still had the vision of Claire's bruised face in my mind, with the rock-solid knowledge of how it got there. So, I pulled my arm back so that my palm was up facing my ear and then watched the complete shock on his face as the back of my hand whistled through the air and connected with the side of his face, throwing him to the side until he was lying at my feet. Blake, unlike me, did not think to dodge. I took one casual step forward so that the ball of my foot stepped on his outstretched hand on the floor. When I bent over slightly to put all my weight through that leg, he whimpered.

"If I ever see a bruise on your wife again, I will fuck you up way worse than this, motherfucker," I said in a low voice. "Yes, I *am* a townie. I'm not like the posh birds you're used to. But I'm *not* weak. I've never been weak. You made a mistake thinking the common, agreeable little girl who doesn't swear could be pushed around, but I'm your worst nightmare – a woman who fights back."

When I took my foot away, he scooted back from me, cradling his hand. "You crazy bitch," he breathed through the pain. "You've broken my hand."

I rolled my eyes and smoothed my hair back. His hand would be fine. When I turned, I realised that we'd attracted a fair bit of attention. The people around us were all wide-eyed, some with drinks suspended halfway to their mouths.

"Ladies. Gentlemen," I said, nodding to acknowledge them as I turned on my heel to where Vicky had disappeared. We were cutting it fine now. But as I walked away, looking in the wrong direction, I collided with what felt like a brick wall.

"Hey," Ollie said, his hands coming out to steady me at my elbows. I winced as his hand closed over where Blake had grabbed me. "You okay?"

I opened my mouth to tell him about Claire and Blake, but then his disinterest from the last time came to mind, as well as his loyalty to his family.

"I'm fine. Just looking for Vics."

"Shit, what's the time?" Ollie said, real panic in his tone now. "You said you were going to make sure she'd left."

I bit my lip. We had five minutes to get out of here. Where the fuck was she? My heart felt like it was beating in my throat as I scanned the room. Finally, I spotted her, and I understood why she wasn't already halfway out of the door. There was only one distraction that could have stopped her leaving, and all six foot four of him was glaring down at her across the room with his arms crossed.

"Sugar," I muttered. Ollie turned in the direction of my gaze and swore under his breath. As we both started striding over to them the organiser's voice filled the room.

"So, if we're all ready. It's that part of the evening where you can start oohing and aahing as we light up this entire county!"

Ollie broke into a run, and I followed suit, but my heels and the crowd held me back. With the first bang, Vicky flinched, and her hands went up to her ears. The sky outside transformed into multi-coloured sparkles, the floor seemed to shake with the force of the explosions, and Vicky's hands at her ears started flapping. Then, one of the rockets must have misfired, and it came flying close to the open double doors, sparks from it shooting out into the crowd. It gave everyone a shock, and most people flinched, but Vicky completely lost it.

Mike's arms had uncrossed now, and his frown was replaced with concern as he focused on Vicky. But the Vicky I knew had left the building. This Vicky was terrified.

The crowd had recovered from the backfiring rocket and were now all moving towards the large balcony to watch the rest of the fireworks, so Ollie and I were suddenly cut off from Vicky. That's when the screaming started. I watched as Mike reached for Vicky, but she was half crouched, screaming, hands flapping and totally in her own world of terror.

"Hold her!" Ollie shouted at him. "Mike, hold her!" Mike's eyes snapped to Ollie's as we pushed through the crowd. "Do it, *now*."

Then Mike moved, striding forward to Vicky and pulling her small body into his, encasing her in his strong arms. The screaming stopped, and a gap became clear for me to slip through to get to them. When I arrived at their side, I reached for Vicky's bag, which had fallen to the floor, and pulled out her noise-cancelling headphones.

"Keep firm pressure," I said to Mike. "Don't stroke to soothe her. Just use the pressure. You can sway her very slightly from side to side. But *no* light touch. She can't stand light touch." Mike's face was pale but determined as he gave me a sharp nod. I put the earphones over Vicky's ears as she burrowed further into Mike's chest.

"Give her to me," snapped Ollie as he put his hand on Mike's shoulder.

"I've got her," Mike said firmly, glaring at Ollie. "Why's she reacting like this?"

"She's Autistic," Ollie said, and Mike's head ticked in surprise.

"Why has nobody ever bothered to tell me that?"

I shook my head. "She doesn't want people treating her differently." I bit my lip and my voice was lower when I spoke again. "Especially you."

His eyes flashed as his gaze cut to me.

"Well, what the fuck is going on tonight? You must have known this was going to happen. Why is she even here?"

Vicky whimpered, and Mike shifted her slightly to encase her even further into the hug.

"Lottie was *supposed* to make sure she left," Ollie said through gritted teeth.

"*You're* her brother, mate," Mike snapped, clearly unimpressed.

"Where were you when *your* sister was hurt?" Ollie snapped back, and Mike's back stiffened.

"Look, can we just concentrate on sorting Vicky?" I asked them both. We were now attracting a fair bit of attention. I knew Vicky would hate to be seen like this.

"Right, well, *I'm* going to be the one sorting Vicky out," Mike told us both, and before either of us could say anything, he scooped Vicky up into his arms, holding her tightly into his chest and strode through the crowd towards the exit. Ollie and I followed at pace. Once we were outside on the driveway, Mike didn't even break stride – he went straight to his massive, ancient Land Rover, wrapped Vicky in his jacket, and deposited her on the front passenger seat. Ollie blocked him as he was about to get in himself.

"I'll take her home," Ollie growled at Mike. "You don't know what you're—"

"No, I *don't* know what I'm dealing with because *none* of you fuckers bothered to tell me," Mike's furious voice cut in. "You've dropped this ball, Harding. It was me she wanted to go to in there. Me that she burrowed herself into, and it'll be me that makes sure she's okay."

Ollie glared at Mike, clearly not going to move, but then Vicky's shaky voice piped up. "I'll stay with Mike," she said. Ollie turned to her.

"Vics, I think—"

"Let her do what she wants to do," I said in a firm voice, and Ollie glared at me. "She's her own person, Ollie. She can make her own decisions."

"Fine," Ollie snapped, moving out of the way to let Mike jump up into the driver's seat. "If anything happens to her, I swear to God…"

Mike rolled his eyes and put his arm over the back of Vicky's seat to look over his shoulder and reverse. Vicky blinked as she watched this manoeuvre, and I could see the panic falling away to be replaced by an entirely different emotion. There's nothing quite like an attractive man reversing a car with the arm-over-the-seat action. I suppressed a smile as he swung backwards and then tore out of the driveway.

"I think she's going to be fine," I said to Ollie, my tone light with relief I felt that Vicky had managed to calm down. But when Ollie turned back to me, I realised that a lighter tone probably wasn't advisable at that juncture. His face was white with worry and fury. His fists bunched at his sides. It was the first time I'd ever felt physically threatened by him, and after what had happened earlier in the evening, I took a shaky step back. That look in his eyes was back again. The look he had after I took the money to stay away from him.

"You *promised* to get her out before the fucking fireworks," he said, advancing on me, and putting his hand on my shoulder to turn me towards him.

"Ollie, listen," I said quickly. "Something happened with Blake and—"

"Not this shit again. Honestly, you're *not* blaming Blake for this. I've already fucked with my relationship with my sister and brother-in-law because of your baggage, making you see things that aren't there, and now you're going to blame Blake for not looking after my other sister when you *promised*?"

"Ollie, you don't understand. Blake—"

"Stop it!" he shouted. "I've had enough. You've turned everything upside down with your bullshit. Vicky was *fine* before you came along."

"She wasn't fine. She was frustrated. I've been helping her."

"She didn't need your goddamn help. Look where your *help* got her tonight?"

"Vicky wanted to be out of her comfort zone. She wanted to—"

He interrupted me with a harsh, humourless laugh. "Well, she sure as shit was out of her comfort zone just now. Do you think she wanted *that*? Do you think she wanted everyone to see her meltdown? I told you not to push her so hard. I've been telling you from the beginning to leave her alone."

"I love Vicky," I said in a shaky voice. "I would never do anything to hurt her."

"Too bad. You've done it. So—"

"Listen, she was already upset by your family. If you'd just listen to me, then maybe you could see that Blake and Claire—"

"Stop talking about my family," Ollie's voice was low and dangerous now. "My family are none of your fucking business."

I blinked at him and snapped my mouth shut. There was nothing I could say to that. He was right. His family were none of my business. These people were not my people.

"Yes, of course," I agreed in a toneless voice, then looked down at where he was holding my shoulder. "You can let go of me now."

His furious expression wavered. "Shit, Lottie, that came out wrong. You just…" He blew out a frustrated breath. "You *know* I'm protective of Vicky and I—"

I shook my head. "I said I understand. Now, take your hand off my shoulder."

When he didn't, I decided I'd had enough, and I jerked out of his grip. When he reached for me again, I took two rapid steps back, and for once, thank the Lord, I didn't trip and fall on my arse.

Panic flitted across his expression for a moment before his features hardened with determination. "This doesn't change anything," he said firmly, and I resisted the urge to shake my head.

"Go and check on your sister," I told him, my voice still neutral. He frowned and tilted his head to the side.

"What do you—?"

I closed my eyes and took a deep breath, letting it out slowly. "Just check on Claire, Ollie."

He huffed, looked to the entrance to the event and then back at me, indecision clear.

"Ollie, check on your *family*."

CHAPTER 35

Feudal rule ended four hundred years ago

Ollie

"Your girlfriend is a fucking psycho," Blake slurred as he grabbed onto my arm. I turned to him and blinked.

"What the hell happened to you?" I bit out.

His left eye was swelling, his shirt was untucked and his eyes were red-rimmed.

"That little bitch happened to me." I shook off his hand as panic gripped me, making my chest feel too tight.

"Blake," I said slowly. "What the fuck are you talking about?"

"Your girlfriend attacked me."

I crossed my arms and narrowed my eyes at him. "Lottie is half your size, Blake."

"Yeah, well, she's a townie psycho, isn't she."

My eyebrows went up. "You're telling me that Lottie attacked you totally unprovoked? Is that what you're saying?"

He looked to the side, clearly reaching for the best lie, and then he shrugged. "I told you not to trust her, mate. Some fucking chav foster kid. She doesn't belong in our world."

"Careful, Blake," I warned in a low voice.

"I can't believe this," his voice was rising, his words slurring together even more as he swayed on his feet. "You're siding with that piece of trash? Where's your family loyalty?"

"Blake? Ollie?" Claire's voice cut through the tension, and we both turned to her. She attempted to smile, but it was tremulous and totally fake. I studied her face for a long moment, and then a wave of rage hit me so hard I felt winded.

"Why didn't you tell me?" I asked her in a strangled voice.

"W-what?" Claire said, her fake smile dropping completely as her hand holding her champagne glass shook. I reached up to her face, touching her cheek for a moment before my hand dropped. She had a full face of make-up on, and I would have missed the bruising if I hadn't studied her so closely. I swallowed past the lump in my throat. My sister was hurt, and I hadn't been there to protect her.

I just have a really bad feeling about him, Ollie. I'm sorry. I know he's family, but he's definitely an alcoholic, and I... I don't think he's safe.

Jesus Christ, I was such an idiot. I moved to Claire and pulled her into me, hugging her fiercely as I tried to tamp down my anger.

"Ollie, what the—?" she started to say, but I cut her off.

"I'm sorry you couldn't tell me, squirt," I said in a low voice into her hair. She stiffened in my arms.

"What are you—?"

"Nobody hurts my sister."

"Ollie, that's not—"

I pulled back to look at her face, framing it with my hands. "Nobody hurts you. Understand me?" She shook her head at first, but as she stared up at me, something shifted in her expression. After a moment, her face crumpled, and she fell into me, burying it in my chest, her body heaving with a suppressed sob.

"What's going on here?" Mum's voice cut in, and I looked over Claire's head to see her flanked by Felix and Lucy. Felix was staring at Blake with an absolutely furious expression. I kissed the top of Claire's head and then gently transferred her to Mum's arms.

"Claire Bear," Mum muttered as Claire sobbed on her shoulder. "What on earth—?"

"Claire, darling," Blake said, belatedly moving to comfort his wife, but I stepped in his path, stopping him in his tracks. He swayed on his feet as he stared up at me.

"You hurt my sister."

"What?" his voice rose to an almost squeak, and real panic flooded his expression. "Hurt Claire? That's ludicrous."

"There's a bruise on her cheek, you piece of shit," I said in a near shout, very close to losing it.

He gave a nervous laugh, taking a few steps back, but Felix had moved to block him, giving him a sharp shove back towards me. That was when I noticed him cradling his hand.

"Did that little townie bitch say something?" Blake shouted, his face transforming from fake concern for his wife to absolute fury. "I told you, *she* attacked *me*. Probably attacked your sister as well. I think my goddamn hand is broken, if you care."

"You should be thankful," Felix put in. "Before Lottie got in there, I was about to beat the shit out of you, and I promise you wouldn't be standing there whining about your hand, and you wouldn't be thinking something was *probably* broken. You'd *know* it was, that's if you were conscious."

"What happened?" I asked Felix whilst staring at Blake, who was starting to look left and right, clearly looking for an escape.

"He grabbed Lottie and shook her so hard her teeth rattled," Felix said through gritted teeth. Blake looked really panicked then. "Then he backhanded her. She dodged but I think he might have clipped her."

"That's bullshit," Blake spat.

"It happened really fast," Felix continued as if Blake hadn't spoken. "Before I could get to her, she'd kicked him in the nuts and backhanded *him* like a fucking awesome ninja before disappearing into the crowd – and then you guys were with Vicky."

"Fucking hell," I muttered, feeling like I might throw up. Lottie had been assaulted? And she wasn't even going to tell me that, was she? No, all she wanted was for me to check on my sister. She didn't think I'd believe her. Or maybe she didn't think I'd care. I blinked, and then that red mark on Lottie's ribs on the day she'd fallen into the pool came into my mind, and bile rose in my throat as her words filtered back into my mind:

I didn't trip. Someone jabbed me, and it knocked me off my feet into the pool.

I moved fast then. Blake's eyes widened as I grabbed him by the scruff of his neck, giving him a brief shake to get his attention.

"You pushed her into the pool that day, didn't you?" I said, and when he didn't answer, my voice rose to a shout as I shook him again. "Didn't you?"

"For fuck's sake," he snapped, still faking outraged fury, but the colour had drained from his face. "Why the fuck would I—?"

"She saw right through you. She's always seen right through you. And you hated that."

Blake's eyes darted around the group of hostile faces, and his face twisted into an ugly mask of real rage that I'd never seen before.

"My elbow slipped, okay? It was an accident."

"She could have drowned, you sick bastard."

"How was I to know she couldn't swim? What grown adult can't actually swim?"

"We overheard her telling Ollie that, Blake," Claire said, her voice shaky but stronger than I'd heard it in a long time.

"Shut up, Claire," Blake snapped.

"You motherfucker," I said, advancing on him as he backed away from me. "I can't believe you—"

"She's a fucking cleaner, mate!" he shouted, and the stupid

bastard actually took a swing at me. But he was drunk, his reactions were sloppy and he was fighting someone his own size for a change. I easily avoided the punch, kept hold of his shirt with one hand, pulled my other arm back, and then let my fist fly into his face.

"You'll move out of my sister's house," I said in a controlled voice as he groaned at my feet. "I don't want to see your face *ever* again." I crouched down next to him then, grabbing a fistful of his hair so that I could talk into his ear. "You might have forgotten this, but I own this city, literally. Nobody lays a hand on my family. London is done for you, mate. You can slink off and live on the rest of your trust fund because you'll never work here again."

I let him go and pushed up to my feet. Two men from the event security team had arrived. I nodded towards Blake, who was struggling to his feet now.

"Get rid of him. I want him off the premises and in a taxi. I don't care where it takes him, but he is not allowed back on the property under any circumstances."

They nodded and grabbed him under his arms to start dragging him towards the exit.

"Ollie, listen. I can explain," Blake started shouting as they dragged him away. "It was all an accident. Claire! Tell him!"

Claire was still sobbing on Mum's shoulder.

I knew I needed to check on Claire, but I couldn't get the image of Lottie's blank expression out of my mind. So, I moved to my sister, kissed her on the side of her head and muttered, "I'll be back," in her ear. As I strode across the room, scanning for Lottie's caramel hair and gorgeous dress, a sense of dread settled over me.

My family are none of your fucking business.

My words from earlier filled my mind as I searched. What had I done?

Right, we were in the middle of nowhere. She couldn't have gone far. How hurt was she? I remembered how she flinched when I'd grabbed her elbow, and the nausea started to rise up again. I moved to one of the guys doing the valet parking.

"Hey, listen, I was out here earlier with a woman in a blue dress. Do you know who I mean?"

The man turned to me and gave me a hard stare.

"I saw you, mate," he snapped.

Okay then. He was clearly not a fan of how I treated Lottie earlier. That makes two of us, *mate*. I took a deep breath to tamp down my frustration.

"Okay," I said through gritted teeth. "Well, did you see where she went? I've searched the venue and I can't find her. She doesn't have a car here, so she couldn't have left under her own steam and—"

"Didn't see her," he interrupted, staring straight ahead. My hands went to my hips. This man was bloody well lying to me. I had to admire his balls, but at the moment I just needed to know where my goddamn fiancé was.

"We had a fight, and I'm worried about her, okay?"

He snorted but hid it behind a cough. I narrowed my eyes at him.

"It's imperative that I find her."

"Oh well, if it's *imperative*, then of course I'll help guv'nor."

This fucking guy was taking the piss. He knew where Lottie went.

"Now see here—" I started, but he cut me off.

"You *see here*, wanker," he said, and I blinked in surprise. Nobody ever spoke to me like this. "If your bird wanted to see you, guess what? She would be here seeing you. From what I saw earlier, she won't be wanting that for a good while."

"Do you know who I am?"

He snorted again. "Yeah, yeah – Duke of Fuckingham. Doesn't give you the right to treat women like shit. Feudal rule ended four hundred years ago, about the same time your bullshit titles should have ended. I'm not telling you dick."

CHAPTER 36

Your love is conditional

Lottie

I set a timer.

Once I'd made it back to our old flat (the walk from the underground now felt dodgy, but I had to tell myself to woman up and get on with it – living in a posh area had made me soft) I texted Hayley to make sure she was okay at her grandparents, and locked myself in.

Then I set a timer for twenty minutes. Twenty minutes felt like the right amount of time. Not quite half an hour, but longer than ten. Once the timer was set, I collapsed onto the bed, curled up into a fetal position and I cried. Not the silent way I normally cried either. No, this was wracking sobs, snot, torrential tears – maximum drama.

But when the timer went off, I sat up, wiped my face, forced my hands to uncurl from the tightly held fists they were in and got ready for bed.

The knocking started about an hour later, but fortunately I had earplugs (you needed earplugs to sleep in this block of flats) so I could ignore it.

By the next morning, there were no more tears. Anyway, I couldn't afford to look a mess, not when confronting Hayley's grandparents that evening.

"That's an interesting jumper," Brenda, Hayley's grandmother, said after she opened the door to me. I tried to smile, but when she frowned down at me, I realised it wasn't very convincing, so I gave up.

"Is Hayley ready to go?" I asked in a flat voice.

Brenda surprised me by opening the door wide and gesturing for me to come in. Usually only Hayley was allowed in their inner sanctum. I was treated as an annoying delivery person — someone whom they had to put up with in order to see Hayley.

Well, I wasn't family, was I? So, what did I expect? I almost let out a hysterical laugh as I thought back to all the effort I'd put in with these people — the bright smiles, the cakes I'd baked, the endless attempts to justify my decisions for my sister when I was the one who knew her the best. The delivering of Hayley on Christmas Day at the exact time they specified with a tray of home-baked mince pies, only to receive a tight smile and have the door slammed in my face after they'd ushered Hayley inside.

Not sure where they thought I could go on Christmas Day as I had no car, and public transport was minimal. In the end, I spent three hours freezing my arse off on a local park bench until I was *allowed* to pick Hayley up.

I wasn't their flesh and blood, so I wasn't welcome. I could count on one hand the number of times I'd even set foot in their house.

Loud footsteps thundered down the stairs, and my startled gaze turned in Hayley's direction just in time for her to collide with me like a hug-seeking missile.

"Hey, lovebug," I said softly, getting down to her level to return the hug. When I pulled back slightly to scan her face, my smile froze. "You okay?"

She looked down at the floor and shrugged, totally closed off and not bloody well speaking. When I dropped her off at the start of the weekend Hayley had been happy. What was going on?

"Hayley," Brenda said, her voice strained. "Go and collect your things. I need to have a chat with your sister."

Tony emerged from the kitchen to stand next to his wife.

"Off you go, love," he told Hayley.

Hayley paused for a long moment before she ran off upstairs.

"Why has she been crying?" I asked them once I was sure Hayley was out of earshot.

Brenda's mouth set in a thin line and Tony shifted uncomfortably on his feet.

"We just wanted to plant the seed that she comes to live here, with us. We thought we should explain things to Hayley before the safeguarding hearing in a couple of weeks. She... er, didn't react well."

"I know she was making progress, but after we talked to her, she's..." Tony shifted uncomfortably on his feet, rubbing the back of his neck. "Well, she's not spoken at all since."

"You're joking?" I snapped, and they both flinched. They knew how much progress Hayley had made. She'd actually spoken to them both when I dropped her off yesterday. I rolled my eyes. "Don't worry, I'll fix it." And I would, just like I always did – on my bloody own. "Come on, Hails," I shouted up the stairs.

"We really didn't mean to set her back," put in Brenda. When I looked at her, I could see real regret in her expression. "I-I don't think we realised how much the suggestion of separating the two of you would upset her."

"Well, now you know." I stared at them both with a steady, unsmiling gaze.

Hayley chose that moment to fly down the stairs with her bag in tow and into my arms. She shied away from Brenda and Tony when they tried to give her a hug. Tony cleared his throat as we were about to walk out of the front door.

"Maybe we could come along to one of Hayley's sessions with that chap you mentioned," he said, his voice gruff.

I frowned at him. Brenda and Tony were always firmly anti the treatment I set up for Hayley. They felt that if we *played up* to her condition, it would perpetuate it. Neither of them acknowledged the trauma of her early childhood as a contributing factor.

I took a deep breath and let it out slowly. My instinct was to tell them both to Fraggle Rock off, but how would that help Hayley? *I* might not have extended family, but *she* did. That was important. They were important – part of Hayley's tapestry of support. That's why I'd arranged for this overnight visit despite their recent push for custody. Hayley had been more comfortable with them over the last two months, and I thought it was time.

I swallowed past the lump in my throat.

"Okay," I said slowly. "There's a session on Tuesday. I'll text the details."

"Okay," Brenda said and shocked the crap out of me by offering me a shaky smile.

Hayley didn't say anything on the tube home, and I didn't try to make her. When she was stressed it was best not to force her to speak. It would come when she relaxed enough. All I did was keep my arm around her, kiss the top of her head and tell her that nothing would keep us apart.

Her tense body did eventually relax, and by the time we arrived at our stop, she was fast asleep. She was so dead to the world that I decided to carry her home. Not ideal given our neighbourhood and the amount she'd grown over the last few months. Just as I paused to readjust her in my arms at the top of the tube steps, a large figure came into my peripheral vision and I started in shock.

"Hey, hey," Ollie said, his hands up, palms forward. "Sorry, darling. I didn't mean to scare you." The people-pleaser in me was desperate to ease the tension between us, but I was done being that girl. That girl just got walked all over and her heart broken. So I just pretended he wasn't there.

I started walking, and he fell into step beside me.

"Lottie, I'm sorry. So, so sorry."

"I know you are," I said, pleased with myself at my ability to keep my voice steady. But I'd promised myself that I'd done all the crying I was going to do last night. I'd given myself those twenty minutes, and I wasn't dedicating any more emotional energy to it.

"Okay," Ollie said slowly. "Well, that's great. So you and Hayley can come home?"

It was then I noticed a black car idling next to us at our walking pace.

"Ollie, I know you're sorry," I told him, readjusting the dead weight that was Hayley in my arms as my muscles burned under the strain.

"Let me take her," Ollie said softly, and I shook my head in sudden jerks.

"No," I snapped. "I can look after her."

"I know you can, Lottie, but let me help."

"Just leave us alone."

"You don't have to do everything and manage everything on your own all the bloody time." Ollie's voice was rising with the growing impatience that was pouring off him in waves.

I let out a humourless laugh so bleak it sounded painful even to my own ears.

"I've been managing everything on my own for my whole life. It's not a choice I made, Ollie. I didn't wake up one day and think: hey, you know what? I'd love to just have to knuckle down and make a life for myself and my sister completely and utterly without help. This is the hand I've been dealt, not a choice I've made."

The burning in my arms was so intense now that one of them almost gave out. Hayley slipped down, and before I knew it, Ollie had taken her. Hayley blinked at him sleepily as he adjusted her in his arms. They smiled at each other briefly before she buried her face in his neck and fell asleep again. And throughout all that he didn't even break his stride. Bloody Ollie, looking amazing in his three-quarter length cashmere coat, wrangling eight-year-olds with ease, making my heart ache with how much I wanted him. Luckily, it was only another fifty yards until we reached my block of flats, so I just wrapped my arms around myself, kept my gaze on the pavement in front of me as we walked there.

"I can take her now," I said when we reached the entrance. My arms were still feeling weak but I was sure I could power through. Ollie was staring at the entrance way with undisguised annoyance.

"Lottie," he said, his voice had softened now. "I know you're angry with me but could you please, please be angry with me at my house where I know it's safe."

"Give me my sister."

He sighed but just turned and started up the stairs, taking them two at a time with Hayley still in his arms. That annoyed me as well. By the time we got to my flat, I was wheezing whilst he didn't even break a sweat.

I attempted to take Hayley from him again but he just raised an eyebrow and waited for me to unlock the door. Once we were in, he took Hayley to her room, laid her down on the bed, tucked her in and left us. I smoothed her hair back and kissed her forehead.

"Sleep tight, lovebug," I whispered against her soft skin.

When I stepped back into the living room, Ollie was standing in front of the sofa, his restless energy vibrating throughout the small space.

"Ollie, I'm too tired for any of—"

"Let me look at your arms."

My eyebrows went up. "My arms? What are you—?"

"Please, baby," he pleaded in a tortured voice. "Please just let me look at your arms."

I rolled my eyes and pushed my sleeves up. Ollie scanned me and zeroed in on where I knew the fingertip bruises were on my left arm. With incredible tenderness, as if I was made of glass, Ollie held my hand to lift it away from my body so he could see the darkening, livid, angry bruising that I knew stretched the circumference of my arm.

There was a low rumbling sound, which I realised was an actual growl building from Ollie's chest. The energy in the room changed. It was now electric – fury, concern and a surprising edge of hopelessness that I'd never felt from Ollie before. He swallowed and let my arm lower back to my side but kept hold of my hand.

"Lottie," he said, his voice hoarse. "Baby, I can't..." he shook his head and closed his eyes. "I know sorry isn't enough. I *know* that. I know I've let you down. You don't have to forgive me now, but please, please, will you consider moving back in? I can't bear—" he broke off, and his jaw clenched tight. When he spoke again, his words were softer. "I can't bear the thought of you and Hayley living here."

I rolled my eyes. "We've been here for over a year, Ollie. And newsflash: we were living here during the months when you were an arsehole to me the first time. You didn't care about it then."

I snatched my hand from his and took a step back. Unfortunately, that was the furthest I could get in the small space without tripping over the sofa. His eyes flashed, but he stayed where he was, holding his hands palm up in surrender.

"God, Lottie, don't you think I know that? Don't you think I've thought about that? About what an absolute prick I was."

He took a step towards me, but I ducked under his arm to walk away.

He watched me from across the room with a wary expression, his hand going up to squeeze the back of his neck. Frustration rolling off him in waves.

"I am not staying at your house," I said, my voice as steady as I could manage. "I need my space, and I need to readjust with Hayley. This is not me trying to punish you or any other nonsense. I know you feel guilty, but actually, if you look at this dispassionately, you've done a lot for me and Hayley. So you should just let go of any guilt and move on."

"Move on?" his voice was rising now as his eyes flashed. "I'm in love with you, Lottie. How do you expect me to just move on from that? I'm not here out of guilt, and I don't give a fuck about how much you think I've *done* for you. I had resources, you didn't, end of story."

He threw his hands up in the air, letting out a short laugh.

"What I did for you and Hayley? It's a drop in the ocean compared to what I'm worth. You would have done the same for me twice over if our financial positions were reversed. You know you would have. Because, Lottie…" He took a couple of steps towards me; I backed up against the kitchen counter but that didn't stop his advance, "… you're in love with me too." He kept coming until he was right in front of me.

I blinked up at him, transfixed by the burning emotion in his blue eyes.

"He hurt you," he said in a rough voice and to my complete shock the blue of his eyes went glassy with unshed tears as he tilted my head back to look at my red chin. "He hurt you just like he hurt Claire, and I wasn't there. I didn't believe you."

I couldn't cope with the intensity of his gaze, so I looked away from him when I asked quietly, "Is Claire okay?"

"She…" He sighed. "She will be."

I nodded as I felt his hand go up to the side of my face. I let myself absorb its warmth for a moment as I closed my eyes – just a second of weakness. Then I jerked back. He stared at me before lowering his hand and shoving both into the pockets of his coat. His voice was hoarse when he spoke again.

"Please come home. I love you. I—"

"Stop saying that," I snapped. I'd had enough. "It's meaningless now. You only love me if it serves your purposes – if I'm helping your family, if I keep my unpopular opinions to myself. Your love is conditional. I've had limits and conditions put on love my whole life and I've had enough of it. I'd rather be alone. And right now I want you to leave."

I pulled the ring off my finger and pressed it into Ollie's hand.

CHAPTER 37

One to go

Ollie

I checked my watch for what felt like the hundredth time then scowled at the tube exit again. Where was she?

"Fuck this," I muttered under my breath as I fished out my mobile.

"What?" Vicky answered in her typical blunt fashion.

"Where is she?"

Vicky huffed. "What you're doing is totally illogical. Lottie is a capable human being. She does not need you to walk her to and from the tube station every day."

I looked around at the neighbourhood, seeing the drug deal that was happening across the road, the fight that had started up outside the pub, and I grimaced.

"You don't know what you're talking about, Vics," I said in my best big brother condescending tone – something Vicky had never reacted particularly well to.

She snorted. "I know a lot more than you, considering Lottie is still speaking to me. If you're so bothered, then why don't you just send a car for her every day like you do for Hayley?"

Lottie had accepted the town car for her sister to take and collect from school, but she absolutely would not accept safe transport for herself. It was completely infuriating. The only plus point was that I could actually see her twice a day, even if that meant standing out in the pouring rain just like I was at that moment. At least I had an umbrella, unlike the majority of these poor people.

"Vicky, just tell me if she's left the office yet or not."

"She left at the normal time like she always does."

"Where the fuck is she then?"

"Oliver, why don't you just call her?"

"I can't call her," I mumbled.

"What?" Vicky pressed.

"I can't bloody call her because she blocked me."

"Oh wow, that's... wow. Well, Mike said—"

"Mike said?" I snapped. "When did you see Mike?"

When Mike had taken Vics home that night I'd been absolutely livid. Who the fuck did he think he was carrying my sister out like that and accusing me of being a shit brother? Okay, so maybe he had a point, but he was the one who'd been turning Vics down and avoiding her for the last few months. Suddenly he's her knight in shining armour, when he'd made it clear that he wasn't interested multiple times? I'd had to watch my beautiful sister get knocked back time and time again by that fucking guy. Why on earth was he giving her the time of day now?

"I don't want to talk to you about Mike."

I growled low in frustration. Vicky was almost incapable of lying, so whenever she didn't want to reveal something she'd have to lie about, she simply shut it down. But then I spotted Lottie.

"Crap, Vics, I've got to go. She's here." I disconnected and shoved the phone in my pocket as I jogged along the pavement towards Lottie's retreating back. She was completely soaked, her hair plastered to her face and down her back as she huddled in on herself with her head down against the freezing rain.

When I made it up alongside her I could see the blue tinge to her lips and how she shivered in her thin raincoat. She started in shock when I held the umbrella over her head and the downpour stopped hitting her full force in the face. But when she saw it was me, she just gave me a side-eyed glance and ducked around some people coming the other way, so I was forced away from her across the pavement. I swore under my breath as I shrugged off my coat and wove my way back to her. She was ignoring me still, her shoulders practically up around her ears as I settled my coat over them. It was huge on her and almost swallowed her whole, but I needed to get her warm somehow.

"For Pete's sake, Ollie. Bog off," she grumbled, but it was a testament to how cold she was that she didn't shrug off the coat. I smiled. Okay, that wasn't the most welcoming greeting, but it had been over two weeks since she'd spoken to me at all, so I considered it major progress. My chest felt tight at her turn of phrase – fully back to swear word avoidance.

"I can't *bog off*, Lottie," I told her the honest truth. "I genuinely can't think of you walking home alone through all this shit. It's simply not possible."

"You found it pretty *possible* for the months you thought I was a grasping bitch," she muttered, and I absorbed that as the well-deserved blow that it was. We walked in silence until we got outside her building, and then she turned to me, both of us standing underneath my umbrella – the rain pounding down on it still. She looked up into my eyes and sighed.

"I'm sorry," she said quietly. "I don't mean to keep raking over that old ground. It's unfair. But Ollie, you can't keep this up. Honestly, who's running the Buckingham Empire whilst you swan off to walk me to and from perfectly safe tube stations?"

"Why did you transfer that money back to Mum? Lottie, she doesn't need it. You didn't have to do that."

"You and your family are already helping me and Hayley with the school fees. I've saved what I could since working for your sister. I would have paid it off sooner if I could have done."

"For fuck's sake," I snapped. "It's pocket change to us. Why bother paying it back? It makes no sense."

Her eyes flashed, and she leaned into me slightly. It was the first real emotion she'd shown me for two weeks. My pulse picked up. Anything was better than the indifference and blank stares she'd given me so far. "It might be pocket change to *you*, but it was life-changing to me and Hayley. However, now I don't want to be obligated to you and your family any more than I already am."

I huffed out a frustrated breath. "If I had my way, you'd be more than obligated to my family; you'd be part of it."

She blinked at me. "W-what?"

"The engagement, Lottie."

"The engagement was *fake*."

"It stopped being fake the moment you promised you were mine when I was deep inside you."

"Ollie!" Her cheeks were bright red now as her eyes darted left and right in embarrassment, and I felt my chest fill with hope.

"No, scrap that. All of this has been very *very* real from the first time I kissed you. No! From the very first conversation we had when you told me not to be a dick."

Her eyes flew wide. "Ollie, that was before any of—"

"I know," I said firmly. "I know it was. And I know I've been a relentless prick since then as well, but it doesn't change the fact that you've been mine since that conversation—"

"You can't—"

I took a chance and reached up with one hand to her face, that warm hope in my chest spreading when she didn't flinch away.

"And I've been yours, Lottie. I've been yours, and I always will be. My family is your family. You and Hayley belong to me, and I belong to you."

For a moment I had her. She leaned into me again very slightly, her breath huffing out of her mouth and her pupils dilating as she stared up at me. Then a car horn sounded, she flinched, and the spell was broken. My stomach hollowed out as she stepped back out of my reach.

"I can't let myself believe you," she said in a whisper that I could only just hear over the rain. "It's dangerous for me to…" She closed her eyes, shutting me out. "I can't fall down again. I'm not sure I could get up the next time."

I reached for her again, but she was ready for me this time. She whipped around to the facial recognition lock on the outer door (the one I had put in last week) and disappeared into the building. I stood looking after her in the pouring rain for what seemed like an eternity, but turned around just as the town car pulled up.

"Ollie!" Hayley said as she sprung out of the car. She ran to me, and I caught her up in my arms for a hug. As well as managing to speak more, Hayley was a lot happier to show physical affection with people she trusted, not just her sister.

"Hey, stowaway," I said to her, juggling the umbrella to keep us both dry as I crouched down to her level. "Good day at school?"

"The best! We had Yorkshire puddings!"

"Wow." I smiled. "That *is* a good day. Any day with Yorkshire puddings is a damn good one if you ask me."

I'd been seeing her regularly like this for two weeks. As well as the times when she came over for play dates with Florrie. Florrie and Claire were living with me now, and for the foreseeable future. It all came out after the fundraiser – the alcohol, the abuse. Claire's shock at Lottie seeing right through it all when her close friends and family hadn't suspected anything.

I know Claire had spoken to Lottie and apologised, but Lottie had been adamant that Claire hadn't done anything wrong. She was just pleased that Claire was safe. She told Claire something she said she'd been told as a child, that "everyone has a right not to be scared". My chest felt tight even remembering that there had been a need for somebody to say that to my Lottie as a child. That there had been reason for Lottie to be scared when she was just Hayley's age.

Blake had gone to Alcoholics Anonymous and spent most of his time either begging my sister to give him another chance or begging me to give him his job back. Neither was going to happen. The fundraiser had shocked Claire into action and she'd cut off contact completely. Florrie for her part was more sad about not seeing as much of Lottie than anything. But then she'd not been Blake's biggest fan for a long time.

I think the fact that my dad had been so uninvolved in my childhood allowed me to make excuses for Blake; allowed me to normalise his poor relationship with his stepdaughter. But the truth was that Dad was a stranger to me when he died, and that's not actually okay. I certainly didn't want that type of relationship with Hayley or Florrie.

Hayley tilted her head to the side. "You gonna come up today?" she asked softly.

I shook my head. "I'm sorry, stowaway." She frowned. "We'll get there, okay? Do you trust me?"

"Yes." She answered immediately, no hesitation. That unquestioning trust was precious, and I was going to do everything in my power not to break my promises to her.

"Everything okay with your sister?"

She bit her lip then and looked to the side.

"You can tell me anything, you know."

"Lottie's sad all the time," she whispered. "She pretends for me but..."

She shrugged. Just like her sister, Hayley knew if someone was unhappy. There was no hiding anything from those girls, even from each other.

"She's worried too. My grandparents want me to—" Her voice broke, and I felt a shot of fury.

"They want you to what, darling?" I asked softly, tamping down my anger.

"They want me to live with them. They asked me about it. I want to live with Lottie. I can't be without Lottie." Her voice was starting to sound a little panicked, and I pulled her in for a hug.

"Nobody is taking you from your sister," I said firmly into her hair, pulling back to look her straight in the eye. "You understand me, sweetheart? I won't let anyone separate you guys ever. Right?"

Hayley tilted her head to the side and then gave me a sharp nod. "Right."

One sister's trust secured; one to go.

CHAPTER 38

You're my numpty

Lottie

"It'll be okay, lovebug," I said as I squeezed Hayley's hand. But my heart was sinking as I took in the sheer number of people filing into the room. It seemed as though it was just myself and Hayley against an army. Her grandparents had brought a solicitor with them. That idea hadn't even crossed my mind. A lawyer? I thought we were deciding where Hayley would be happiest? We didn't need a lawyer for that, did we? And for some reason, everyone was invited into the room before us. We were left waiting outside whilst they'd been in there for over twenty minutes. How could they be deciding anything without speaking to me and Hayley? Laura, our social worker, popped her head around the door then and gave us a tight smile.

"Right, you're okay to come in now," she said with a forced, bright tone, and my panic ramped up again.

I'd seen that expression before. It was the expression people used when they had to let you down. I'd been let down a fair bit since childhood, so I knew what the mixture of pity and resignation meant.

Hayley and I followed behind her into the room. Looking at Brenda and Tony there wasn't the normal defiant anger I'd seen from them before. Instead, Brenda was fiddling with her sleeves and looking uncomfortable. Tony only made brief eye contact with me.

"Do you have anyone else with you today?" Laura asked almost hopefully.

I shook my head and was about to answer when the door into the waiting area slammed open, and Ollie stormed through it. He looked utterly panicked, windswept and totally gorgeous. I knew it shouldn't, but at the sight of him, relief, so strong I almost collapsed under the weight of it, swept through me. His eyes flicked between me and Hayley, and I saw the same relief reflected in his expression. He came straight to me, grabbed my hand in both of his, and I felt something slide onto my ring finger. He kissed the side of my head before moving his mouth to my ear.

"Trust me," he whispered before moving back to give Hayley a hug.

"Stowaway! Fancy seeing you here," he said brightly. "Let's get this boring stuff done, and then we can go get pancakes, right? At least you get to skive a day off school."

Hayley smiled for the first time that day and my heart clenched.

"Terribly sorry we're a touch late." I startled at the sound of Margot's voice, as she, Vicky and Claire all crowded into the space then proceeded to hug me and Hayley in turn.

Laura took in my now huge entourage with increasing bewilderment.

"Shall we?" Ollie said smoothly, extending out his arm for Laura to precede us into the conference room.

"R-right," she stuttered. Ollie opened the door for her, and we all filed past him. Brenda and Tony's eyes were wide as they took in the number of people that filled my side of the table. After many previous meetings with just me on this side, they were probably finding the shift in the power imbalance impossible to process.

Denise, the safeguarding lead, cleared her throat. "Okay," she said, using a bright tone to hide her shock. "I knew we were expecting Hayley as well as Lottie today. Hi, Hayley."

Hayley gripped my hand harder but didn't say anything in response, which didn't surprise me – she was now talking to small groups, but this was way too intimidating an atmosphere for her to say anything. I felt a surge of anger that she was even put in this position but tamped it down.

"But I don't think we were aware of the additional support accompanying Lottie today. Shall we go around the table introducing ourselves?"

Once all the introductions had been made, Brenda and Tony were starting to look a little pale. When Ollie introduced himself as Oliver Harding, the Duke of Buckingham, the silence that followed was thick with tension. It was the first time I'd heard Ollie use his title as a weapon since the school incident. His aristocratic tone told everyone in the room that he was the one in charge, that hundreds of years of breeding meant that his authority should go unquestioned. Even in the toughest business negotiations, he'd never sounded quite as commanding.

"Right, okay," Denise said gamely into the stunned silence. "So, if we're ready I'll start. This meeting is to help assess what would be best for Hayley. After speaking to Brenda and Tony I think that it might actually be better to have a quick chat whilst Hayley pops out for a bit with Laura for a hot chocolate, then Hayley can come back and say her bit too. Okay, Hayley?"

Hayley had shrunk into my side, and her grip on my hand was almost painful.

"It's okay, lovebug," I muttered into the side of her head before kissing her on the temple. "Have a hot choccie and then you'll be back in no time."

She shook her head, but then Claire came around to crouch down next to her.

"Come on, sweetheart," she said softly. "How about Vicky

and I take you? I've got some Skittles in my bag. We can sneak them together."

Hayley's eyes flew to Ollie. She pressed her hand to the centre of her chest then to the centre of mine. I had to blink rapidly to stop tears forming. Ollie turned away from everyone in the room as if we were on our own. He pressed his hand to his chest then to mine then to Hayley's.

"I'll look after her, darling," he said firmly. She kept eye contact with him for a long moment before she slowly nodded, let go of my hand and allowed Claire and Vicky to lead her out of the room.

"So, Brenda, Tony," Denise said. "Did you want to start?"

Brenda cleared her throat, shooting a nervous glance at Ollie, who was sitting back in his chair now, giving the impression that he was completely relaxed, but I could feel his coiled tension and razor-sharp focus as he stared Brenda down.

"Well, as I've said before, the child is—"

"Hayley," Ollie said, his voice cracking across the room like a whip. "*Not* the child, Hayley."

"Y-yes, of course," Brenda said, clearing her throat before continuing. "Hayley would be much better off in our care. Lottie's proven she's too young for this type of responsibility. She's not meeting Hayley's needs like she should be. That child still isn't speaking most of the time, and Lottie just lets her get away with it. She clearly needs more boundaries in the home environment. She does not have the resources to adequately support our granddaughter. It's a child looking after a child. Totally inappropriate. And then there's this newspaper article. God knows what she's involved in. Taking a large amount of money for... well, I wouldn't like to say what it was for."

I froze in my seat in shock. It was only then that I noticed the newspaper sitting in the middle of the table. Before anyone could say anything, I flew to my feet and snatched it up.

"Oh my giddy aunt," I breathed as I sunk back down into the chair, staring at the now-crumpled paper in my hand. There was a photo of Ollie and me in the corridor of the fundraiser. He was kissing my neck, my head was thrown back, and my mouth was slightly open. The headline read, "Duke Pays Cleaner Fifty Grand for Services Rendered".

For a moment I felt like I was going to throw up. There was a low ringing in my ears, and all the faces in the room started to blur. Then I felt Ollie's large, warm hand around mine, heard his voice through the fog, and it anchored me into the present.

"Breathe, Lottie," he murmured. "Trust me, remember?"

I took a deep breath and let it out slowly. Ollie cleared his throat and straightened in his chair. I was just about aware enough of my surroundings to notice the atmosphere in the room shift when he started speaking.

"I wasn't aware that the musings of tabloid newspapers featured heavily in discussions regarding custody arrangements for children," Ollie put in smoothly, staring Brenda and Tony down. Tony swallowed, and Brenda's face flushed red. "Mum?" He held up the newspaper over his shoulder, not breaking eye contact with Brenda.

"No problem, darling," Margot piped up happily as she grabbed the newspaper from him, took it to the bin in the corner of the room, screwed it up with undisguised enthusiasm and dumped it inside.

"But seeing as tabloid gossip *has* been brought up," Ollie went on, "we may as well discuss it before moving on to the *real* issues. My mother came to know Lottie and Hayley during Lottie's time in my employ. Miss Lottie Forest took a loan from my mother. This loan was to cover the extra tuition costs for her sister. I believe you have the educational reports from nine months ago describing the recommendations for Hayley? Hayley's school was not able to meet these educational needs. Indeed, her SEN money was never used specifically for Hayley – it was put into a pot with the rest of the specialist funding. This was totally inadequate. Hayley was not making progress, and at that time Lottie did not have the means to fund private educational psychology. The loan she took covered these additional expenses, and it has now been fully repaid. I have my mother's bank statement proving this. My relationship with Miss Forest has nothing to do with any financial transaction between her and my mother."

"I am not in the business of buying women for my son," Margot put in. "As you can imagine, he has always been quite capable of attracting interest from that quarter without my input or any money changing hands."

"Well, I—"

"Let's cut to the chase, shall we," Ollie put in smoothly, his tone turning lethal now as he leaned forward over the table. "Are you suggesting that I paid Miss Forest for sex?"

"Lord Harding," Denise said in a high voice. "I'm sure we don't need to go into—"

"It's *Your Grace*."

"W-what?"

"The correct way to address me is, Your Grace."

"Oh, I just meant that—"

"Do you think I have to pay for sex, Mrs Corbett?" he asked Denise, whose mouth fell open in shock. A snort from across the table drew my attention. Laura's face was bright red, and her lips were pressed in a tight line, clearly trying to stop herself from bursting out laughing.

"I very much doubt it," Denise finally said in a choked voice, and Ollie inclined his head in acknowledgement.

"No, the real question here is why Hayley's grandparents, with the much better *resources* they purport to have at their disposal, did not offer Miss Forest financial help for this extra psychological and educational support for Hayley?"

Tony cleared his throat and shifted uncomfortably in his chair. "Well, we didn't really think that... we didn't know..."

"You didn't know what?" Ollie asked, raising a single eyebrow. "Were you unaware of the extra costs Miss Forest was incurring?"

"We didn't think all that nonsense was necessary," Brenda spluttered, and the room fell silent.

"Did you *read* the educational reports?" Ollie put in, his voice now low and dangerous, real anger bubbling underneath his tone.

Brenda rolled her eyes. "That's all just a bunch of tosh. The girl just needs boundaries. Not some fancy therapy. Load of American rubbish."

At that, I'd had enough. I was going to take my lead from Ollie. It was time to stop walking on eggshells with this woman.

"Because boundaries and emotional unavailability worked so well for your son?" I put in.

"How dare you!" Brenda snapped.

"The reason my sister doesn't speak is not because of a lack of boundaries." I was surprised by how clear my voice was, but this was my family I was fighting for, and I could feel Ollie's hand around mine. I could do this. "It's nothing to do with how *I've* looked after her. She wasn't speaking *at all* when she came to me. She was damaged. Now, why is that?" There was a heavy silence as Brenda looked at Tony, and Tony seemed to shrink in his chair. "Where is your son now?"

"That's not fair," Brenda spat. "If he hadn't got involved with *your mother,* he never would have—"

"I am *not* defending my mother," I said. "Believe me, I will never defend my mother. But *your son* chose to have a child with her, and your son also chose to leave his family when my sister was only five. He left her with an unstable woman who slipped back into alcoholism. Something he knew would happen. He did not ring me to tell me he'd done it. He just left. I was the one to go and check on my sister. *I* was the one who found the flat a complete disaster. To find my hungry sister sitting in filthy clothes, her voice hoarse from crying, whilst my mother was passed out on the sofa. *I* reported it to social services. *I* took my sister home with me, and I looked after her. *I* jumped through all the hoops I had to in order to foster her. *I* pushed and pushed for psychological assessments when she stopped speaking. And, by the way, she may have stopped speaking to other people, but she *never* stopped speaking to me. I comforted her at our mother's funeral. I've been there for her since she was a baby, unlike your son and the both of you."

"We couldn't see her when she was with your mother," spluttered Tony. "She was completely unreasonable, and we didn't approve of any of her—"

"My mother was not a reasonable person," I said. "Sober, she was a very difficult woman. *Very difficult*. Drunk, she was hell on wheels. She consistently let me down, neglected me and emotionally abused me. However, she was deemed responsible enough to retain custody of my sister after she was born. At that time she was sober, but I knew that wouldn't last. So, *I* made sure I maintained a relationship with her. I did this to look after my sister. The alternative was estrangement, and where would that have left Hayley? Did I have to jump through my mother's hoops? Yes. Would I have walked through fire for my sister? Also, yes. The fact is that both of you washed your hands of my mother and, in turn, your granddaughter for years."

"It appears to me that the only adult to have put Hayley's needs first in all of this is Lottie," Ollie put into the silence that followed. "You've made it clear how much you dislike Lottie. Yet she *still* facilitates your relationship with your granddaughter. She still brings Hayley to see you. She even brought Hayley over for Christmas Day last year. Didn't she? She trekked all the way out to your house on public transport on Christmas Day."

Brenda and Tony started to look uncomfortable at this point. I wondered where Ollie was going with this.

"Did Lottie spend those hours in your house also?" Ollie asked, it was then I caught the shot of white-hot anger running through his tone.

"No, of course not," Brenda snapped. Tony looked down at his hands.

"Do you know where Lottie spent the three hours that Hayley was with you?"

"How is that any of our business?"

"Did Hayley ask you if her sister could come too?"

Brenda looked away at that. "I don't remember."

"It was below freezing on Christmas Day last year. Did you know that?" Ollie turned to me. "Lottie, where did you spend those three hours?"

"In the park round the corner," I said.

"Right, because everything is shut or fully booked on Christmas Day, isn't it?"

"We should have asked the girl in," Tony blurted out. "Hayley begged us, and we…" He looked up at me then. "I'm sorry, love. We should have asked you in. We should have—"

"Tony, for God's sake," Brenda snapped. "What are you doing? She's nothing to do with us! She's—"

"She's Hayley's sister. Bloody hell, woman. Can't you see what he's trying to point out to us? She's *family*. Maybe not by blood, but we should have treated her like family. We didn't deserve the effort she made to include us in Hayley's life."

A hush fell over the table, Tony's words still hanging in the air, and for a moment no one spoke. Then, at last, I broke the silence.

"Apart from your attitude to her therapy, you're good grandparents to Hayley," I said eventually. "Of course I wanted you involved in her life. The more family she has, the better."

Brenda shocked me then when her eyes filled with tears. "Oh," she managed before she turned onto Tony's shoulder and started sobbing.

"Er… right," Denise said, sounding unsure. "So, I'm not sure if we should—"

"I'm sorry," Brenda interrupted, her gaze fixed on me, completely ignoring Denise. "Your young man is right – Tony's right. We should have treated you like family, and we didn't. We lumped you in with her, and we were so very, very angry that…" She started crying softly again.

"The last weekend we had Hayley, we upset her so much that she stopped speaking again," Tony told everyone. "And we're sorry. We thought Lottie was part of the problem, and we were too blind to see what was really going on. Of course, Hayley should be with Lottie. We're sorry that we suggested separating the girls."

"Okay," said Laura slowly. "So what custody arrangements are we going to have moving forward? I see there were concerns here about lack of support and stable home?" Laura glanced briefly around at my entourage and hid a small smile. "I'm not sure that is a *huge* concern. Wouldn't you say?"

"Accommodation-wise, Hayley and Lottie can choose between my three UK residences, my villa in Tuscany, my apartment in New York or my chalet in Verbier," Ollie said. Laura snorted again but managed to smother it with her hand. He took my hand in his, lifted it to the table so that the ring was showing, catching the light from the bulb overhead.

"I have also secured another rental property in Kensington. It's a garden flat which we are due to move into in two weeks," I told them.

"You aren't living together?" Laura asked with a confused frown.

"I am not a married woman yet," I told her. "Until that time, we will have our own property separate from the Buckingham Estate."

Denise sighed, slammed her file on me and Hayley shut with a decisive thump and turned to stare at Brenda and Tony.

"I deal with a lot of child protection cases," she told them. "Our caseloads, as you can imagine, are unbelievably full." Her eyes flashed. "I'm sorry, but this is beginning to look like a waste of our time. Is it really your assertion that this child is unsafe in the care of her sister?"

Tony looked down at his hands, and Brenda swallowed as she met Denise's furious gaze.

"Are you in contact with your son currently?"

Both Brenda and Tony shook their heads.

"Other children? Other family?"

Another head shake.

Denise cleared her throat. When she spoke again, her voice was softer. "Might I suggest then that a better plan would have been to make room in your family for not only your granddaughter, but also her sister?"

The silence stretched out after that statement until Tony looked up and caught my eye.

"Sorry, love," he said in a quiet voice.

I felt my eyes sting but blinked to clear them as I gave him a small nod of acknowledgement.

Denise sighed then went out to fetch Hayley and Claire back into the room. Before anyone had a chance to speak, Hayley stood up and slammed her little hand down on the table.

"I live with my sister," she said in a loud, clear voice which carried around the room. A tear did slip down my cheek then. It was partly pride, partly relief, but primarily pure joy. For Hayley to stand up and speak to a room full of adults was something I would never have thought possible a few months ago. "We are the *Sister Team*. I'm gonna let Ollie, Claire, Vicky, Margot and Florrie on our team. Oh! And Lucy, Felix, Mike *and* Legolas. It's a big team now. Granny and Grandpa, you can join our team too if you want, but not if you're going to be mean to Lottie. No mean people are allowed on the Sister Team."

"We're not going to be mean to your sister, love," Tony said softly.

Hayley crossed her arms over her chest and narrowed her eyes at him and Brenda. "You've been super mean to her before. You say you love me, but there's no me without Lottie. So you hafta love her too."

Brenda stood up and walked around the conference table to get to Hayley. When she reached her, she crouched down to her level.

"I'm sorry, darling," Brenda said softly, pushing Hayley's hair back from her forehead and behind her ear.

"We'll do better, love," said Tony, who'd come around to stand next to his wife.

Hayley tilted her head to the side and hesitated for a moment before she took the step forward into Brenda's arms. Brenda's breath hitched as she hugged Hayley back, her eyes screwed up, a tear leaking down her cheek and a fierce expression of relief on her face. When Hayley was transferred to Tony's arms, Brenda turned to me.

"I was wrong," she said, her voice stiff despite the tears now free-falling down her face. She swallowed. "I'm sorry."

Tony and Hayley had separated now. Everyone seemed to be holding their breath as Brenda and I stood watching each other. Then Brenda did something I would never have expected. She grabbed me into a hug. It took me a few seconds to work through my shock and hug her back, but I managed it.

"You kept her safe," Brenda said, her voice now broken with her sobs. "You were just a baby yourself, and you kept her safe."

"It's okay, Brenda," I muttered, completely overwhelmed. Then Tony hugged me as well, talking about how he was a "stupid bugger" and how sorry he was.

"Right, well, that sorts that," Denise said as Tony and I separated. Her voice was thick, and when I looked at her and Laura, there were tears in their eyes.

"Wonderful," Margot put in. "Well, if that's all wrapped up, might I suggest lunch at The Ivy? Ladies, you're welcome to join us."

Laura smiled. "I must say I have never had one of these meetings conclude with an offer of lunch at such a fancy restaurant!"

"Darling, their salmon en croûte is to die for."

Denise laughed. "We've another meeting, so we'll have to settle for a pasty from Gregg's, but thanks."

We all filed out of the building. After the last emotionally charged hour, it was more than a little awkward. I'd assumed Tony and Brenda would rush off, but the biggest surprise of that day was yet to come. Because once we were on the pavement, Tony moved to Ollie and put his hand on his arm.

"I... er, well—" He broke off to clear his throat, clearly working up to something. After a moment, he puffed out his chest. "Lottie doesn't have other family so—"

"Yes, she does," Margot interrupted. "We're her family."

"He's not married her yet," Tony put in and Margot pressed her lips together in frustration. Tony turned back to Ollie, his face set with determination. "What I mean to say is that we're her family now." He looked away for a moment, clearing his throat again. "Y-you should know that I won't have some rich fly-by-night messing her about. I know you've upset her. Clearly, she's let you off the hook, but we'll be watching you now too. So your intentions better be honourable."

I blinked in shock. How had we gone from Tony looking at me as if I was dirt on his shoe to him blasting Ollie in case he might *mess me about*?

There was a pause. I thought Ollie was going to let rip at Tony again. But instead, his expression softened. "Okay, consider me thoroughly warned. And, just so you know, I might have let Lottie down before, but that is not going to happen again. I love her and Hayley very much."

Tony swallowed and gave him a sharp nod.

"Right, we'd best be off," Brenda said into the uncomfortable silence.

"Of course not," Margot put in, linking her arm through Brenda's. "There's lunch to be had. We'll all be going together, then we can talk about you and Tony popping up to the country estate next month."

Everyone started walking down the pavement with Tony and Brenda swept along for the ride. I was having trouble keeping up, what with going from the fear of this morning, to the shock of the entire Harding clan showing up at the hearing, to the relief that Hayley wasn't going to be taken from me, to the utter mind-boggling shift from Brenda and Tony being my enemies to them wanting me as their adopted granddaughter. And then there was Ollie…

"Bringing the entire family might have been overkill," I told him as he took my left hand in his, holding it firmly. We were both at the back of the group. Hayley was walking between Claire and Tony, Vicky was walking with the dowager and Brenda.

He shrugged and grinned down at me, totally unrepentant. "I didn't want there to be any doubt in anyone's mind who you and Hayley belonged to."

I rolled my eyes. "I haven't agreed to anything yet."

"But maybe you'll give me a teeny, tiny, wafer-thin chance?"

I bit my lip, looking out onto the road and thinking back over the last few weeks. Ollie walking me to and from the flat. Him keeping his promise to Hayley. Showing up for me today with his family in tow. And, I mean, the sex from before wasn't half bad either… Okay, sue me! Any woman would have to factor that in – look at the man, for Fraggle Rock's sake.

"Maybe, just a wafer-thin one," I said softly.

He jerked to a stop.

"Ollie?" I said in confusion, turning to him. His expression was fierce as his hand went up to the side of my face.

"D-do you mean it?" It was the first time I'd ever heard this man sound anything other than supremely confident and it was that thread of hope in his voice that made my heart swell. It was like I could feel some of my broken pieces fly back together, and the numbness seeping away. "Lottie, baby. Do you mean it?"

"Yes," I whispered.

His eyes closed slowly as he rested his forehead against mine and breathed out a long, relieved breath, totally ignoring the London pedestrians streaming past us on either side.

"Thank fuck," he said, his voice rough with emotion as he pulled me into him in a fierce hug, kissing the top of my head. "I love you. You know that right? You know how much I bloody love you?"

I smiled into his chest. "Of course I know it, you numpty," I said as I pulled back slightly to look up into his eyes that, to my shock, were glassy with unshed tears.

"You're right. I *am* a numpty."

"Well, you're *my* numpty. Because I love you too."

One of his hands went around my back, the other slid into my hair, and right there in the middle of one of London's busiest streets, right in the middle of the day, the Duke of Buckingham kissed me.

There were of course paparazzi, but Ollie knew that, and he didn't give a Fraggle Rock.

EPILOGUE

Because that was family

Lottie

"Posh people are weird," Hayley whispered, and I gave her a fervent nod. We both had black circles all over our faces from burnt corks and we were watching Bertie, one of Ollie's many cousins, do his forfeit, which consisted of running five times around the outside of the house in his underwear (no mean feat considering the size of the country pile). It was below freezing and Bertie did not appear to be in the best shape. We both followed his progress as he streaked past the vast living room windows, with only the smallest union jack pants barely covering his modesty.

Apparently this was what happened at Christmas in posh houses. You exchanged gifts in the morning – most of them homemade and all of them under a fiver. You ate a huge amount of turkey, watched the King's Speech of course, and then spent the rest of the afternoon playing games, hence the black circles and streaking cousin.

Other than the huge game of Twister spread out on the floor and the karaoke machine, I suspected most of these games would have been played by this family for hundreds of years. We'd been eased into this last year. At that point, we still weren't living with Ollie full time, much to his annoyance.

But I had to take the time to trust him again. Plus, I'd taken a six-month lease on the flat. I wasn't going to lose that money, despite Ollie grumbling that I "didn't need the bloody money" and he'd "buy the bloody flat if I was that worried about it". He blustered about whilst I serenely ignored him until the other flat in my building was burgled, and Ollie declared the area "practically a ghetto" (we were in Kensington near him, so that couldn't have been further from the truth).

But he begged me, Claire begged me, Florrie begged me and then, finally, Hayley begged me. Hayley never asked for anything, and seeing as she was asking for something I wanted, I decided to give it to her. So, we moved in. Claire and Florrie were still living there then. By this stage Blake was out of the family home, but she still preferred to live with Ollie for now. The divorce was finalised now. Blake leaking that story about me and Ollie to the press had just firmed Claire's resolve to get him out of her and her family's lives as soon as possible.

I hadn't realised how worried Claire was about the living situation until she asked me if they were intruding in my home. *My* home. Totally confused, I'd told her this was the Harding family home, and for someone who rarely lost her temper, she really went nuclear. Ollie and his family did not like me suggesting Hayley and I weren't part of them.

Six months after I moved in, we were married in Little Buckingham church. Hayley, Florrie, Vicky, Claire and Lucy were bridesmaids. Legolas broke into the church and ate my bouquet (well, the official story is that it was a break-in – Hayley and Florrie had been asking for weeks if he could be an honorary groomsman, and he was wearing a bowtie in his mane, so I had my doubts).

Felix offered to walk me down the aisle, but in the end, I decided to walk on my own. After all, I'd been looking after myself all my life – no reason not to do it down the middle of a church with my head held high.

Ollie hadn't even let me walk the full length of it anyway. His eyes lit as soon as he saw me in the lace gown I'd chosen with Lucy and his sisters. I only got about halfway before he'd had enough. He strode down the aisle, snatched me up into a hug, kissing me in front of all the guests. The rest of the walk to the altar was with my hand in his as he propelled me forward with me only just able to keep my balance on my heels.

The vicar raised his eyebrows. "We haven't got to that part yet, young man," he told Ollie.

"Sorry, old chap," Ollie said with his standard charm. "But this one has kept me waiting for long enough. Needed to make sure she made it up here."

When it came to the vows, we said all the traditional ones, and then Ollie surprised everyone by calling Hayley over to us. He took one of her hands in his, keeping one of mine in the other and crouched down to her level.

"Hayley," he said, smiling at her. "I know I'm marrying Lottie today, but I want to make some promises to you too, okay?"

Hayley nodded, her eyes shining as she looked at this amazing man. He took a deep breath then he blew our world apart.

"I promise to love you even when you eat the last of the Nutella," he started, and Hayley giggled with the rest of the church. "I promise to keep telling rubbish jokes to embarrass you in front of your friends for the rest of your life."

"Oh great," groaned Florrie, sparking more laughter from the congregation.

"I promise I'll love you bigger than the whole sky," he said in a softer voice, his hand taking her hand to her chest covered with his, before moving them both to the centre of his chest. "I promise that you, your sister and I will always be a team. And Hayley, my little stowaway, I promise I'll never let you go."

Hayley lost her battle with tears then, along with most of the congregation, as she flung herself into Ollie's waiting arms. The rest of the ceremony was performed with Hayley on Ollie's hip and me tucked under his other arm. The picture I had blown up for our kitchen is that exact pose outside the church with Ollie smiling a massive proud smile into the camera like he couldn't believe his luck, me beaming up at him from under his arm, and Hayley's smiling face tucked into his neck.

"Oh balls!" Claire shouted as her plate spun off her egg. Plate spinning on hard-boiled eggs was another posh-people parlour game that I was struggling to understand. "Lottie, it's your turn."

I'd never thought Claire was particularly quiet, more subdued, but I was coming to realise that she was just as loud and out there as her daughter. Clearly Blake had been holding her back. After their divorce came through last week, she'd seemed even lighter. She'd stopped asking if we wanted her to move out after I told her very firmly one evening, "Claire, Hayley and I have had *years* of being a small family of two. We made it work, but you could never understand how much it means to us to live with family. And for Fanta's sake there's still more bathrooms than people in this joint!"

As I was spinning a plate on an egg, not something I thought I would ever need to be doing in my life, Hayley tugged on my sleeve.

"Is it time yet?" she whispered. I looked up at Brenda and Tony, who were across the room, having their faces covered in the cork soot as well, and lifted the envelope that Hayley had passed to me. Brenda nodded, and Tony took her hand, giving me a smile and a thumbs-up.

"Yes, lovebug," I said. "Let's do it." I grabbed a champagne glass and tapped it with a spoon I'd swiped from earlier to get everyone's attention.

"Hey, everyone," I said, feeling a bit unsure now that everyone was silent. I forced a smile and cleared my throat.

Ollie frowned at me from across the room. He could tell my forced smiles from my real ones.

"So, Hayley has something to say. She wanted to say this herself, but as you know, her voice isn't the loudest, so if we could have a bit of quiet just for a couple of minutes, we'd be super grateful."

Ollie's long legs had eaten up the distance between us, and he was now by my side when Hayley got to her feet.

"Hi," Hayley said in such a small voice a few people had to lean forward to strain to hear her. My heart felt like it was in my throat. "I wanted to give Ollie my present and…" she trailed off, then tugged on my hand. I leaned down to her, and she whispered in my ear. "It seems a bit silly now. Is it silly?"

My throat closed over, and I took her face in my hands.

"It's not silly, lovebug," I said fiercely. "Nobody will think that. Least of all, Ollie."

"What's going on?" Ollie said, worry in his voice now. "Hails? You okay, darling?"

Hayley squared her shoulders and turned to him, losing the nerve now to address the entire room.

"I wanted to give you a present, but maybe it's a bit silly," she said in a small voice.

"I would never think that anything you give me is silly, stowaway," Ollie told her, crouching down to her level.

Hayley ducked her head and looked down at her feet as she handed the envelope to Ollie. He took it and ripped it open, then looked it over briefly. When he realised what it was, his eyes closed for a moment, and when he opened them, the expression on his face was savagely beautiful.

"Hayley," he breathed before pulling her in for a hug, the papers clutched in his hand.

"You don't think it's stupid?" Hayley whispered in his ear, and he pulled back slightly to rest his forehead on hers.

"No, sweetheart," he told her. "This is the best present I've ever had in my life. It's anything but stupid."

"What is it?" Claire shouted. Standing up from her game of Twister with her hands on her hips.

"Mum, you numpty," Florrie said in her patented exasperated tone. "Those are adoption papers. Hayley gave Uncle Ollie *her*. Gosh, you adults are so dense sometimes."

"Brenda and Tony managed to obtain the consent we needed."

They'd finally tracked down their son. It had broken their hearts, but he'd been only too happy to sign away his parental rights.

"We'll be her legal guardians together," I told Ollie hesitantly, and he transferred his fierce expression to me. Lifting Hayley in his arms between us, he wrapped us both in a hug.

"There's another present," I whispered in his ear. "But not for another seven or so months." He froze, his shocked eyes flying to mine before a massive smile took over his face and he lifted us both off our feet and spun us both around as if we weighed nothing at all. Hayley and I squealed, and everyone there clapped and cheered.

And that photo, snapped by Margot, who, despite being in floods of tears still knew a good shot when she saw one, went next to our wedding shot. Every morning, I'd drink my tea from my fancy cup and stare at those photos. Most mornings, when Ollie would catch me doing it, he'd kiss me back to the present, drawing disgusted groans from Claire and the girls.

Because that was family.

You wound them up, you drove them crazy, but, above all, you loved them.

BONUS EPILOGUE

Found my voice

Ollie

"Margot bit me!"

I looked down at Theo's unimpressed face and then over to Margot's cheeky one.

"Margot, honestly," Lottie whispered, glancing nervously around us and giving the other parents apologetic smiles. Lottie had never quite got the memo that the Duchess of Buckingham does what the fuck she likes, and she doesn't have to apologise to anyone, even if her kids *are* biting each other. "You're eight years old. You shouldn't still be biting your brother. Can't you behave for the next thirty minutes? Just until after the speech."

Margot huffed. "Snitches get stitches," she muttered darkly to her brother. "I didn't bite him that hard *and* he's got a jumper on. Legolas bit me on the arse last week, and I didn't cry about it like a little bitch."

"We've talked about this, Margot," Lottie hissed through gritted teeth. "You cannot swear in public."

Margot's eyebrows went up. "Since when is arse or bitch a swear word?"

"Oh my God," Lottie muttered, sinking further down into her seat in embarrassment. The marquee they'd set up in the school grounds was packed with hundreds of parents, and we were right at the front of the audience.

"I have to agree with my granddaughter there," Mum put in from the other side of the kids. "I really don't think arse or bitch are swear words, darling."

Lottie rolled her eyes. "The trouble with you posh people is that you don't live by the same set of rules as the rest of us commoners."

"You're hardly a commoner, Lottie," Mum told her with a frown.

Lottie sighed. "I'll always be a common—"

"You're a bloody duchess is what you are," I told her firmly, taking her hand in mine and giving it a squeeze. "*My* duchess. So you can say whatever the fuck you like."

"Ollie!" she whisper-shouted. "You're not helping, you know?"

I turned to her and smiled. When she focused on me, her expression went from pissed off to that slightly dazed look she still sometimes got when I turned on the charm at close range. She closed her eyes for a moment, clearly trying to shut me out and reclaim her cross mood, but I couldn't have that. So, I lowered my head to close the short distance between our mouths and I kissed her.

"Ugh, gross," groaned Theo in a pained voice. "Margot? Bite me again. I need the physical pain to distract me from the emotional distress of watching this disgusting PDA."

I pulled back to smile down at Lottie's stunned face again, then, without looking away from her, my hand flew out to hold Margot back from her brother and hug her into my side.

"There'll be no more biting, darling," I said as Margot cuddled into me, and I squeezed Lottie's hand.

Lottie swallowed, pressing her lips together to stop herself smiling back at me.

"Can we just behave like a normal family for the next thirty minutes?" she snapped, the reluctant amusement on her face resetting to her previous panic. She squeezed my hand back so hard my knuckles cracked.

"It's going to be okay, baby," I whispered in her ear. "Hayley's got this."

She hummed, biting her lips and nodding her head slowly as she stared up at the stage. I could feel the tension and worry rolling off her. She'd been working herself up all week about this, but I knew my little stowaway could do it. Hayley could do anything.

"If I could have everyone's attention," Mrs Bramell, the headmistress said into the microphone in her standard commanding tone that made the whole place fall silent. "So it's the end of another academic year, and, sadly, we have to say goodbye to our wonderful Upper Sixth. I've been so proud of this year's group of young people, and none more so than the exceptional young lady who's about to come up to the stage. She has been a pleasure to teach, excelling academically, socially and on the polo field. But her finest qualities are her quiet strength, her kindness and her absolute determination. It was that determination that led to the new initiative we've put in place, offering free school places to children in care. I have to say that there was resistance to such an ambitious plan from the board of governors and myself, but to be honest, we were steamrollered. In our defence, I challenge anyone not to give in to the unstoppable force that is Hayley and Florence Harding."

"We love you, Mrs B!" Florrie shouted from the side of the stage, and a ripple of laughter went through the crowd.

"Yes, thank you, Florrie," Mrs Bramell said in a long-suffering tone. "Now, if I could welcome to the stage our head girl, Hayley Harding."

Hayley stood from her seat on the stage, pushing her caramel curls behind her ears as she smiled at Mrs Bramell and made her way to the lectern with her head down, amidst polite applause from the audience. When she stopped behind the microphone,

I saw her take a deep breath in and let it out slowly before she looked up at the crowd.

"That's it, stowaway," I muttered under my breath. "Just like we practised, darling."

She scanned the crowd once and then froze, all the colour draining from her pretty face.

"I-I..." She broke off and closed her eyes tight.

Count to five and start again. Come on, Hayley.

Lottie tensed beside me, rising slightly out of her chair and I gave her hand another squeeze to tell her to settle. Hayley's big rugby-playing bastard of a boyfriend also half rose out of his seat on the stage, a frown on his face as he watched Hayley struggling. I caught his eye and shook my head once. His jaw clenched in frustration, but he sat back down as he bloody well should.

"I'm not a massive fan of public speaking," Hayley's voice cut through the tension in the room. Her eyes were still shut, but after a moment she swallowed once and opened them to scan the audience again. When her gaze fell on us, some colour returned to her cheeks, and I let out a breath I hadn't realised I'd been holding. I gave her a smile and a nod which she returned subtly. Her voice was stronger when she spoke again.

"In fact, I wasn't really a fan of speaking at all a few years ago. But I was lucky. I had a sister who wouldn't give up on me, and she found a man who wouldn't give up on either of us. My family is everything to me. But some people aren't so lucky. Everyone deserves a chance. If it wasn't for my family and this school, I don't know how I would have found my voice, and I hope in some way this initiative will help other kids to find theirs." Hayley paused to take in a breath and that's when the applause broke out, the entire marquee erupting into joyful, noisy support. Margot, spitfire that she was, wriggled out from under my arm and jumped up on her seat.

"Yeah!" she shouted, punching the air. "Go, Hayley!"

Theo followed suit, putting his fingers in his mouth to let out a loud whistle.

That seemed to be everyone's cue to stand as they continued to clap, and Hayley blinked in shock at the audience's response. She smiled a shaky smile and took a small step back from the lectern before turning to Florrie and gesturing for her to come up to the front. Florrie smiled and bounded over to Hayley, throwing an arm around her, pushing her back to the lectern and taking hold of the microphone.

"Right, you lot," she said into it. "Hails hasn't bloody finished yet, so settle down."

The applause died down enough that I could hear Hayley's laughter and, just like it always did, it made my fucking day. Florrie shoved the mic back at Hayley and tried to head back to her seat, but Hayley grabbed her hand, keeping her there. Then she looked straight at me.

I laid my hand on the centre of my chest.

She laid her hand on the centre of hers.

Her eyes filled with tears, and I could feel my own sting.

Then, my strong little stowaway, she blinked them back.

And she finished her speech, with her hand in Florrie's and her eyes on her family.

The End.

Read on for Florrie & Jonah's story.
Exclusive paperback content.

FLORRIE AND JONAH

Too much

Florrie

"Oh no," I groaned. "Who invited his grumpy arse?"

"Florrie," said Hayley in a warning tone as she turned to follow the direction of my gaze. "He works for the Buckingham Estate, just like everyone else here."

I rolled my eyes. "He'll bring down the mood. No one wants his stick-in-the-mud, holier-than-thou, rule-following, curmudgeonly arse here. I want everyone to have a good time. Him glaring and stomping about is going to give the whole event a shonky vibe."

As if Jonah could tell I was talking about him, his gaze snapped to mine across the room. And just like that, I was hurtled back to being that sad, lovesick sixteen-year-old who thought she'd never seen anyone or anything more beautiful than Jonah Grayson. Even back then, when he was a fresh-faced twenty-six-year-old straight out of law school, he'd had this aura of power, competence and sharp intelligence, which put everyone else in the room at a disadvantage. Couple that with his tall, well-built frame, his dark brown eyes and thick dark hair, and I was a goner.

My uncle Ollie had always had a knack for picking the best people to work with, hence Jonah rapidly rising through the ranks and now being the main legal counsel for the Buckingham Estate.

Even scowling and far away, he looked so unfairly gorgeous that a wave of irritation washed over me. Screw him and his perfectly tailored suit. Jonah lived in suits, the stuffy bastard. He probably even wore them when he played football every Saturday with Uncle Ollie, Uncle Mike and Felix. (I knew I shouldn't be as familiar with the man's hobbies and movements as I was, but he was my addiction, and I was clearly a masochist.)

From the first moment I met Jonah, all I'd wanted to do was rip that suit off him and crack through his ultra-serious persona. In fact, at the time I'd seen it as something of a challenge. That was, until I was put in my place on my seventeenth birthday. Nobody had ever made me feel quite as small as Jonah Grayson had. No one had ever knocked my self-confidence as badly.

Before that night I had been employing my tried and tested flirting techniques with him. They worked well enough with the boys at school, so why not Jonah Grayson? When he was at Buckingham House for business meetings, I made sure to be in my tightest activewear, flirty little dresses, short denim skirts or any of my other myriad of revealing outfits, which I knew drove normal human males to distraction. It wasn't completely out of the ordinary for me to chat to Uncle Ollie's employees when they came over. Okay, so *maybe* serving them their tea, cracking jokes and just *happening* to be doing Pilates in the library when they walked in wasn't all totally organic. And *maybe* I looked at Jonah more than I should have done and occasionally leaned over him further than was strictly necessary. But I didn't deserve his vicious put-down that night of my birthday.

It had been the first time I'd really ever tried alcohol, and the two glasses of champagne I drank went straight to my head. So when I saw Jonah I threw myself at him, kissing his cheek to say hello, and smiling brightly up at him with my body pressed against the length of his. For a moment, I thought I had him. His gaze had dropped to my mouth, and something dark passed through his expression. But then he shook his head to clear it, took me by both my arms and set me firmly away from him.

"Don't do that again," he clipped, his northern accent stronger in his anger. "You're a spoilt brat, used to getting your way in everything. Prancing around Buckingham House in your little outfits, driving everyone insane. But you won't have your way with me. You're too bloody much, Florrie. That's what you are: *too much*."

He stormed away then in a cloud of his self-righteous anger, leaving me standing in the middle of my own party, feeling like a stupid child.

I think it hurt me even more because deep down I had a small inkling that he might be right. I *was* too much. Up until then I hadn't necessarily thought or considered my over muchness. I mean, at school I was popular. At home, my family, although admitting I had a lot of personality, never made me feel like that was a negative thing.

For a few weeks after my party I had actually tried to tone myself down somewhat. Finally Hayley had snapped and demanded to know what was the matter with me. Hayley rarely demanded anything, so it had been a bit of a shock.

I'd asked her if she thought I was *too much*. She was furious, wanting to know who had said that to me, fully ready to go on a Hayley Rampage to defend my "bloody brilliant personality", as she put it. I refused to tell her who said it, but I think she may have eventually worked it out. She knew about my crush on Jonah and my subsequent unexplained hatred of him.

The truth was, I was ashamed. I didn't want my best friend in the whole world to look at me differently, to think that maybe I *was* a bit much. But then Hayley's absolute fury that *anyone* could *ever* suggest anything of the sort, and her insistence that I go back to full-power Florrie restored some of my confidence.

Okay, so my personality wasn't everyone's cup of tea, but I couldn't change who I was. So I went back to being unapologetically me again, but I still resented those weeks I wasted attempting to tone myself down.

What I found particularly unfair about the whole situation was that I *still* could not find anyone as attractive as I found Jonah Grayson. Even now, as he scowled at me across the room with that hint of disdain in his expression, there was no one else who made me feel almost dizzy with desire. No one else who made my hands shake with the adrenaline that flowed through me when I saw him. It was really bloody annoying.

I smoothed down the tulle of my skirt and straightened my shoulders. When I looked back up, there was still disdain in his expression, but one side of his mouth was very slightly quirked up. Great. He was laughing at me, laughing at my outfit, which no doubt he also thought was *too much*. I mean, it wasn't exactly subtle. My dress was strapless, bright pink and had a sequined encrusted bodice with a full tulle skirt coming out from my hips. Anyone who stood too close to me was actually involved in my outfit. I'd paired it with four-inch heels which, due to my pipsqueak stature, were absolutely necessary. They were also bright pink.

He was in all black. Even his shirt was black.

Ugh, it's not a funeral, mate.

At least he wasn't wearing a bloody tie.

"Condescending prick," I muttered under my breath.

"How do you know he's being condescending?" Hayley said. "You've only seen him across the room. You haven't even spoken to him yet."

"I can tell from his face. Right, come on. I'm not going to let him drag everything down. I've got a party to organise."

I looked across the room at Auntie Lottie, who was standing without a drink in her hand.

"Gosh, there're a lot of people here tonight," Hayley said, and I could hear a thread of uncertainty in her voice. Hayley was much better than she used to be, but she was never going to be comfortable with a ballroom full of people. This was not her natural habitat.

Luckily I had a plan. I always had a plan. And all six-foot-four of him was walking in through the side entrance.

"Look who's here!" I said brightly, linking my arm through Hayley's and leading her over to where her boyfriend Marcus was standing.

Marcus, like me, was almost pathologically social, and, also like me, adored Hayley. Truth be told he'd adored Hayley for years. All it took was a little push from me and now look at them – happy as clams, as he tucked Hayley under his massive arm and kissed the side of her head.

"Right, kids," I told them both. "Stay out of trouble. I've got some sorting to do."

As I moved through the crowd towards the bar, I could feel his eyes on me, and I wished he'd bugger off. Unfortunately, the party coordinator I needed to speak to was within a few feet of him. I gritted my teeth and powered through. There was no point wimping out now. I was not a wimp. Hardings were tough. So I pasted a smile on my face and stepped forward.

"Hi, Lawrence," I said brightly through a smile.

"Lady Harding. Everything okay?"

"Lawrence, please. I've told you, it's Florrie. Everything's great. Your staff are an absolute credit to you. The only slight adjustment would be that the duchess needs non-alcoholic drinks. They should be circulated first to her. No alcoholic drinks should be offered to her, especially *not* wine. She can't tolerate the smell of alcohol."

"Ah, right. Yes. Sorry, my mistake."

"No problem at all. Like I said, you're doing a super job."

I aimed my smile at him full beam. As a general rule, if I wanted to get my way, I unleashed my smile. I'd been doing it since I was a toddler.

Just then, one of the waiters came past with a tray of mushroom-topped blinis, and I stepped into his path with another smile.

"I'm *so* sorry," I said, as he looked down at me with a slightly dazed expression. "Actually, there is a guest who's allergic to mushrooms. Could you do me a *huge* favour and please take this back to the kitchen and inform the other wait staff of the problem. Thank you so so much. I really owe you a massive debt of gratitude."

"Y-yes, Lady Harding," he breathed, still looking dazed. "Right away."

"Oh, you are the most *wonderful* man."

I heard a cough which sounded suspiciously as though it was disguising a laugh from Jonah's direction but decided to ignore it.

"Florrie?" I turned at the sound of my cousin Margot's voice, and looked down to where she was tugging on my skirt.

"Yes, darling?"

She bit her lip and my heart sank. Margot Harding biting her lip was not a good sign.

"What have you done?"

Her eyes narrowed at me, and her hands went to her hips. "Why does everyone always think it's me? I haven't done anything. It's that stupid boy"

"Okay, what has he done?"

She sighed dramatically. "I'd better show you."

I considered getting Hayley, but she was totally engrossed in her boyfriend. Uncle Ollie was right across the room talking to some of the Estate farmers, Auntie Lottie finally had a drink she could enjoy and Mum was laughing with Callum. I made it a rule never to interrupt my mum laughing, especially not with her husband. Mum being happy was one of my greatest triumphs since I'd been the one to engineer that particular relationship in the first place. She deserved to be happy. My mum had had enough bullshit to last a lifetime.

So I followed Margot through the ballroom and out of the double doors onto the lawn on my own. It was dark now, and the lawn was soggy from the earlier rain.

"Bloody hell," I muttered as my pink heels sunk into the ground. "Margot, honestly, I don't think this is—"

"Should I get Mum?" she asked as I wrenched my heel free of the mud, but I shook my head. Auntie Lottie had been stressed about this event for weeks, I was not going to have her traipse out into a soggy lawn when she needed to be entertaining her guests. Being the duchess was stressful enough as it was. My job was to make sure that everything ran smoothly and that she didn't have to worry.

That was my job with everyone, really. I just wanted everyone to be happy.

"Over here," Margot called, and I trudged after her across the lawn until we were standing under one of the huge oak trees.

"Well?" I asked, yanking my heel out of the soft grass again.

"Look up." Margot was pointing into the branches over our heads. And there was an upside-down Henry Moretti.

"Oh my God, Henry!" I shouted. "What the hell are you doing?"

"It's all right, Florrie," said Henry, fairly nonchalant for someone hanging upside down from a branch suspended high enough that he'd definitely break his neck if he fell. "I'm fine. Just sort of stuck."

"What do you mean you're stuck?" I cried in horror. "You're upside down!"

"Yeah, well, I know I'm upside down. I was *meant* to be upside down. It's just, now I can't really get right side up."

Visions of Henry falling out of the tree and breaking his neck filled my mind, and without any further thought, I kicked off my shoes, tied my hair back, shoved the tulle of my skirt into the tops of my hold-ups and grabbed onto the tree.

"Hurry up, Margot. Give me a boost," I said as my foot slipped across the slippery surface of the wood. "Come on!"

"Er… Florrie. I don't think…"

Just then a large hand clamped around the top of my arm.

"What the hell do you think you're doing?" that familiar voice snapped, and I tore my gaze away from an upside-down Henry to a furious-looking Jonah.

"What does it look like I'm doing?" I snapped back. "I'm going to save Henry before he falls and breaks his neck."

"You will do no such thing," he said, but I wrenched my arm away from him and started climbing anyway. Years of know-how of this particular tree worked in my favour, but unfortunately I hadn't factored in how slippery the bark was from the earlier rain, or the fact I was in stockings and not trainers. So when I lost my footing, my leg slipped, slicing over a branch, and then I fell backwards.

I braced for impact, but instead of hitting the ground I was caught in a pair of strong arms and then held against a broad chest. Jonah looked down at me, I looked up to him, and it was like time stood still. I could see every one of the thick eyelashes framing his beautiful brown eyes as his pupils dilated. I could see the muscle ticking in his jaw as he searched my face. Christ, for such a grumpy arsehole, he certainly smelt good.

"Hey, people!" Henry called, breaking the spell. "I'm still stuck up here upside down, you know."

Jonah blinked and set me down on my feet away from him like I was an unexploded bomb before clearing his throat.

"You're not going up there," he said to me and then turned to see Margot scrambling her way up the tree instead. He plucked her off and set her down on the ground with a long-suffering sigh.

"Neither are you, Margot," he said firmly.

"You're not the boss of me," she snapped as she rolled her eyes.

"You Harding women are impossible," he muttered under his breath.

"I can't just leave him up there," I protested.

He huffed and shrugged out of his jacket.

My mouth went dry as I saw the way his shirt clung to his muscular torso. God, a physique like that was wasted on this man. A breeze blew across the lawn then and I shivered. Before I knew what was happening, he was right there in front of me, throwing his jacket around my shoulders and then pulling the lapels together at the front so that it completely enveloped me.

With him that close and his gorgeous, fresh Jonah smell even stronger now, I almost felt weak at the knees like some sort of pathetic romance heroine. Margot gave me a well-deserved look of disgust, and I shook my head to clear it. But before I could shrug off the jacket, Jonah had spun around to the tree and started to climb.

"Be careful," I said, telling myself that I was concerned purely for the potential legal case against the Estate should Jonah fall and decide to sue. "This old girl is tricky if you're an inexperienced tree climber."

"I've climbed a fair few trees in my time, Florrie," he grumbled, making surprisingly good progress up into the branches.

"You surprise me," I called back through a strained smile. "I would have thought you were born in a three-piece suit and answering legal questions. I doubt you had time for climbing trees as a little boy."

"A lot of things about me would surprise you, Florence Harding," he told me as he reached Henry. "Right, I'm going to lever you up, mate, and then you're on your own, once you're right-side up."

Using one hand, he pushed Henry effortlessly up onto the branch above him. And then they both started to climb down. I bit my lip. Okay, I definitely wouldn't have been able to manage that with my puny upper body strength. Henry and I probably would have both broken our necks by now.

When they made it to the safety of the ground, all Jonah got in terms of thanks was a brief "cheers, mate" from Henry as he and Margot ran off, no doubt to create more havoc elsewhere.

Oh, God, now I'd have to thank the man myself.

"Uh, yeah, so thanks for that," I said then narrowed my eyes at him. "What are you doing out here anyway?"

I started to take his jacket off, but my breath caught in my throat when he stepped forward into my space to secure it back across my shoulders. He looked me up and down and then frowned when he looked at my leg.

"You're hurt." The way he said those two words was strange, as if me being hurt was an unimaginable, terribly horrific event. I glanced down at my leg and winced. There was a long scratch with blood trickling down through my stocking, which was now shredded on my thigh.

"Bollocks," I muttered.

"You never should have tried to climb that tree," he snapped. He was still in my space, still holding onto the lapels of his jacket, which was around me.

I rolled my eyes. "I'd have been perfectly fine. I'd have made it up there eventually–"

"You would not have been fine. You're so reckless."

"I'm not reckless!"

"Why didn't you go and find Ollie or Lottie or your mum or stepdad or *anyone*? Why did you have to just go and sort it out yourself? Why are you always looking after everyone else?"

"They don't need the stress. This is a massive event and—"

"Which you organised."

"Yeah, *I* organised it. So if there are problems, *I* can sort them out."

"A kid being stuck upside down in a tree is not a problem related to organising the event. It's not something you need to solve on your own."

"I want everyone to have a good time. I don't want them stressing about bloody Henry. He's always getting into one scrape or another."

I stepped back from him, not willing to endure another lecture. He kept hold of his jacket, so I simply ducked down and out of it. When I glanced down at the blood, which was already drying on my leg, I decided I didn't want to waste any time on it. So I started to pull the tulle back out of the tops of my stockings. Meanwhile, Jonah stood holding his jacket, his eyes laser-focused on the tops of my thighs as I completed this inelegant manoeuvre.

"Get a good enough look?" I snapped. His eyes went straight up to mine then and two flags of colour appeared high on his cheekbones. Good, I embarrassed him. Maybe now he would bugger off.

The skirt came way past my knees so the scratch was completely covered.

"This'll be fine." I slipped my shoes on and then started to turn in the direction of the party, but I froze in shock when his hand closed over mine. Hand holding was not in our repertoire of interactions.

"You're just planning to waltz back in there?" he said, giving my hand a sharp tug to pull me towards him. "You're not going to see to your leg?"

"It's a scratch. Jonah. I've had way worse injuries from climbing trees before."

He blinked at me. "You could get tetanus and die," he said.

Ugh, he was such a pessimist. He was the same way with the Buckingham Estate, always looking for problems, always looking for things that might go wrong. I was the total opposite, a complete, unadulterated optimist.

"I've got to get back to the party, you numpty. I'm not buggering about with my leg. I don't have time."

"You bloody well are," he said.

"I bloody well am not."

I yanked my hand from his and started stomping across the lawn. Unfortunately, I forgot about my heels and that stomping wasn't really an option when you were wearing four-inch spikes on your feet on muddy ground. When one of them sunk into the grass I nearly toppled over, and then I was in his arms again.

"What are you doing?" I said as he hoisted me up against him bridal style.

"You are not leaving that leg to fester," he snapped and simply started stalking across the lawn in the opposite direction of the ballroom, towards the service entrance.

"What's my leg got to do with you?"

"It has everything to do with me, Florrie," he snapped. "I'm going to be looking after you."

"You have absolutely no—"

"You look after everyone else all the time, and you never think about yourself. Ever," he bit out, and I snapped my mouth shut. "I watched at Hayley's twenty-first when you didn't even eat *one bite* of food. I watched you run yourself ragged for your family. I watched you make everyone feel comfortable. Even when that total dickhead kept cornering you, you didn't tell your uncle or stepdad. *I* was the one who had to punch that git in the face."

"What?" I whispered. I wondered why Piers had a black eye and an attitude change the next time I'd seen the sleazy bastard. There weren't any more boob grazes and cornerings after that incident.

"So I'm going to be the one to look after you now. I'm tired of watching you look after everyone else, no thought for yourself. Now you could get tetanus or an infection in your leg; anything could happen. You don't think through the consequences."

He strode with me into the small side kitchen of Buckingham Manor, which was much cosier than the main kitchen where all the catering stuff was, and put me on the warm wood table.

"Jonah, really, this is completely unnecessary," I said breathlessly. "I don't know what's got into you."

"*You've* got into me," he snapped as he went into one of the cupboards and grabbed a first aid kit. Bloody hell, I hadn't even known we had a first aid kit in there. But that was Jonah, the ultimate in practical resourcefulness.

"Listen, I don't know what you're doing, but I'm leaving." I started to shuffle forward to the edge of the table in order to jump down, but he lifted me by my hips and placed me back again.

Then suddenly, I was looking up at him, my hand on his chest which was rising and falling rapidly with his heavy breathing as he stared at me. His hands were on each side of my hips. And he was *so so* close.

"Oh my God, you're almost painfully beautiful," I whispered.

He froze. Shit. I closed my eyes, as that feeling of shame washed over me. The last time I'd thrown myself at this man, he'd made me feel about two inches tall.

"Forget I said that," I said frantically.

Jonah wrenched back from me and started fiddling with the first aid kit. I looked at his large, tanned hands. They were shaking slightly, and I frowned.

"You need to pull your skirt up," he said, his voice not quite steady now and that muscle ticking crazily in his jaw. The atmosphere in the kitchen had changed. It was almost electric. As if in a trance I pulled up the puffy, full skirt. Then he focused on my leg. His hands reached for the top of my stocking and then he brushed the skin of my inner thigh as he pulled it down.

"Holy shit," he breathed to himself. A fierce expression crossed his face before he swallowed, threw the stocking onto the floor, and then moved back to the first aid kit.

His hands were gentle as he wiped along the scratch. It stung, and I sucked in a short breath, but it was more the shock of his hands on my inner thigh than the sting of the antiseptic. After he'd cleaned the scratch, he found a long plaster and pressed it down to cover the whole thing.

"Right, okay, all done," he said, his voice was hoarse now. "I-I… you can go back to the party now." But instead of moving away from me to allow me to do just that, he moved even closer. My legs widened as he stood between them. I was looking up at him, my breath coming in short pants as he scanned my face, and then his eyes dropped to my mouth.

"Fuck it, just fuck it," he muttered. One of his large hands cupped my jaw, the other drove into my hair, and he was kissing me.

Finally, Jonah Grayson was kissing me and it was absolutely bloody fantastic. Five years of pent-up longing was unleashed. I couldn't get close enough to him. One of my hands pressed against his hard chest as the other slid up until my fingers were in his thick hair. My mouth opened under his, and his tongue swept inside.

He held me against him like he was terrified I'd disappear, his hand so large that it spanned my entire back.

"Jesus Christ," he breathed when he broke the kiss to move his mouth to the shell of my ear, then skimmed his lips down my neck. "My God, I've wanted you for so long, I feel like I'm coming out of my skin. Florrie, tell me to stop." His voice was hoarse with desperation now as his hand closed over my breast and I gasped into his mouth when it moved back to mine.

"I don't think I ever want you to stop," I said breathlessly against his lips.

But then the first aid kit clattered to the floor. Jonah froze before pulling his hands away and taking a step back. I could tell as rationality returned to him. The flush on his cheeks drained, leaving him pale under his tan.

"Fucking hell," he said as he ran both his hands down his face, "Florrie, I—"

"It's okay. It's fine," I muttered as my face heated with acute embarrassment. Realising my dress was askew and the skirt still rucked up high on my thighs, I frantically started pulling myself together, feeling completely humiliated. The culmination of five years of sexual fantasies had ended in yet *another* rejection. "You don't have to say anything," I said quickly, hoping to abate the verbal onslaught I knew was coming. "You made yourself clear the last time. You think I'm a spoilt brat. I understand that. You don't have to tell me again how I'm *too much*."

"Oh, God, no," he groaned. "Florrie, I—"

"It's fine. Honestly, you didn't say anything that wasn't true. But there's nothing I can do about my personality. It's just who I am, okay? And—"

"Jesus, Florrie, please listen to me," he said, his voice had an urgent quality now. "All that bullshit I spouted back then was just me being an absolute prick who felt like a total piece of shit for wanting a sixteen-year-old girl so badly. I mean, you *were* too much." I stiffened and he rushed forward to take both my hands in his. "But I didn't mean it like that. I just meant that you were too much for me to resist. Jesus, resisting you has felt like a full-time job for the last five years. And I can't handle it anymore. All I think about is you from morning to night. Everything I do is for you. The reason I care about the Buckingham Estate so much is because of you."

I frowned at him. "You hate me. You're always frowning at me. You're like a bear with a sore head around me."

"I'm frustrated around you," he admitted. "At first, it was because you were too young, and then it was because it was obvious *you* hated *me*. And I knew that was my fault. It was on me. But there was no way past it." He huffed. "I'm not social and good with people like you are. I don't know the right thing to say. Everything I did seemed to annoy you. How could I tell you I was in love with you?"

I blinked up at him. "B-but you think I'm spoilt."

"No, I don't. You're the opposite of spoilt. You'd do anything for your family and anyone you care about. You're selfless beyond all comprehension."

"You're always scowling at me."

"Because I want you so badly."

"I offered myself to you!"

"You were sixteen! I was twenty-six!"

"Sixteen is the legal age of consent in the UK, you pompous arse."

His eyebrows shot up. "So your uncle would have been happy with me fucking you on the regular for the last five years, would he? A teenager. He'd have been happy with that?"

"Oh God, you're so bloody sensible."

"Sensible?" he said, ripping his hands from mine to tear them through his hair. "When it comes to you, I'm anything but sensible. I'd do anything to get even a glimpse of you. I'm always offering to come for meetings in the house at all hours just so that I could maybe see you in passing or smell your perfume. Florrie, I'm totally obsessed with you. It's completely out of hand."

I tilted my head to the side, not quite ready to believe him yet.

"So you don't think I'm too much?" I said quietly.

"My God, Florrie, I could never, ever get enough of you. You could never be too much. You're just the right amount. I'm the one that's too much, too obsessed, too… Christ, the things that I want to do to you."

I grinned and launched myself at him, both my legs coming around his hips and my arms around his neck.

"Florrie, your leg," he said as he supported me under my thighs with one hand, the other going into my hair at the side of my head. "You'll hurt your—"

"You worry too much," I told him through a grin, then silenced him with a kiss. When I pulled back to rest my forehead on his, his expression was a little dazed again. "Screw formality. Screw the Buckingham Estate. Take me upstairs right now and screw *me*, Jonah Grayson."

That's when it happened. I'd only heard the sound a few times before. So when his rich, full laugh filled the kitchen I felt like I'd won a war.

"I'm in love with you, Florrie," he said as his laughter subsided. "I'm in love with you and I never want to let you go. You should know that before you go offering yourself to me. Because I *won't* be able to let you go."

"Well, that's bloody convenient because I'm in love with you too. So take me upstairs to my room right bloody now."

He laughed again, and I decided my life's mission would be to make this man laugh as much as humanly possible. He was way too serious. He needed way more Florrie in his life, as did everyone. Because I was just the right amount of awesome, and so was he.

**If you enjoyed reading *Gold Digger*,
you will love *Outlier* –
the next book in the *Daydreamer series*.
Read on for an excerpt now.**

CHAPTER 1

Six minutes and forty-five seconds

Vicky

I glanced at the large digital clock next to my front door and frowned. He was three minutes and forty-eight seconds late. Maybe he wasn't coming? I shook my head in short jerks—that was an illogical assumption. Of course he was coming. The man needed to make money – I'd looked into his company accounts and verified that this was the case – and I was paying him *a lot* of money.

The fact that he still did his own deliveries made absolutely no sense. This was something he needed to contract out. His time would be much better spent creating the beautiful furniture he made.

My mind flashed to the glimpse I'd had of him in his workshop a couple of months ago, and my mouth went dry.

I'd been with Lucy, Lottie and Hayley in Little Buckingham looking for a small, runaway pony (a bizarre but actually not uncommon occurrence in Little Buckingham). Lucy had thought that Legolas might have made a beeline for her brother's workshop to "piss him right off". The pony wasn't there, but Mike was, and as always, he looked incredible. His flannel shirt was wrapped around his waist, and he had a tight thermal covering his upper body as he sanded down a large table, his muscles rippling under the material with each pass. He'd smiled at Lucy, Lottie and Hayley, but also as always, when he looked at me, his smile dropped. Mike didn't really like me. To be honest, not a lot of people did. But I was hoping maybe I could change that. Lucy and Lottie had bolstered my confidence enough over the last few months to start believing it was possible at least.

When I brought my hand up to smooth my hair, I noticed it was shaking. I clenched my jaw in frustration. I could not have a meltdown. Not now. Not with him four minutes and twenty-two seconds late.

So I did the breathing exercises Abdul had taught me and balled my hands into fists to stop the tremors. When I shifted on my feet, I felt my muscles protest. I'd been standing in this same spot facing my front door for the last forty-nine minutes, so still and tense, that now, everything had stiffened. I was aware that standing still in one's corridor for nearly an hour, staring at a door, was not normal behaviour, but normal behaviour was not exactly my forte.

When I became hyperfocused on something, my quirks slipped into downright weird territory. And it was fair to say that when it came to Mike, I was *extremely* hyperfocused. I was almost more obsessed with Mike Mayweather than I was with hedgehogs.

Almost.

The problem was that the more hyperfocused I became, the more my behaviour deteriorated into the less-than-normal zone. I did not want Mike to think I was less than normal when he already didn't like me.

My throat tightened as I went over one of the causes for his aversion to me. My memory can be very useful. I can recall events, conversations, and everything I've ever read or seen with perfect clarity. Academically, this is a huge advantage. However, when you've done something so awful and incorrect that you'd rather forget it completely, the ability to replay it entirely, down to the tiniest detail is not useful; it's a curse.

I could still picture Lucy Mayweather's face the day we threw all those awful accusations at her and then threw *her* out of the office. I could also picture the surveillance footage we recovered of Lucy being assaulted only seconds before. My brain tended to dwell on upsetting things despite how illogical that might be. As a consequence, I'd replayed Will Brent throwing Lucy against the office wall, and her head bouncing against the plaster too many times to count.

So no, Mike did not like me, not after that. When he'd later stormed into the office, stomping through the carefully controlled environment in his steel-capped work boots, all six-foot-four inches of him vibrating with fury over what we'd allowed to happen to Lucy, I'd never seen anything as magnificent in my entire life. I thought I was defective in that area. Well, I was defective in a lot of areas, truth be told, but with men, particularly so.

Until I saw Mike Mayweather that day, I couldn't imagine ever voluntarily letting someone put their mouth on mine, let alone all the *other stuff*. But when it came to Mike, all I could think about was what his lips would feel like, whether his beard was scratchy or soft, and how his large body would feel on top of mine.

After years of believing that I was dead when it came to attraction, my attraction to Mike had become all I could think about. Hence, my standing stock still in the corridor, staring at my front door.

For fifty-two minutes.

I closed my eyes to focus on my breathing again, but they snapped open when the door suddenly shook with two loud pounding knocks. Without thinking, I instantly pulled it open to stare at a huge, flannel-covered chest.

He was right there. So close, I could smell him.

Now, I was very sensitive to scent in general and quite intolerant of most, especially when related to other human beings. But Mike's clean, woodsy, manly scent was so good, it made me feel light-headed for a moment. That, combined with the outline of his muscular chest in another tight thermal under said flannel shirt, worked together to short-circuit my brain. All I could do was stare at his chest. Which was weird, and I so, *so* wanted *not* to be weird in front of this man.

He cleared his throat, and my gaze shot from his chest to his angry brown eyes with their thick eyelashes. The eyelashes were incongruous with the rest of his extremely rugged appearance— thick beard, which was in no way sculpted like the other men of my acquaintance, messy brown hair a few days past needing a cut, tanned skin weathered from all the time he spent outdoors.

I'd never seen anything so beautiful.

"You going to stand there staring at me all day, princess?" he asked in his growly voice. He didn't say *princess* in a nice way, but he did at least leave off the "ice" part.

I hated that nickname. *Ice princess*. I knew what it implied— that I was stuck-up, aloof, and I thought I was better than everyone else. I knew that was Mike's opinion of me too. But this encounter was supposed to change all that. I was wearing actual jeans, for God's sake. Granted, Lottie had had to trial dozens of pairs for me until she found one soft enough for me to tolerate, and even then, I was still really uncomfortable and desperate to be back in my fleece-lined tights, or even better, my buttery soft leggings. But the idea of these jeans was to make me look normal.

In fact, my entire carefully crafted appearance was trying to achieve that aim, from my "messy bun" which had taken me the best part of an hour and involved processing no fewer than five hours of YouTube videos, to my "natural look" make-up, to the relaxed cream jumper, which was just on the wrong side of itchy – itchiness was a real problem for me but I decided that if could put up with the jeans, then I could tolerate the jumper as well. I'd even debated whether I needed to wear sexy underwear. There was no way I would have been able to tolerate lace or any underwiring, but I could maybe, *maybe* have dealt with satin if push came to shove. Instead, I decided to stay with my normal seamless cotton super-soft bra and knickers for now.

I didn't think Mike would accept my proposal initially. He'd likely have a period of consideration, and I could then work up to tolerating uncomfortable underwear so that I'd be ready to wear it at a predetermined place and time.

"You're six minutes and forty-five seconds late."

Yes, that is what I said to him. I am a socially incompetent person, but that was bad, even for me. The trouble was I had a terrible habit of stating facts as they popped into my head. And in my experience, people didn't want to have the unabridged truth foisted on them regularly. It was just one of the various ways I lacked social skills. I did not have the ability to lie, not even white lies.

Now, if everyone functioned like me, that would be fine. With white lies and half-truths eliminated, we could all live in honest harmony, being completely straight with each other at all times, and not taking offence to other people simply stating facts.

But the world was not full of Vickys. We were a rarity. And we were considered rude.

Mike crossed his impressive arms over his chest, his muscles bunching under his shirt as he did it, and his expression darkened.

"Christ, can we just get this over with then?" he snapped. "I wouldn't want to waste any more of your precious seconds than strictly necessary."

I stared up at him and blinked. "I have cleared my entire day for this delivery," I said, yet again, blindly stating the truth without thinking through the consequences.

His eyebrows shot up. "For fuck's sake, why?"

I opened my mouth to speak but then closed it again, just catching myself in time before I could blurt out that I'd spent the entire morning making myself look "normal," and that I was hoping he would be willing to negotiate terms with me this afternoon.

"You say the f-word a lot." This observation is what popped out of my mouth instead, and from his eye roll, it wasn't a lot better than the other options. It's not that I minded swearing; I didn't. But for me, it was too difficult a minefield to negotiate. If you incorporated swear words into your regular vocabulary, you had to have the social awareness and emotional intelligence to know when it was appropriate and when it was not. I had neither social awareness nor emotional intelligence, so I chose to simply avoid swearing altogether.

"Sorry if I've offended your delicate sensibilities, Lady Harding. But if we could move this along, my sweary uncouth carcass will be out of your hair a lot sooner."

He said *Lady Harding* the same way he'd said princess—with undisguised contempt. I wasn't sure if it was just contempt for me or for the peerage system as a whole. I mean, he was friends with my half-brother Ollie, who was the Duke of Buckingham, so I doubted it was only the peerage he objected to. No, Mike Mayweather simply didn't like me.

I doubt he remembered, but he'd never liked me. It had been obvious even on the handful of occasions I was around him as a child. And, back then I had been far less objectionable. I didn't go around stating obvious truths as a child. In fact, I did not speak at all. It was one of the many ways in which I was a disappointment to my mother.

After I stopped speaking, she decided she'd had enough of my constant silent presence in her new family and started dropping me off at my biological father's house for part of the summer holidays.

The trouble with that was that my biological father, the previous Duke of Buckingham, wasn't that keen on me either—and he also wasn't home a lot. This meant that I became his wife Margot's problem, which seemed supremely unfair, seeing as I was the product of the affair Margot's husband had while still married to her. But she couldn't very well put a six-year-old child out on the street, so I was welcomed, however grudgingly, into the family home for a maximum of two weeks every summer.

The first time I saw Mike Mayweather was at Buckingham Manor, and he was carrying a hedgehog in his bare hands.

"Sorry, Lady Harding," he'd muttered to my stepmother, when blood dripped from his hands onto her rug. "It's just, I found it out in the daytime, and that can mean it's sick." The sight of that large, rough boy gently cradling a tiny creature and not caring that the spikes were ripping his hands to shreds has stayed imprinted on my brain ever since.

The handful of times I followed Ollie to the Mayweather cottage, Mike scowled at me from across the small kitchen, clearly unhappy that I was invading his space. Mike's mum was an extremely kind woman and didn't seem to mind that I didn't talk, or that I only ate the tops of the Jaffa Cakes and would only drink tea out of one specific mug. She also gave the type of hugs I could tolerate—brief, tight side hugs.

I really, *really* liked Hetty Mayweather.

Despite Mike's obvious dislike of me, even back then, he still fascinated me. And unfortunately, I hadn't fully mastered my habit of staring at things I found fascinating as a child. In fact, I hadn't really been able to mask at all—my only saving grace being the mutism.

"I'm not a Lady," I told Mike as he continued to stare down at me.

He shook his head once. "What are you—?"

"I'm not Lady Harding," I explained. "My father didn't pass his title onto me because I'm illegitimate."

His scowl dropped slightly, and he shifted on his feet. "Oh," he said as his arms uncrossed, before he reached back to grip the back of his neck, revealing that glorious chest even more, as his flannel shirt pulled to the side. He cleared his throat. "Right, sorry, love. Didn't think."

At the use of the word love, my gaze shot from its fixation on his chest, to his eyes. There was a softness about them now as he looked down at me, which hadn't been there before. That, combined with his use of an actual endearment, short-circuited my brain again. I could feel my pulse beating in my ears as a wave of light-headedness swept through me. Seconds ticked by until eventually, Mike had enough.

"Okay, if you could move back a little, then I'll…"

It happened when he put his large hands on my shoulders in order to manoeuvre me out of the doorway, as I'd clearly lost the ability to do this myself. He didn't grab me; his touch was gentle, and there was nothing threatening about it. But I wasn't prepared. I *have* to be prepared when people touch me. So, despite how much I'd been dreaming about Mike putting his hands on me, when it actually happened, I yelped and wrenched away from him.

My hands went up, and it took all of my effort and training to stop them from flapping and pressing onto my ears. When I finally got my breathing under control and was sure I wasn't going into a meltdown, I looked up at Mike to see he'd backed away from me with his hands up, a horrified expression on his face.

I swallowed and tried to speak, but as was often the case when I was stressed, no words would actually make it past my tight throat.

"Bloody hell," he snapped. His horror now bleeding into anger. "Chill the fuck out. I wasn't going to attack you. You're the last woman I'd—" He broke off then, but I knew what he was going to say.

I desperately wanted to explain my reaction to him, but aside from the fact I physically couldn't speak at that moment, even if I could, what would I have told him? That I wanted him to touch me more than I've ever wanted anything in my life, but that I needed warning because I was so unbelievably weird? The whole point of today was to try to convince him I *wasn't* weird so he'd agree to my terms. Admitting to all my ridiculously complicated quirks would hardly be working towards that aim.

To read the rest of Vicky's story,
preorder *Outlier* now to secure your copy.
Coming to a book store near you in August 2025.

ACKNOWLEDGEMENTS

A special thank you to Ollie. Your arrogance in declaring you wanted yourself in one of my books but not just as "any old bastard". No, you wanted to be a Duke, and you inspired me, people pleaser that I am, to write one.

Massive thanks also to my readers. I never dreamt that people would take the time to read the stories I have thought up in my freaky brain, and I am honoured beyond words. I am also eternally grateful to the reviewers who have taken a chance on me – your feedback has made all the difference to the books and is the reason I've been able to make writing not just a passion but a career.

Susie's Book Badgers - you are wonderful humans, and your support means the world.

My fantastic alpha readers – Jess, Small Suse, Aurelia, Carly, Jane, Ruth, Katie and Andy – your feedback was essential and much appreciated.

Thank you to my agent, Lorella Belli, for your support and encouragement.

To Jo Edwards my fantastic editor and dear friend – thank you, thank you and I'm so sorry about all the semicolons!

Thank you to the wonderful team at Keeperton for believing in the Daydreamer series and bringing the books to a wider audience.

Last but not least, thanks to my very own romantic hero. I love you and the boys to the moon and back.

ABOUT THE AUTHOR

Susie Tate is a #1 Amazon bestselling author of addictive, feel-good contemporary romance. She can be counted on to deliver uplifting but also heart-wrenching stories that make her readers laugh and cry in equal measure. Her charismatic but flawed heroes have to work hard to earn their heroine's forgiveness but always manage to redeem themselves in the end.

The real and raw themes that underpin Susie's books are often inspired by her experiences working as a doctor in the NHS for the last twenty years. Susie worked in a range of hospital specialities before becoming a GP, during which time she looked after a women's refuge for victims of domestic violence as well as being child safeguarding lead for her practice. Susie's medical career gives her a unique insight and understanding of the social, psychological and physical issues some of her characters face, lending authenticity to her writing.

Susie lives in beautiful Dorset with her wonderful husband, three gorgeous boys and even more wonderful dog. Her very own romantic hero and husband, Andy, suffers from Motor Neurone Disease (aka ALS). Susie's career as an author has allowed her to spend more crucial time with Andy and their boys after this devastating diagnosis. Susie and Andy work to raise awareness about MND/ALS and support charities like the MNDA and My Name5 Doddie, who are searching for a cure and supporting sufferers.

 Arndell

Connect with Arndell
Love this book? Discover your next romance book obsession and stay up to date with the latest releases, exclusive content, and behind-the-scenes news!

Explore More Books
Visit our homepage: keeperton.com/arndell

Follow Us on Social Media
Instagram: @arndellbooks
Facebook: Arndell
TikTok: @arndellbooks

Stay in the Loop
Join our newsletter: keeperton.com/subscribe

Join the Conversation
Use **#Arndell** or **#ArndellBooks** to share your thoughts and connect with fellow romance readers!

Thank you for being part of our book-loving community. We can't wait to share more unforgettable stories with you!